DOOMSDAY FOR DEMOCRACY?

On the obscreen, Royce watched the shimmering haloed image of an unidentified decelerating starship.

Carlotta punched the replay button. The strong, calm, slightly intimidating face of a gray-haired man appeared on the access screen: "I am Dr. Roger Falkenstein of the Transcendental Science Arkology *Heisenberg*. We are entering your solar system and will make orbit around Pacifica in twenty days. Our mission is peaceful and will greatly benefit your people. I request permission to land on your planet and open negotiations with your government."

Both Carlotta and Royce knew that no planet had ever said no to the Institute. And if the *Heisenberg* was arriving, a Femocrat mission could not be far behind.

Like it or not, the Pink and Blue War had come to Pacifica!

D1010329

NORMAN SPINRAD

A WORLD BETWEEN

A KANGAROO BOOK
PUBLISHED BY POCKET BOOKS NEW YORK

Distributed in Canada by PaperJacks Ltd., a Licensee
of the trademarks of Simon & Schuster, a division of
Gulf+Western Corporation.

Another *Original* publication of POCKET BOOKS

POCKET BOOKS, a Simon & Schuster division of
GULF & WESTERN CORPORATION
1230 Avenue of the Americas, New York, N.Y. 10020
In Canada distributed by PaperJacks Ltd.,
330 Steelcase Road, Markham, Ontario.

ISBN: 0-671-82876-2

First Pocket Books printing October, 1979

10 9 8 7 6 5 4 3 2 1

Trademarks registered in the United States and other countries.

Printed in Canada

For DONA SADOCK

"And you can tell everybody
this is your song . . ."

A WORLD
BETWEEN

1

Riding the west wind on the edge of an onrushing thundersquall, Royce Lindblad sat barechested in the open cockpit of the *Davy Jones*, conning the sailboat by the tiller, the boomline, and the seat of his green velour pants. Lightning hissed and crackled in the black thunderheads behind him, but no rain fell on the choppy azure surface of the Island Sea. High above the single mast, a flock of bright yellow boomerbirds rode the same wind on their great motionless wings, hooting their good-natured defiance of the elements in tubalike tones. As long as the boomerbirds remained aloft, there was no imminent danger of the squall transforming itself into a vornado, and therefore no need to retract mast and sail and go to power.

Unplugged from the net and his responsibilities by choice, Pacifica's Minister of Media was in no particular hurry to rush home to Carlotta and affairs of domestic life and state. Although it was only two hours from Gotham to Lorien Island even under sail, time had a different meaning out here; you could expand or contract it at will. Flung across half a million square kilometers of shallow ocean, the thousands of isles that made up the Island Continent could be either the suburbs of Gotham or a vast outback of sea and sky and untouched beaches, depending upon your chosen speed.

Twelve million people, nearly a third of the planetary population, lived out here, none of them more than an hour and a half from the center of Gotham under powered flight. From a commuter's point of view, the towns on many of the larger islands and the private villas that hugged smaller bits of land were all a quick jump from each other and from the Pacifican capital. When the island of your nearest neighbor was only minutes away, you forgot that those minutes could be thirty kilometers of open sea. When you could jump from Gotham to the furthest island in the archipelago in under two hours, you forgot that the twelve million Islanders and all their works were but a thin dusting of humanity sprinkled over a virgin immensity of sea and wooded islands on a planet fifty light-years from the sun that gave their kind birth.

But down here on the surface of the sea, the Island Continent became a vast world entire, more empty than inhabited, more Pacifican than human, and you were a lone sailor on an alien sea, the clock of your mind keeping the oceanic time of wave and wind.

Horvath Island loomed fuzzily on the far horizon, and Royce thought he could make out the blue fusion flame of a liner coming north from Thule arcing in for a landing at Lombard. As if to distract his attention from this reminder of the world of men, a big marinerdyle breached the surface not a hundred meters from his boat in a sudden explosion of foam. The huge reptile raised its spindly forelimbs into the air, and the translucent membranes of its twin sails unfurled and caught the wind with an audible snap, to the hooting derision of the boomerbirds. Cupping the wind with its sails of skin with a precision and delicacy that Royce could not hope to match, the creature paced the boat for several minutes, and was pulling away when it finally sounded with a nose-thumbing flip of its great tail-flukes.

Royce adjusted his course, steering well clear of the powered traffic around Horvath Island and the liner port of Lombard. Beyond Horvath Island was a long sickle-shaped chain of small islets with only half a dozen estates scattered among them, and in the middle of the chain, about twenty-five kilometers away now, was Lorien.

Royce had homesteaded Lorien long before he met Carlotta Madigan. Carlotta had changed the vector of his life in most ways, drawing him into orbit around her rising star. Carlotta might have been on her way to her first term as Chairman even then, but if she wanted to share her bed with Royce Lindblad on a long-term basis, that bed was going to be on Lorien, not in that tower apartment smack in the middle of Gotham where they had first met. They still kept the city apartment for convenience's sake, but Lorien was home—they had designed the house together, and Royce had insisted that the deed to the place be a joint contract, too. He was traditionalist enough to believe that a man must choose the home, even if his lady was destined to head the government. *Especially* if she was a power in the world—a bucko had to be king of the castle when the lights went out, didn't he?

Truth be told, the Island Continent was Royce's first love, something that perhaps only another child of Mainlanders could fully understand. His parents were wheat farmers in the rich lower Big Blue River valley, but even as a small boy, romances of the Island Continent had been his favorite entertainment channel fare. By the time he came into his citizen's stock at seventeen, he had sailed these seas thousands of times on the net and in his dreams, and he had long since known that on his seventeenth birthday he would put the mainland of Columbia behind him.

His father—a big graceful man whose thoughts ran slow but deep—had understood this for a long time. That last afternoon, they had sat together on the mossy bluffs overlooking the Big Blue. Behind them, the yellow carpet of ripening wheat rippled contrasting textures in the breeze like ruffled velvet. Below them, the river poured between banks rich with kelly-green Pacifican lawnmoss. Spiderwebs of white cloud whisped across the sky. The air was golden with the perpetual warmth of the eternal Columbian summer. Hydrobarges laden with grain and vegetables from further upriver jetted down the river southeast toward Gotham, scoring the turquoise water with the white wakes of commerce. It was peaceful, it was beautiful, it was home, but . . .

"Don't be down, bucko," his father said. "You're only blueing it because you feel you should be. For your mother and me, or so you think."

3

"You don't feel I'm letting you down, dad?"

His father shook his head and smiled. "This is *my* piece of the planet," he said. "This is what sings its song to me. You hear a tune from somewhere else, you've got to dance to it. It's a roomy planet, Royce. What sort of bucko would you be if you stuck yourself in one corner of it just because you happened to be born there? Look at me, *my* father was an engineer in Thule, and here I am. Now, if you were telling me you intended to go eat ice half your life, *then* I'd tell you you were whackers!"

They laughed in unison, men together.

"You don't think I'm whackers for calling a place I've never been 'home?' " Royce asked.

"Ah, we're all whackers that way, now aren't we?" his father said. "We all get itchy for somewhere else until we land someplace that scratches us right. And those islands— ah, yeah, those islands . . . nothing like the Island Continent on any world I ever heard of. You ever wonder why the Founders left 'em alone and put their roots down here in Columbia?"

"Now that you mention it . . ."

Royce thought he knew his history as well as the average Pacifican. The Founders had colonized Pacifica directly from Earth some three centuries ago, and for the first couple of generations, humans had stuck pretty much to their farms on the rich plains of eastern Columbia. But come to think of it, how *could* those people have stood on the shore, looking west across these flat plains, and east across the vast and mysterious sweep of the Island Continent, and still have chosen to ignore the beauty and complexity of the great archipelago for the fertile sameness of the continental veldt?

"Well, I'll tell you what I think, bucko," his father said. "The Founders were people with a dream, and this was it." He spread his big arms wide. "Back where they came from, land like this was only a memory and a promise. So when they saw these plains, they knew they were home. But they were no simple folk, our ancestors. They were smart enough to invent electronic democracy and the net and all the rest of it. And they knew about dreams. They knew that people don't dream about where they grow up even if their parents did. Maybe especially if their parents did . . ."

He hunkered forward and wrapped his arms around his

knees, staring across the Big Blue at the far bank. "So what I think, Royce, is that they saw those islands, and they knew that their children, and their children's children, wouldn't dream of being farmers out here on the plains. So they left the Island Continent alone for someone else to dream on when their time came."

He stood up and put his arm around Royce's shoulders. "So I don't want you to dream my dream bucko," he said. "It's right that you dream your own. That's what Pacifica's all about. That's why I'm going to be proud tomorrow when you leave for your islands. Hang loose, bucko, and listen to your own song."

Though no man could dance entirely to his own music around a woman like Carlotta Madigan, Royce had never forgotten that going-away present from his father. Though his father might have been an unsophisticated Mainlander in the eyes of Gothamites, he had still managed to teach Royce what it was to be a real bucko, a male human, subspecies Pacifican.

And out here on the open waters, holding the power of the wind through the boomline, the inertia of the sea through the tiller, and experiencing himself as the controlling interface between them, Royce always felt time, history, and karma slip away, paring him down to his essential maleness, reconnecting him to that young bucko saying his goodbye on the bank of the Big Blue.

For being a bucko was much like being a lone sailor on this protean sea. You could choose your wind, set your tiller against the resistance of your own karma, and by playing the two against each other, use both to propel you along the course set by your own will.

It was this essentially bucko secret that Carlotta could never quite grasp. That was why they moved under power when they traveled between Gotham and Lorien together, and it was also why, despite her intelligence, her experience, her statecraft, and yes, her wisdom, it was he who conned their political boat through the quicksilver winds and currents of Pacifican electronic democracy.

He had tried to teach her how to sail, but the trouble was that she had no feel for the art of tacking.

Now Horvath drifted by far off to port. Clear of this human settlement, Royce changed course again, pointing his bow along a straight vector toward Lorien, the wind directly astern now, blowing him along at maximum sailing speed, skipping homeward across the surface of the sea like the discrays that leapt clear of the wavecrests and bounced along on their flat bellies like thrown stones with loud, crisp smacks.

Just as well that Carlotta isn't into this, Royce thought. A man shouldn't share everything with his lady; he's got to have a quiet place to hear his own song. Without that, there'd be nothing within him to give in the softness of the night, and that's what makes the world go round, bucko.

The villa that Carlotta Madigan and Royce Lindblad had designed together was a low crescent hugging the inner shore of Lorien Island's small lagoon. The exterior walls were latticeworks of chocolate-brown stonemeld and slightly bluish windows, and the shallow-peaked roof was of deeply grained royal blue bongowood from the Cords, weatherproofed with a microglass glaze. A wide veranda shelfed out onto the lagoon from the front of the house on pilings with the boat berths beneath it. The landward side of the building faced the heavily forested hills of the island across a rather formal garden—a small fountain, a manicured Earth-grass lawn, bongowood garden furniture, and beds of Earthside roses, tulips, and chrysanthemums in red, white, blue, and yellow.

Royce's netshop overlooked the lagoon, with a glass door leading directly out onto the veranda, but Carlotta's was on the other side of the house, looking inward on the garden and the virgin native woods beyond.

In theory, this was supposed to afford her a tranquil and changeless natural backdrop for conducting affairs of state, but in practice she hardly ever even glanced out the window when she was plugged into the net.

Indeed, the screens of her outsized net console faced the big window, so that her back was to the garden when she sat in one of the two loungers facing them, enfolded within the curve of the emeraldwood-paneled cabinet. The standard Pacifican net console was a six-screen job: one for the personal communication channels, one for the hundred broadcast channels, one for computer interfacing, one for the accessbanks, one for the gov channels, and a sixth for general utility functions like grounds surveillance, video games, and general electronic doodling. Carlotta's console, like Royce's, had four additional screens: one for intragovernmental communications, one for continuous Web-monitoring, one for interfacing with the Parliamentary computer, and one for the planetary observation system.

When Carlotta plugged into the electronic universe of the Pacifican media network, the immediate ground-level world outside faded almost at once from the surface of her mind as her sensorium went multiplex and electronic. Through cameras, microphones, and screens, her sight and hearing became not only planetwide but multiplex and compounded like the vision of an insect. The face and voice of virtually everyone on Pacifica—and indeed on worlds beyond—could be called before her with a quick verbal command. All of human history since the invention of videotape might march before her eyes at whim. Computers would advise her on anything from simple arithmetic computations to the long-term trends in the balance of payments between Pacifica and fifty other human worlds. Anyone on the planet with an ax to grind or a philosophy to expound would harangue her directly if she chose to hear. Ninety channels of entertainment vied for her idle attention, and if nothing in realtime piqued her fancy, there was half a millennium of taped programming in the accessbanks. Current news was available from the points of view of the government, the administration, the oppositions, Marxists, Free Libertarians, Transformational Syndicalists, Sardonic Fatalists, and Platonic Absolutists, among a whole zoo of others. If Pacifica was not world enough, the Galactic Web brought in shrill Femocrat propaganda from Earth, travelogues from thirty worlds, Transcendental Science musings, the latest vicious gossip from Thunderball, a tachyon-borne smorgasbord from the scattered planets of men.

All this was the electronic universe of every Pacifican, except those who unplugged from time to time with severe cases of media cafard. But as incumbent Chairman of Pacifica and a Parliamentary Delegate for nearly sixteen years, Carlotta Madigan had an even more complex and intimate feedback relationship with the media net.

For on Pacifica, media was politics, and politics was media, and had been from the days of the Founders. Geographically isolated farmsteaders could only cohere into a political whole through the media network and the instantaneous plebiscites of electronic democracy. In the beginning there had been no Parliament and hardly any real politicians—just a computer complex in the little town of Gotham to record and tally the electronic votes and a small staff of bureaucrats to implement the directly expressed will of the people. Now, however, that initial simplicity had evolved, along with Pacifican society, into a complexity that nevertheless still cohered through the net at electronic speed.

Now there was a Parliament, and Delegates, and administrations, and elections, and electronic votes of confidence, and government corporations both temporary and permanent, and export industries, and currency controls, and economic planning, and full-time politics and full-time politicians with a vengeance—all of it in perpetual flux and most of it transpiring electronically via the net.

As Carlotta Madigan sat alone on Lorien, tens of kilometers from the nearest human and further still from the capital at Gotham, it all flowed through her via screens, microphones, speakers, controls, satellites, laserpipes, and computers.

Lean and bodily youthful in her mid-forties, Carlotta was graced with a face that on the comscreens of subordinates, colleagues, and political adversaries was an ageless image of authority that flowed not so much from her office as from who she was. Though her fair skin was barely lined at all under flowing black hair, her blue eyes were old steel, and her proud nose and full expressive lips might have been those of an ancient Doge of Venice. With Royce Lindblad as her helpmate, she was the best damn Chairman Pacifica had had in two generations, and no one knew it better than she did.

Carter Berman, the current Minister of Industries, a gray-haired man in his seventies who had shuffled in and out of that office more often than probably even he cared to remember, was on the comscreen now, in something of a defensive dither, trying to persuade her to establish a Pacifican Skyliner Corporation to bring down the fares on the routes between Gotham and the Cords, and Carlotta was getting that familiar sphinxlike look which should have told him that it was a lost cause.

". . . as things stand now, there are only two lines operating between Gotham and the Cords, and the competition is virtually nil, Carlotta . . ."

As he spoke, Caroltta punched up the traffic figures on her access screen. "So is the traffic," she said. "The two lines operating now are averaging only 61 percent of capacity."

"But check the fare structures."

Carlotta punched up the figures. TransColumbia was charging 180 valuns for coach and 230VN for first class. Zipline was charging 167VN and 240VN. "So?" she said testily. "There's absolutely no evidence of price-fixing."

"Look at the charge per passenger-kilometer and compare it to routes of similar length."

When Carlotta punched up the figures, she saw that the charge per kilometer *was* nearly 30 percent higher than Gotham-Valhalla or Valhalla-Lombard and even 17 percent higher than Gotham-Godzillaland. But on the other hand, the profit margins didn't really seem excessive.

"Look at the figures yourself, Carter," she said. "The profits aren't out of line."

"They're 25 percent above what they should be. A government corporation could cut the fares 20 percent and still show a respectable profiit."

"At the same capacity figure?"

"Of course," Berman said, squinting quizzically.

"Well hell, Carter, what makes you think we could run that line at 61 percent?" Carlotta snapped. "Demand's inelastic. Compete with TransColumbia and Zipline, and *all* the liners will be running less than half-full, and the govcorp will run at a loss along with the freecorps. Then they'll drop their routes and we'll be stuck with them."

"Have you modeled that or are you just winging?" Berman asked, beetling his brows in annoyance.

"Winging it," Carlotta said. "And so are you, right? You don't have a computer projection on that, do you?"

"No," Berman admitted.

"Well, when you come up with one, plug me in again," Carlotta said, unplugging herself from the circuit. She sighed. For all his Technocrat pretensions, Berman was an Interventionist at heart. If he had things his way, there'd be a new govcorp every time someone's profit margin went half a point above 10 percent. For her part, Carlotta preferred to leave the free market alone until something got really flagrant.

The Constitution gave the government monopolies in energy production and mining, which was more than enough to let the government run at a profit, pay a decent dividend on citizen's stock, and keep the total economy on an even keel by manipulating energy and metals prices. Within those parameters, the free market could pretty well run by itself.

The govcorp business had started only a century ago, when the freight-booster companies had been caught fixing prices. Profit margins of 40 percent had been excessive by anyone's standards, but regulating the free market went against everyone's grain. Instead, Parliament had set up a government freight-booster corporation to drive down prices by competing in the free market. It worked so well that the gov was able to dispose of its stock in the corporation within five years at a nice capital gain for the citizenry.

But what had begun as an emergency program inevitably became institutionalized. Now there was pressure to set up a competing govcorp every time the profit margin in an industry exceeded about 10 percent and pressure to sell it out to free-market interests the moment the profit margins dropped below that arbitrary figure, whether it made sense in current stock exchange terms or not .

As far as Carlotta was concerned, it was a visionless, rigid way to run a planetary economy, and she had been willing to lose the Chairmanship over just such issues several times. Not without a vote of confidence you don't, Carter! she decided. She smiled her Mona Lisa smile. And we both know the votes aren't there, she thought, calling up a status report on agricultural prices and production.

Now here's an area where the free market doesn't work at all without constant finagling, she thought. The five million Columbian farmsteaders could grow enough food to feed quadruple the planetary population if they had any incentive to do so. But most of them could grow all their own food and take care of their other economic needs out of their citizen's dividends. As a result, the free market in foodstuffs would heterodyne wildly without continual government intervention. Shortages when overproduction dropped prices so low that the farmsteaders stopped producing surpluses for the money economy, followed by sudden rises in prices, followed by more overproduction, another price drop, another shortage, ad nauseum. An agricultural govcorp would have made the most sense, but the Mainlanders had too much political clout for any such proposal to get through Parliament. So the Ministry of Agriculture was forced to buy and sell commodities in huge amounts in order to keep prices relatively stable.

According to the current figures, wheat production was down, and soybeans were going into a glut situation. Carlotta plugged in to Cynthia Ramirez, the Minister of Agriculture.

"Buy a hundred million bushels of wheat futures at 12VN," she ordered. "Sell soybean stocks at 6 until the price drops to 9."

"We're going to have to release wheat soon at 9," Cynthia pointed out. "And we bought those soybeans at 8. We'll take a beating all the way around."

Carlotta shrugged. It was virtually impossible to run the Ministry of Agriculture at anything but a loss. "Do it," she said. "We can always boost the price of iron to make up the loss."

If that's not too inflationary, she thought as she unplugged. The job of Chairman was essentially a juggling act. The gov as a whole had to run at a healthy profit or the voters would swiftly boot out the administration that reduced their citizens' dividends. But the gov also had to keep the total economy and the currency in balance, which often meant doing things that were totally counterproductive in profit-and-loss terms. The Chairman had to walk this fine line continuously while juggling the entire economy, which was why any Chairmanship that lasted a full fiscal year was cause for smug self-congratulation.

Carlotta had already been in office for two quarters this time around, but her smugness about it was tempered by the knowledge that Royce was at least half-responsible. There had never been a Minister of Media better than Royce, and never a team like the two of them in the top two offices . . .

Idly thinking of Royce out there in the *Davy Jones,* Carlotta programmed a general weather review from the

11

planetary observation system. The obscreen split vertically. On the left, temperature, humidity, and barometric readings; on the right, realtime images from standard observation cameras scattered around the planet.

A heavy windless rain fell on the western slopes of the central Sierra Cordillera mountains, soaking down through the laden branches of the towering trees and turning the loamy forest floor to chocolate-colored muck sprinkled with brilliantly colored fungi . . .

Rain always reminded Carlotta of that party at her Gotham tower apartment where she had first met Royce. It had been pouring that night, great driving sheets obscuring the lights of the city below and drumming against the windows. It was supposed to be one of those political gatherings put on by a rising hopeful—a great stew of power with just a flavoring of sex. And then she saw him, barechested in the then-current bucko fashion, skin-tight white pants, high black boots, a short red cloak flung casually over his bare shoulders, long brown hair, and that silly, endearing droopy mustache—a transparent attempt to look older that only made him seem even younger, even more desirable. For a moment, politics suddenly seemed so unimportant—

A merciless sun fried the perpetually cloudless sky over the Wastes. Heat waves shimmering above the dun-gray sands caused the far-off slate-colored mountains to waver like a mirage of themselves . . .

—They had spoken only once during the party, and that only briefly. Carlotta had been holding court with a small group of older Delegates, impressing them with her grasp of the issues, whatever they had been at the time, with her momentum, her easy disdain of their temporarily higher status. She turned to get a drink, and saw him, leaning up against a wall, pelvis arched forward, looking at her.

"Like what you see, do you?" she said with as much imperiousness as she could muster.

"You're a winner," he said. "I'm at your mercy, lady. You can have me if you want me." He laughed—boyishly, ironically. "You might even persuade me to vote for you."

"You certainly consider yourself a hot little bucko, don't you?" Carlotta said.

12

Royce laughed, arching himself languorously toward her. "Don't *you?*" he said, looking into her eyes.

Carlotta moved closer, piqued by his classic bucko narcissism, leavened as it was with a saving self-irony. "I might be interested if your bark's not better than your bite."

"Oh, I never bite," Royce said. "Do you?"

Carlotta laughed and flicked a finger at the V of his pants. "That's for me to know and you to find out," she said, snapping her teeth together—

A sprinkling of snow drifted down from the leaden skies over Thule, lightly powdering the eternal glare ice of the frozen antarctic continent. Only the far-off domes of Valhalla fractured the endless flat white monotony of the polar cap like carefully placed dots of contrasting pigment on some minimalist abstract painting . . .

—Two moments at a party like hundreds of others. A good-looking woman turning thirty and climbing up the power curve had endless young buckos offering themselves up to her, some just for the night's pleasure, but just as many angling to make orbit around a rising star, and Carlotta had supposed that this was just another handsome and available young body in the crowd. She had thought little of it, and had gone back to politicking, perhaps with a slightly enhanced sense of her own personal charisma, certainly not thinking of that young bucko as anything more than a tasty possibility for some idle evening—

A strange howling windstorm roared through the dense verdant jungle of Godzillaland, rainless, whipping showers of brightly colored blossoms through the tangled undergrowth. Flitbats bounced from tree limb to tree limb in skittish panic, and something huge crunched through the jungle near the edge of the obscreen . . .

—Carlotta had been tired but exhilarated by the time the last of her guests left; fatigued, talked-out, but emotionally buoyed by how well it had gone, filled with a sense of impending triumph at the thought of what now seemed like her certain election to Parliament when the present administration fell.

Absorbed in political calculations, she walked into the bedroom—and there he was. Stretched out naked on the carefully turned-down bed with a glass of wine in his hand and his red cloak draped with minutely calculated carelessness over his loins, the quintessence of bucko insouciance.

13

He sipped his wine and stared at her over the rim of the glass. "Are you through conquering the world for tonight, Carlotta Madigan?" he said.

Carlotta choked back a laugh. It was too much, it was like some silly porn opera, and yet . . . And yet, when he crooked his finger at her imperiously, she went to him. When he kissed her, her lips opened to his, and whatever she had been thinking about was forgotten.

It was the perfect bucko performance, so physically perfect as to seem almost soulless, a porn opera for sure. Afterwards, he propped himself up on one elbow and regarded her with classic insolent smugness.

"Who are you?" Carlotta said softly, playing her own part as the script would have it.

"Royce Lindblad," he said huskily.

"And what manner of creature are you, O mysterious and masterful stranger?"

"Well, truth be told, I'm an assistant producer for the Web," he said sharply, abruptly changing verbal tone. "Porn operas for export." And he broke up into gales of laughter.

"You fucking son of a bitch!" Carlotta managed to shout before she started laughing with him—

White clouds scudded across a clear blue sky over the eastern end of the Island Continent. Far off toward the horizon a single bright blue sail billowed between two forested islands . . .

Sitting in her lounger, Carlotta smiled almost girlishly. They had spent the rest of that night not making love but talking media and politics, and almost from that moment that had been half of their relationship, she the master, Royce her helpmate.

But she couldn't look at a sail moving across the open sea without thinking of Royce out there in his boat, that young bucko still. And she couldn't think of Royce sailing without remembering that first night, for that was the young and ever-ageless part of him that only she and the sea knew, her silly young bucko in the sweetness of the night—

Suddenly all her net console screens went blank and then began strobing in blinding scarlet while the speakers battered her ears with a shrill electronic hooting. A priority security override! What the—

Leaning forward nervously, Carlotta punched the "accept" button, wondering what in hell could have happened.

The strobing of the screens and the alert siren abruptly ceased. The agitated face of a youngish woman appeared on the private govchannel screen.

"Well?" Carlotta snapped. "Who the eff are you? What's going on?"

"Laura Sunshine, Ministry of Media, Web Monitoring Bureau," the young woman said in a tightly controlled voice. "We're getting a tachyon transmission from inside the solar system."

"What?" Carlotta grunted, her mind suddenly racing along in high gear. It made no sense. Modulated beams of faster-than-light tachyons were used strictly for interstellar communication—they were the medium of the Galactic Media Web. Tachyon transmission was much too expensive to use for shorter-range communication; besides, Pacifica was the only habitable planet in this solar system.

Therefore, it had to be a starship from outside, and that was truly a historic event. The instantaneous tachyon transmissions of the Web held the human worlds together, but physical travel was restricted to sub–light speeds, and the nearest inhabited solar system was a decade and a half away.

Furthermore, why would a starship wait until it was inside the Pacifican solar system to announce its impending arrival? Most starships carried would-be immigrants, and the standard procedure was to announce intentions from the home planet before the ship left, so that a welcome could be bought with rare items of interstellar trade —Earthside life-form embryos and seeds, unique biologicals, secret technologies—coveted by the world at journey's end. These things were negotiated before-hand, unless— *Oh, no!*

"Is this transmission in clear or in code?" Carlotta asked brusquely.

"In clear," Laura Sunshine said. "And you're not going to like it."

"No shit?" Carlotta muttered sardonically to herself. Then, aloud: "Plug me in, and for God's sake, scramble this circuit."

The govscreen went blank for a few moments and then

a new face appeared on it: an older man with long, neat, steel-colored hair, an angular face with hard brown eyes, and a great beak of a nose. He was wearing an all-too-familiar midnight-blue tunic with a high stiff collar edged in silver.

"I am Dr. Roger Falkenstein of the Transcendental Science Arkology *Heisenberg*," the man said in a cool, measured voice. "We are entering your solar system and will make orbit around Pacifica in twenty days. Our mission is peaceful and will greatly benefit your people. We intend to establish an Institute of Transcendental Science on Pacifica. As Managing Director of the *Heisenberg*, I request permission to land on your planet and open negotiations with your government."

The screen went blank for a moment and then Falkenstein reappeared. "I am Dr. Roger Falkenstein of the Transcendental Science Arkology *Heisenberg* . . ." The damned thing was a continuous tape-loop.

Angrily, Carlotta unplugged it and plugged in Laura Sunshine. "That's the whole thing?" she asked.

"That's it, they're transmitting it continuously," Laura Sunshine said. She grimaced nervously. "The Pink and Blue War?"

"Looks like it, doesn't it?" Carlotta said grimly. "Hold this circuit and plug into planetary observation. I'll see if we can get a visual."

She plugged in the planetary observation system and got a dark-haired young man on the obscreen. "This is the Chairman," she said. "Scramble this circuit. Scramble another circuit to Laura Sunshine, Ministry of Media, Web Monitoring Bureau."

"Huh?" The young man gaped at her quizzically.

"Just do it," Carlotta snapped. "And remember, this is priority security, not a blatt to anyone." When the circuits were safely scrambled, she said: "We're getting tachyon transmission from a ship inside the system." She didn't bother to allow the ob-tech a moment to digest that. "Laura will give you the coordinates. I want you to lock a long-range orbiting scope on the beam and give me a visual at max magnification, *and keep all relevant circuits scrambled.*"

A few moments later, a hazy object swam across the

obscreen: a silvery cylinder against a black backdrop of space and hard pinpoint stars. A thin blue fusion-flame spouted from the near end of the thing, nearly transparent, but unwavering and perfectly conical. The ship was surrounded by a rainbow aura, as if its image were imperfectly electronically superimposed on the starfield, or as if it were surrounded by some unknown kind of energy field.

"Can you give me some kind of speed estimates?" Carlotta asked.

"It's moving at about a tenth the speed of light now," the voice of the ob-tech said uncertainly. "But . . . but it's decelerating at about ten gravities . . . that's . . . no one inside could survive . . . it's impossible . . ."

"Not for *those* buggers," Carlotta muttered. "They don't know the meaning of the word." Then, crisply: "Okay, keep the scope locked on, keep it on this circuit, keep the circuit scrambled, and keep your mouth shut."

"Now what?" Laura Sunshine asked.

Carlotta pondered the haloed image of the *Heisenberg* for a long silent moment. Sit on it? Release it to the general news channels? Announce it via the gov news channel? *What?* Once the damned thing went into orbit, nothing could keep the knowledge from becoming public. If I try to sit on it till then, I'll face a vote of confidence for concealing information. But if I release the news now, before we formulate a policy, we'll have to come up with some kind of policy in the middle of a planetwide shouting match. Damn! Either way, it was going to be political circus-time!

I'd better not make a move without Royce, Carlotta realized. He's supposed to be the expert at this kind of thing. And where the hell is he now? Out there on his boat with nothing but a clear com-channel, communing with the drooling boomerbirds! I *told* him he should put a scrambler on the *Davy Jones*, but no, my young bucko has to have his place to unplug!

"Answer their transmission," she told Laura Sunshine. "Audio only: 'Transmission acknowledged. Request you maintain silence until further contact.' Send that six times, cease transmission, keep this circuit open, and keep your fingers crossed."

17

Carlotta frowned at the image of the *Heisenberg* for another quiet moment. Here comes the Pink and Blue War, she thought. Why did it have to happen to *me?* Then, petulantly, she plugged in the *Davy Jones.*

2

A FEW STRAY DROPS OF RAIN STUNG ROYCE'S BARE BACK, whipped almost horizontally by the wind of the darkening storm behind him, but the boomerbirds had not yet abandoned the sky for the surface of the sea, and the first little islets of the chain leading to Lorien were already passing off to starboard. It might be a close thing, but he reckoned that he would be able to make it home without resorting to power.

The wind suddenly gusted a few points further south, scattering the flock of boomerbirds for a moment and rippling the mainsail of the *Davy Jones*. The boomerbirds honked their indignation as they formed up again, and Royce adjusted the angle of his boom slightly, offsetting the change with his tiller so as to maintain his present course. Funny how a storm that drove the boomerbirds from the sky would drive human sailboats into the air, as if there were some strange reciprocal relationship between the humans and the native Pacifican life-forms—

Suddenly the com-terminal built into the control console at the front of the cockpit began chiming at him insistently.

"Arrr . . ." Royce grunted irritably as he leaned forward

and punched the "accept" button. Carlotta's face appeared on the screen, tense and impatient.

"What is it?" he said. "Can't it wait? I should be home in half an hour if the wind holds."

"No, it can't wait," Carlotta said brusquely. "It can't wait at all. And forget about your precious wind and torch back here as fast as you can."

"What's the hurry?" Royce asked. "What's so cosmically important that a half-hour's going to make a difference?"

"I can't tell you."

"Why can't you tell me?"

"Because you're too godzilla-brained to install a scrambler on that damn boat of yours and this is a priority security matter, that's why!" Carlotta snapped. "Now stop talking and get moving!"

"Hey . . ."

Royce watched Carlotta pause to cool herself before she spoke again. This *must* be serious! he thought. "I'm sorry, Royce," she said much more quietly, "but this is really serious and I need you here five minutes ago."

"Okay, okay, I'll be there before your blood pressure can drop five points."

"Thanks, bucko," Carlotta said with the faintest trace of warmth, and unplugged from the circuit.

Royce slid his seat forward on its rails a meter or so in order to reach the flight controls more easily. He threw a switch and electric winches quickly sucked the sails into the hollow mast. He activated the float units, and pulsed fusion engines beneath the waterline lifted the *Davey Jones* two meters into the air, clear of the wavecrests. He set the thruster at minimum throttle and the boat was under power, skimming along above the surface of the sea at 30 kph. He punched a button and mast, boom, and rudder were retracted into the aerodynamically smooth hull of the boat. He threw another switch, and the gunwales of the open cockpit extruded a clear microglass canopy over him. Now the *Davy Jones* was ready to jump.

Royce set the autopilot for Lorien, set the speed for max, and waved goodbye to the boomerbirds. "Watch your tailfeathers!" he said, and gave the con over to the automatics.

The hum of the fusion engines rose a little louder and

the *Davy Jones* shot a hundred meters straight up, scattering the outraged boomerbirds again. At the apogee of the lift, the fusion thruster accelerated rapidly to 1000 kph, slamming Royce against the back of his seat.

The boat climbed rapidly at a forty-five-degree angle, and the islets below dwindled to green specks on a flat plane of azure glass. Almost before Royce could look down through the canopy at the dwindling world below, the boat nosed over and descended to a hover two meters above the sea, not a quarter of a kilometer west of the narrow mouth of Lorien's lagoon.

That boomin' autopilot sure cuts it close! Royce thought as he cut out the automatics, turned on the thruster, and steered the boat for the lagoon, zipping along at a good 80 kph above the chop.

In a few minutes, he was pulling up beside Carlotta's boat, the *Golden Goose*, in the docking area under the veranda of the house. Another minute, and the boat was secured, and he was dashing two steps at a time up the gangway topside.

Rugo, their fat brown bumbler, met him at the top of the gangway—a rotund, waddling bundle of self-centered affection. He rubbed up against Royce's leg, regarded him with great soulful violet eyes, and nuzzled the bottom of his buttocks with his soft yellow beak. "Sorry, Jocko," Royce said, ruffling the bumbler's furlike feathers as he gently nudged the creature aside, "we appear to have a planetary crisis going, and mommy needs daddy."

"Whonk!" Rugo exclaimed with skeptical indignation as Royce pushed by him. Through the glass doors, Royce saw that Carlotta was waiting for him in his own netshop, sitting on the edge of one of the loungers, so intent on the screens that she appeared not to have yet noticed his arrival.

Royce slid open the doors, pecked her on the cheek, and sat down in the other lounger. "So?"

Carlotta nodded silently at the array of screens before them. Royce saw Laura Sunshine from his own Web Monitoring Bureau on the gov comscreen, and on the obscreen, the shimmering haloed image of some kind of decelerating starship.

"A visitor . . ."

"The Transcendental Science Arkology *Heisenberg,* to

21

be precise," Carlotta said. "And it makes orbit in twenty days."

"Oh-oh," Royce muttered. He leaned back in the lounger and pondered a moment. "Any contact?" he asked.

"Just this on a continuous tape-loop," Carlotta said, punching a replay button.

The strong, calm, slightly intimidating face of a gray-haired man appeared on the access screen—ancient with wisdom, yet somehow agelessly youthful. Royce felt immediately attracted yet also repelled—*formidable* was the word. "I am Dr. Roger Falkenstein of the Transcendental Science Arkology *Heisenberg.* We are entering your solar system and will make orbit around Pacifica in twenty days. Our mission is peaceful and will greatly benefit your people. We intend to establish an Institute of Transcendental Science on Pacifica. As Managing Director of the *Heisenberg,* I request permission to land on your planet and open negotiations with your government." The voice was authoritative, oceanic, and something in it called to Royce, promised the ineffable. The political considerations, however . . .

"How did this come through?" he asked.

"Tachyon transmission," Carlotta said. "I requested they maintain silence until further notice, and they complied."

"Who knows about this?"

"Laura Sunshine and one tech at planetary observation."

Royce let out his breath slowly. Only the Ministry of Media had the equipment to pick up tachyon transmissions. Only two other people knew. "Seems as if it's effectively sat on," he said.

"For the next twenty days, anyway."

"No good," Royce said flatly. "We can't do that. If we don't break the news soon, there'll be a Parliamentary vote of confidence."

Carlotta frowned, indeed almost pouted. "I figured that much out myself," she said rather plaintively. "But if we release this before we have a policy, we'll be in the middle of a full-scale planetary debate when those bastards arrive, and my hands will be tied."

"I believe that's called democracy," Royce said dryly.

Carlotta glared at him. "It's called the Pink and Blue War," she said.

Royce studied her face, and saw a very un-Carlotta-like defensive tension there. "Don't you think you're overreacting a little?" he said.

"What do you mean?"

Royce nodded toward the image of the *Heisenberg* on the obscreen. "What we have at the moment is *not* the Pink and Blue War," he said. "We have a Transcendental Science mission. We have no Femocrats. We don't even have an Institute of Transcendental Science, only some people who want to talk about establishing one."

"I don't quite follow," Carlotta said. But her expression had softened, and she really seemed to be looking to him for advice and guidance now.

"I'm looking at this strictly on a current political level, because that's what we've got to handle *right now*," Royce said. "The options are limited and so is the problem. We can't not talk to this Falkenstein and we can't refuse him permission to land, because that would violate interstellar protocol. So you have to negotiate, but at the moment, that's *all* you have to do. So between now and then, all you need politically is to line up Parliament behind some negotiating position. Right now the issue isn't the Pink and Blue War, it's putting together political backing for a talking position with Falkenstein, period."

Carlotta's expression brightened. "I see what you mean," she said. "Call a closed session of Parliament and line them up behind a negotiating position between now and the time the *Heisenberg* makes orbit."

"Right."

Carlotta stared out the window at the lagoon for a moment. "And I know just what that has to be," she muttered. Oh-oh, Royce thought.

Carlotta turned to Royce again. "But what do we do in the meantime?" she asked. "We can't sit on the news for very long, but we can't release it until we've hammered out a consensus position in Parliament either."

Royce nibbled on a thumbnail. It was all a matter of timing and nuance. "Okay . . ." he said slowly. "So we have to do something immediately to cover ourselves. A simple press release by a low-level Media official to the effect that a starship has entered the system, nothing about contact, the gov is trying to determine its identity. We can get away with that for a day or two . . ."

"And two days from now . . . ?"

Royce grimaced. "By then, we'll have to release the whole story or be charged with denial of media access when it finally breaks. No choice."

"Which gives me less than two days to call a closed session of Parliament together in Gotham and line up a majority of the Delegates behind some kind of tentative policy . . ."

" 'Fraid so."

"Shit."

They sat together silently for a long moment. *"How?"* Carlotta finally said. "If I tell them why I'm calling a closed session, do you think a hundred and three Delegates can keep a secret like that for two hours, let alone two days? If I just casually call an ordinary session, they'll take a week to dribble in."

Royce laughed. "You're the Chairman," he said, "but if I were you, I'd just tell them I was calling an immediate closed session on a matter of priority security. Nothing like that kind of curiosity to encourage max speed."

Carlotta smiled her Mona Lisa smile. "They'll be jumpy as flitbats, but they'll be there practically before I can unplug," she said. She got out of her lounger and gave Royce a quick wet kiss on the lips. "Gotta jump to it," she said. "You take care of the press release in the meantime." She ruffled Royce's hair. "What would I do without you, bucko?"

"Offend the electorate twice a week and masturbate a lot," Royce answered dryly.

It took only a few minutes to arrange the press release through Laura Sunshine (no sense in letting anyone else in on the secret), and Carlotta would be busy in her own netshop for hours setting up the Parliamentary session, so Royce decided he might as well use some of the time to refresh his hazy knowledge of Transcendental Science and the Pink and Blue War.

Pacifica had steered as clear of the conflict between Transcendental Science and Femocracy as was possible on a planet where media access to all points of view was a sacred constitutional right; at best, the conflict was regarded as light farce, as witness the snide local term for what on most other worlds was considered an ideological battle of grave cosmic import.

As a result, however, Royce found that his understanding of the Pink and Blue War was strictly in comic opera terms. Something like two centuries ago, militant feminists had come to power on Earth in the aftermath of the Slow Motion War, and now, apparently, the women were all godzilla-brained lesbos who kept a small supply of ball-less wonders in cages for breeding purposes, at least if one took the incomprehensible but massively solemn propaganda they poured into the Web at face value.

Meanwhile, back on Tau Ceti, a colony of double-domed geniuses had founded the first Institute of Transcendental Science which began to spew forth a bottomless cornucopia of scientific wonders, or so they claimed, and then began to spread through the human worlds via per-ambulating artificial worldlets they called "Arkologies," establishing new Institutes wherever they went, promulgating their scientific vision of a hyperevolved *Homo galacticus*.

The Femocrats considered the Transcendental Scientists "faschochauvinist Fausts," and the Transcendental Scientists considered the Femocrats "misguided primitives" several light-years beneath their intellectual contempt. These were the roots of the Pink and Blue War, an ideological conflict too silly to be taken seriously by sophisticated Pacificans, enlightened citizens of the media capital of the human galaxy.

However, Royce realized, there had to be more to it than material for historical comedies. Several planets had actually turned Femocrat after visits by missions from Earth, and Institutes of Transcendental Science on per-haps half a dozen planets were launching Arkologies of their own these days. Royce gazed out his window. The sun was beginning to set into the deepening blue of the sea. The western sky was a sheet of purpling orange flame, but toward the east the heavens were already darkening, and the first bright stars of night were winking into existence as a flock of birds passed like shadows across the trun-cated disc of the setting sun. It was hard to imagine that up there in the galactic night strident voices were scream-ing godzilla-brained propaganda at each other, ideologues were subverting long-established cultures, a war of sorts

25

was going on, and out there beyond his unaided vision, the Arkology *Heisenberg* was speeding toward Pacifica, bringing the whole unwanted mess to the planet that he loved, a harmonious world at peace with itself.

Rugo slapped at the glass door with his big webbed swimming feet, demanding admittance. Royce got up and let the bumbler in. "Whonk-ka-whonk, ka-whonk!" the big brown bird opined as he followed Royce back to the lounger and stood beside it for his head to be scratched.

Royce laughed as the bumbler cocked his head at him solemnly. "You've got a point, Jocko," he admitted. *And I told Carlotta she was overreacting? he thought. Nothing's really happened yet. Surely we can handle these clowns.*

Still, it behooved him to know something more about what was speeding toward Pacifica than a few stale jokes and the bilge that the Femocrats and Transcendental Scientists put out on the Web.

He called up the basic briefing tape on Transcendental Science from the accessbanks. "Transcendental Science is a philosophy, a technology, and one of only two human transtellar political entities," a female voice said as the Transcendental Science ensign, a four-pointed silver star, appeared on the access screen. "Some contend that it is also an ideological religion." The image of a middle-aged man with short blond hair appeared on the screen; there was something vaguely unsettling about his intense blue eyes. "The movement was founded two hundred and fifty years ago by Dr. Heinz Shockley who established a colony on the fourth planet of the Tau Ceti system. Citizenship was open only to scientists who passed a rigorous screening and their immediate families. Shockley's basic philosophy is still the *raison d'être* of Transcendental Science today . . ."

Shockley began to speak in a deep, urbane, almost syrupy voice. "We are living at the end of human prehistory. Though we travel haltingly from star to star, communicate instantly across the light-years, and have unlocked the secrets of the stellar phoenix, we are still circumscribed by the universal parameters of matter, energy, time, and mind. Science is our method for understanding those parameters and maximizing our mastery of the universe within them. But this is prehistory. *Homo galacticus*, true star-roving man, must learn to *transcend* the so-called

natural limits of the universe through a *transcendental*
science. He must not be confined by the speed of light,
or the so-called natural human lifespan, or the consciousness he evolved with. He must seize this sorry scheme of
things entire and mold it *totally* to the heart's desire . . ."

"Deep," Royce admitted aloud. But not exactly relevant
to the current problem. "Let's have the capsule history,"
he told the access computer.

A schematic map of the human galaxy appeared on the
access screen—inhabited systems represented by white
dots, a single blue dot for Tau Ceti. "Fifty years after the
founding of the first Institute of Transcendental Science
on Tau Ceti, the first Arkology, the *Einstein,* left the system," a male voice said. A blue dot moved away from Tau
Ceti toward the system of Ariel. "Twelve years later, the
Ariel Institute of Transcendental Science was established,
and ten years after that, Ariel launched its first Arkology.
Meanwhile, Tau Ceti launched three more of its own." The
dot representing Ariel turned blue as the dot representing
the *Einstein* reached it. Other dots moved off into space
from Tau Ceti, then one from Ariel. "Since then, five
more systems have established their own Institutes of
Transcendental Science and have begun launching Arkologies . . ." White dots began to turn blue as blue dots
moved across the schematic like a swarm of insects. "Sirius,
Zeus, Barnard . . ."

"And so forth," Royce muttered, stopping the tape.
"Query: how many Arkologies are now in existence?"

"Seventeen, plus or minus five," the computer voice
said. "This is an estimate, exact figure unknown."

"Query: has any system visited by an Arkology failed to
establish an Institute of Transcendental Science?"

"Unverifiable. Hypothesis one: answer no. Hypothesis
two: Transcendental Science only releases data on its suc-
cesses."

I'd buy hypothesis two, Royce thought. As he remembered, Transcendental Science didn't put anything on the
Web except straight propaganda, and Pacifica's "News of
the Galaxy" stringers were barred from their planets.

But the key question was the so-called "Transcendental
Science." These jockos were obviously Machiavellian political meddlers, but they couldn't have run up against anything like the Pacifican political system before, and Royce

27

didn't seriously believe that *anything* could subvert Pacifica's peculiar brand of dynamic stability. But did the cargo of the *Heisenberg* include anything that could benefit Pacifica sufficiently to justify whatever risk there was in letting them hawk their wares planetside?

"Program," he ordered the access computer. "Report Transcendental Science and technology in advance of Pacifican or general galactic levels."

"Verified: Transcendental Science Arkologies are capable of traversing a given distance 40 percent faster than any other known starships, method unknown," the computer voice said. "Verified: inhabitants of Arkologies have survived prolonged 15-gravity acceleration with no ill effects, method unknown. Reported but unverified: possible extended lifespans, cloning, organ regeneration, telekinesis, telepathy, artificial sentience, time travel, matter transmittal, simulkinesis, methods unknown."

"Query: have any of these technologies been offered for sale on the Web Exchange by any planet with an Institute of Transcendental Science?"

"Answer: negative. Elucidation: all relevant planets have ceased to buy or sell technology via the Web within three years of establishment of an Institute of Transcendental Science."

Now that *is* ominous, Royce thought. If any of this superscience is real, the buggers are deliberately keeping it a monopoly of their effing Institutes. You can't buy it, you can only join the club. They seem to be using it as some kind of political weapon.

Royce scratched Rugo's head mechanically, regarding the image of the *Heisenberg* on his obscreen with a newly soured expression. He was beginning to see why it was called the Pink and Blue *War*. In a situation where physical invasion was a logistical impossibility, this kind of behavior was about as close to interstellar aggression as you could get. It violated one of the basic principles of civilized interstellar conduct: free commerce in science and technology.

In a more somber mood now, Royce called up a briefing tape on the Pink and Blue War, using not the public access banks but the Parliamentary computer; he wanted the bottom line, not the surface stuff that everyone knew.

A schematic of the human worlds appeared on the Parliamentary access screen—neutral systems as white dots, Transcendental Science systems in blue, Earth and four other systems in pink.

"The Pink and Blue War," said the computer voice. "Pacifican vernacular for the ideological and political conflict between Transcendental Science and Femocracy. Vectors: Transcendental Science Arkologies, four known Femocrat interstellar missions, Web propaganda. Avowed Femocrat goal: the establishment of Femocratic social systems on all human worlds. Analyzed Femocrat goal: same. Avowed Transcendental Science goal: dissemination of advanced science and technology to all human worlds. Analyzed Transcendental Science goal: establishment of a unified Transcendental Science dominion over all human worlds through Institutes of Transcendental Science. Cause of conflict: mutually incompatible political goals. Current status: four solar systems converted to Femocracy, six solar systems dominated by Institutes of Transcendental Science, thirty-nine neutral. Vector analysis: Web propaganda ineffective, maximum result, Femocrat political parties on twelve planets. Known Femocrat missions: 100 percent effective. Known Transcendental Science missions: 100 percent effective. Projection, one century . . ."

Two of the white dots went pink, six more turned blue. "Projection, two centuries . . ." Four more white dots turned pink, seven turned blue. "Projection, three centuries: data insufficient."

"Query," Royce said. "Impact on Pacifica, immediate, medium-term, long-term."

"Immediate impact: nil. Medium-term impact: decline in interstellar markets for Pacifican Web exports, collapse of 'News of the Galaxy' news service, inability to purchase off-world science and technology due to balance-of-payments problems and partial collapse of market in same. Long-term impact: collapse of the Galactic Media Web, planetary isolation, possible political polarization along ideological lines, possible overthrow of Pacifican Constitution."

With a grunt of displeasure, Royce unplugged from all channels, including the obscreen image of the Arkology *Heisenberg. "Whonk!"* Rugo squawked indignantly, startled by the angry punch of buttons.

"No shit, Jocko?" Royce muttered. You're right, he

thought, suddenly this doesn't seem like such a joke. He gazed out the window, abruptly overcome with a temporary case of media cafard.

It was fully dark now, and though the sea was whipped into a chop by the arrival of the thundersquall that had chased him home, most of the sky was still clear. Far from the lights of Gotham, undisturbed by any moon, the sky over the Island Continent was a blaze of stars against the velvet blackness of the heavens, and a silvery, ever-shifting sheen on the churning surface of the waters.

What went on up there in the cold hard blackness was reflected on the quicksilver surface that lay below. How many other people on how many other planets were at this moment looking out over the serene nightscapes of their worlds while the storm moved stealthily and unnoticed toward them among the pinpoint lights of the common sky?

Lightning crackled in the thunderheads over the lagoon. There was a crash of thunder, and a hard rain began to fall.

3

CARLOTTA HAD SET THE WAKE-UP PLATE IN THEIR GOTHAM bedroom for the predawn hour the night before, but instead of being eased electronically into full wakefullness, she was awakened by Royce's body moving on hers, by an insistent tingle between her legs, by the unconscious motions of her own body responding to his from the other side of the veil of sleep.

"Whuh—? Huh—? What the hell are you doing?" Physical pleasure vied with early-morning grouchiness. Her body was awake and enjoying itself, but her mind was half-asleep and grumbling.

"What does it feel like I'm doing?" Royce muttered slyly in her ear without breaking rhythm.

"You're raping me, bucko," Carlotta grunted, blinking away the vestiges of sleep.

"Oh," Royce said. "Sorry." He stopped his body in mid-thrust, holding himself stiff and lifeless as a corpse. "I thought you were enjoying it."

Carlotta moved her hips against him. "Cut this shit out."

"Say please."

"Please," she whispered with a giggle, sticking her tongue in his ear. Royce laughed, and they moved together

31

once more, fully awake to each other's rhythm now, building swiftly to a rather well-timed mutual fulfillment.

Afterwards, Carlotta leaned back lazily against a pillow and pressed a button on the nightstand, which drew back the curtains to admit the wan gray light of impending dawn blearing down on a barely stirring Gotham. Fully awake now at this loathsome hour, she longed to drift back to sleep at least until the sun was a civilized distance above the horizon. Royce, as always, was filled with his loathsome and incomprehensible first-thing-in-the-morning energy, punching out an order for a bedside pot of kaf.

"What was the idea of that?" Carlotta asked.

"Just a silly way of starting what promises to be a very unsilly day," Royce said, suddenly serious.

"Yeah," Carlotta said somberly. "It's not going to be easy. You coming along with me?"

"Be there before noon," Royce said, as the kaf popped out of the servetable, hot and steaming. "Got to go to the Ministry first and prepare a press release so we can have it out the moment the session's over." He poured two cups of kaf and handed one over. "You still intend to ask for a free hand?" he asked.

"For sure. I don't want that Falkenstein addressing Parliament. It's got to be private negotiations with me so I can turn him down without a vote beforehand."

"Even so, there's a good chance there'll be a vote of confidence afterward," Royce said. "And if you lose it, I wouldn't care to predict how the electronic vote would go afterward, either."

Carlotta sipped at her kaf, shrugged. "It's worth losing the Chairmanship over this if I can get rid of the *Heisenberg* in the process," she said. "If I get plenipotentiary powers beforehand, my decision can't be countermanded later, all they can do is throw me out of office."

"There *is* a possibility you've overlooked . . ." Royce said slowly.

Carlotta cocked an eyebrow at him.

"Falkenstein could demand media access," Royce said. "Appeal directly to the body politic. It's his right under the Constitution, you couldn't deny it to him—if he knows about it."

Carlotta shuddered. "Oh, come on Royce," she said.

"You think the Transcendental Scientists are experts on Pacifican constitutional law?"

"Who knows? I just don't think it's smart to assume their ignorance."

"There isn't any other choice," Carlotta snapped. She studied Royce narrowly. There seemed to be something peculiar sneaking into his attitude. "You *are* with me on this, aren't you, Royce?"

"You make the policy, boss-lady, I just sell it," Royce said, without a trace of rancor.

But as she dressed hurriedly, Carlotta was left with a feeling of slight unease, as if somehow the mere presence of the *Heisenberg* moving inexorably toward Pacifica was already disrupting harmonies, both political and domestic.

Her mind was already girding itself for combat as she took the elevator down into the garage of the tower apartment building. Here was a typical collection of the quirky personal transport favored by confirmed Gothamites. Little motorcycles and scooters powered by small fusion motors, jump-harnesses, powerskates and skimboards, one- and two-place floaters—all concrete technological expressions of the unspoken Pacifican motto, "Getting there is *all* the fun."

Growing up in the city, Carlotta had tried them all at one time or another. As a teenager, she had taken her life in her hands on powerskates and skimboards; with her first citizen's dividend, she had purchased a jump-harness which soon scared her into shifting over to a series of cycles and scooters; now, as Chairman, with a slightly higher regard for her own personal safety, she got around the city by floater.

Carlotta's floater was a one-place model. She stood on a small metal disc containing a float unit and a little thruster. Her hands gripped a fixed set of handlebars that rose from the front of the circular platform. Under her left thumb was a simple on-off switch; the right handlebar grip was a twist-throttle. That was all there was to it, a simple machine, and a complex sense of vector and balance.

Carlotta turned on the float unit and the floater rose the standard one meter off the floor. She cranked on a little throttle and the floater moved forward. She turned to the right by leaning her body in that direction, and the floater zipped up around the curving ramp and out onto the street.

Carlotta had called for an early morning opening of the Parliamentary session, figuring it might take all day, and the sun hovered just above the horizon, a pale glare filtering through the residential towers on the eastern islands of Gotham. The air, as always at this latitude, was warm, but the early morning light had a chill quality to it as the city blinked its way into wakefulness in the long shadows. The building fronted on a main avenue, but at this unseemly hour the traffic was still light: a few older people sedately riding the glideways on either side of the roadbed; kids careening along to school balancing precariously on their powered skimboards with slow liquid hip-swivels, or rolling by in low racers' crouches on powerskates; cycles and scooters weaving in and out of this slower-moving traffic; floaters, like Carlotta's, maintaining a calmer course in the center of the street.

Carlotta followed the street as far as the bridge to the next island, but there she veered to the left, across a narrow margin of beach, and out over the water, due west toward the shoreside Parliamentary Building.

The eastern half of Gotham was built on scores of small islands connected by an almost incomprehensibly complex maze of bridges, and it was possible to get from anywhere to anywhere else by negotiating the transisland streets, which made glideways, cycles, skimboards, and the like practical intracity transport. However, the shortest street route from here to there was always a matter of fierce and inconclusive debate, to be settled only temporarily by impromptu races, and the floater, equally at home over water or land, was the only way to proceed from point A to point B in a more-or-less straight line, unless you were the sort of maniac who *enjoyed* leaping from island to island in a jump-harness like a giant flitbat.

Carlotta weaved in and out through the islands, under bridges, around boat traffic, by other floaters, at her top speed of 70 kph, without paying conscious attention to the route she chose or the automatic shifts of weight, having made this run from her apartment to Parliament so many times down through the years that she was her own autopilot. Her mind was elsewhere, looking ahead to the Parliamentary session.

We've never faced anything like this before, she thought as the floater rounded the curve of Paradise Island and the green and gold dome of the Parliament Building hove into view, shimmering in the sunlight at the edge of the mainland shore. We've got the smoothest-running political system there is; we've never had civil unrest, or economic chaos, or even an ideological split that's gone much beyond polite table-talk.

The floater sped across the wide expanse of clear water between the island half of the city and the shore. This bay was the hub of Gotham, the central void. The island half of the city spread itself behind Carlotta in a great jeweled crescent, a confection of gleaming residential towers in a riot of bright colors, rambling business and entertainment districts crammed with the eclectic architecture of thirty planets and as many ages. Parks, zoos, gardens, theaters, midways, luxurious townhouses, all linked together by a faerie latticework of bridges. Fantasy-town, Carlotta thought. Fun-town. Downtown.

But shoreside, Gotham was all functional business. Wharves, booster-pads, low ugly factories, warehouses, and hoveryards, the utilitarian plainness broken only by the Parliament Building, placed there half on the shore and half on pilings over the bay as a political compromise between the Mainlanders and the Islanders over a century ago. *That's* what passes for a grave political decision on Pacifica, Carlotta thought sardonically. Are we the untouchable sophisticates we think we are? Or are we eternal adolescents who have never really been tested?

Carlotta eased her floater off the surface of the bay and zipped across the green-and-gold-tiled plaza in front of the Parliament Building toward the entrance to the Delegates' garage. It looks like we're going to find out, she thought nervously, gliding down the ramp into the cool murk of the subsurface parking area.

Most of the parking spaces were already occupied by Delegates' transport; Royce had certainly been right about that. Nothing like the mysterious aura of a closed session to fill the benches in triple-time.

Carlotta took the elevator up to the circular corridor that surrounded the Parliamentary chamber. Although the public had been kept out, the newshounds had somehow already gotten word of the closed session, and the corridor near the entrance to the chamber was clogged with reporters and mobile TV units from most of Pacifica's dozens of competing newsnets. Ironically, only the official gov newshounds seemed to be missing. In the time-honored fruitless tradition that probably extended back into Terran prehistory, cameras, microphones, and shouting newshounds' faces were shoved at Carlotta as Parliamentary ushers wedged her through the tumult while she murmured a litany of "No comments" to a babel of incomprehensible questions.

This is bad, Carlotta thought as the ushers closed the doors to the Parliamentary chamber on the shouting chaos behind her. No way I can get out of here without issuing a full statement. Who in hell talked?

The circular Parliamentary chamber reminded Carlotta of a theater-in-the-round, or, she thought sardonically, of an ancient Roman arena. Visitors' seats with a capacity of about a thousand, mercifully empty now, formed a curving grandstand above the circular floor of the chamber for about two hundred degrees of its circumference. A semicircle of Delegate seats, two rows deep, enfolded the Chairman's hot-seat. The Delegates sat facing the Chairman with their backs to the gallery; the Chairman, therefore, faced *everyone*. Behind the Chairman was a series of large screens controlled from her console, but also capable of being used by individual Delegates from their seats, or remotely by those who couldn't be there in the flesh. Above the screens was a large glassed-in media booth—darkened and empty for this closed session.

Carlotta walked quickly down the central aisle, sat down behind the Chairman's console, and surveyed the Delegates silently for a moment before calling for order.

Two-thirds of the seats were filled. Glancing at her voting board, Carlotta saw green lights under the slots for all those not physically present, Royce included. The missing Delegates were all plugged in, so there would be no unseemly "Not Presents." No one could say afterward that the decision she was hopefully about to maneuver was unrepresentative of the Pacifican people.

Delegate districts were deliberately gerrymandered to represent not merely rough population equivalents but pragmatically recognized social and cultural realities. Thus, while roughly a third of the Delegates were plain-dressed

Mainlanders and another third were Gothamites and
Islanders in their usual idiosyncratic flamboyance, there
were somewhat demographically disproportionate numbers
of whackers from Godzillaland in shorts and token tank-
shirts; Good Old Mountain Boys in earth-colored leathers
with long unruly hair; and Thule ice-eaters elected in their
work-districts, not from the off-months playgrounds. Coherent political parties as such did not exist; this was a
collection of one hundred and three individualists representing the current attitudes of thirty-five million more mav-
ericks, almost all of whom believed that stable political
parties or even ideological coalitions were somehow un-
Pacifican. About the only generalization that you could
make was that a small majority of the Delegates were
women.

Who leaked the news of this closed session? Carlotta
thought sardonically. I've got a hundred and three probable choices, and every last one of them could be right.

Ceremoniously—and entirely unnecessarily in the hush
that had greeted her entrance—Carlotta rapped her gavel
and said: "Parliament is now in session." She smiled sarcastically. "I suppose you're all wondering why I gathered
you here today." She punched two buttons on her console.
"Well, to make a long story short . . ."

One of the screens behind her came to life with a realtime image of the Arkology *Heisenberg* moving toward
Pacifica. Then the taped image of Dr. Roger Falkenstein
appeared on the screen beside it and began to speak. The
Delegates listened to th whole thing in stony silence, but
the moment it was over, everyone was speaking and shouting at once and Carlotta's board lit up with dozens of
requests for the floor.

"Order," Carlotta shouted, rapping her gavel. "Order!
Order!" When that didn't work, she forthrightly yelled
"Shut up!" at the top of her lungs.

The Delegates shut up.

"That's better," Carlotta said sweetly. "Chair recognizes
Delegate Willmington." Nora Willmington was a Gothamite and former newshound; she could be counted upon to
take umbrage at the slightest hint of denial of news access,
and it was best to get that question out of the way immediately.

Nora rose as if to make a speech and indeed began to

declaim in slow ironic tones. "I should like to ask the Chairman by what right, under what constitutional authority, she withheld the news of this contact with the Arkology *Heisenberg* from the news channels and issued instead a patently phony press release to the effect that the ship entering our solar system was unidentified and had not announced its identity to Pacifica—"

"By right of common sense and under the authority of sweet reason," Carlotta said. "The moment this august body saw the message, you were all screaming at once like godzillas with burrmites up their tails. How would you have liked to have had the whole planet bellowing like that before we had a moment to decide anything? We wouldn't have been able to hear ourselves think. And we *do* think, don't we?"

"If the Chairman thinks that snide remarks can justify—"

"Tell you what, Nora," Carlotta interrupted, "I hereby move that we release the Falkenstein message with full details immediately following the conclusion of this session. And I further move that it be considered a formal vote of confidence in me, okay?"

"I'll second *that*," Nora said.

"Good," Carlotta said. "Now do we have to waste valuable time debating this resolution or can we get it out of the way right now and deal with the real issues at hand?"

"Vote! Vote! Vote!"

"Thank you, people," Carlotta said as Nora sank back into her seat. "Ayes for the resolution, nays against."

The central wall screen behind her lit up with the running tally as the Delegates pressed their "Aye" or "Nay" buttons. It took about thirty seconds, and the count was 99 to 5 in favor, Carlotta not voting. So far, so good, Carlotta thought. That was a neat little maneuver, avoiding a possible no-confidence vote on withholding the message by turning it into a vote on releasing it. We're over the first hurdle.

"Now to the issue at hand," Carlotta said. "Falkenstein will be here in about eighteen days. Interstellar protocol demands that we allow him to land, and common sense dictates that he be allowed to present his case to some official entity or person. Since we've already voted to release everything we know at the end of this session, I submit that by then we must have decided who will meet with Falkenstein and what their policy directives from this body will be. Any dissent to that?"

There was general silence. Lacking political parties, the Pacifican Parliament was not in the habit of debating the self-evident.

First things first, Carlotta thought nervously. First whatever plenipotentiary powers I can extract, then the policy question. "I'd like to suggest that whoever meets with Falkenstein be empowered *only* to transmit whatever policy we decide upon today and that they *not* be empowered to discuss any deviation from that position without a full Parliamentary vote." That's a cagy way of putting it, she thought: no discussion, my hands are tied, I'm only expressing the will of my government. "Debate?" she asked.

Carlotta's board lit up with a dozen requests for the floor. At random, she recognized Jarvis Tatum, a beefy, red-haired Good Old Mountain Boy from the Cords.

"Shouldn't we decide our policy before we decide who's going to speak for us?" Tatum suggested. Oh-oh.

"A good point," Carlotta said, "but I think not. We don't want our spokesman to emerge from the winning side on the substantive issue, we want a neutral voice representing a consensus. Therefore, I rule that we consider the procedural point first and the substantive issue second."

There was a muted murmur of discontent at this, but the Chairman had the unquestioned right to decide points of Parliamentary order, and there could be no vote of confidence on such ostensibly procedural matters. But I'd better not be too heavy-handed about this, Carlotta realized. "Chair will entertain motions on the procedural question," she said, hoping that she was not going to have to be the one to nominate herself.

The board lit up, and she recognized Ian Palacci, a Columbian farmsteader, at random, not daring, at this point, to recognize any Delegate closely identified with herself.

"I move we appoint a three-person delegation," Palacci said. "One Delegate representing the eventual majority on the substantive issue, one Delegate representing the eventual minority, and the Chairman, if she is willing to so serve."

Carlotta pondered that for a moment. It was not quite

what she wanted, but it *was* fair, both in substance and in eventual appearance. It would be hard for anyone to raise a serious objection, and it would serve her purpose well enough. "Chairman agrees to so serve and seconds the motion," she said. "Any other suggestions?"

Two lights on the board. Carlotta recognized Warren Guilder from Thule.

"I move that instead of appointing a delegation, we invite Dr. Falkenstein to address Parliament directly," Guilder said.

Oh, shit!

Twenty lights on the board. Carlotta ignored them for the moment and spoke herself. "Closed or open?" she asked, hoping to trap Guilder.

"Uh . . . open, I guess . . ."

Carlotta recognized Catherine Buhl from Gotham, whose light had come on after Guilder's reply, figuring that her response would therefore have to be negative.

"Do we really want this person addressing the whole planet before we even know what he's going to say?" Buhl said. "Does this Parliament trust a Transcendental Scientist that far?"

"Well . . . uh . . . closed then . . ." Guilder muttered, to general laughter and more lights on the board. Again, Carlotta chose a Delegate whose light had come on in response to Guilder's answer—Nora Wilmington, who could be counted upon to oppose any further move toward secrecy.

"The notion of inviting *any* off-worlder to address a closed session of Parliament is unprecedented, repulsive, and will surely create nothing but thoroughly justified public outrage! Besides, we just voted to end secrecy in this matter!"

There were general shouts of approval and Carlotta felt she could risk recognizing Cynthia Cronyn now, even though she was generally identified with the Madigan administration.

"I call for a vote on Delegate Palacci's motion!"

The board lit up with about twenty seconds. Once again, Carlotta had managed to shift the vote to where she wanted it, this time without even having to take a position.

"Very well, then," she said. "Ayes for the resolution, nays against."

The vote was 71 in favor, 32 opposed, not as overwhelming this time, but still a better than two-to-one majority. "Motion carried," Carlotta said. "Now the Chair will entertain motions as to how this body will instruct the delegation." Now, she thought, comes the crunch.

Royce Lindblad made his way to his front-row Delegate's seat as unobtrusively as possible, exchanging only a quick covert glance with Carlotta as Delegate Maravitch continued to drone on.

". . . reasonably reliable sources further indicate that extended lifespans, perhaps as much as three centuries, have been achieved by . . ."

Royce had followed the general drift of the debate on the delegation's instructions on his office net console with half an eye while he prepared the basic press release and the backup media line, and it seemed to him the the Delegates were now just repeating themselves endlessly. The three basic positions had coalesced during the first hour, and what had been going on for the past two hours was just so much redundant hot air.

Perhaps a third of the Delegates who had spoken were, like Maravitch, entranced by the reputed scientific wares of Transcendental Science. Who wouldn't want to live for centuries, be able to transmit matter instantaneously, regenerate damaged organs, and all the rest of it? This pro-Institute faction had a strong argument, and blithely assumed that Pacifican society was inherently strong enough to resist becoming a de facto satrapy of Transcendental Science.

Another large faction was obsessed with the Pink and Blue War, even though there was no Femocrat factor in the current political equation. These Delegates equated a Pacifican Institute of Transcendental Science with inevitable involvement in the conflict, and stood foursquare for telling Falkenstein to remove his unwholesome presence from the Pacifican solar system. Strangely enough, many of them were male. It seemed to Royce that what they really feared was not the presence of an Institute of Transcendental Science, but the Femocrat response they assumed it would bring, as if they doubted the ability of Pacifican manhood to maintain its position of equality in the face of a Femocrat onslaught. This smelled unwholesomely unbucko to Royce, and, in a curious way, a slur against Pacifican women, too. Nevertheless, the political reality was that these Delegates were going to vote the way Carlotta wanted. Sometimes politics made rather effete bedfellows.

The rest of the Delegates, the swing vote, were caught in the middle. They wanted what Transcendental Science had to offer, but they feared involvement in the Pink and Blue War. It seemed to Royce that this group basically wanted Transcendental Science without the Transcendental Scientists, and simply didn't want to believe that such a thing was impossible.

It also seemed to him that everyone was missing the real point, the line that the media campaign he had already set in motion was going to take . . .

". . . a planet that refuses to ride the leading edge of scientific advance must inevitably become a backwater of inbred nostalgic . . ."

On and on went the debate, to no purpose that Royce could comprehend. Thus far, Carlotta had confined herself to chairing the session, and hadn't spoken out on the issue at all, when a strong statement from the Chairman would probably have swung the vote her way, and almost certainly would have done the trick if she made it a vote of confidence in herself. Was she simply letting them wear themselves down—*or did she want to avoid taking a personal stand entirely?*

Could that be it? Royce wondered. Does she want to conceal her own position so as to strengthen her hand in the forthcoming negotiations?

Royce caught Carlotta's eye and cocked his head slightly in a subtle gesture that only she would recognize. Carlotta returned the same signal, glanced down at her Delegate board, then looked directly into his eyes for a long moment.

So that's it, he thought. She wants me to do it. Uneasily, Royce pressed his request button, asking for the floor. It wouldn't be the first time he had fronted for Carlotta this way, nor would it be the first time he had supported a policy of hers with which he was not in total agreement. But he wondered if what he was going to say would be quite the words she wanted to put into his mouth . . .

"The Chair recognizes the Minister of Media . . ."

Royce felt the attention of the Delegates focus on him
with greater-than-usual intensity. The Minister of Media
was ordinarily the second most influential figure in the
gov, even when he was not the intimate of the Chairman.
Royce, as Carlotta's closest political ally and her lover,
usually but not always spoke for the Madigan administration as well as the Media Ministry. It was the most powerful possible combination in Pacifican politics.

"Speaking as a Pacifican," Royce said slowly, "I must
agree with those who want our planets to have the full
benefits of Transcendental Science. Only a fool would not
want to triple his lifespan, enhance his consciousness, and
attain the max mastery of his total environment. Pacifica
should have this knowledge."

He paused to let a low murmur whisper through the
chamber, to let the Delegates glance at Carlotta, who was
trying rather unsuccessfully to conceal her displeasure.
Royce laughed to himself—it was the oldest rhetorical
trick in the book.

"Speaking as a man," he continued, "I must agree with
those who want to avoid embroilment in the idiocy of the
Pink and Blue War *at all costs.*" There was a scattering of
applause and much confusion at this apparent reversal;
only Carlotta seemed to have caught on to what he was
doing. "Speaking as a Delegate, I must agree with those
who fear the subversion of Pacifican society by an Institute of Transcendental Science, Femocrats or no Femocrats."

Audible rumblings of confusion now. Even Carlotta was
looking at him peculiarly, as if trying to figure out where
he might be going. Perfect, Royce thought. I've summed
up all three positions and managed to support them all.
"If that sounds confusing, well, it is," he said. "It's like
wanting rain for our crops but not wanting to get wet.
We're all caught in the middle of the same paradox. Our
disagreements aren't with each other but within our own
selves."

He paused again, sensing that he had bled the conflict
out of the debate now, tied them together in an emotional
community by uniting the divergent viewpoints within himself. Now they were waiting hopefully for him to resolve
the paradox; even Carlotta seemed to be hanging on his

next words, as if she were no longer merely counting on him to serve her tactical purpose but to resolve a real confusion of her own.

"However," he said, hardening his voice, *"as Minister of Media,* I see the position this Parliament must take with crystal clarity. Pacifica's Web exports are the key to our continued prosperity. 'News of the Galaxy,' our entertainments, and our unique transport designs give us an overwhelmingly favorable balance of interstellar payments and provide jobs, directly and indirectly, for perhaps a quarter of our adult population. Other planets can afford to buy our Web products and keep us in the style to which we are accustomed only by exporting science and technology. Without free interstellar trade in science and technology, the interstellar economy based on the Web will eventually collapse, and if that happens, *we* will be the biggest losers."

Royce rose deliberately to his feet and began using his hands for dramatic emphasis. "Transcendental Science withholds its knowledge from the free Web market," he said sharply. "Transcendental Science uses its advanced knowledge not as an item of trade but as a *political weapon* with which to build a monopoly at the leading edge of science and technology. The price of their knowledge is measured not in interstellar credits but in loss of political autonomy. If Transcendental Science succeeds in its ultimate goals, interstellar free trade will be destroyed and Pacifica will pay a heavy price in economic depression and mass unemployment."

Royce sat down slowly to a guttural rumble of angry approval. There could hardly be a Delegate in the chamber who disagreed with *that!* Carlotta's face was unreadable as she studied him with a somewhat bemused expression. She now knew that he was giving her what she wanted tactically, but only by deflecting the Delegates from what she considered a matter of principle onto a bread-and-butter issue which would make them vote her way, and Royce wondered whether she might not be resenting that somehow.

"Therefore, as Minister of Media, I say that even if there were no such thing as the Pink and Blue War and no such ideology as Femocracy, Pacifica should do *nothing* that in *any way* furthers the monopolistic practices of

44

Transcendental Science. Therefore, I hereby move that our delegation be instructed to tell Falkenstein and his people that, while we are eager to buy any knowledge he may have to sell at a fair price, any such knowledge will then become a free item of interstellar trade, and that any Pacifican Institute of Transcendental Science must be run under Pacifican law—most specifically including the media access laws. And if they choose not to abide by these conditions, they are to remove themselves from this solar system forthwith!"

Decorous but spontaneous cheering broke out. "Second the motion! Second the motion!" Dozens of Delegates were calling for the vote. Royce smiled at Carlotta smugly, knowing that he had cunningly recrafted the issue at hand into a resolution that no one could seriously argue against and hope to remain in office. Closed session or not, he thought, that was one hell of a speech, and I'm going to release the tape to the news channels—it's perfect for our purposes.

Carlotta's face was utterly sphinxlike as she gaveled the Delegates to order. "If there are no objections, I call for a vote on the Minister's motion," she said evenly.

Of course there were none, and the motion sailed through, 80 to 23. And in a move that surprised even Royce, he himself was voted onto the delegation as the majority opinion member, along with Carlotta, and Lauren Golding from the Cords for the small minority, even though he was usually considered Carlotta's shadow.

It filled Royce with a rare sense of totally private pride to think that the Delegates had recognized his independent existence to such an extent. But on the other hand, Carlotta had been able to avoid taking any strong position at all, so as things stood now, it was *he* who publicly represented *her* position as if it were his own, and *she* who appeared to remain above it all, the obedient servant of a Parliamentary consensus that he had marshaled behind her. It was hard to figure out who was the puppet and who the puppeteer.

The disc of the setting sun behind them was cleanly bisected by the razor-sharp western horizon, and the surface of the sea was a glaze of deepening gold as Carlotta Madigan sat thoughtfully in the open cockpit of the

Golden Goose watching Royce sail the boat back to
Lorien. Dozing boomerbirds rode the light swell, their
heads tucked peacefully into their bright yellow breast
feathers. Far away to port, the translucent hump of a big
jellybelly glowed eerily in the twilight.

The world seemed at peace as it edged into night, and
Royce was like a little boy, thoroughly absorbed in the
delicate task of extracting the maximum speed from the
light following wind. Carlotta had secured the mandate she
wanted from Parliament, and the unforeseen election of
Royce to the delegation had even given her a welcome but
unexpected effective control. The ship of state seemed to be
making its way through its troubled waters almost as
smoothly as the *Golden Goose* gliding along the surface of
this tranquil sea. Yet something disturbed the peace of this
moment on a deep level that she could not quite plug her
conscious mind into, and the elusiveness of it made it
doubly annoying.

And somehow it was focused on Royce. He had been
so damned pleased with himself, so much the triumphant
bucko, that there had been no way to deny him this slow,
crawling surface sail back to Lorien. Surely this isn't too
much for me to endure for the sake of my bright young
bucko, Carlotta thought. Especially when he's served me
as well as he has today.

But that *is* what's bothering me, she suddenly realized.
Not the sail, but the *way* Royce steered that resolution
through today. And the way he built the press release
around his own speech afterward. He maneuvered Parliament the way he sails a boat, tacking with the wind, gliding frictionlessly through the storm, without ever facing
the real issue head-on and powering through it.

What if this Falkenstein is a political sailor like Royce?
What if he fools us all and *accepts* the conditions Royce
assumed would be unacceptable? If he says yes—no matter
what it really means—how can we say no—especially with
Royce so publicly identified with the line we're taking?
Wouldn't it have been better to have gotten a loud no vote
on principle up front, even though the margin of victory
would've been much smaller than this overwhelming but
ambiguous consensus?

But Royce had made the decision for her. He had acted

unilaterally, and now he at least appeared publicly to be the pilot of a policy he had created. This was something new in their political relationship, and she didn't like it. And truth be told, she didn't much like herself for not liking it. Are you some kind of crypto-Femocrat at heart, Carlotta Madigan? she asked herself half-seriously. Does your bucko *always* have to walk two steps behind you?

"Do you really believe everything you said today, Royce?" she asked.

Royce glanced at her peculiarly.

"I mean, what if Falkenstein *accepts* the conditions in the resolution? How do we say no to an Institute of Transcendental Science then?"

Royce laughed. "First of all, I think the chances of that happening are zip," he said. "Secondly, if he *should* accept our conditions, what would be wrong with having an Institute anyway?"

"*What?*"

"What do you mean, *what?*" Royce snapped. "I meant what I said. If we can have Transcendental Science without political strings, without interference in our way of life, and without helping to maintain their monopoly, then why not? Give me one good reason!"

"Why . . . ah . . . I guess it's just a gut-feeling, Royce," Carlotta said lamely, unable to explain it even to herself. "I mean, who wants the Pink and Blue War . . . ?"

"But if Falkenstein accepts our terms—which he won't anyway—how does that involve us in the Pink and Blue War? If anything, it'll help *end* the damned thing. Without the Transcendental Science monopoly, the dynamic for the war no longer exists. Truth be told, that's what I'd like to see happen. Wouldn't you?"

"Ah . . . er, I suppose so," Carlotta said distantly. "I guess I'm just a little edgy . . . Something about that Falkenstein bothers me on an irrational level, is all . . ."

"Hmmmm . . ." Royce muttered, and turned his attention back to the set of the sails and the sea before him. As the first stars of night began to dust the darkening sky, the two of them sat apart, brooding on their own private thoughts.

That in itself disturbed Carlotta as she gazed up at the night sky. For truth be told, Carlotta hated the thing that was moving toward them with a passion beyond all rational political logic. It seemed that the shadow of the Arkology *Heisenberg* had already darkened their own intimate landscape.

4

DR. ROGER FALKENSTEIN FELT THAT HE STOOD AT THE brink of a mission that might be a major inflection point in the upward curve of human history. Or a break-point in the steady hyperbolic rise should he fail.

Rising through the liftube at the long axis of the *Heisenberg* from his quarters on 12-deck to the main briefing room on 2-deck, Falkenstein passed through nine typical decks of the Arkology, which he thought of as neither vehicle of transit nor home.

Three of the decks through which he passed were nothing more than human warehouses: tier upon tier of Deep Sleep chambers in which, at any given time, the majority of the Arkology's inhabitants spent the years between meaningful activities in suspended animation, editing their long lifespans into continuous dramas of peak experiences by removing all periods of boredom and waiting.

Partially as a result of this instant access to Deep Sleep, where both body metabolism and memory track could be frozen into a timeless moment while objective years or even centuries flowed by unnoticed, the residential decks of the Arkology were for the most part starkly functional. Circles of spacious apartments surrounded the central drop and lift tubes with only a token formal garden here and there. Color schemes varied, but generally ran to bright primaries, golds, whites, and metallics—colors well calculated to energize the mind and brighten the spirit, but equally well calculated to avoid the earth-tones that would psychologically simulate growing things or the surfaces of planets. Even the paintings in the apartments, the murals in the public areas of the Arkology, and the motifs of the artificial "skies" above each deck tended almost entirely to the astronomical—star fields, great banded gas giants, complex multiple-star systems, stylized black holes, blazing novas. Growing things were for the most part confined to the hydroponic decks, where the vats were arranged in neat rows and the plants provided food, animal fodder, and oxygen; fuel for the human metabolism, not a narcotic for the soul.

The psychic heart of an Arkology consisted of the lab decks and the computer deck and the communications deck that linked all planetbound Institutes of Transcendental Science and all Arkologies into a unified culture that could truly be said to be galactic, at least in a primitive sense. *Homo galacticus* had at least evolved to the point where he needed no psychological simulacrums of his planetary past any more than planetbound humans needed to live in simulations of the treetop world from which their remote ancestors had descended.

And now we are poised for the next step, Falkenstein thought as he reached 2-deck. And fate has chosen me as the nexus of evolutionary forces, as the instantaneous instrument of the process which has taken our species from the trees to the stars, and which is now battering against the very limits of the naturally evolved universe. Now we must evolve beyond evolution itself or sink inexorably backward into the primordial slime.

The main briefing room was a circular domed chamber; a round white table filled the center of the room, the floor was carpeted in light gray, and the walls were a seamless expanse of pale blue broken only by a large computer display screen and a speaker grid. Computer access was strictly voice-activated here, so that the Arkmind could take part as just another collegue.

The domed ceiling was a single great screen that could be opaqued to a soothing pearl gray or illumined with an appropriate abstraction from the artbanks, or, as it was now, turned into a "window" onto the space outside the Arkology's inertia screen.

Now the great globe of Pacifica hung above the table, a cloud-swirled ball of greens, browns, and brilliant blue suspended in the perpetual blackness of star-filled space. White icecaps gleamed at either pole. The great curving horn of the main continent of Columbia half-cradled the vast Island Continent as if it had just flung an armful of green jewels eastward across the azure sea. The Big Blue River and its tributaries were clearly visible like a network of blue veins draining the green and gold eastern plains. The Sierra Cordillera cleanly divided the western portion of Columbia, furred with green on the western slopes, outlining the sere brown of the desert interior. At this magnification, even the city of Gotham winked at the edge of visibility at the delta-mouth of the Big Blue, like a tiny chip of shiny metal intermittently catching the light of the sun. The immense ball above utterly dominated the room. It was a tangibly living planet, huge, verdant, and, with its perpetual slow swirl and ebb of white cloud patterns, organic and breathing, palpably alive.

Five men and a woman sat around the white table. Carlos Miranda, one of the *Heisenberg's* Link Officers, had been out of Deep Sleep for a year on his regular tour. The other four men were specialists who had been awakened when the *Heisenberg* entered the Pacifican solar system specifically to background this mission: Lar Dalton, Psychopolitician; Harry Eisen, head of the Survey Update Team; Winston Cornelle, Historical Analysis, and Artur Polichev, Legal Advisor.

Together, these five men represented the apexes of five Situation Task Forces of up to twenty men apiece specifically formed to deal with all aspects of the Pacifica mission. The men in this room gave Falkenstein access to more depth information on Pacifica than the Pacificans had on themselves.

And then there was Maria. Falkenstein's wife was one of the few female graduates of an Institute of Transcendental Science, specialty Projection, which had no immediate relevance to the Pacifica mission. But Psychopolitics had determined that a husband-wife negotiation team was the optimum sync with the Pacifican psychopolitical matrix. One lone ambassador-plenipotentiary would offend their democratic ideology, and a team of experts would tend to arouse their paranoia and point too sharply to their total scientific inferiority. Further, the Pacifican sexual power balance leaned subtly toward the female—though the Pacificans themselves kept this just below the level of full conscious awareness—and a sexually balanced negotiating team was therefore highly desirable.

Besides, Falkenstein knew that he functioned best with Maria at his side—he was a rare and lucky man to have a wife of her intellectual quality—and he would have brought her along no matter what analysis Psychopolitics had come up with.

"Very well," Falkenstein said, taking his seat next to Maria with a quick private glance of greeting, "this will be our last chance to run through the scenario before Maria and I go planetside. Arkmind, please monitor. Maria, please summarize."

A strange look passed briefly across Maria's even features—annoyance, pride, perhaps both. Annoyance at being treated like a student at an oral exam, pride at being accorded the status of aide-de-camp to the Managing Director, who happened to be her husband. Falkenstein's motivations were also mixed. He wanted to be sure she had internalized the scenario thoroughly, but he also wanted to assure the others of her competence. Despite the projections of Psychopolitics, there was still a certain reluctance to entrust a woman with this level of responsibility, and the fact that Maria was his wife only added another layer of ambiguity.

"Roger and I will be negotiating with a delegation consisting of the Chairman, Carlotta Madigan; the Minister of Media, Royce Lindblad; and Lauren Golding, a Good Old Mountain Boy Delegate representing the minority faction most favorable to our position," Maria said crisply. "Lindblad is Madigan's lover and political ally; therefore, she is in effective control of the delegation."

"Correction," said Eisen. "It was Lindblad who proposed the motion their Parliament passed, and Lindblad who has done most of the speaking for the administration position. Madigan has carefully avoided taking a public position. Therefore, he may very well be acting independently."

"Almost certainly a political ploy on her part," Dalton insisted. "Their personal relationship syncs into the dominant Pacifican female-superior mode, and Lindblad has never opposed her on a significant political issue."

"But historically, the Pacifican Minister of Media has been a political figure of significant independence, frequently in opposition to the Chairman," Cornelle said.

"But the current situation is an anomaly and therefore historical analysis does not—"

Maria smiled thinly at Eisen. "Is this psychopolitical analysis, Harry, or do you just find the concept of a dominant female political figure in an egalitarian society hard to swallow?"

Eisen flushed. Falkenstein laughed, but no one else laughed with him. "This is irrelevant," he said. "The operative fact is that the Pacifican Parliament has overwhelmingly instructed the delegation to reject an Institute of Transcendental Science on anything like reasonable terms. Whether this was engineered by Madigan or not, she is bound by the instructions of her Parliament. Maria, will you please continue from there . . ."

"Therefore, the Arkmind has projected the almost certain failure of the negotiations," Maria said in flat professional tones. "Even if Lindblad or Madigan should unexpectedly side with Golding and the delegation should accept our proposal, Parliament would have to ratify it, and if an immediate vote were taken, it would certainly be negative, and that would be the end of it."

"Correction," said Polichev. "If Madigan supported the Institute and Parliament then turned it down, there would then be a planetwide electronic vote of confidence. If she won, a new Parliament would be elected which would likely overturn the previous vote."

"A train of events which the Arkmind projects as virtually impossible," Falkenstein said testily. "Can we please stick to the main lines of the scenario? Maria . . ."

"Therefore, we must avoid an immediate confrontation when our proposal is turned down," Maria continued. "We ask for time to study their counterproposals. We formally request permission to remain in orbit around Pacifica in the meantime. With the utmost politeness and reasonableness. The Arkmind predicts that the Madigan delegation cannot deny such a request without risking a vote of confidence on the wrong side of the issue of simple galactic protocol." Maria smiled, knowing she had stated it all well. "That concludes phase one of the scenario."

"Very good," Falkenstein said. "But perhaps we had better look ahead and clarify phase two. Artur, will you verify the timing for me again?"

"Once the fact that we've been given permission to remain in orbit has been released to the Pacifican media, it will be irreversible except by vote of Parliament," the Legal Advisor said. "Say overnight, for safety's sake."

"At which point I invoke Article 12, Section 3 of the Pacifican Constitution . . ." Falkenstein said.

"Section 2, Roger," Polichev corrected. "*No one*—and the phrasing clearly does not exclude non-Pacificans— may be denied a public net channel or may be prevented from purchasing time on free market channels except by reason of judicially declared criminal intent or in order to advocate the overthrow of the Pacifican government or Constitution by extralegal means."

"They won't like it, but they'll have to swallow it," Dalton said. "Aside from the legalism, the Pacificans are absolute fanatics on the subject of free media access— it almost has the psychic force of a religious commandment. We'll have them caught by their own deepest convictions."

Falkenstein drummed his fingers on the table nervously. "There's one hole that I can see in phase two," he said. "They can't deny us media access once we invoke their own Constitution, but they're not going to like it. Might they then not simply revoke their permission for us to remain in their solar system? Arkmind, a projection on that, please . . ."

"Sixty to forty negative under the present scenario," said the cool, soothing voice of the computer.

Falkenstein frowned. "Not nearly good enough," he said. "How can we raise the odds to at least 75–25 in our favor?"

"Politicize the issue immediately," Dalton suggested. "In local psychosexual terms."

"Elucidate."

"Transcendental Science's image is male-dominant—"

"I wonder where they got *that* idea?" Maria muttered. Falkenstein shot her an angry glance.

"—as a result of Femocrat propaganda," Dalton continued, speaking through her, "Lauren Golding is a so-called 'Good Old Mountain Boy' from the Sierra Cordillera, where the local culture is almost entirely male and dominantly homosexual. Any hint that expelling us is a female attempt to surpress free access to the ideas of a male-dominant culture will arouse strong political support for us there, and we seem to have his vote anyway—"

"But if the homosexual male culture supports us openly, won't that cancel itself out by polarizing Pacifican lesbians against us?" Maria interrupted.

Dalton frowned in annoyance. He glanced at Falkenstein for support. "If I may continue . . . ?" he said somewhat frostily.

"She *does* have a point, Lar . . ." Falkenstein said.

Dalton sighed. "Actually not," he replied. "You forget that we're dealing with a subtley female dominant culture on Pacifica, Maria. Which means that since lesbians are thoroughly integrated into the existing power structure, there is no female equivalent of the male homosexual sub-culture of the Sierra Cordillera. Besides, since this *is* a female dominant society, there are no psychopolitical pressures towards lesbianism, and therefore the demographic equation is *not* evenly balanced." He smiled wanly at Maria. "*Now* may I return to the main line of the sub-scenario?"

Maria said nothing, but Falkenstein could sense a resistance in her that seemed only peripherally involved with this minor technical point.

"*To continue,*" Dalton said, after an uneasy moment of silence. "Golding's vote can be considered assured. The swing figure thus becomes Royce Lindblad. Befriend him. Appeal to his manhood. Treat him as Madigan's equal or even her inherent superior. Drive enough of a wedge between them so that he won't support any move by Madigan to expel us immediately. Even if she takes it to Parliament —which I doubt she would with a majority of her own delegation against her—there would then be enough political division to postpone a showdown vote for at least a week, during which time our psywar teams will concentrate on linking the expulsion issue to the freedom of media access issue. It will then be too late to expel us."

Maria's features tightened. "I don't like it," she said. "Don't you recognize any limits, Lar?"

"It's well within the Pacifican psychosexual parameters, Maria," Dalton said mildly.

"I mean limits of human decency," Maria snapped.

"This is war, Maria," Falkenstein said testily. "And the stakes are ultimate. You know what the alternative is. Arkmind, a projection on the probable success of this sub-scenario, please?"

"83 to 17 favorable," the computer said.

"Well, that settles that!"

"Roger—"

"Enough, Maria!" Falkenstein snapped. "The decision has been made." Maria nibbled at her lower lip, then stared down at the table. For all her unquestioned intellect, she had as much capacity to make these things difficult as the next woman.

"Now then," Falkenstein said more calmly, "it occurs to me in the light of what Lar has said that it might be useful to establish a political base in the Sierra Cordillera during our long-term psywar campaign. Might we not persuade the Pacificans to let us land a small party while we're in orbit—on humanitarian grounds? They know nothing of our culture and the planetbound mentality would surely sympathize with the supposed need of our people to get off the Arkology and smell the flowers, as it were . . ."

"A good idea," Dalton said. "Try to put it specifically to Golding in a way that will make him believe he thought of it himself. A personal invitation from his constituency, and so forth. Then, during the three-month period before the Femocrat mission arrives—"

"I'm afraid we have a little problem there," Miranda said. "The Femocrat ship has delayed deceleration. Projections show they'll have to pull a steady four gees when they begin, which will bring them here within six weeks. Probably keeping most of their personnel in Deep Sleep and doing it either with automatics or a volunteer skeleton crew."

"Damn!" Falkenstein muttered. "That's pretty drastic. Does it mean they know we're here?"

Miranda shrugged. "Could be. We've scrambled all our tachyon traffic, but tachyon beams are directional. They could've detected scrambled transmissions moving toward Pacifica and extrapolated the correct conclusion."

56

Well that's certainly how we found out what *they* were up to, Falkenstein thought. The *Planck* had picked up scrambled transmissions from a Femocrat ship moving toward Pacifica at their maximum speed, eight years from planetfall, and it had taken a couple of rather extreme black hole flybys plus the inertia screen which the Femocrats lacked to beat them to the planet at all.

And now we find out that we only have six weeks to maneuver freely in instead of three months!

"Does this mean that we should change our phase three scenario?" Falkenstein mused aloud.

"You mean tell the Pacificans that there's a Femocrat mission on the way from the outset and immediately sync the establishment of an Institute into an anti-Femocrat movement?"

"Yes."

Dalton shook his head. "It might prove useful in the long run, and if we don't work fast enough we may have to do it anyway once they arrive," he said. "But in the phase one and phase two timeframes, it would just sync the issue of expelling us into the issue of staying out of the 'Pink and Blue War,' as they call it here. The Pacificans would then be overwhelmingly in favor of throwing both us and the Femocrats off the planet. Winston . . .?"

"I concur absolutely," the Historical Analyst said. "If the Pacificans found out about the Femocrat mission, they'd expel us immediately so they could treat the Femocrats the same way when they arrived. Becoming embroiled in the ideological conflict is absolute anathema to this planet."

Falkenstein leaned back in his chair and sighed. "Then we stick to the original scenario through phase three," he said. "Should the Femocrats arrive before we succeed in establishing an Institute, we act as surprised as the Pacificans and consider adjustments to phase four at that time. Lar, your people had better begin working out the contingencies now, though. Six weeks of a free hand is better than no time at all, I suppose."

"So it is," Dalton said.

"So it had better be," Falkenstein replied. "I think this meeting is concluded. Arkmind, you may cease monitoring."

As the staff filed out of the room, Falkenstein slumped

further back in his chair, tilting his head backwards so that the huge image of Pacifica on the dome above him filled his field of vision, a vast and intimately synergizing organic complexity of geography and ecosystems, matter, energy and process.

How hopelessly complex a living planet is, he thought. This one, with its nearly circular orbit and minimal axial tilt—easy enough to predict its constant seasons, but would an Arkmind model have ever extrapolated that mammalian life-forms would never evolve in such a context? Add a sentient human culture, and the complexities multiply exponentially, and so therefore do the uncertainties.

And this . . . *this* . . . The Pacifican culture seemed almost malevolently designed to maximize uncertainty and minimize predictability. Mass trends given instant political expression through electronic democracy. A psychosexual balance so complex and ambiguous that the Pacificans themselves don't really understand it. Total media saturation of maximum diversity, partially government controlled, partially a total chaos of whim and fashion.

Although Pacifica sat at the psychic and economic center of the Galactic Media Web, although Pacifica in a sense held the atavistic system of separate planetary governments together in dynamic but static stability, despite the Pacificans' unchallenged mastery of the media arts, despite the fact that Pacifica was therefore in a sense the pinnacle of the previous human evolutionary state, the Council had long since decided to leave this damnable planet alone. There were too many uncertainties to be utterly confident of success, and failure here could turn this most aggressively neutral of planets into the most dangerous enemy conceivable.

But now, Falkenstein thought, we have no choice. By itself, Femocracy was an evolutionary dead end, a pathology that would collapse of its own internal contradictions long before the dawn of the true galactic age. But should Femocrat ideology come to dominate the planet that dominated the Galactic Media Web . . . Falkenstein shuddered. Through Pacifica, Femocracy could dominate the human worlds in a timeframe of decades, metastasize like a runaway carcinoma, set human evolution back a thousand years within a century . . .

And now Pacifica *has* become a Femocrat target. We're

forced to fight them here. And *I'm* the man standing at this evolutionary crossroads, with the future of the species riding on every move I make . . .

Falkenstein shook his head ruefully. I wouldn't have asked for this, he thought, but truth be told, I wouldn't want it in anyone else's hands either.

"Having second thoughts, Roger?"

Maria had come up beside him unnoticed, and stood there with her left arm around the back of his chair. Instinctively, Falkenstein straightened his posture, composed his features, and cleared his mind of these uncertain ruminations. "About what?" he said crisply.

"About meddling in a personal relationship for political purposes," Maria said. "After all, how would you like it if someone ran a scenario like that on us?"

Falkenstein looked up into her even, ageless features, the face he had known and loved for half a century. "They would surely fail, would they not?" he said.

Maria nodded up at the image of Pacifica looming above them. "Those people down there are not thee and me," she said.

"Noblesse oblige?" Falkenstein said sardonically.

"You could call it that."

Falkenstein's features hardened. I hope my faith in your ability to function optimally on this mission isn't misplaced, Maria, he thought. I hope pride and love haven't clouded my vision. "We have a higher obligation," he said. "What is the possibility of destroying one personal relationship when measured against a catastrophe like a Femocrat Pacifica?"

"What if the relationship in question were *ours*, Roger?"

Falkenstein's eyes softened, but his face became a mask of sternness in compensation. "I know what you'd like me to say," he said. "But we both know what the truth is, don't we?"

Maria looked away from him, down at the floor. Tenderly, Falkenstein touched her hand. "There's another way to look at it," he said. "Royce Lindblad hasn't come into his full-manhood. Is it wrong to give him that? If their relationship can't survive his equality and political independence, will anything worthwhile have really been destroyed?"

Maria looked into his eyes. Words froze on her lips. She shook her head and kissed him lightly on the cheek.

"I suppose you're right, Roger," she said in a subdued voice. "Yours is the long view and the deep view. As always."

Falkenstein patted her hand, wondering why her simple acknowledgment of the truth filled him with such annoyance.

5

WELL THEY CERTAINLY ARE AN IMPRESSIVE COUPLE, CAR-lotta Madigan thought as she, Royce, and Lauren Golding led the Falkensteins away from the newshounds on the lawn and into the lodge. The question is, a couple of *what*?

Dr. Roger Falkenstein, lean, gray-haired, and almost theatrically self-assured in a midnight-blue high-collared suit tailored for authoritarian effect like an ancient military uniform, seemed ageless. He could have been fifty or a hundred and fifty, or a thousand and fifty. It would not be hard to believe that those bright unreadable eyes had seen centuries go by. His wife fitted the same mold; trim, age-less of body, ancient around the eyes, and wearing a green skirted suit cut in the same fashion, only unmatched colors pointing up the fact that neither of them were really wear-ing uniforms. Perhaps there was a shade less arrogance in her bearing. Although they seemed to make a point of walking side by side and treating each other as equals, he had done all of the talking to the reporters. It fitted with the male-dominant reputation of Transcendental Science, but it also appeared that they were making a somewhat fumbling effort to counter that image. Well, you'll have to do better than that on Pacifica, Jocko, Carlotta thought, freely admitting to herself that she had taken an instant visceral dislike to the Managing Director of the *Heisenberg*.

She led the party through the lobby and up two flights of stairs to the roof garden atop Koma Lodge. As casual as the choice of this rented villa might seem, it had been the result of some careful political calculations. From the roof garden, the towers, domes, and bridges of Gotham were dimly visible to the northwest over a calm blue sea and a sprinkling of tiny uninhabited islets. Koma Lodge was close enough to Gotham so that there could be no charges of holding the Transcendental Scientists incommunicado at some isolated locale, but far enough away from metropolitan Gotham and small enough to make the restrictions on the number of newshounds seem reasonable. Royce had wanted to hold the meetings at Lorien as a gesture of personal hospitality, but that was exactly the sort of personal identification with the Transcendental Science delegation that Carlotta was determined to avoid.

Five bongowood loungers had been arranged around a table of refreshments under a potted umbrella-fern, and Carlotta poured iced floatfruit wine for everyone as they seated themselves. Golding immediately took a long swallow. Royce toyed with his glass without drinking. The Falkensteins ignored the wine, the view, the breeze, any attempt at preliminary small talk, and sat there regarding Carlotta with unreadable eyes, formally waiting to open negotiations.

"I'm not exactly sure where to begin," Carlotta said, after what seemed like an endless staring contest. "I mean, this is a bit uncomfortable. We know what you're here for, and you know what our government's position is . . ."

"And perhaps we're all drawing unnecessary conclusions," Roger Falkenstein said, cracking a friendly smile that set Carlotta's teeth on edge. "You seem to believe that an Institute of Transcendental Science would represent some kind of intrusion in your internal affairs . . ."

"And you're saying that it wouldn't?" Royce said.

Falkenstein directed his false smile at Royce. "Not through any intention of ours," he said. "We Transcendental Scientists don't consider ourselves a nationality or an ideology or even a political unit. We're research scientists and teachers, nothing more. We are simply proposing to set up a kind of university on Pacifica. We'll disseminate our knowledge to Pacifican students, train local people in the Transcendental Sciences, and eventually teach Pacificans to run the Institute by themselves and leave your planet entirely. You'll be left with a functioning Institute able to elevate the technological and scientific level of your planet and equipped to do its own research at the frontiers of human knowledge, and run entirely by indigenous personnel." Falkenstein shrugged ingenuously. "Why should anyone feel threatened by that?"

"Sounds harmless enough to me," Golding said.

"Totally altruistic," Carlotta cracked sardonically.

Roger Falkenstein cocked an inquisitive eyebrow at her. "I mean, what's in it for you?" she said.

Falkenstein laughed. "Oh, I see," he said. "You distrust apparent lack of self-interest. Rightly so. Actually, there's a great deal in it for us, if you define 'us' correctly."

"And this correct definition is . . . ?"

"Mankind," Falkenstein said, with an embracing, inclusive gesture. "The species. Our common destiny. Each time we establish a new Institute we gain *colleagues*. Science is, after all, a vast collective effort. The more people working at the edges of the scientific frontier, the more rapidly the race as a whole progresses. Everyone has a self-interest in that. Our system of Institutes combines the most useful aspects of both diversity and common effort. Each Institute draws upon the unique genius of its planet, but all are bound together in a network of free and instantaneous information exchange, so that projects are not needlessly duplicated, so that the total research effort synergizes into a whole that is greater than the sum of its parts."

Spread it on bread and feed it to Rugo! Carlotta thought. Melts in your mind, not on your fingers. But it was Royce who applied the grease-cutter.

"That sounds like the gift of the Magi, Dr. Falkenstein," he said. "But if that's really your vector, why do you withhold your knowledge from the Web? Why don't you sell your science and technology freely like everyone else? Or if you're really all that selfless, give it away?"

That's my bucko! Carlotta thought, slipping Royce a sidelong glance of appreciation which he seemed to ignore.

Falkenstein's composure cracked for an instant, but he re-erected his confident, friendly mask quickly enough.

"We'd like to be able to do just that," Falkenstein said. "It would certainly make our ultimate task that much easier. Unfortunately, that would be the height of irresponsibility."

"Oh, really?"

"Really," Falkenstein said earnestly. "The knowledge we possess even in the current timeframe would be disastrous in the wrong hands. For instance, we could, if we chose, reproduce ourselves entirely by cloning, and genetically tailor the clones, too. What would the Femocrats do with *that?* Eliminate the male of the species entirely, perhaps, or worse, produce a subsentient slave species. For instance, our Arkologies can traverse interstellar distances 50 percent faster than conventional starships, and some day, we hope, research in this area will lead to a faster-than-light drive that will enable men to travel from star to star in *weeks* instead of years. This will either bring about a true galactic culture, the next step in human evolution . . . or the unthinkable."

"The unthinkable?" Golding said.

Suddenly Falkenstein seemed genuinely sincere for the first time. "The possibility that men will once again wage *war* against each other," he said softly. "The human race only ceased its incessant warfare when planetary governments became the political norm. Not because human consciousness had evolved beyond the possibility of this suicidal behavior pattern, but because the distances between solar systems, the years-long voyages necessary, made war a logistical impossibility. But given a faster-than-light drive, given our present capabilities in the areas of cloning and genetic engineering, and given the psychopathology of Femocracy, could not an army of genetically tailored amazon warriors sweep through the human worlds? Would not the rest of humanity resort to force of arms to combat such a threat? And if such a galactic war were fought with the powers even currently at our command, we would probably destroy ourselves as a species. Our knowledge of astrophysics would enable us to nova suns. We could create plagues that no protoplasm could survive . . ."

Falkenstein lapsed into silence. A cold wind seemed to blow in, and not from the ocean.

"So you see," he finally said, "we can't simply disseminate our knowledge cavalierly and wash our hands of the consequences."

Lauren Golding's bluff red face seemed unnaturally pale. His booming voice faded to a whisper. "The man is right," he said.

"I'm not sure that you're not leaping to a whole set of unnecessary conclusions, Dr. Falkenstein," Carlotta said uncertainly. "Seems to me you consider the rest of the human race idiot children . . ."

Maria Falkenstein spoke for the first time. "Of course we're projecting conclusions. That's the whole point. For most of human history, science has been fragmented from politics, morality, ultimate concerns. Scientists produced knowledge and power, considered both ethically neutral, and turned their backs on the consequences. But we believe—"

"Not believe, Maria," Roger Falkenstein interjected, *"know."*

"—we *know* that reality is a unity of matter, energy, time, and mind. Psychosocial and political projections are therefore as much a valid area of scientific concern as astrophysics or genetic engineering because they're interrelated aspects of the same whole . . ."

"That all sounds very deep," Carlotta said, "and maybe it is. But I don't see its relevance to the issue at hand— your insistence on controlling access to your knowledge instead of making it the common property of the human race."

"Our long-range goal *is* to make Transcendental Science the common property of the human race," Falkenstein said. "But one does not become a Transcendental Scientist without encompassing the *whole*, without developing a transcendental consciousness. And *that* is what we do at our Institutes. To graduate from an Institute of Transcendental Science is to join an interstellar brotherhood of evolved human consciousness that *transcends* planetary nationalism or ideological mind-set, that seeks to evolve the whole race to its own level in time. That's why we build Arkologies—because we consider ourselves citizens of a galactic culture yet to come which will transcend the parameters of our naturally evolved planetary consciousness."

Falkenstein glanced at Carlotta, but then seemed to be directing his next words to Royce. "That's also why we can't allow anyone but Institute graduates access to partial knowledge. Transcendental Science is not separable. Would *you* hand over a fusion bomb to an unsocialized child?"

Royce locked eyes with Falkenstein for a long moment. Then he looked out to sea, where a small covy of bumblers paddled just offshore, bobbing their heads under the surface in search of fish. But he didn't seem to be watching the big birds; his eyes seemed unfocused, as if staring off into Falkenstein's distant yonder. This has gone just about far enough! Carlotta decided.

"You've given us your position in considerable depth, Dr. Falkenstein," she said. "You've made your points most cogently. Now I had better clearly state ours. We'd like to have an Institute of Transcendental Science. We're willing to let you send teachers planetside. *However,* any Pacifican Institute of Transcendental Science must be considered a corporation chartered under Pacifican law. Which means that anything imparted to Pacifican citizens on Pacifican soil becomes governed by *our* laws, not yours. Specifically that means our information access laws and our Web trade regulations. Pacifican Institute graduates may sell anything they know to the Pacifican government or to private corporations who in turn may also resell information to the government. Any knowledge sold to the government goes into the public accessbanks, where it may be retrieved free of charge by any Pacifican citizen. Anything in the public accessbanks may be traded on the Web under the discretion of the Ministry of Media."

Carlotta smiled sweetly at Falkenstein, confident after what she had just heard that she had effectively slammed the door. "If you can live with that, we have a deal," she said. "Otherwise, we have nothing to discuss but philosophic pleasantries."

Surprisingly, Falkenstein seemed not to react at all. No surprise, no annoyance, no nothing. He just sat there calmly pondering her diktat for a long thoughtful moment. "Interesting," he finally said mildly.

"Interesting? Is that all you have to say?"

"Well, we always expect to have to conform to local law," Falkenstein said in the friendliest of tones. "What you propose obviously has complex ramifications, both legally and philosophically. Obviously, I cannot accept your offer until we have had some time to study the full implications . . ."

What? Huh? Carlotta was caught completely off balance. "You mean you're not rejecting it?" she blurted. "After all you've just said?"

Falkenstein smiled at her. Ingenuously? Sardonically? It was impossible to even guess. "The difference in our respective positions seems to boil down to a question of trust," he said. "Do we have enough trust in the efficacy of our own Institute to be confident that all Pacifican graduates, without exception, will behave responsibly after they are fully trained? A deep question for us to ponder. If we are able to answer in the affirmative, it will represent a great step forward. Of course, we will have to give the matter thorough study, consult our Arkmind, and put it to the Council of the Whole.' Obviously, this is a matter of high policy, and neither I nor the people of the *Heisenberg* can make such a decision independently . . ."

He glanced at Royce, then at Golding. "Personally, if it were up to me . . ." He shrugged, sighed. "But then, it isn't. We should be able to have a decision for you in a week or two, if that's acceptable. Obviously, I can't get the Council to alter such a policy without considerable debate. But I'll try . . ."

"That sounds reasonable," Golding said. "Maybe more than reasonable."

Royce nodded, and Carlotta, though she longed to, could find no reason to object under the Parliamentary mandate, especially with both Royce and Golding apparently taken in by this slick brand of jellybelly oil.

"Then I gather you'll bear with us a while?" Falkenstein said. "We have permission to remain in orbit?"

"I can't see why not," Carlotta said grudgingly.

"Thank you," Falkenstein said. He picked up his glass of floatfruit wine, took a sip, nodded appreciatively. He stood up, stretched, gazed out to sea, took a deep breath, walked around in a small semicircle, stood behind Golding's chair, took another sip of wine. It all seemed like choreography to Carlotta.

"I'd like to ask one small favor," he said. "We don't get to spend much time on planetary surfaces, you know, and this one is particularly beautiful. Perhaps we might stay here tonight, refresh ourselves with your good sea air, and postpone returning to the *Heisenberg* until morning?"

"For sure," Royce said. "We'd already planned dinner, and breakfast will be no problem. Right, Carlotta?"

"Of course . . ." Carlotta muttered uneasily.

"You like the sea, do you?" Royce said, sipping his own wine.

"It's refreshing," Falkenstein said. "Of course Maria and I were born on a planet that's mostly mountains. Tall rolling chains covered with forests, high clean air, waterfalls from glacial overruns . . . I feel more of an affinity for that sort of terrain . . ."

"You'd like the Cords," Golding said, looking up at Falkenstein. "Rainforests. The sun rising through the forest canopy at dawn. And we have quite a seacoast too. Didn't think you folks would be mountain types . . ."

Maria Falkenstein laughed. "We're not exactly outdoors types," she said. "But some of us do have our memories . . ."

Golding ran his eyes up Roger Falkenstein's lean ageless body; Falkenstein seemed to strike a pose, lithe and aristocratic in his tightly tailored suit. "Perhaps you might find time to see the Cords, Dr. Falkenstein."

Falkenstein smiled at him. *"Roger,* please, now that our official business is done," he said. He shrugged ruefully. "I'd like that, but I'm afraid there are too many people on the *Heisenberg* who'd also like to stretch their legs on some mountain slope. They might accuse me of invoking personal privilege."

"Well I don't see why we can't afford your people a little vacation in the Cords," Golding said. "Those that feel . . . sympatico, anyway. Of course, our accommodations might be a little rough and ready . . ."

Falkenstein turned a positively brilliant smile on Golding. "That would be marvelous . . . Lauren," he said. "And you wouldn't have to worry about accommodations, we can throw up housing for a hundred people within an hour. That's the maximum number the *Heisenberg* could spare at any given time anyway. We'd shuttle our vacationers back and forth, we wouldn't want to flood you with a horde of tourists. After all, half the enjoyment would be . . . experiencing your way of life."

"We'll enjoy showing it to you," Golding said, smiling broadly.

"Just a minute!" Carlotta snapped, finally able to accept her own reading of the game Falkenstein was playing. He's actually *cockteasing* this bucko, unless he really is mano. He's practically setting up a mass assignation. Or at least Golding thinks he is!

"What's the matter, Carlotta?" Golding asked.

"There's no policy on letting these people planetside," Carlotta told him.

Falkenstein arched his eyebrows. "Oh? Well, then perhaps we'd better forget it, Lauren, I didn't realize—"

"Forget it, my hairy ass!" Golding snapped. "Do we need a vote of Parliament to extend simple hospitality to travelers? Is that the kind of people you are back East? Well, we're friendlier folk in the Cords, mistake that not, Roger. If you're going to insist on a vote on something as silly as this, Carlotta Madigan, you'll have it, and a vote of confidence it'll be, too!"

"I only mean—"

"You think I don't know what you really meant, woman?" Golding said. "You easterners don't want our visitors to see the Cords. For all your talk, you still really don't consider mano men fit representatives of this planet!"

"Now look here, Lauren, if you're accusing me of being prejudiced against mano—"

"Shut up, both of you!" Royce yelled. "You're bellowing at each other like godzillas and with about as much intelligence behind it. What are these people going to think of us? Lauren, I assure you that Carlotta has not one damn thing against mano men. Carlotta, you're being bloody silly about this. What possible harm can there be in letting a few people off the *Heisenberg* smell the flowers? You're surely not seriously suggesting that this sort of thing is a matter for Parliament, are you?"

Carlotta flushed in anger, then amazement, then acute embarrassment. Royce had never spoken to her like that in public, and indeed seldom in private. And, of course, he was right. What an ass I'd make of myself if I turned something as trivial as this into a political issue! Let Falkenstein and Golding bugger each other comatose if they want to, she thought. "I'm sorry, Dr. Falkenstein," she said. "It was just a little misunderstanding."

"I'm sorry I was inadvertently the cause of it," Falkenstein said goodnaturedly. "If I had known—"

"Let's all forget it, shall we?" Royce said. "Let's just go give those newshounds outside what they're waiting for so we can all relax before dinner."

Subdued, Carlotta let Royce lead the party downstairs to the lawn and the waiting media people. Why did I make such a big thing out of nothing? she wondered.

Dr. Roger Falkenstein smiled warmly at her for the benefit of the cameras as they stepped out of the lodge into the sunlight. She smiled back mechanically. A big thing out of nothing? she thought. Then why do I feel so effing certain that we've just been expertly snockered?

Wrapped in his own thoughts, Royce Lindblad stood at the railing of the roof garden, staring out across the brooding black sea at the distant lights of Gotham, a brilliant string of jewels shimmering on the northwest horizon under the cool and distant canopy of the stars. A flock of sleeping boomerbirds rode the waves a hundred meters offshore. Bumblers, curled into fat balls, slept on the narrow margin of beach, gurgling occasionally in their alien dreams. The lights of the world of men seemed like an intrusion, a pimple of presumption on the face of the Pacifican night.

"Thinking deep thoughts, or just getting some air?"

Roger Falkenstein had come up behind him, and was leaning against the back of one of the loungers, looking up at the stars. How long has he been standing there watching me? Royce wondered. And what's the game now?

Dinner had been a peculiarly strained affair. The conversation had been dominated by Falkenstein and Golding, with Falkenstein egging Golding on with a profession of great interest in his rambling travelogue for the Cords, an interest that lacked real credibility, considering the source. Maria Falkenstein had thrown in just a line here and there, playing the dutiful foil to her husband. Carlotta had bristled with well-concealed hostility. Royce was reasonably sure that only he had recognized her long silences and her attempts at cross-conversation with Maria and Golding for what they were. Carlotta simply disliked Falkenstein on a deep gut-level, and no amount of logic, display of intellectual depth, or cool charm was going to change that.

Royce knew that he had behaved uncharacteristically, too— laying back from the conversation and observing the noninterplay of personalities, trying to sort out his own true reaction to Falkenstein from his reaction to Carlotta's reaction, and not really succeeding.

"I guess maybe I'm just trying to figure you out," Royce said, turning to face Falkenstein. "Carlotta really dislikes you, you know."

Falkenstein smiled ruefully. "I'm not a machine," he said. "I can sense that as easily as the next man. And you, Royce . . . ?"

"I don't know enough about you to decide. In fact, when you come right down to it, I don't know a damn thing about you at all."

Falkenstein walked over to the railing beside him. "Well, that's one of the differences between men and women, isn't it?" he said.

"Is it?" Royce asked. What in hell was this jocko talking about now?

"Carlotta has no more data than you do," Falkenstein said. "Yet she's frozen into an emotional stance while you reserve judgment. Call it a differential attitude toward logical uncertainty."

Roger laughed. "I'm beginning to see why the Femocrats call you people faschochauvinist Fausts," he said.

Falkenstein turned to face the sea, but his eyes gazed upwards at the stars. "Half-guilty," he said. "We're proud to identify ourselves with Faust. What was the man after, after all? Knowledge. Mastery of the universe. Transcendance of the naturally evolved order. The supremacy of man over matter, mind over unreason. Look up there, Royce. It goes on and on forever in space and time, and here we are, confined to a handful of stars, a few paltry years, a rulebook of physical parameters written without our consent and hardly for our benefit. Faust wasn't satisfied with that, and neither are we. Look up there and think about it, Royce, and then try to tell me that Faust was no hero."

Royce looked up into the interstellar abyss for a long moment. time without end, stars without number, worlds that had not yet felt the tread of man stretching away to infinity. This, he felt, was real, this was from the heart.

71

Falkenstein had taken him to the mountaintop of his own vision and tried to show him the view. Whether he had entirely succeeded or not, he had at least made the effort. Still . . .

Royce lowered his eyes from the brilliant hardness of the sky to the softly rolling sea, where boomerbirds slept peacefully on the waves awaiting the sunrise's call to the air, where birds, fish, reptiles, and yes, men, might trust themselves to the embrace of a world they called home.

"And are you willing to sell your soul for it, too, Roger?" he asked.

Falkenstein laughed. "That part of the story is just the backbrain speaking," he said. "Devils and demons, and gods and commandments, and things men were not meant to know. We've evolved past that, Royce. Now we know that all there is is ourselves, an empty infinity, and what we choose to make of both."

He lowered his gaze, smiled at Royce, and now he seemed like some kind of older brother, a man that one day might be his friend. "You know, one of our people once wrote a play about Faust, and the tape is still popular. Faust as hero, with no heaven, no hell, no God, and no Mephistopheles. Perhaps we might run it on one of your net channels. It would explain us to your people better than a lot of dry rhetoric, and if nothing else, it'd be entertaining."

"Why not?" Royce said. "I'd like to see it myself." He laughed. "Do you have an apologia for your faschochauvinism on tape too?"

Falkenstein grinned and wagged a mocking finger at Royce. "I pled *half*-guilty, if you remember," he said. "Men and women have absolute equality of opportunity in our culture—legally, economically, educationally, professionally. We simply allow the natural evolutionary divergences to shape our psychosexual balance instead of bending reality to conform to some ideological concept of mental asexuality."

"But isn't it true that few of your women are Institute graduates?"

Falkenstein shrugged. "True," he said. "I suppose a Femocrat would say that that proves we're a male chauvinist society. Actually, all it proves is that there *are* in fact characteristic mental divergences between men and women."

"But your own wife is an Institute graduate, isn't she?"

Falkenstein nodded. "We're lucky enough to have a personal relationship that transcends the norms of our culture. Like you and Carlotta, I think."

"Like us?"

"Maria and I are equals. That's rare in our culture. You and Carlotta are equals, and that's rare in yours."

"It is?"

"Isn't it? Don't most Pacifican men have relationships, frequently transient, with older, more powerful women?"

"Well yes," Royce said uncertainly. "But . . . but a real bucko is master in the bedroom, where it counts . . . and we're not exactly second-class citizens, you know. Many men wield power on Pacifica. The sexes are truly equal here." But somehow, Falkenstein was making him feel defensive, a bit less the real bucko.

"*Are* they?" Falkenstein said. "Then why is Carlotta reacting so defensively to us?"

Royce shrugged. "Go figure why a woman—" He caught himself short. Falkenstein grinned at him sardonically.

"Yes, indeed," Falkenstein said. "They *do* tend to act more on their emotional reactions than we do, don't they, bucko? Ideology aside, that's a scientifically verifiable fact. And in this case, from a purely female viewpoint, perhaps her instincts are right."

"They are?"

"She senses that our cultures are alien to each other," Falkenstein said. "Maybe the woman behind the politician feels threatened by a society where men . . . well, lead by a process of natural selection. Maybe she fears that Pacifican men will become more . . . shall we say, assertive, if they have too much contact with us. Why else would she become so upset at Lauren's simple invitation? Do you really think that the fact that the invitation came from a *male* subculture had nothing to do with it? All this on a subconscious level, of course . . ."

"Carlotta's not like that," Royce insisted somewhat wanly. Then, more positively: "And I'm no woman's pet bumbler, either!"

Falkenstein clapped his arm around Royce's shoulder.

"Of course not," he said. "You're the Minister of Media, aren't you? The second most powerful human on Pacifica. The fact that Carlotta is the first . . . well, that's just a happy coincidence, isn't it? Some day, no doubt, *you'll* be Chairman, eh?"

Royce eyed Falkenstein narrowly. "Just what are you trying to do to me, Roger?" he said.

Falkenstein shrugged. "Just bucko talk," he said. "And as a fellow bucko, I'd just like you to be aware of things you probably know already. In case you should become puzzled by certain things your woman may do. They *are* a mystery to us, aren't they? And no matter what the psychosexual nature of the culture, there are times when a woman needs . . . guidance from her man, right?"

"Are you trying to drive something between Carlotta and me?" Royce asked testily.

"Far from it, Royce," Falkenstein said. "I'm merely pointing out that there are times when a man must make allowances. You were right to break up that argument between Lauren and Carlotta, for instance, but if you had understood what we've just talked about, perhaps you might have been more gentle about it."

Royce nodded. "I suppose you have a point," he said.

Falkenstein smiled. "Applied Transcendental Science," he said. "But I'd best be going now, or my wife may start feeling neglected. Perhaps we can talk again later on."

"I'm sure we will," Royce said. And he stood there for a long time after Falkenstein left, trying to sort out his feelings. He had never met a man quite like Roger Falkenstein before. Alien, yet close to some homeland he could not quite define. Cool, and sometimes obviously manipulative, yet also, he sensed, a man of great depth and authentic feeling. A bucko, and yet not a bucko. Devious, yet open in some way that Pacifican men were not. Repellent in some ways, and yet *I feel drawn to him*, Royce thought. *Does he misunderstand women entirely, or does he possess some masculine wisdom that we buckos have lost?*

A bright point of light moved among the stars: the Arkology *Heisenberg*, the hand of man sweeping across the darkness. Only one thing was certain: Falkenstein, with his Faustian visions and his brotherly advice, represented the forces of change, a new constellation in the Pacifican sky.

And something within Royce responded with eagerness to the radiance of that new star.

Capped by its gleaming expanse of northern ice, the green and brown sweep of the Columbian continent dwindled rapidly in the viewport as the shuttle arced upward toward its rendezvous with the *Heisenberg*. The planet swiftly became a globe of unreal loveliness against the black background of space, jewellike, limpid, and deceptively serene. Beside Maria, Roger relaxed in his seat, a thin smile of self-satisfied contentment lighting up his features with his own cool sort of joy.

But Maria Falkenstein was troubled, and she could not quite project the reason why. The scenario was well into phase two now, and rolling along smoothly. Reality had followed the projections with a satisfying nominality. Time had been bought, the foothold in the Cords had been secured, and even the invoking of the Pacifican media access laws had been done with that casual smoothness that was Roger at his best.

He had waited until after breakfast—in fact, until they were about to board the hover back to Gotham. The media people had departed, and only Carlotta Madigan, Royce Lindblad, and Lauren Golding were there on the dock to see them off in the bright morning sunlight. ·

"By the way," Roger had said to Lindblad, "do I make the arrangements with you to broadcast that Faust tape?"

"Unless you want to sell it to a free market channel," Lindblad said.

"Oh, no," Roger said smoothly. "I'd rather have it be a gift from our people to yours. In fact, I think the best thing would be for us to purchase a full-time channel for, oh, say three months. We have many things we'd like to show your people, and we'd feel better contributing them freely rather than turning a profit."

Lindblad looked only mildly surprised. "Well . . . ah, that *would* be the province of the Ministry of Media . . ." he muttered.

But Carlotta Madigan flushed angrily. "What is this?" she snapped. "We haven't negotiated anything like that!"

Roger looked at her mildly. "Perhaps we've misunderstood your laws?" he said. "I was under the impression that your Constitution specifically guaranteed the right of

anyone to purchase time on your media net. I didn't think
it was a political matter. Am I mistaken?"

Lindblad and Madigan looked at each other. Something
in Lindblad's eyes seemed to say, "I told you so." Had he
projected just this contingency?

"I think you've been less than candid with us, Dr. Falkenstein," Madigan said in clearly hostile tones.

"How so?" Roger answered with a total show of innocence.

"When we agreed to let you remain in orbit pending
your decision, we hardly anticipated that you'd use the
time to pump propaganda into the net! If we had known—"

"Well *I* hardly anticipated that you would violate your
own Constitution by denying us media access when I
agreed to give your own terms the most careful consideration," Roger said evenly.

"Of all the —"

"It *is* his right under the Constitution, Carlotta," Lindblad said.

Madigan whirled on him angrily. "Are you *defending*
this tacky little maneuver, Royce?" she asked.

"I'm not defending anything," Lindblad said testily.
"I'm just pointing out that we have no legal choice." He
shrugged, as if to say, "I told you this would happen."

"Oh, don't we?" Madigan said. "We can rescind your
permission to remain in orbit if you persist in using our
own Constitution against us, Dr. Falkenstein."

"Not without a formal vote of Parliament," Golding
said. "Not after we announced it on the net."

"You think I wouldn't risk a vote of confidence on this,
Lauren?"

"On *what?*" Golding said. "On withdrawing permission
we've already granted as a weapon to circumvent the
media access laws because *you're* afraid to let these people
make their case?"

Madigan turned to Lindblad, as if seeking guidance,
reassurance for her own position—much as Roger often
turns to me, Maria Falkenstein thought, sympathizing both
with Lindblad's personally awkward position and Madigan's sense of frustration.

Lindblad glanced quizzically at Roger before he spoke.
"It's a lost cause, Carlotta," he said. "If we've really been
snockered into this, it's a job well done."

76

Madigan seemed to choke back an angry reply. She turned to Roger and saluted him ironically. "Congratulations, Dr. Falkenstein," she said. "As one political animal to another."

"I assure you there was no trickery involved," Roger lied ingenuously. "I'm sorry if this little misunderstanding has created that impression."

"Sure you are," Madigan said. Then Roger shook hands with the three of them. Golding had shaken his hand enthusiastically, Lindblad with more reserve, but still without apparent rancor. But Madigan had touched his flesh gingerly, as if fearing the transmission of some loathsome disease.

And so we have had our way with the political leadership of Pacifica, Maria Falkenstein thought. We've manipulated their laws, their psychosexual structure, their homosexual subculture, all according to a well-layed-out scenario prepared by teams of experts with the aid of the Arkmind. What chance did they really have against us? And it's only just beginning. We'll give these people an Institute of Transcendental Science, and the question of whether they want it or not won't even enter the equation.

It's necessary that we do this, Maria thought, as the planet dwindled to an abstraction in the viewport. I really do believe that. It's necessary, and it serves their own higher good. When that Femocrat mission headed for this planet, Pacifican independence and self-determination became an illusion.

Yet Maria had seen something on Pacifica that clouded her certainty with empathic confusion. She had seen a woman in command and a man who served her and yet in some elusive way was her equal. It was, in a somewhat distorted way, the mirror image of her relationship with Roger. Roger, as much as any man could, treated her as an independent being and an intellectual equal. True, he commanded, but he commanded the men of the *Heisenberg*, too. In that way, she found herself emotionally identifying with Royce Lindblad, consort of the Pacifican Chairman.

But Carlotta Madigan was a woman of strength and intelligence, and a woman who ruled, not in the pathological Femocrat mode, but within a complex psychosexual structure that seemed to respect the equality of men and women. She was a woman who ruled equal men and women. How could any woman who had graduated from an Institute despite the long odds fail to identify with a Carlotta Madigan?

It seemed to Maria that what Madigan and Lindblad had was something precious, rare, and perhaps quite fragile. Something that, at least in a private microcosmic sense, was superior to any male-female relationship she had ever seen, including, perhaps, her own.

She knew with cold clarity that it was foolish to measure such a small thing against the political necessities of a struggle that would ultimately determine the future course of human evolution. Should she express such a notion to Roger, he would take it as proof of the inherent limitations of the female psyche.

Still, it disturbed her beyond all reason to think that Roger—even out of the most dire political necessity—might shatter that delicate personal balance in the service of a higher good

As the clean uncluttered cylinder of the *Heisenberg* appeared in the viewport, she hoped that somehow it would not be necessary to destroy that elusive and precious thing she had sensed among these Pacificans in order to save them.

She glanced at her husband, his unfocused eyes pondering internal vistas that she could never be sure were totally shared. Perhaps, she thought, in their own small way, these Pacificans have something to teach us, too.

❧❦❧

6

THE INTERIOR OF A FARMSTEAD LIVING ROOM, DATED AS second-generation Pacifican by the single-screen net console. The rude extruded concrete walls and ceiling meet at crazy angles; the rough-hewn furniture looks as if it has been nailed together by an astigmatic; grimy ancient Terran farm tools are scattered at random, creating an unreal cartoony effect—a Pacifican hayseed reality that never was. Mother, in a red-and-white gingham dress, sits in a rocker watching a gross porn opera on the net console—an orgy sequence involving a Terran goat, a baby godzilla, and several humans of assorted sexes. Father, wearing muck-smeared denim overalls, feeds a baby pig with a bottle. Son sits in the corner working on a model sailboat and sneaking looks at the screen. Daughter makes a grand entrance from the left, dressed in an exaggeration of a then-current Gothamite mode—skin-tight silver shorts and a monohalter exposing one breast, which has been painted around the nipple to resemble a flower.

Daughter (world-weary): "Be it ever so humble, there's no home like *this!*"

Father: "So you finally got tired of playing a porn opera queen in Gotham, Lu-Anne?"

Daughter (brushing hay off a chair and sitting down

79

gingerly): "How many times must I tell you that I'm working in *government*, Daddy?"

Father: "Same damn thing, ain't it? Screwin' people in public is screwin people in public, I always says." He mugs at the camera, breaking himself up to canned laughter.

Daughter: "Daddy, you're incorrigible!"

Father: "Then don't incorrige me! Hee-hee-hee!" He throws the baby pig at her. "Why don't you feed Horace his slop?"

Mother: "Shut up! They're coming to the good part!" She rocks faster and faster, giggling to herself.

Father: "See what you Islanders are doing! That porn opera channel is turning your poor old mom into a demented sex-maniac."

Son (rubbing the handle of his knife obscenely): "Different strokes for weirdo folks!"

Daughter (snidely): "Still stroking *yours* behind the barn, Jody?"

Father: "Them goddam net channels is turning my whole family into shit-brains!"

Mother: "Then why you always watching them god-zillas biting each other's asses off, Hiram?"

Father (indignantly): "That's a native Pacifican art-form. Doncha have any respect for *culture*, Ma? Seems to me we could do with more of that and less of the brain-rot that's comin' through the net these days. I mean, I'm as much in favor of free media access as the next man, what made our planet great, and all that hog-slop, but next thing you know we'll be watching Femocrats in brass underwear goin' at each other with carrots and telling our women-folk to wear jockstraps."

Daughter: "Oh, Daddy, you're such a fascist!"

Father: "Well, I'd vote for any Delegate who'd clean up the net!"

Mother: "Oh shut up, Hiram, you'd vote for your goat!"

Cut to a closeup on Son, who licks his lips reflectively.

Son: "Mmmm . . . Femocrats in brass underwear going at each other with carrots . . ."

A closeup of the baby pig, who suddenly squeals and spits up his milk.

A closeup of Daughter, who groans wearily.

Daughter: *"Everyone's* a media critic these days!"

The frame freezes, and then the farmstead scene is replaced by a tall dark man in an ancient magician's tuxedo.

Magician: "Yes, you never know *what* you'll see on the Pacifican net next, and there's probably some people like old Hiram right out there now who'd zap *this* channel if they could.. But fear not, good friends, thanks to your own enlightened media access laws, Transcendental Science will be right back with the rest of today's installment of *"Founding Father"* after this straightforward pitch from your sponsors, namely *us.*"

He rolls up both his sleeves to reveal . . . nothing.

Magician: "Now there's nothing up our sleeves . . . except a few little tricks we'd like to teach you." He waves his hands and produces a bouquet of flowers as the camera pulls back. "Like for instance the instantaneous transmission of matter." The bouquet disappears from his hand and reappears instantaneously, floating in the air a few feet away. He smiles feyly. "Control of gravity, too. I'd do our live-three-hundred-years trick now for you, folks, but that'd be a *looong* commercial, wouldn't it?"

As the camera moves in for a closeup, his clothes disappear, and he's standing there naked, shrugging.

Magician: "Of course, there's no such thing as magic, as we all know. Only science that you don't understand yet. But you will, folks, you will, unless, of course, you're going to listen to old Hiram. Speaking of whom, let's see if Femocrats in brass underwear are really going to materialize via the net and give the old boy a hard-attack! Or has baby piggy *really* had the last word . . . ?"

"Godzilla-brained sillyness," Wenda Rentzlauf said. "We're not like that on the Mainland, and we never have been." Still, Rauf Rentzlauf couldn't help noticing that she was suppressing a giggle despite herself as the splenetic Hiram slipped and went ass-over-backwards into the manure-pile.

"Of course it's sillyness," he said, keeping one eye on the screen and the other on his wife. "It's not supposed to be realistic comedy. Ancient form. Backslip, or slapstick, I think they call it."

"Well, I think it's *crude*, Rauf."

"It's *supposed* to be crude."

"Well, I also think it degrades Mainlanders and the

Founders," Wenda said. "It was Mainlander Founders who *created* the media access laws—they weren't a bunch of godzilla-brained social fascists like that old shitkicker."

"Course not," Rauf said. "That's why it's funny. You got to admit those Transcendental Scientists aren't the humorless borks everyone seemed to assume they were."

"Guess not, they're sure good at laughing at *us*."

"Ef it all, Wenda, they're laughing at themselves, too," Rauf said. "That scientific magician with the disappearing clothes . . ."

"I suppose you're right, but I still think it's pretty low-level humor."

On the screen, Hiram staggered to his feet, tripped on a squealing pig, and fell on his face in the muck. Wenda choked back a laugh. "Low . . ." she stammered. "Really low."

Rauf made a pig-face at her and squealed indignantly. *"Everyone's* a media critic these days!" he said.

They both broke up laughing.

A split-screen shot. Roger and Maria Falkenstein sit on a breezy, rough-hewn porch, sunlight filtering down through a dappled green forest in the background. They wear loose white blouses, and their hair ruffles in the breeze, very outdoorsy and informal. In the upper right quadrant of the screen is a bluff-looking man in the coveralls of a Thule mining tech.

Miner: ". . . you people *really* have three hundred year lifespans?"

Roger Falkenstein (shrugging ingenuously): "Well now, we really don't know *how* long these techniques will let people live, since we've only had them a hundred years or so. We're all going to have to wait to find out. You wouldn't mind waiting three or four hundred years for an answer, would you, Jon?"

Miner (smiling): "I guess I could stand the suspense. But how old *are* you?"

Maria Falkenstein (archly): "A lady never tells."

Roger Falkenstein (breezily): "And a gentleman never asks. Good talking to you, Jon, and now we'll take another plug-in from our audience."

The miner's face is replaced by a young woman in a slash-cut red tunic, very up-to-date Gotham.

Woman: "I'm Hildy Berwick, and I'm a transport designer . . ."

Roger Falkenstein: "Good talking to you, Hildy . . ."

Woman (somewhat belligerently): ". . . and I'd like to know why you people have taken a whole net channel and put on all these entertainment shows. I mean, documentaries or straight propaganda, I could understand . . ."

Maria Falkenstein: "Why does Pacifica put all *its* entertainment on the Web?"

Woman (laughing): "For money!"

Roger Falkenstein: "But surely also because everyone is a bit of a prima at heart. We all get a boost out of seeing our art, such as it is, transcend cultural boundaries. What better way for two peoples to make friends with each other?"

Woman (somewhat skeptically): "You're telling me you're not trying to convince us of anything with all this stuff?"

Roger Falkenstein: "Sure we are. We want to entertain and tell you about what we have to offer, too, but we keep the two separate, because, as we all know, propaganda is the death of art. That's why we have shows . . . and commercials. Speaking of which, I do believe it's time. Been nice talking to you, Hildy . . ."

Just the Falkensteins now, smiling warmly from the screen, with a smooth announcer's voiceover: "And we'll be back with more *'Talk to the Falkensteins'* after this straightforward blast from Transcendental Science . . ."

"They do seem like real human beings, don't they?" Carver Brown said, as something about organ regeneration ran on the screen.

His brother Bob laughed. "What did you expect, pointy-eared demons with filed teeth?"

Carver shrugged. "I don't know," he said. "Somehow I had the impression that these people were . . . colder, less open. I mean, I didn't expect them to be this much like *us*."

"Maybe they didn't expect *us* to be this much like *them*," Bob said. "*If* they really are just what they seem."

"What do you mean by that?" Carver said uneasily. Bob, who had sold one godzilla epic script, fancied himself something of a media sophisticate, a behind-the-scenes cynic.

83

"Well the *rest* of the stuff on this Transcendental Science channel is for sure slick as jellybelly oil," Bob said. "And nothing appears so artless as really sophisticated art."

"My brother, the godzilla-artist!" Carver said. He made a pig-face. *"Everyone's* a media critic these days!"

Bob's face puckered in distaste. "That's *exactly* what I mean," he said enigmatically.

A closeup of a weary red-eyed man hunched over a programming console pecking desolately at the keys. The lighting is dim and bleak.

Announcers' voiceover: ". . . yes, we all have those days when the creative faculty just refuses to function. But Transcendental Science has proven that creativity need not be at the mercy of metabolism or some mysterious muse. Individually tailored eptifier formulas will enable all of you to function at your creative peak *when you choose . . ."*

The man gobbles a few pills. The lighting brightens, his eyes clear, he perks up and begins manipulating the keys with speed and assurance.

Announcer's voiceover: ". . . and this technology will be available to all Pacificans as soon as the Institute has trained enough people to dispense it. And now . . . back to *'Space Opera'!"*

A panoramic view of a fleet of Arkologies against a brilliant starfield, the starships festooned with unlikely brass ornamentation in a florid neobaroque style. Heavy, fully orchestrated fugal music plays a paean to glory.

Cut to the interior of a spaceship, a bridge ornamented in the same overripe style. The captain, in a midnight-blue uniform trimmed with gold braid and jewels, sings an aria to his crew:

> "Now in a twinkling
>   Ere our glorious star be sinking
>   We traverse the starry fen . . ."

Cut back to the panoramic view of the fleet of spaceships as the stars blur out of existence, and a beautiful planet, all emerald green and loamy brown under a fleecing of lavender clouds, fades in below them.

Captain's baritone over:

"Beyond all human ken
To a world both fair and living . . ."

Cut to a ground-level view of a faerie city, crystal
spires under purple clouds, dazzling with multicolored re-
flections, golden-winged bipedal creatures soaring like
birds on high.

Captain's baritone over, with an orchestral tremolo
shimmering to a crescendo:

"A people wise and giving
Far from the lands of men."

Dressed only in white briefs, Royce Lindblad sat on the
edge of his lounger staring at the three live screens of his
net console. Outside the glass netshop doors, a thundersquall roiled the dark waters of Lorien lagoon, partially
obscuring the stars with angry black clouds, one of nature's grander displays on Pacifica.

But not even this could bring Royce's attention back to
ground-level reality. His broadcast screen was plugged
into the Transcendental Science channel, where a documentary on hypnolearning had just given way to the
latest installment of "Space Opera." His compscreen,
plugged into the Ministry computer, displayed the realtime audience rating of the Transcendental Science channel, which had risen to a fat 30 percent when the entertainment show replaced the documentary. His utility
screen showed the total rating profile of the Transcendental
Science channel over the eight days that it had been in
operation, and it was an interesting rating profile indeed.

At first, curiosity value had given everything broadcast on the Transcendental Science channel the same
rough 25 percent. Soon, the ratings for the informational
programming had dropped like a stone—propaganda was
propaganda, no matter how slickly produced, and the
Pacifican boredom threshold for such stuff was low. But
the ratings for most of the entertainment shows had
held at 25 percent or so, and a few of them, like "Space
Opera," had even shown a slow upward drift during the
last week. Even "Talk to the Falkensteins," after dipping
from its peak, seemed to be maintaining a steady 19.

If they were running this as a free market channel and

selling commercial time, they'd be number one, Royce thought. But the only thing they're trying to sell is Transcendental Science, and with these ratings, they've got quite an audience for their commercials.

He wondered, though, whether the commercials were really being effective. So far, the polls showed a big increase among the undecided on the question of allowing the establishment of an Institute, and little movement from the nos to the yeses. It seemed to Royce that they had grossly underestimated the sophistication of the Pacifican audience; people were watching the shows for the hell of it, but the commercials, at best, seemed to be generating merely a tolerant indifference to the product.

A neat media analysis—*too* neat. What it didn't explain was why the ef the entertainment shows themselves were so popular. They were reasonably well done, but not exactly outstanding by Pacifican standards. It had to be something in the content, something that the audience wasn't getting elsewhere at any level of quality.

"Space Opera" I can see, Royce thought; I like it myself. The music is pretty awful, but all those fanciful planets and alien civilizations stretch the mind in directions we're not accustomed to. "Science fiction," it was called according to the accessbanks, an old prespace form. But "Founding Father"? "City Streets"? "Them Good Old Mountain Boys"? What's the appeal there? Why do Pacificans get such a flash out of watching cartoon figures of themselves acting like assholes?

Okay, it was obvious that the idiot characters served a simple propagandistic purpose—the figures of fun were all social fascists who opposed total media access in one way or another. Fair enough, such people were legitimate targets of satire, and it obviously helped keep the Transcendental Science channel on the air. But how can that be all that's going on? Royce wondered. Keep the channel on the air just to keep the channel on the air? This stuff is reaching the audience in some way I don't quite understand . . .

"Bloody hell, Royce, are you still plugged in to that stuff?" Carlotta had entered the netshop unnoticed, wearing only a loinclout in the warm night.

Royce hardly glanced up at her. "Mmmm . . ." he muttered. "I just can't figure out what they're up to . . . if they're really up to anything."

"Oh, they're up to something, all right," Carlotta said, draping herself over the back of his lounger. "It's quite obvious."

"It *is?*" Royce said, looking back up at her.

"You'll notice they're still stalling. Obviously, they have no real intention of establishing an Institute on our terms. They're going to turn us down and make a big political push for an Institute on *their* terms."

"You read *that* from the programming?" Royce said dubiously.

Carlotta smiled her Borgia smile. "I read that from my political instincts," she said. "If they turned down our terms now and started using this channel to sell an Institute on *their* terms, what do you think public reaction would be if I tried to rescind their permission to remain in orbit in order to shut them up?"

"*Everyone's* a media critic these days!" Royce said, in sudden comprehension.

"Precisely love. Too dicey to risk a vote of confidence on already. You're trying to read too much into their current programming. What they're really after now is high ratings and guaranteed continued media access no matter what they do. This harmless, simple-minded stuff is only the opening gun in their media blitz. Give it time and watch it change."

"Assuming they're not really seriously considering our terms," Royce said uncertainly. Assuming you're not just reacting off your emotional dislike of Falkenstein, he thought.

"Oh shit, Royce," Carlotta snapped, "you're not really that naïve!"

"Maybe not," Royce admitted irritably. "But maybe *you're* being a little simpleminded too."

Carlotta scowled at him.

"Maybe you're being a little chauvinistic. You seem to assume that it's all a Machiavellian plot, period. You don't consider for a moment the possibility that these people may have something real, that what they want to sell us may be something we need to buy."

"Lord, you *have* been plugged into this channel too long!"

"Maybe *you* haven't been plugged into it enough. Have you seen this 'Space Opera' thing, for instance?"

Carlotta held her nose and nodded.

"That's all you get off it?" Royce snapped. "You don't see past the bad music and silly plots?"

"To *what*, may I ask?"

"A feeling . . ." Royce said, groping for words to describe something vague and incoherent, even in his own mind. "A more dynamic sense of the future . . . a vision of man's galactic destiny . . ."

Carlotta studied him as if he were some strange new species of animal. "This has gone even further than I thought . . ." she muttered to herself.

"*What?*" Royce snapped. He didn't like being looked at that way, he didn't like it at all, that smug condescension, that certainty that her own perhaps incomplete vision was the whole truth and nothing but, that . . . that . . . *that Pacifican female arrogance?*

Carlotta's expression softened. She touched a finger to his nose—an old familiar signal—but now the usual electric connection between her fingertip and his groin was short-circuited somewhere. "Come on, bucko," she cooed. "I didn't come here to fight." She glided around to the front of his lounger, snapped off the net console, and flipped away her loinclout. "Or to plug into that thing." She knelt before him. "You know what I want to plug into, bucko."

"Is that what I am?" Royce said. "Just another pretty body?"

He said it petulantly, half-seriously, but Carlotta laughed, determined not to notice. She pulled off his shorts, took his hand, rose, and led him toward the glass doors. Paralyzed by the disjunction between the reaction of his mind and the response of his body, Royce let her have her way with him.

Carlotta flung open the doors to the veranda, and a swirling blast of wind and rain shocked Royce's body into sensuous alertness. "It's wild out tonight," Carlotta said, and led him out onto the rain-soaked deck.

After the first cold shock, the wind-whipped rain became the subtle massage of a thousand tiny fingers. The surf roared and foamed beneath them and the sky fell away to infinity as stars peeped down through the dance of the clouds. It seemed to Royce as if he was a pinnacle of hypersensitive flesh at the center of a vast elemental world of rain and sky, an organ of sense thrust up by insensate nature in order to experience its own mindless majesty.

Carlotta smiled knowingly at him—perhaps all too knowingly—her rain-soaked hair pouring over her shoulders like black syrup, rivulets of water beading off her nipples. She put her arms around him, kissed him wetly on the lips, and pressed their rain-slickened bodies together, her curving softness meeting his angular hardness along a gliding interface of moistened flesh.

Then she slowly sank to her knees, sliding breasts, and then teasing, trailing hands along the length of his body, pushed him somewhat roughly up against the wall of the house, and gobbled up the last vestiges of his resistance in the warm cave of her mouth.

Royce leaned back against the pebbled roughness of the stonemeld wall, a delicious textural contrast to the sucking rhythmic softness of Carlotta's lips, arched himself into her, stared up at the stars through the swirling clouds, felt the rain pouring down his chest onto Carlotta's hair, and gave himself over to this sweet arching moment of bucko perfection.

And yet . . . and yet something inside him stood back from this stage-managed sexual production—this ecstatic synergy of sky, wind, lips, bone-hard narcissistic gratification, and yes, real love. Something whispered in his ear that this was what it was to be a bucko, but it took this and something more to be a man.

The interior of a combination barbaric throne-room and opulent boudoir. A beautiful red-haired woman wearing a golden crown and a filmy red robe lies on a green velvet divan. Her legs are spread and exposed to midthigh, one red-nippled breast is exposed by a fold in her garment, as she watches with sullen hot eyes as three men sword-fight with three amazon warriors before her.

The amazons wear only metallic brass-colored shorts; their high breasts and muscular torsos glisten with sweat. The three men are tall, lean, and dark, poured into gleaming skin-tight black suits which outline every muscle of their finely sculptured bodies.

The queen's right hand strokes her inner thighs as two of the men in black suddenly disarm their opponents by dashing in past their blades and twisting the swords out of the women's hands by brute masculine force. The two men fling away their swords, grab the amazons by the hair, and throw them to their knees. The queen's hand moves higher as the men in black unzip silver flies and angrily forced their defeated opponents' to suck their enormous erect cocks. The amazons seem to lose their will and go about their task with moaning enthusiasm.

Cut to a tighter shot on the queen, her eyes hot with anticipation, as the third man, slightly bigger than the other two, clangs the sword from his opponent's hand with a tremendous backhand blow, and smashes her to the floor with a swipe of his hand. He unzips his fly, but, ignoring the defeated amazon, he leaps to the divan, grabs the queen by her ankles, flips her over onto her stomach, tears off her gown, and enters her from the rear. As the queen writhes and groans in outraged ecstasy, the fallen amazon crawls to the divan and begins kissing and licking the buttocks of the man in black.

The camera pulls back to a wider angle on the divan, including the two other couples. Now the other two men have the amazons spread-eagled, faces to the wall, their shorts down around their knees, panting and screaming as they are taken from behind. The frame freezes into a motionless tableau of angry lust.

Announcer's voiceover: "And we'll be back with more 'Soldiers of Midnight' after this word about genetic design and environmental control . . ."

"That is truly vile," Dori Holvak said as she and Cort Varder lay naked on the bed in the pale glow of the entertainment channel screen.

"Ah come on, Dori, it's just a porn opera," Cort said, his hand stroking her thigh, his body inflamed with a strange and unfamiliar aching lust, so sweet as to be almost nauseating.

"Just a porn opera!" she said, pointing haughtily between his legs. "It's vile, it's disgusting, it's vicious, and you're enjoying every minute of it!"

"So what if I am?" Cort said throatily. "It's only a fantasy." He moved his hand higher, and Dori twitched, pulling away from him. Somehow that filled Cort with a cold rage.

"Only a fantasy?" Dori said. "But *what* a fantasy! So that's the kind of slime that goes through your head when we're making love?"

"That's not true!" Cort said angrily.

"Oh isn't it? Tell me you're not turned on!"

Cort laughed. "All right, I admit it, it turns me on," he said, rolling over onto her. "So what? Variety makes the heart grow fonder."

"Not mine it doesn't! Not *that* variety!" Dori said as he tried to enter her. She pushed up at his shoulders and tried to pull herself away from him. "Get off me, Cort, I'm not exactly in the mood!"

A weird power coursed through Cort's body, a totally unique sense of engorged buckohood that he had never quite experienced before. He grinned at her, trying to make it a sex game, a light fantasy, something paler than what he felt, something less feral and sinister than his own strange lust.

"Well *I* am," he said, grabbing her wrists and pinning them to the bed with the full weight of his upper body. "Come on, Dori, it's only a little fantasy," he added uneasily. "Give in, and you'll enjoy it."

Muttering imprecations to herself Carlotta Madigan snapped off the comscreen and marched into the garden. The night was cool, the blossoms fragrant, and the starry sky as clear as crystal, but none of it could soothe her anger and frustration. Falkenstein had put her off again, made excuses, further delayed his decision, and by now any doubt she had had about the true nature of his game had been quite thoroughly removed.

The new programs that had appeared on the Transcendental Science channel definitely represented a new phase in their media blitz—psychological preparation for a political showdown. 'Every Mother's Son.' 'Soldiers of Midnight,' 'Men of Science'—comedy, porn opera, biographical drama, they were all designed to reach something twisted, atavistic, and ugly buried deep within the bucko psyche. Instinctively, Carlotta knew that this stuff was antifemale, designed to arouse the murky drive for male supremacy that had disfigured all of prespace human history, to sync that unwholesome force into support for an Institute, to use it to build a male demographic base for political purposes. And if Royce considered that analysis mere "female emotionalism," the latest depth-polls and ratings proved it with hard figures. The audience for this crap was two-thirds male. The Institute issue was already polarized along sexual lines: 21 percent of the women in favor, but 42 percent of the men. And in the Cords, the figure had reached 76 percent! What was going on in the Cords, anyway?

Well, whatever it is, this is the Pink and Blue War with a vengeance, even without Femocrat involvement. And the longer the showdown is postponed, the more time they have to do their dirty work . . .

Rugo waddled around the corner of the house, came up to Carlotta, and nuzzled her thigh with his beak. "Whonk-ka-whonkity?" he asked.

"Yeah, I'm getting torched, Rugo," Carlotta said, scratching the bumbler's head. "What do you think, Jocko? Is it time to tell old Falkenstein to put up or get out?"

"Whonk!" the bumbler opined loudly.

"That's what I think, too," Carlotta said. "Enough is enough, right? Next thing you know, this stuff is going to starting getting to *you*, male creature that you are."

Rugo waddled back a few steps. "Whonk-ka-whonk-ka-*whonk!*" he protested.

"Okay, okay, I was only kidding . . ."

Royce appeared at the living room door, a dark male silhouette outlined by the light from within. "Hey, Carlotta, come inside!" he called. "They're running that 'Faust' Falkenstein told us about. You really should see this. I've got it on the living room screen."

Damn that! Carlotta thought as Royce disappeared inside the house. Even *he's* starting to act a little strangely. Plugged into the Transcendental Science channel religiously in the name of doing his job. So quiet sometimes, like a sullen little boy. And we've been arguing; we hardly ever used to do that. Even making love seemed a little peculiar lately. There were times, even at the moment of orgasm, when his mind seemed to be totally elsewhere, lost along some peculiar masculine vector she neither understood nor cared to understand.

Great grunting godzillas, Carlotta thought as she started resignedly toward the house, are they starting to get to *us?*

A very long shot on a bleak and jagged chunk of steel-gray rock floating in the interstellar void. The camera zooms in with ever-increasing speed, centering finally on an ancient and scarred dome of golden metal on the surface. A recognizably human starship is parked nearby. The zoom dissolves to a shot inside the dome. A man and a woman stand before an organically recurved alien computer console shimmering on the interface between energy and matter—weathered and yet somehow insubstantial under the shadowy vaulted dome the color of old gold and carved into abstract gothic alien gargoyles. The man—lean, dark-haired, and saturnine—is dressed much in the manner of a Transcendental Scientist in black trousers and a black tunic with a high-cowled collar that almost gives the effect of a cloak. The beautiful young blond woman wears a flowing robe of virginal white.

Woman: "I fear this place, great Faust, for surely this is all that remains of that demon race which conquered the starry realms only to vanish with all its works before our own sun coalesced from the primal mists."

Faust (contemplating the alien artifact): "Surely, indeed, fair Marghuerita. What ultimate knowledge was theirs! To traverse the marches of the galaxy in an instant, to know the worlds of ten million suns, to discourse with the mages of ten thousand wise and ancient races, while we poor humans slowly crawl about a few paltry barren parsecs, our great life's journey not yet fairly begun before we are snuffed out by implacable and pitiless time. Gods they were, or godlike enough so as to render the distinction between flesh and the ultimate meaningless—and all by virtue not of the anointment of some nonexistent deity but of their own vast and indomitable wills. *By their own wills!*"

Marghuerita: "Demons, Faust, in their limitless pride, not gods in their wise and humble obeisance to immutable law. Great in their mastery of matter and energy, pitiful in their ignorance of the limits of the sentient soul, for are not they and all their works vanished into the great nothingness from whence they evolved?"

Faust (contemptuously): "Neither, in truth—for both

gods and demons, Great Jove and Lucifer himself, are but the literary maunderings of the childhood mind. For throughout the limitless universe naught exists but matter, energy, and the laws that bind them. That, and the great mystery of sentience itself—at once the creature of these blind and immutable forces and yet quickened with the striving to transcend the parameters which gave it birth. I would discourse with this last and lonely sentinel of those who dared to challenge those final frontiers. For surely even I, whose long and fruitful life has wrested more from the great impenetrable unknown than any other Earth-born woman's son, might drink in wonder, long and deep, like a thirsting babe, from this well of wisdom whose bottom lies so deep as to recede from view beyond the birth-veils of our paltry human age."

Marghuerita: "Long have I loved you and long have I followed from star to star as you pursued this quest whose final goal recedes forever down the corridors of time, but into this nether pit I followed neither you nor any man, not for the sake of centuries of love in perfect bliss . . ."

Faust (ignoring her and addressing the alien computer): "Speak and reveal to me the wisdoms, knowledge, and cosmic lore which you enfold!"

The alien computer dissolves into a rainbow mist of shimmering energy and speaks with an other-worldly voice compounded of electronics and keening strings—immense, cold, and profound.

Computer: "Who seeks to learn that which those who spanned ten million suns could not in sanity contain?"

Faust: "I am Faust, image of the race of men, born on a mote of dust circling an insignificant sun, who yet dares to challenge time itself and wrest from the universal nothingness the keys to dominion over matter and energy, time and mind."

Computer: "Your mind to me is clear as pristine glass yet opaque as ever my masters' were. For filled as I am with data beyond your imagining, I am but a mere concatenation of matter and energy, knowledge and pattern—no quickened sentient flesh which too is these things and yet seeks to make itself ineffably more. But this I know: stride into the vortex I contain as man if so you must, you shall not as human flesh emerge."

Slowly, as if in a trance, Faust moves toward the mist of shimmering energy. Marghuerita grabs at his arm and tries to hold him back.

Marghuerita: "Leave me not, for if you enter there, you will find me forever gone when you as man or demon prince emerge."

Faust (looking at her with regret): "I must, for if I do not, all my life will have been a lie."

Marghuerita tears off her dress and stands before him naked, stroking her own bare flesh.

Marghuerita: "Would you leave these arms who half a lifetime have held you in love's soft embrace for sake of cold knowledge which will not for an eyeblink warm your transformed demon's heart?"

Faust: "So be it, then, lost love, for no more would I be a man if I constrained my questing spirit for sake of some constricted timebound thing I fancied my immutable soul. A man is but the will to yet again transform. Nothing less and nothing more."

He gently disengages himself from her and walks resolutely into the shimmering field of energy. His body touches it and dissolves into a silhouette of rainbow fire . . .

Slowly, conveyed by an altering emphasis in the lighting of the scene, the life-energy drained from the figure on the lefthand slab—the cyborged Faust, half-protoplasm, half-metal prostheses and electronic circuitry. Simultaneously, the lighting heightened on the perfect human body on the righthand slab—Faust's new corpus, cloned from a snippet of flesh. The dead cyborg was totally in shadow by the time the human body quickened to life, sat up, and declaimed directly at the camera, its face glowing with an eerie triumph.

"Now does Faust return full circle to the worlds of men, clothed once more in the sweet frailties of human flesh, possessed of all once sacrificed upon the altar of ultimate knowledge, reborn transfigured and transformed with all knowledge, lore, and wisdom snatched by daring's hand from the deep beyond contained within my new brain's folds." Faust rose from the slab as the scene darkened, then shone with the blaze of a myriad suns. "Now go I forth to greet the new dawn and lead beyond the universe's pale paradigm all those whose courage bids them follow where unknown destiny beckons, beyond the star that gave them birth, beyond in all good time even those forbidden marches where now Faust's lone footsteps have broken path for those who dare to follow and expand the bounds of that which calls itself the heart of man."

Faust's face on the screen froze into a still shot, as an announcer's voice said: "And let's see how much of Faust's dreams are fancy and how much is already within the bounds of Transcendental Science—"

"Spare us the commercial, at least," Carlotta said, turning off the living room screen.

Royce blinked once, slowly and deliberately, a conscious effort that brought him back from wherever it was that he had been. "Wow," he muttered. "That was really something, wasn't it?"

Carlotta half-turned on the couch beside him; she was studying him again, with that calculating look he had noticed all too frequently lately. "For sure it was," she said. "Enough of *something* to make my mind up once and for all."

Royce cocked an inquisitive eyebrow at her, still trying to sort out the nature of this vague residue of change that what he had experienced seemed to have left in his mind. The archaic and elusive language of the program, the stilted declamations, the murkiness of it all, seemed to have soaked right through the forefront of his mind without leaving a clear trace, working instead some alchemical change in the deeper reaches of his backbrain, a glimpse of cosmic grandeur shimmering just beyond his conscious grasp, vast and vague. Is it just a clever trick? he wondered. Or is it something real? *Or both?*

"Made up your *mind* . . .? he muttered.

Carlotta nodded. "It's time for a showdown," she said, "and that thing proves it. Falkenstein has to either accept our terms or reject them—and *now*. We can't afford to let them keep pumping stuff like that into the net indefinitely."

Now Royce found himself studying Carlotta—her cold assurance, her seeming lack of all confusion or doubt. "Stuff like what?" he asked. "What did you get off that anyway, Carlotta?"

"A pattern," Carlotta said. "A progression. First they

assure themselves a media with those comedies. Then
they start working on the male psyche with sexual power-
trips like 'Soldiers of Midnight.' Then they sync the
twisted sexual energy they've called up into a male
Faustian archetype which neatly symbolizes themselves."
She laughed mirthlessly. "You know, in their way, I
think the Femocrats are right about those bastards."

"Oh, come on, Carlotta!"

"Oh, come on yourself, Royce! You're the effing *Minister of Media!* Tell me you don't see it! Tell me that this
blitz isn't deliberately designed to play sexual politics.
This is their half of the Pink and Blue War, bucko, and it's
also an excellent example of why we've got to keep it off
Pacifica."

Royce couldn't deny that what she was saying seemed
true. The latest stuff on the Transcendental Science channel *was* rather blatantly male-oriented, and this *Faust* did
seem to follow the progression she saw. Faust, the male
scientist-hero daring to seek transcendence, while the female figure, representing the conservative values, tried to
stop him, and finally had to be left behind.

But was all this simply an appeal to male faschochauvinism, or was Falkenstein also right? *Was* there an
inherent genetic differentiation between the male and female psyches? Was Carlotta's truth the whole truth, or was
there something else deep and vital that she simply couldn't
feel?

"Is that *all* you got off it, Carlotta?" he asked. "I mean,
okay, I can accept your political analysis, but what about
the deeper meaning?"

"Deeper meaning?" Carlotta snapped. "Science must
march forever on, in high-heeled jackboots and skin-tight
black underwear!"

Royce regarded her sullenly now, masking his full feelings. She really *doesn't* understand, he thought. She can't
see beyond the psychosexual political games to the essence
of what they're trying to tell us, what they really believe,
what may be a deeper truth.

Truth be told, *I'm* not exactly sure what it is, either,
Royce admitted to himself. All he had was a feeling,
vague and formless, but gut-real, that what men and
women had built on Pacifica, precious though it was, was
not the human ultimate, that residing up there in the

Heisenberg and "vacationing" westward in the Cords were people who knew something that Pacificans did not. Something beyond more advanced technology and greater scientific knowledge—a grander perception of the human soul and its place in the universe. He was beginning to feel like a child, a provincial, and he longed to understand what it might mean to truly become a cosmopolitan adult.

"What are you thinking so deeply about, Royce?" Carlotta asked, studying him again, an attitude of superiority he was really beginning to actively resent.

"About what you said," he muttered. "I've got to admit that everything you said is true, but I think there's something else you just don't understand . . ."

"And what might that be, oh deep-delving Faust?"

Royce laughed ruefully. "Damned if I know either," he admitted.

Carlotta continued studying him, but now there was something more empathetic to it, an attempt, perhaps, to truly understand. "I think maybe I'm beginning to understand where you're coming from a little," she said. "They've hooked you a little with this stuff, haven't they, and you have to find out what's really behind their game for yourself, right, bucko?"

Royce shrugged in agreement.

"Well, then let's satisfy both of us," Carlotta said more sharply. "I've decided to issue an ultimatum to Falkenstein: he must either accept or reject our terms *now* and submit his position to a vote of Parliament. So why don't *you* fly out to the Cords and deliver it? Look around for a day or so, satisfy your personal curiosity, and bring back his answer." She smiled at him. "I trust you not to come back mano," she said dryly.

Royce laughed and moved closer to her. "But do you trust me to not come back in black underwear spouting cosmic truths?" he said.

She looked at him wryly, then seriously, then wryly again. "I guess I'll just have to take my chances on *that*," she said.

7

ROYCE LINDBLAD HAD BEEN IN THE SIERRA CORDILLERA
only twice before: once, further north, to power-ski the
great glaciers that covered the mountainslopes up close
to the polar icecap; and again, further south, he had
attempted to cool his temper in the high mountains of the
fringe country between the true Cords and the dense jungle
of the Horn after an altercation with a producer in Godzillaland. But he had never been in the rain forests of the
middle latitudes before, and he had never really been
thrust into the mano milieu of a major Cord town like
Bongo.

Falkenstein himself had met Royce at the coastal liner
port in one of those archaic helicopters that were favored
here for reasons Royce didn't care to contemplate. The
noisy thing clattered like a giant angry insect inches above
the lush green crowns of the bongo trees, dipping and
rising precipitously as the maniac pilot—a wiry-muscled
young mano with soft-flowing black hair, a waxed mous-
tache, and clad only in tight godzillahide shorts—followed
every subtle rise and fall of the terrain, grinning slyly
at the discomfiture of his passengers.

Conversation was impossible until the helicopter landed
in a large cleared area just outside the town. Here great

swathes of the bongo forest had been cut down, and near the helipad the huge blue logs were being processed into boards at an outdoor sawmill, coating the loamy ground with sapphire dust. A large freighter sat on the ground on its tubes while teams of Good Old Mountain Boys, naked to the waist and filmed with the blue fairy dust, loaded boards by hand. They wore the famous Cord Superigs—articulated steel exoskeletons, arm-and-leg struts connected to a dorsal spine, and powered by small packs in the pit of the back. The power-rigs not only enabled a logger to effortlessly lift five times his own weight, but to move at triple his natural speed. The loading teams moved with coordinated demon energy and seemed to be getting a real blast out of tossing around huge ten-meter boards like so many toothpicks.

The pilot laughed as he watched Royce watching the mad dance of the loaders. "You should see us climb trees!" he said. He eyed Royce up and down speculatively. "Maybe you'd like to try it yourself. I've got a spare rig, and I think I'd enjoy taking you up into the tops."

"Uh . . . if it's anything like our flight here, I think I'll pass," Royce said, uneasily trying to politely ignore the invitations, both overt and implied.

The pilot laughed slyly and winked at Royce. "Well, if you change your mind and decide you want to climb our trees, just ask around for Gary Gravin.. For a visitor from Gotham, I'm always available."

"Thanks, Gary," Falkenstein said quickly. "Maybe we'll see you later at the lodge." He shrugged good-naturedly at Royce as he led him out of the clearing and along a wide path that led upslope between tall rows of bongo trees, shaggy-barked giants of purplish brown that broke into an overarching green canopy thirty meters above the deeply shadowed forest floor. High in a copse to the right, Royce saw humanoid shapes skittering up a great trunk with blurry speed. A moment later, he heard a high-pitched biting whine, a shout of "Coming down!" and a great leafy crown came smashing down through the foliage and fell to earth to wordless human shouts, snapping branches and scattering a green cloud of leaves which drifted slowly to the bare brown earth through the cool fragrant air.

About three hundred meters up the slope, the forest

gave way to a natural-looking oblong meadow, and the path became the main street, such as it was, of the town of Bongo. Low one and two-story buildings of bright blue bongowood lined both sides of the upward-sloping street for about five hundred meters. Most of them were cunningly carpentered in organic flowing curves, all of them had large window areas facing the street, and most of them were stores, restaurants, cafés, and theaters, with bright electronic signs and somewhat garish display screens —a honky-tonk midway that seemed weirdly out of place in this bucolic setting. The residential cabins, houses, and chalets were nestled more inconspicuously in the woods that surrounded the business district.

Beyond the twin lines of buildings, the slope of the meadow steepened, and two hundred meters up, the forest began again, rising into a dramatic wooded peak capped with perpetual snow. At the top of the meadow, partially overshadowed by the forest, but dramatically emphasized by the white peak that rose far beyond it, was a large disc of a building made of some silvery substance that reflected the blue of the sky, the greens of the forest and lawnmoss, in a shimmering crazy-quilt pattern.

"*That's* your lodge?" Royce asked, nodding at the silvery disc. "It seems a bit . . . conspicuous."

"Standard temporary planetside structure," Falkenstein said, leading him up the street. "We put it up in a few minutes, and we can take it down just as fast. Don't worry, we don't intend to leave an eyesore here, once its purpose is accomplished."

"And when might that be?" Royce asked hesitantly. What the hell, this was as good a time to make the gov's position clear as any.

"When we build a permanent Institute," Falkenstein said. "Wherever we do it, we'll consult a local architect so it won't disturb the indigenous style of the environment, if you wish."

"Very thoughtful of you," Royce said. A man in a Superig raced past them at breakneck speed. Falkenstein waved at him as he zipped by, and the Good Old Mountain Boy waved back. Royce took a good second look at the people on the street, in the stores, sitting at the outdoor café tables. Most of them, of course, were Good Old Mountain Boys, wearing shorts or leather-textured

101

tight pants, with dramatic long hair, flamboyant beards or moustaches, and conspicuously displaying their naked upper torsos. But there were quite a few men in high-collared Transcendental Science tunics or loose blouses and pants. And although they looked conspicuously alien and unmano in this company, they seemed to be mingling freely with the locals with a decidedly untouristlike cama-raderie.

"Your people seem to be getting along very well with the locals . . ." Royce said.

"We've got a lot of cross-cultural experience," Falken-stein replied neutrally. He studied Royce speculatively. "You seem disturbed . . .?"

"Not personally," Royce said half-truthfully. "But I'm here as an official representative of the gov, and as such, I must warn you that . . . well, politicking would not be looked upon with official favor." Especially by Carlotta, he thought.

"I quite understand," Falkenstein said airily. "But is there something else? You seem a bit . . . tense."

They had reached the end of the town and began climbing toward the lodge across the velvety lawnmoss. The sky was a clear blue, the air was cool and redolent of growing things, and Falkenstein seemed to be trying to be open and friendly. It hardly seemed the setting or the moment in which to deliver an ultimatum, and Royce began to feel like a bit of a shit. Nevertheless, it might as well be gotten over with.

"Yeah, there is, Roger, I might as well tell you. Car-lotta is tired of waiting for your decision. I've been in-structed to return with your answer. Either you now agree to accept our conditions for the establishment of an Institute or . . ." Royce shrugged in embarrassment.

But Falkenstein smiled warmly at him. "I quite under-stand," he said. "No hard feelings, bucko. As a matter of fact, I expect a final decision from the Council tonight. You'll have your answer before you leave, I promise you."

Now they had reached the lodge. The building seemed to be a seamless, featureless construct, lacking windows or even a door. "Shall we leave politics for later, Royce?" Falkenstein said. "I thought you might like to look around."

"Sure," Royce said. "But how . . . ?"

Falkenstein laughed. "If you'll just follow me . . ." He

102

walked a few paces around the circumference of the
building to a spot where the silvery substance seemed
somehow less substantial, more shimmery. "A shimmer-
screen," Falkenstein said enigmatically, and he suddenly
stepped halfway through the "wall" of the lodge, the
interface between his body and the shimmer-screen outlined with a pale rainbow glow. "It's quite safe, Royce," he
said. "If you'll step this way . . ."

Hesitantly, Royce followed Falkenstein through the
shimmer-screen. It was like stepping through nothing at all,
and once inside, Royce saw that the exterior wall of the
building was transparent from the inside. They were
standing in a kind of glassed-in circular balcony that
seemed to run halfway around the interior circumference
of the building. Inboard, a series of conventional doorways
led into interior rooms. There were opaque silvery walls
at either end of the tubelike curving balcony.

The view was grandly impressive. They seemed to be
standing in the open air. Before them, the verdant lawnmoss meadow rolled downslope to the bright blue toy
buildings of the town, and beyond that the forest began,
humping up into a series of green-furred foothills that
fell away to a sheening sliver of sea just at the horizon
line. It was one hell of a front lawn.

"Okay," Royce said good-naturedly, "so I'm impressed."

Falkenstein looked at him quizzically. "By what?" he
said matter-of-factly. "We haven't even started the guided
tour yet."

"And this is the clinic," Roger Falkenstein said, leading
Lindblad inside. There were four Pacificans being treated
by *Heisenberg* personnel. One was having a broken arm
bone-welded in a stimufield, a second was receiving anti-
selfing shots for a colonic cancer, a third was undergoing
an eye transplant to correct a retinal rupture, all com-
paratively minor treatments, not entirely beyond the capabilities of Pacifican medicine.

But the fourth patient was a showpiece designed to
impress the locals with the benefits of Institute science.
A tall, gray-haired fellow in early senescence, he lay on
the table, naked to the waist, once-heavy muscles gone
to oleaginous flab, his face seamed and scaly, his liver
cirrhotic with decades of hard drinking, his arteries hard-

ening, his other internal organs in a general state of aging decay. Henderson from genetic chemistry was injecting tailored RNA and enzymes cloned from the patient's own genetic material.

"You're treating the locals?" Lindblad said dubiously. "I'm not sure you really have permission to do that . . ."

"Oh, come now, Royce," Falkenstein said. "We naturally brought along medical facilities for our own people. What harm can it do to extend the benefits of our knowledge to your own people? Would you have us sit by and watch them suffer?"

"We *do* have our own medical facilities, you know," Lindblad said. "We're not exactly primitives."

"To be sure," Falkenstein said. "But can you heal a broken arm in three hours? Or transplant an eye in one?" He nodded at the aging man on the table. "Or regenerate worn-out organs and bodies *at all?*"

"*That's* what you're doing?" Lindblad said, suitably impressed.

Falkenstein nodded with a show of diffidence. "In a few weeks, his body will be as young as yours."

"How long will it last?" Lindblad asked, contemplating the aged wreck.

"Until the body ages to the point where it needs to be regenerated again," Henderson replied.

"You mean you can keep people young *indefinitely?*"

Falkenstein shrugged. "Who knows?" he said. "We've only had this technology for a century or so, so no one's been regenerated more than three times. But in theory, yes."

"Fantastic," Lindblad muttered.

"Hardly," Henderson said. "We're fairly close to a procedure that will enable the body to keep regenerating itself without further treatment. A much more elegant solution to the aging problem, don't you think?"

" 'And death shall have no dominion . . .' " Lindblad said.

"I'm not sure we've quite reached *that* point yet," Falkenstein said, with a little chuckle. "Accidents *do* happen, and while we *could* clone a new brain and transplant it, the personality and memories would be lost. Once we perfect the electronic storage of human consciousness, however . . . but come, let's have a look at the Think Tanks."

And he whisked Lindblad out of the clinic, maintaining the once-over-lightly pace of the tour, which seemed to be having the desired effect. Lindblad had been quite goggle-eyed at the matter transformer. Falkenstein had had the techs dematerialize a gold vase and recreate it across the room out of raw matter, down to the enamel seascape painted on it. It appeared to be the broadcast transmission of a material object, though no actual mass was being moved, only data. The computer scanned the object, atom-for atom, and then reassembled a perfect replica out of the raw material at the receiving end. The pattern could be transmitted by an instantaneous modulated tachyon beam, so this was a sort of faster-than-light transport of material objects.

And so the tour continued, from the matter transformer to the pharmocomputer to the sleep-synthesizers to the clinic to the Think Tanks, throwing the wonders of Transcendental Science at Lindblad in rapid fire, inundating him with some of the obvious advantages of Transcendental Science, those which the planetbound mind could most easily relate to.

And it seemed to Falkenstein that Lindblad was responding well. Indeed, as men of non-Institute planets went, these Pacifican "buckos" were unusually intelligent and open-minded. Not surprising, really, considering that this planet was the media capital of the galaxy, living essentially off its wits. However, one might have expected more resistance to outside influences from a people that in some ways considered themselves the hub of the human worlds, the masters of the Web.

There was some dispute among the psychopoliticians on this point, which the Arkmind had not yet definitely settled. Some held that the very fact that Pacifica dominated the Web made for a culture that interacted easily with outside influences. Others clung to a psychosexual model: the female-dominant psychosexual balance here caused the somewhat adolescent men to eagerly identify with an alternate model. Falkenstein leaned heavily toward this theory. The highly successful media blitz mainly worked that vein, the masculine society of the Cords had responded best of all, and Royce Lindblad himself seemed to be a perfect example of the psychosexual dynamic.

The prevalent cultural matrix had elevated Carlotta

Madigan over him, but Lindblad was essentially a dominant personality—a possible alternate planetary leader—
and he had already shown signs of taking an independent
position in favor of the Institute.

You're no woman's tame yes-man, Royce Lindblad,
Falkenstein thought as he led him into the Think Tank
room. You may be a boy among the women of this planet,
but you have it in you to be a man among men. All of
you do. All you buckos need is a little push in the right
direction.

After a full afternoon's guided tour conducted by Roger
Falkenstein and what could almost have been called a state
dinner presided over by Falkenstein and his wife, Royce
Lindblad felt that he simply had to get away by himself
to do some digesting—both of the heavy four-course meal
and of all he had seen and heard.

The night air was as cool, fragrant, and heady as a good
white wine as he wandered downslope from the lodge toward the lights of Bongo. The preternaturally bright stars
of the mountain sky silvered the forest crowns below with
pale highlights and gleamed on the snowy mountain
peak behind the lodge. Piper-lizards chirped their whistling
nightsong, skittering across his path through the soft lawnmoss. Isolated for the moment in the dark immensity of
the night, Royce's mind cleared into that sharp focus he
felt as a lone sailor on the open sea.

And the winds of change were blowing at gale force
from the Transcendental Science lodge above him.. The
human future was sitting up there in an alien building
plunked down on Pacifican soil, and there was no doubt
about it. That now seemed as clear and uncompromising as
the hard pinpoints of light in the clear black mountain
sky . . .

But that sense of clarity began to elude Royce when he
reached the edge of Bongo and returned to the world of
men. The main street was crowded now, music poured out
from the restaurants and cafés, Good Old Mountain Boys
sauntering along in shorts and night-cloaks mingled with
breakneck demons in Superigs, conflicting food odors
wafted on the breeze, and the complexity of a living human
culture seemed far removed from mountaintop certainties
and metaphysical absolutes.

A World Between

And this was just one small town in a region of Pacifica only half as complex as the rest of the planet, for this was the world of manos, of men alone. Men walked arm-in-arm with men, stared into each other's eyes across café tables, whispered endearments in each other's ears, fondled each other in the shadows and in the light. All the subtle interplay of lust and love existed here, but not the psychic dialectic between male and female minds.

Royce felt a curious ambivalence toward these manos now, something he had never been conscious of before. The male body held no attractions for him, but the same could be said for a lot of female bodies, too. But beyond physical sex, it was the subtle, fascinating mental differentiation between men and women that had caused him to center his life around women in general and Carlotta in particular. He supposed that he had always pitied manos on some level for this missing thing in their lives, but now, walking down this street where men were men among men and nothing more, he wondered if there wasn't something to be said for the bucko-to-bucko ties that could not quite exist in the same way among men who competed for the favor of women.

As he wandered down the street, Royce noticed male Transcendental Scientists scattered among the manos of Bongo. They didn't seem to be engaging in the sexual by-play, but they did seem part of the general man-to-man camaraderie. How weird! Royce thought. *They're* the off-worlders, but *I'm* the one who feels like a stranger.

His eye caught the hand of someone waving at him from a sidewalk table. It was Gary, the helicopter pilot, and two other men were sitting with him—a great hulk of a fellow with long black hair and a shaggy beard that merged into a seamless mane, and a slim young man with a shaven skull and a fringe of blond beard. On impulse, and figuring there was safety in numbers, Royce pulled up a chair and sat down.

"Brian and Dave," Gary said, indicating the giant and the bald man respectively, "and this is—"

"Royce Lindblad," Brian said, extending a huge hand. "We all know who he is." He laughed as Royce hesitated, then shook his hand. "Don't worry, I don't bite."

"Not strictly true," Dave said archly.

"Yeah, well I know the difference between one of these

107

eastern boys and your tender buns, Jocko," Brian said. "This bucko is a lady-lover in his bones. He's been having it off with Carlotta Madigan for years, hasn't he?"

"Does that make you uncomfortable?" Royce asked uneasily.

"Do *we* make *you* uncomfortable?" Gary asked slyly.

Royce nodded at a passing Transcendental Scientist. "Not as much as *those* buckos do," he lied.

Brian frowned. "What do you have against the space-eaters?" he said.

"Maybe he listens to his lady more than he should," Gary suggested. "A common easterner weakness."

"You *like* them?" Royce asked.

"Why not?" Brian answered. "They're *real men,* not mama's pets." He smiled fatuously at Royce. "Nothing personal."

"And they're giving us plenty and taking nothing in return," Dave said. "What's not to like?"

"You're not worried that they'll upset our way of life?"

"Woman's talk!" Brian said. *"Whose* way of life? Aside from the way they're going to update this planet, it might do you boys good to listen to *men* for a change. You won't take it from us because we're not lady-lovers, but the space-eaters know how to be men and have it off with women at the same time. You might ponder that, Jocko."

"I have . . ." Royce muttered. "But you mean they're not . . ."

"Mano?" Gary said. "Oh, there are a few bigmouths who claim to have climbed a few space-eater trees . . ."

"But they're full of jellybelly oil," Brian said. "You think we all think with our wongs, like you boys? We don't have to climb a man's tree to *like* him, Jocko. And those space-eaters are as bucko as you or me. Maybe a little more so than some easterners I could mention . . ."

"Such as certain lady-lovers who let their women do their thinking for them," Gary said.

"You mean *me?*" Royce snapped.

"If the rig fits . . ."

Does it? Royce wondered. If it came down to a split between Carlotta and me on this thing, what would I do? He didn't know. He didn't even want to think about it. "I haven't really made up my mind," he said. "And neither has Carlotta," he added lamely. "All she's done is set *Pacifican* terms for establishment of an Institute."

"And you think *Roger Falkenstein* is going to take crap like that from Carlotta Madigan? And risk having the effing *Femocrats* getting their claws into Transcendental Science?"

"He hasn't said no . . ."

"And he hasn't said yes," Brian snapped. "Shit, Lindblad, you're an effing lady-lover, but you're still a *man!* Would *you* take a chance like that?"

"So you think Falkenstein is going to end up dictating his own terms?" Royce asked.

"For sure," Gary said. "It's the only bucko thing to do. And then you lady-lovers are going to *have* to speak for yourselves, or admit that you're hanging it up."

"What about it, Royce?" Brian said. "You man enough to tell us where you stand without waiting for clearance from the great Carlotta?"

"I've seen what they have, and I know we've got to have it one way or another," Royce blurted. "I'll go that far."

"Well, well," Brian said, "a lady-lover with balls! Maybe there's hope for you boys yet."

"Maybe we could even teach him to climb trees," Dave said.

"Torch it, Dave!" Brian snapped as Royce flushed with embarrassment. "This lady-lover is a real bucko, and that's more important than cooling your effing rod. Days to come, we manos and the lady-lovers are gonna have to learn how to be buckos together without letting our wongs get in the way. Whatever we like to prong, we're all *men*, and we've got to be brothers if we want to keep our spheres. Isn't that right, Royce?"

"Maybe it is," Royce said slowly. These buckos believed that Falkenstein was going to insist on his own terms, and so, ironically, did Carlotta. If it came to that, where would the true betrayal lie? In opposing the woman he loved, whose wise policies he had faithfully executed throughout his political career? Or in opposing his own instincts in the service of the woman he loved, who, wise as she was, was not only a fallible human, but seemingly blind to the vision he shared with these men, and perhaps with Roger Falkenstein as well?

Let it not come to that, Royce thought, rising from his chair. It was definitely time to demand Falkenstein's unequivocal answer. He was beginning to dread what he was going to hear, but waiting to hear it had suddenly become exquisite torture.

"I'm overdue for a meeting," he said. "It's been enlightening, buckos. I just hope you're wrong about what's going to happen."

"We won't be," Gary said.

"Leave the man alone," Brian snapped, standing up and offering his hand. "Can't you see he's got a personal conflict here?" He smiled warmly at Royce. "It's not exactly my vector," he said, "but I can feel for you."

Royce shook his hand. "Thanks brother," he said, feeling a surge of genuine warmth pass between them, even as a shadow of impending sadness drifted like a storm-cloud across his heart. How are you going to tack across *this* stretch of sea, Jocko? he wondered.

"I'm sorry, Royce, that's just the way it is, I have no discretionary power in the matter," Roger Falkenstein said.

"Really?" Lindblad said, eyeing him narrowly. "Or is this the way you planned it all along? At the moment, I feel like a monumental asshole. Carlotta was sure this would happen; even some buckos I just talked to on the street knew it would happen. I seem to be the only one stupid enough to have given you people the benefit of an honest doubt. I don't like being made a fool of, Roger."

They were sitting alone in the indoor balcony of the habitat. Down at the end of the meadow, the lights of the town had already dimmed. It was the tag-end of the night; soon Lindblad would retire, Falkenstein thought, and then it would be morning, and he would fly back to the capital, out of immediate reach. It's important that he not go to bed angry. If he can't leave here *for* us, at least he shouldn't leave *against* us.

"I can sympathize with your anger, Royce," Falkenstein said. "Policy often conflicts with personal feelings, for me as well."

Lindblad cocked an inquisitive eyebrow. Good.

"Perhaps I've been less than honest," Falkenstein said.

110

"Perhaps I really knew all along that the Council would insist on its own terms." He smiled ironically at Lindblad. "And perhaps you were practicing much the same self-deception, and for similar reasons."

"Oh really?"

"Come now, Royce, we both know you're at least as intelligent as Carlotta, and you must have known on some level that it would come to this, just as I really knew I had no real chance of persuading the Council to accept your terms. So we both double-thought our way around the inevitable as long as we could because we both really want the same thing and we both have policy problems with our superiors."

"I'm not sure I follow you," Lindblad said, in a tone of voice that seemed to indicate that he did.

"We both understand that the forces of human evolution can't be stopped in the long run, that your planet must have our knowledge simply because the knowledge exists, that we must give it to you because to withhold it would be a futile attempt to hold back our common destiny."

"I guess I can agree with that," Lindblad said. "But—"

"But politics. But the inevitable fear of ongoing change. Your political superior is concerned with preserving your planetary culture against transformation by outside forces, and I can respect that. My political superiors are concerned with keeping our knowledge and power from falling into the wrong hands. I hope you can respect that, too."

"Yeah," Lindblad said, "I see your point."

Falkenstein shrugged. "If it were up to the two of us, there wouldn't be any problem," he said. "Our priorities are the same; I think perhaps we even trust each other, and we don't have the pragmatic political responsibilities."

"But that's not reality, Roger," Lindblad said sympathetically. "Reality is that our governments are now going to insist on conflicting policies."

Falkenstein nodded. "And I must implement the policy of the Council while you must do your best to thwart it. . ."

Lindblad looked away, out over the darkened meadow. "Maybe . . ." he said slowly. "But maybe not. Your Council may dictate policy to you, but Carlotta and I are a team, we listen to each other, and beyond us is a Parliament that can overrule our decisions, and a populace that can overrule Parliament. So our positions will be thrashed out between Carlotta and me, subject to what we think Parliament will accept, subject in turn to the Delegates' estimate of the will of the voters, which in turn will be influenced by your own media blitz . . ."

"Which Carlotta will attempt to remove from the net?"

Lindblad eyed him ironically. "No way," he said. "You know damn well you've already made that politically impossible, and besides, I wouldn't stand for that myself. Cutting off media access to preserve our way of life would be a contradiction in terms, and unconstitutional as well."

"You mean you're going to support us?" Falkenstein asked hopefully.

Lindblad laughed. "I mean I'm going to try to keep an open mind and support your right to make your case," he said. His eyes suddenly became shrewd and measuring. "And realistically, that was the purpose of this artful little conversation in the first place, now wasn't it, Roger?"

Falkenstein laughed spontaneously, without calculation. "Perhaps we both understand each other better than we like to pretend," he said. "Perhaps that makes us friends."

"Maybe we like each other," Lindblad said. "But as things stand now, we can't afford to be friends."

Falkenstein nodded. "Too much policy between us," he said. But he did feel a surge of something very like friendship for Lindblad. Childlike in some ways, vastly sophisticated in others, these Pacifican buckos had it in them to be men of true galactic stature, and Lindblad himself seemed to be awakening from the arrested adolescence in which his cultural matrix had trapped him. Perhaps I'll liberate him from this planetary parochialism yet, Falkenstein thought, and the planet with him. What, after all, are friends really for?

"I still think you're making a big mistake, Carlotta," Royce said, as they sat in his office in the Ministry of Media watching her taped announcement running on the gov channel. "Why get yourself booted out of office over the inevitable?"

Carlotta's attention was multiplexly fragmented as she

watched the four live screens of Royce's net console. Part
of her was watching her own image calling for a Parliamentary vote on establishing an Institute on Falkenstein's
terms in seven days. Another part of her was watching a
taped playback of Falkenstein himself, as he transmitted
the diktat of his possibly nonexistent Council in yesterday's
press release. Yet another segment of her attention was on
the Parliamentary computer's projection of the outcome of
such a Parliamentary vote, and the fourth screen displayed
the latest depth-poll figures. In addition, there was Royce's
attitude to contend with.

Her own taped voice was that of a neutral technocrat
announcing a procedural matter. Falkenstein's attitude
seemed falsely regretful and smarmy. The Parliamentary
computer projected a ten- to fifteen-vote majority in favor
of an Institute. The depth-polls showed 37 percent in
favor of an Institute, 31 percent opposed, a whopping 32
percent undecided; a deep split along male-female lines;
and 81 percent of the Cords now in Falkenstein's pocket.
Royce's attitude seemed sullen, contentious, and perhaps
even hostile.

Nevertheless, Carlotta had already integrated the data
into a total gestalt and reached a decision. Now, she
thought, I've got to try to explain that process to my own
bucko.

"By making it a vote of confidence in me, I may swing
enough Delegates to squeeze a no vote through," she said,
not really believing it herself.

"Not a chance," Royce said. "This issue transcends
political charisma, and you know it."

"You're probably right," Carlotta admitted. "But if I
lose the Parliamentary vote of confidence, it'll force an
electronic vote of confidence, and if I win that, there'll be
Parliamentary elections, and probably a majority in the
new Parliament for rescinding permission." She shrugged.
"That's what I'm really after. The rest is just maneuvering."

"Oh, crap!" Royce snapped, pointing at the depth-poll
figures. "Look at those figures! You'll lose the electronic
vote of confidence, too, and then what will you have accomplished?"

"I see 32 percent undecided, Royce, and those votes will
be decisive."

"They sure will," Royce said, "and the trend is from the nos to the undecideds and from the undecideds to the yeses. It's moving Falkenstein's way already, and he hasn't even made full use of his ammunition yet. What do you think the prospect of eternal youth will do to those undecided votes?"

Carlotta got up, walked to a window, and looked out over the islands of Gotham, so normal-looking from this height in their midday bustle. The sky was a crystalline blue, the bright sun shone on the waters, the bridges and buildings sparkled in a rainbow of colors, and floaters skipped blithely over the waves like discrays. To the east, the Island Continent speckled the ocean with fair green isles. This world was beautiful, life here was good, what men and women had built together on Pacifica was precious, it was home, and no matter what the personal cost, it was worth defending.

"A lot can happen between now and a final electronic vote of confidence," she said, turning to Royce. "And you're the bucko who can make it happen."

"You mean using your own campaign to stick it to Falkenstein?" Royce said.

"That's exactly what I mean," Carlotta said. "In an electronic vote of confidence, we can go after the bastards in a way we can't as gov officials. Falkenstein's had the media blitz business all to himself so far—that's why the trends are all in his direction." She smiled warmly at Royce. "But when *Royce Lindblad* has a chance to go after those undecided votes with no holds barred . . . well, bucko, we both know who the master is."

Royce looked across the room at her with a most peculiar expression—narrow around the eyes, laughing around the mouth.

Carlotta walked across the room and put a hand on his shoulder. "We can do it together, Royce," she said. "Not just the standard political treatment, but muckdigging, scripted interviews, entertainment satires of Transcendental Science, I could even challenge Falkenstein to a debate . . ."

Royce frowned. "It's my considered professional opinion that it won't work," he said.

"Why?" Carlotta snapped. "This defeatism just isn't like you."

Royce stood up, pulled away from her, and began pacing in small circles. "Damn it, Carlotta, I've *been* there, I've seen some of what they really have. As far as anyone knows, no planet has ever said no to an Institute. Have you asked yourself why? I think not even the best media blitz can beat them because even *I'm* not convinced that they *should* be beaten."

"Are you telling me you're going to oppose me on this, Royce?" Carlotta said softly, finally voicing the unthinkable.

Royce stopped pacing and stared right at her. He hesitated. He shook his head. He shrugged. "No . . . not exactly . . . I mean . . . sophomoric as it may sound, I just want to let the system work. Pacifica is supposed to be a democracy, so let the people really decide. Not you and me predetermining a position and then trying to use the net to engineer public assent. I think I belong in the undecided column, too, Carlotta."

"You're a high gov official, Royce. You can't avoid taking a stand on an issue like this. When it comes down to a Parliamentary vote of confidence, you'll have to vote either for me or against me."

"Torch it, Carlotta, you *know* I'd never vote non-confidence in you!" Royce blurted. "If we really do disagree, it stays here in this room. You're the Chairman, babe, and when you take a public position, I'll back you up . . ."

"But your heart won't be in it," Carlotta said. You'll do it because you love me, she thought. Because I'm your lady.

Royce sat down on the arm of the lounger where she stood. "I'm not even sure of that," he said. "Because I'm not really sure what you're against—Transcendental Science or the effing Transcendental Scientists."

Carlotta looked down at him, finally beginning to understand, groping for some middle way. "It's the Transcendental Sciences you think we can't afford not to have, right?" she said.

"Yeah, that's the bottom line."

"And I *know* we can't afford to have some Machiavellian Institute mucking up the life of this planet. Thing is, the Femocrats are right about the Transcendental Scientists—they *are* faschochauvinists. They're playing the dirtiest sort of psychosexual politics. Maybe they can't even help themselves; maybe they don't even know what they are. They're a disease, and as long as their faschochauvinist pathology is synced into their Faustian goodies, that disease will spread into every male psyche, into every bedroom on Pacifica." And I'm beginning to wonder about *us,* she thought nervously.

Royce stood up. He fingered his lower lips thoughtfully. "If we could have Faust without the faschochauvinism . . ." he said. "Could you buy that?"

"Sure," Carlotta said. "But would Falkenstein sell it?

"No way," Royce said ruefully. He snapped his fingers. "But maybe *we* could," he said. "Define the issue as narrowly as possible. No to their terms for an Institute. But without kicking them off the planet."

"And then what?" Carlotta said. "As long as they have media access, they'll keep playing the same game."

Royce shrugged. "But it would buy us time, it would put them on the defensive, and if we couched it that narrowly, I think you might be able to squeeze through an electronic vote of confidence. Make it a vote to expel them, and the result will be an Institute and a new Chairman backing it."

Carlotta's political instincts were all against the idea. As far as she was concerned, the real issue at this point was Falkenstein's meddling. And this would only extend the present situation indefinitely, *if* it worked . . .

Unless, she told herself, it made Falkenstein decide to leave on his own. He just might, she thought uneasily. We have no way of really knowing, do we? "I suppose it's worth a try," she said dubiously.

Royce's expression brightened. He took her hand, and beamed at her like a little boy. "Great!" he said. "Now we can *really* work in sync on this thing."

Carlotta smiled at him, a mere mask over the doubt she felt. Don't kid yourself, she thought. This isn't a political decision, it's a personal one. You're doing it for Royce. You're doing it for *us.* Politically, it's a lousy compromise, it's just postponing the crunch, hoping it'll go away.

Thanks to Falkenstein, politics had invaded the bedroom. And now, for the first time in her career, she had compromised her political judgment for a simulacrum of domestic peace. Was it a compromise with the Minister of Media or with the man she loved? Had love invaded politics as surely as politics had invaded love?

8

"PRIORITY ALERT! PRIORITY ALERT! PRIORITY ALERT!"

Carlotta Madigan was jolted rudely into abrupt head-pounding wakefulness by a klaxon and a shouting voice emanating from the bedroom's auxiliary net console. The single screen was strobing an angry eye-killing red in the darkness. "Oh shit . . ." Carlotta groaned, disentangling herself from Royce's arms and propping herself shakily up against the bedboard.

"PRIORITY ALERT! PRIORITY ALERT! PRIORITY ALERT!"

"What the fuck—" Royce sat up beside her, rubbing sleep from his eyes. He fumbled for the bedside controls and finally found them. The racket ceased, and a distraught face appeared on the screen.

"What's going on?" Carlotta demanded. "It had better be at least a major earthquake! Do you have any idea what time it is, whoever you are?"

"Madison, Net Monitoring," the man said brusquely. "What's going on is *this*." A woman's face appeared on the screen, yellowish complexion, almond eyes, a short cap of black hair, her voice soothing in register, but harsh with underlying tension.

"This is Cynda Elizabeth of Starship B-31, out of Earth. Our ship has been struck by a meteor, our propulsion system is damaged, we have crew members suffering from gee-fatigue, we need medical assistance and permission to land at once. Planetfall in five days. This is an emergency. Starship B-31 in distress . . ."

"Great grunting godzillas," Royce muttered as the Net Monitoring tech appeared on the screen again, "effing *Femocrats!*"

With a conscious effort, Carlotta shook the sleep from her mind and made her voice sharp and authoritative. "Is this channel scrambled?"

"No," the tech said.

"Why in blazes not?" Carlotta snarled. "Do you want this damned thing leaked all over the planet?"

"It is already," the tech said. "They're broadcasting this on ten different wavelengths—comchannels, news channels, gov channels, the works, all unscrambled and in clear."

Goddamn bitches! Carlotta thought. They've got to be doing this deliberately. Disabled ship, my sweet ass! A blanket distress signal to make sure they leave us no choice.

"Cute," Royce muttered. "Very cute."

"You think it's a phony, too?"

Royce grimaced. "You can bet they'll produce some gee-fatigue cases when they land, and you can also bet it's going to take some time to repair their propulsion system, too," he said.

"When they land? *If* they land, bucko!"

Royce shrugged at her in the darkness. "We have a choice? With the whole planet listening to them scream for help?"

"Arrr!" Carlotta snarled wordlessly. "You're right, damn it!" she said. "Tell them permission to land is granted and all medical assistance will be rendered," she told the tech. "Send that via their ten bloody broadcast channels. Then send them another message by tight tachyon beam. Tell them to maintain total silence until further contact. And tell them if they don't, they can bloody well stew in their own juices and suck vacuum."

"Shall I phrase it somewhat more diplomatically than that?" the tech asked.

"Yes," Carlotta sighed. "Say it as sweetly as you please as long as you make yourself abundantly clear."

Royce unplugged the circuit. Carlotta turned on a soft yellow night light. They sat there side by side in the warm glow for a muddled moment.

"Now what?" Royce asked.

Carlotta took a deep breath and exhaled with slow deliberateness. "Now," she said more calmly, "we'd better take some time to think."

First things first, Carlotta thought. What has to be done immediately? The Parliamentary vote on the Institute was scheduled for two days from now, three days before the Femocrat ship was to land . . . "We've got to postpone the vote on the Institute," she said. "Indefinitely."

Royce nodded in agreement. "I find it hard to believe that the timing of all this is coincidence," he said. "Odds on, Falkenstein knew these Femocrats were on the way here all along, and I'd give even money that the Femocrats already know the *Heisenberg* is here. Since interstellar voyages take so long, they both must've known for a long time, which means that contingency plans have been worked out in detail already."

"So?" Carlotta said.

"So I know what *I'd* do if I were Falkenstein. My media blitz would go as follows: Carlotta Madigan opposes the Institute, Carlotta Madigan has allowed the Femocrats to land. The Femocrats oppose all Institutes of Transcendental Science. Therefore, Carlotta Madigan is a crypto-Femocrat. Therefore, a vote against the Institute is a vote for Femocracy. He's thoroughly established the psychosexual vector already."

"Oh, shit!" Carlotta muttered. "And there's really nothing we can do about it. The Femocrats are sure to demand media access, and we can't deny it to them as long as they're on the planet." And since their ship is "disabled," we can't expel them either, she realized. "Welcome to the Pink and Blue War," she said bitterly.

But Royce seemed less somber. "We've *already* done something about it by omission, thanks to my ineffable wisdom," he said. "You still haven't taken a public position on the Institute, and until you do, Falkenstein and the

A World Between

Femocrats can beat each other over the head, but they can't catch you in the middle."

Carlotta smiled wanly. "You're right, bucko!" she said. And maybe it's not all bad either, she thought. The Femocrats will certainly fight the Institute and help mobilize women against Falkenstein. If we lay low until their ship is repaired and we can get rid of them, maybe we can add enough male votes by expelling the Femocrats to defeat the Institute in Parliament. "It looks like procrastination is the better part of valor in this case," she said.

Royce nodded. "The best thing for you to do now is nothing," he said, climbing out of bed. "I'll prepare a press release on the Femocrats and an executive order cancelling the Parliamentary vote." He kissed her lightly on the cheek. "You might as well go back to sleep, babe."

Carlotta smiled at his bare retreating ass and snuggled back under the covers. Maybe this isn't so bad at all, she thought, turning off the light. For suddenly it seemed that she and Royce were back in sync again, just like the old days of a few weeks ago. Sometimes, she thought, strange politics could make for more familiar bedfellows.

The B-31 lay like the bleaching bulk of an immense beached whale in a verdant green field on the bank of a swiftly flowing river about twenty kilometers northeast of the Pacifican capital. The weeks of waking time she had spent aboard it were already beginning to seem like a distant purgatory to Cynda Elizabeth as she waited to board the Pacifican hydrofoil under the warm sun, her nostrils filled with the subtle perfume of the lawnmoss meadow and the shoreline aromas of the gurgling river. This planet hit the senses with an immediacy that the briefing tapes had not quite prepared her for. Verdant, empty, untouched by the radiation scars of war or the millennia of human effluvia that made even the renascent Femocrat Earth seem like a half-moribund cinder, Pacifica seemed like a lost Eden, bursting with the germinating seeds of a better future.

"Look at all those *men*," Bara Dorothy said, gesturing toward the Pacifican security force that had cordoned off the ship. "Not a sister among them."

Cynda suppressed a scowl—partly to avoid ideological

121

conflict with the mission's Mentor, partly to keep from being brought down, the victim of another of Bara Dorothy's formidable negative abilities. "I'd handle it the same way if I were them," she said.

Bara Dorothy looked down at her suspiciously, hands on her strong wide hips. A full head taller than Cynda, with dark black skin, a blunt prow of a nose, piercing brown eyes, and the heavily muscled body of a woman who fanatically exercised for an hour every morning before breakfast, the Mentor had a way of striking such superior poses at the slightest provocation. "What are you doing now?" she said humorlessly. "Advocating Pacifican faschochauvinism?"

Oh, Mother, I've done it again! Cynda thought. As Team Leader, she was titular head of the mission, at least for diplomatic purposes, but Bara Dorothy spent most of her time making it clear that not even she—*especially* not even she—was immune from the Mentor's interpretation of Femocratic doctrine.

"I'm not advocating anything," Cynda said, donning her official persona. "I'm analyzing the local social pattern, doing my duty. We've *forced* them to allow us to land, so naturally they're somewhat suspicious and hostile. All the official studies indicate that Pacifica is *not* an overtly faschochauvinist planet; in fact, the head of government is a sister. Therefore, it's *her* policy to keep sisters away from our ship for now because she knows they'd be fertile soil for Femocracy. Whereas men . . . are *men.*"

"You may have a point," Bara Dorothy admitted grudgingly. "But bear in mind that a woman head of government does not a Femocratic society make," she added, unable not to have the last word. "As witness the way she allows these men to dress themselves up in uniforms and even to bear arms."

Cynda nodded noncommittally. There *was* something unsettling about these strong, confident-looking Pacifican men in their tight-fitting blue pants and tunics. These were male animals totally unlike the breeders back home; swaggering, self-contained, like the faschochauvinist machos of the history tapes, utterly undomesticated. Fear she did feel, but the approved contempt was tempered by something she could not quite grasp, something queasily unsettling.

A Pacifican male approached them: tanned, blond, long-haired, and half a head taller than even Bara Dorothy. "Ready to board now," he said, without a hint of deference. "The ambulance 'foils will be here in another few minutes." He stepped closer and insolently looked the two of them up and down. "This way, ladies," he said with an ironic little bow.

"Watch your manners, breeder!" Bara Dorothy snapped.

The Pacifican grinned strangely. *"Breeder,* is it?" he said. He laughed. "Well, that's certainly the quickest invitation I've gotten yet!"

Bara Dorothy's hands balled into fists. She took a menacing step forward. But the Pacifican just laughed again. "Want to wrestle, eh?" he said. He winked at Bara Dorothy. "Can't it wait till we're alone? I've got a nice little boat, we could have dinner in Gotham at the Windhaven, and then take a nice slow sail—"

"I think we misunderstand your customs and you misunderstand ours," Cynda said quickly. "I'm sorry if there's—"

"No need to apologize," the Pacifican said airily. "You ladies have been confined in that can without any buckos for a long time; it's only natural that you'd be a little less than subtle about your needs." He smiled at Bara Dorothy. "But *really,*" he said, "out here in front of everyone while I'm *on duty* . . . ?"

For the first time in memory, Bara Dorothy was left without a word to say. Cynda thought she might just attack the Pacifican, and as amusing as that might be to watch, it would be an awful way to begin a diplomatic mission. "I think we'd better board now," she said loudly.

"Yeah, I guess so," the Pacifican said, glancing at Bara Dorothy, chuckling to himself, and turning his broad back to both of them.

I do believe that breeder knew exactly what was going on, Cynda Elizabeth decided as they followed him on board the hydrofoil. He didn't really expect Bara to breed him right then and there; he was having *fun* with her.

"Faschochauvinist vermin!" Bara Dorothy snarled under her breath as she stepped aboard. "Rutting animals!"

"Not exactly like the breeders we're used to," Cynda said as solemnly as possible. "But try to remember you're on Pacifica, not Earth, Bara. If you try to command the breeders here like the tame ones on Earth, they'll like as not give you a beating like the old machos used to do."

"I'd like to see one try!"

So would I, Cynda thought, watching the muscles ripple on the shoulders and backside of the Pacifican breeder. I'll bet they know how to *breed* like the old machos, too! She flushed under the hot sun, then sighed. Maybe my sisters are right about me, she thought sadly. Maybe I *am* a secret breeder-loving pervert at heart . . .

Thinking these dark thoughts, Cynda followed meekly as Bara Dorothy led her to the open foredeck, safely away from the Pacifican breeder crew. A few moments later, the hydrofoil eased away from the bank, then rapidly accelerated to a giddy speed, slapping through the choppy river, spraying both of them with a fine mist of foam as they sat on the hot metal deck watching the green banks zip by in a dizzying blur.

Bara Dorothy screwed up her face in her chronic expression of distaste. "I'm getting wet," she said. "Let's go into the cabin."

"You go ahead if you want to," Cynda said, quite enjoying the heat of the sun, the rhythm of the waves, the rush of the fragrant planetside air, even the cooling spray on her face. "I'd rather not mix with all those breeders."

"Suit yourself," Bara Dorothy said, walking away shakily toward the stern. Cynda sat there alone for several minutes, glancing at the farmsteads along the banks pouring by, watching a flock of big blue birds pacing the hydrofoil for a few moments, straining her eyes forward to catch the first glimpse of the Pacifican capital, enjoying the sense of isolated motion through the alien landscape. For the first time since she had been selected for this mission, she thought she might end up enjoying it.

"Hi, there, I don't think your friend likes me very much, how about you?" The tall blond Pacifican breeder had come up from the stern. He stood towering above her, balancing himself against the motion of the 'foil with his hands on his hips, in Bara Dorothy's characteristic domineering pose. Glancing toward him, Cynda found herself staring straight at the tight crotch of his blue pants. Flushing, and not entirely with embarrassment, she looked away.

"She's not exactly my friend," Cynda said. "More a colleague."

The Pacifican smiled and sat down beside her. "That's nice," he said. "I mean, she's an obvious lesbo, and I thought maybe the two of you . . ."

"Lesbo? I don't believe I know the word."

"A woman who has it off with other women," the breeder said. "What do you call it?"

"Why . . . why, we don't call it anything. What do you call a woman who . . . *breeds with men?"*

The Pacifican inched closer. "Nothing in particular," he said, "but I'd be glad to whisper a few nonspecifics in your ear."

"What do you think I am!" Cynda snapped with an indignation a good deal stronger than what she felt.

The Pacifican frowned. "So you *are* lesbo," he said.

"Of course!" Cynda said self-righteously. "You think I'm some kind of breeder loving *pervert?"*

The breeder's expression lightened. "Aha!" he said. "Methinks the lady doth protest too much."

Cynda Elizabeth froze, stared down at the rushing waters, away from the breeder, paralyzed by fear, and perhaps something else. *How can he possibly know?* she wondered. Can these Pacificans be *telepathic?* For what this breeder had so casually surmised was something buried so deep in the core of her that she only half-admitted it to herself, and then only when confronted with an absolutely unavoidable moment of self-revelation. As far as she knew, she had never actually overtly manifested these . . . these loathsome perverse fantasies. A certain coldness in bed with sisters, a dearth of long-lasting or meaningful affairs —that surely only revealed itself as a tendency toward asexuality. The true perversion took place only in the privacy of her mind—the way she imagined an atavistic macho atop her when engaged in a mandatory contribution to the fetus-banks with some cretinous inept breeder, or fantasizing a macho piercer inside her.

But the psychs recognized that even these fantasies were normal atavistic throwbacks to the primitive age, evolutionary detritus from the animal backbrain. Doctrine clearly stated that *all* sisters experienced them from time

125

to time; they were nothing to worry about until they were acted out. Only the *act* of unauthorized sexual contact with a breeder was punishable as perversion, and such crime was rare, though the twisted impulse was scientifically recognized as relatively common. Cynda had never been in real danger of succumbing to such loathsomeness in *deed;* she had never even seriously considered the possibility of acting out her atavistic fantasies. They had always remained a private shame, locked securely inside her own skull.

Yet this Pacifican breeder had read them as clearly as if they were written in letters of fire across her face! Mother! Cynda thought. Can it really show so plainly?

"I've offended you?" the breeder said softly, an amazingly unbreederlike tenderness in his voice. "I'm sorry. We've all heard that you Femocrats are all lesbo, but . . . well, looking at you I found it hard to believe . . ."

Cynda looked at the Pacifican. There was neither ordinary breeder servility nor atavistic macho arrogance on his face. What she saw there was simple concern, a desire for sentient contact as human as that of any sister. Even a certain strange strength edged with softness that did peculiar things to her stomach.

She smiled at the Pacifican. "It's all right," she said. "I think we have more to learn about each other than anything that can be put on tape."

Up ahead, the towers, islands, and bridges of the Pacifican capital appeared in ghostly distant silhouette where the river widened into the sea, an alien city shimmering in the mind's eye.

"Maybe we can help each other learn," the Pacifican said. "My name's Eric Lauder. Look me up if you have time, and I'll show you the sights, lesbo or not." He nodded slyly toward the stern. "If your friend will let you."

"I told you, she's no friend of mine," Cynda snapped. "And *I'm* the Leader of this mission, not Bara Dorothy. *I'm* in command."

"*Sure* you are," the breeder said challengingly. "Well, since you say you're the boss-lady and a free woman, do we have a date?"

"I'll think it over," Cynda said neutrally. But inside, she was a turmoil of impotent anger. Oh, yes, she thought, I'm

officially in command! But Bara Dorothy was the direct
representative of the Comity of the Sisterhood; on matters
of doctrine, her word was supreme, she could place *anyone*
in suspended status for any uncorrected violation. And
who decided when something was a doctrinal issue? *Bara
Dorothy!*

Now, for the first time since this mission had been put
together on Earth, Bara Dorothy was beginning to grudgingly appreciate the wisdom of the Sisterhood in choosing
a questionable character like Cynda Elizabeth as official
Leader. *I* certainly couldn't deal with these people this
way, she thought. I'd never have the stomach for it.

The Pacifican hydrofoil had taken them to an anonymous little building on an isolated outlying island of the
capital, and there they had been kept under virtual house
arrest until this meeting with Carlotta Madigan in her
office in the Parliament building. Hydrofoil crew, guards,
even the cooks in the building where they were held were
all strutting atavistic breeders, machos straight out of the
history tapes. The Pacificans seemed to be deliberately
isolating them from all contact with the local sisters.

At Cynda's suggestion, they had spent their confinement
monitoring the Pacifican media net. As Bara had expected,
the Transcendental Scientists were already campaigning
for an Institute, and by the foulest imaginable appeals to
the faschochauvinist tendencies present in all breeders.
Well, that was excellent! The more those faschochauvinist
Fausts worked on the male Pacifican psyche, the more bla-
tant and obvious the macho loathsomeness of the Pacifican
breeders would become in the eyes of even these unenlight-
ened sisters. The classic strategy was to polarize the sexes,
and then lead the sisters in the struggle to seize their rightful dominion; by polarizing the breeders in support of their
Institute, the Transcendental Scientists were only serving
as the unwitting allies of Femocracy.

And now Cynda Elizabeth was doing an excellent job of
securing the necessary freedom of action from the Pacifican government—you had to give the little breeder-
lover *that!* The four of them had been sitting in Madigan's
little office for half an hour now, and Bara had swallowed

her distaste and let the official "Leader" do most of the talking for her.

"I suppose it *would* be a bit unreasonable to confine your entire crew to your ship until repairs are completed," Carlotta Madigan was saying. "Assuming everything is as you say it is."

"Feel free to inspect the ship if you like," Cynda said ingenuously. "You'll find everything as I've described it. Two hundred sisters in Deep Sleep. Our ships just aren't large enough to maintain life-support and living space for so many passengers."

"And it would be cruel and inhuman not to allow them to wake up and stretch their legs," Madigan's breeder said sardonically. The presence of this Royce Lindblad—a particularly loathsome specimen of the male animal—had been the hardest thing for Bara to take thus far. Perhaps it was because she had been instantly attracted to Madigan herself—a proud sister brimming with sexual magnetism and charismatic power, a natural aristocrat in the raw. How I'd like to show her what sisters should be to each other! Bara thought.

But it was all too disgustingly obvious that this Lindblad habitually violated Madigan's flower with his vile piercer. To make matters worse, Madigan allowed her breeder to take part in this discussion as a near-equal, and far from deferring to her obediently, he seemed to regard this untoward privilege as his natural right.

"I'm glad you agree," Cynda said, smiling at Lindblad. "We're not asking for official hospitality. We'll pay our own way and we'll stay in ordinary facilities and take care of our own."

Bara Dorothy shook her head subliminally. Now *that's* why using a Leader like Cynda Elizabeth is a stroke of genius! she thought. True, she's loaded with atavistic breeder-loving tendencies and he's ideologically unreliable, but what *other* kind of sister could adapt to dealing with the locals this smoothly, even to the point of smiling at this arrogant breeder and treating him like an equal? Certainly not me!

"All well and good," Lindblad snapped with incredible macho insolence. "But what are you doing here in the first place?"

"I told you," Cynda said benignly, "we were struck by a meteor and—"

"Yeah, but what right did you think you had to come to Pacifica without prior clearance in the first place?"

Bara could tolerate this insolence no longer. "We weren't on our way to Pacifica," she snapped. "We were on our way to Alcheron, on a technical assistance mission, when our ship was disabled. This was the nearest solar system and—"

"Alcheron's a Femocrat planet, isn't it?" Lindblad said harshly.

"So?" But Bara saw that this damnable breeder had guessed the truth. If they checked with Alcheron, Alcheron would back up the cover story that had been worked out long in advance, before the damage to the ship had been faked. This creature was saying that confirmation from Alcheron would be credible proof of nothing.

Madigan glanced at Lindblad, as if they were confirming some unstated psychic agreement, as if she were consulting him. Lindblad shrugged, and only then did Madigan speak. She had actually looked to him for guidance!

"I suppose we have to take your explanation at face value, then," Madigan said. "Since we have no charge to hold your people on."

"I'm sorry you feel you must put it on such a legalistic basis," Cynda said with amazing glacial calm, still playing the unruffled diplomat.

"We're a democratic society," Lindblad said. "We have laws and a Constitution and we abide by them—even when our instincts tell us to do otherwise."

"Is that why you've allowed the Transcendental Scientists to spew their faschochauvinist filth into your media net?" Bara said. Cynda Elizabeth shot her a disapproving look. Couldn't the little fool see that the breeder had just given them the opening they were waiting for? For a mad moment, Bara almost envied the way Madigan and her breeder seemed to be able to coordinate wordlessly, to speak and think as one.

"That's precisely why," Lindblad said, staring her down.

Cynda Elizabeth finally picked up on the situation. "Then I suppose you won't mind if we do something similar?" she said rhetorically. "True, we're here by accident, but we feel it our duty to counteract such faschochauvinist propaganda whenever we encounter it. A free exchange of ideas is the essence of democracy, isn't it?"

The breeder laughed sardonically.

"I said something funny?"

Madigan smiled ruefully. "Your request wasn't exactly unanticipated," she said ironically. "What are you asking for, a full-time net channel?"

"That won't be necessary," Cynda said. "We'll buy time on the regular free market channels as we need it. In return for your cooperation, we'll be glad to make a donation."

"A donation?"

"We have a large library of tapes on our ship," Cynda said. "History, philosophy, cultural material, and so forth. We'd be happy to read them all into your public access-banks—free of charge."

"Most magnanimous," Lindblad said.

"We don't believe in making a profit off knowledge," Cynda said. "We don't have a capitalistic economy. Do you agree to these arrangements?"

"As you no doubt know, we have no legal alternative," Madigan said.

"I'd hoped we could interact in a spirit of friendship," Cynda said. "Not on the narrow basis of legality."

"You've gotten what you wanted, so spare us any further jellybelly oil!" Lindblad snapped. "We're not idiots. We know why you're here, we know you've trapped us in our own Constitution, we don't really believe your ship was forced down by accident, and we don't like any of it. You've been allowed to remain because of our humanitarian instincts, you've been granted media access because on Pacifica the rule of law supercedes political expediency and sometimes even plain common sense, though I wouldn't expect *you* to understand the reasons why."

Bara Dorothy bolted to her feet, hands balled into fists, and glared at Madigan. "This is intolerable!" she shouted. "Are you going to allow a *breeder* to speak to a fellow sister like that in your presence?"

Madigan looked back at her with eyes of frozen ice. "Royce is the Pacifican Minister of Media," she said coldly. "He has every right to speak his own mind. Moreover, in this case, he is speaking for my administration."

130

"You mean to say that this—"

"Shut up, Bara!" Cynda Elizabeth snapped unexpectedly. She shrugged at Madigan; she actually forced a smile. "You'll have to excuse my colleague," she said. "Our ways are not your ways, and she's experiencing a bit of culture shock."

Lindblad smiled a glacial smile. "On Pacifica, even *she* has the right to mouth off as she pleases," he said. "Perhaps some day you'll come to see the wisdom of that."

"Perhaps . . ." Cynda said in a most peculiar tone of voice. Slowly, Bara's anger subsided. The little breeder-lover *is* a diplomat, she thought, and I certainly am not. From each according to her abilities . . .

Madigan rose. "You've been granted freedom of the planet and free media access under Pacifican law," she said formally. "I believe we have nothing further to discuss at this time. This meeting is therefore ended."

The curt dismissal left Bara Dorothy with highly ambiguous feelings about the outcome. Legally speaking, they had gotten everything they sought to obtain.

But although Bara had expected unyielding hostility from the Pacifican breeders, Carlotta Madigan's hostility had surprised, disturbed, and confused her. Here was a woman who ruled a whole planet, a paradigm of the sisterly virtues, and she seemed almost as hostile to Femocracy as some macho breeder! A natural Femocrat herself, she had allowed this breeder to control the tone of this meeting like some pre-Holocaust wisp. It didn't add up, it didn't make sense, and worst of all, Cynda Elizabeth seemed to sync right into this alien situation.

Whatever the flaw in Cynda that made this possible, it was clearly necessary and useful, at least for the moment, as long as the psychological tendency did not translate itself into loathsome deed. With the deliberate exception of Cynda Elizabeth, the entire staff of this mission had had unusually rigorous depth-screening to weed out sisters with potential deviant tendencies. Nevertheless, Bara realized that on Pacifica, ideological discipline was going to have to be even more tightly maintained than she had supposed. The planet reeked of perversion, and of a peculiarly subtle and insidious kind. The place seemed almost deliberately designed to bring about the worst in the best of sisters.

In a strange and sinister way, the example of a Carlotta Madigan, sexually perverted, but politically potent, was more dangerous than any male faschochauvinist could be.

9

THE MISSION HAD RENTED THE THIRD FLOOR OF THE SIRIUS, a modest hotel on one of the bigger islands in the heart of downtown Gotham. Most of the rooms had been converted into dormitories for the staff who remained in Gotham by the simple process of jamming them with cots, and the others were converted into office space by installing the necessary net consoles, files, desks, and computers among the original furnishings of the suites. Bara Dorothy had insisted upon doing it this way—not only were Femocracy's galactic credit reserves slimmer than it was politic to reveal, but it made good sense to keep the central operation as inconspicuous as possible, at least during the current phase.

While Cynda made the grand tour of Pacifica, Bara remained in Gotham, coordinating the campaign and planning the media blitz with Mary Maria, the psywar expert, who dealt with the local Pacifican production companies and the Ministry of Media.

The opening phase of the campaign was two-pronged. Cynda traveled from place to place in a rented liner with an entourage of about twenty Tutors. At each stop, she was met by a few other Tutors who traveled singly on public transportation. When Cynda's party traveled on, a local cell was left to function; with such complex comings and goings it would be difficult for the Pacifican authorities to realize that a planetwide network was being set up.

Meanwhile, the media campaign was run from Gotham Central, the local Tutors set up cells within the city, some subtle lobbying of female Delegates was begun, and Bara Dorothy coordinated the total effort from her office in the Sirius, avoiding all contact with the locals. She had enough insight to realize that she simply couldn't interact diplomatically with the Pacificans, nor did she have the stomach to try.

So here I sit, she thought, isolated in this office almost as if I were back on the B-31, functioning entirely through subordinates. Her office had been the largest and perhaps most garishly furnished suite on the floor—burgundy walls, a tented white ceiling, a huge gilded oval bed, a large holo-mural of a mountain scene that cycled from sunrise to sunset to a surreally bright night to sunrise again in sync with local Gotham time, ornate bongowood tables, a brown velvet couch, and a magnifying mirror over the bed. The original Pacifican furnishings were still in place—she even slept in the obscene bed—but the boudoir effect had been mercifully destroyed by the functional additions: a plain gray net console, a small computer, a cheap no-nonsense desk, three tape-files, and a big demographic map of Pacifica.

Bara studied the map with growing satisfaction. Areas of densest female population—Gotham, the Island Continent, the antarctic city of Valhalla—were in pale red. The eastern third of Columbia was an intermediate yellow, the Wastes and the jungles of the barely habitable Horn were neutral white except for the small yellow dot of Hollywood, and the Cords were a sinister deep blue. Silver pins indicated Tutor cells already in place and green pins indicated planned locations. The pins were clustered heavily around Gotham, throughout the towns of the Island Continent and Valhalla, and sprinkled along the length of the Big Blue River. There was one pin at Hollywood and none at all in the cords. About two-thirds of the pins were already silver.

Wanda Claudine entered the office through the permanently open door, a slim little blond who had gotten off twice with Bara since they had landed on Pacifica. She smiled at Bara, twitching her trim little backside as she went to the map, took out a green pin along the north-eastern shore, and replaced it with a silver one. Bara felt a twinge of desire.

"Eat a little honey tonight, Wanda?" she asked.

Wanda beamed at her—perhaps, Bara thought, a little falsely. "Always a pleasure and an honor, Bara," she said. "After dinner?"

Bara nodded. "Nothing like a little sweetness for dessert," she said pleasantly. But she wondered, as always, how many of her lovers responded to her superbly honed body and subtle mouth, and how many simply got off with the mission's Mentor to maintain her good will. Well, she thought philosophically, just as plenty of willing lovers are an inevitable prerogative of power, so uncertainty of their sincerity is an inevitable byproduct. "Would you send Mary Maria in?" she said.

While she waited for the psywar expert, Bara Dorothy punched up the current cell stats on the computer. Each cell was a team of three: one overt Tutor and two coverts. The overt Tutor set up a Femocracy study group as quietly as possible, and all three team members tried to persuade locals to attend the biweekly meetings on an individual basis, with the coverts posing as Pacificans who were already attendees.

This insured that even if only one Pacifican sister attended initial meetings, she would see that at least two of her fellow citizens shared her interest, and it also provided "instant converts" as role-models for the locals. When a cell reached an attendance level of about twenty, the coverts would fission off and start new cells, masquerading as Pacificans who had been entrusted with the assignment by their cell sisters. In the next stage, real Pacifican sisters would be allowed to start new cells, so that by the third stage, further growth was already indigenous and could not be easily traced back to off-worlders. Thus would Femocracy spread in an ever-widening geometric progression, swiftly becoming a truly Pacifican mass movement independent of the off-worlder mission, except for coordination, ideological education, and the supporting media blitz.

The figures that the computer displayed were excellent

for this early phase. A third of the functioning cells had fissioned off two secondary cells, and there were already seven tertiary all-Pacifican cells in operation. All of which meant that there were now nearly two thousand sisters at least tentatively interested in the cause. I think we're ready to begin the media blitz now, Bara Dorothy thought as Mary Maria entered her office.

Mary was a tall, bosomy, red-haired sister, and since she interacted directly with the Pacificans most of the time, she had taken to dressing in Pacifican modes, in this instance, a billowy green-skirted tunic that bared one brown-nippled breast. It was a style that disturbed Bara on an ideological level, appealing as it did to the atavistic breeder breast-fixation. Mary Maria would have to be watched closely. It was necessary for her to sync into the Pacifican matrix to some extent, but care must be taken that she didn't become infected by the role she was called upon to play.

"I think we're ready to begin our media blitz, Mary," Bara said. "What do we have ready for the net channels?"

"Quite a bit," Mary said briskly. "In addition to all the prepared tapes we brought with us, we've completed about ten hours of stuff with local actors——including breeders, who seem to be willing to act in *anything* for money." She grinned. "And a flash of tit."

Bara scowled. "You're not to encourage that," she snapped. "I don't want any of our sisters perceived as potential sex-objects by these local breeders."

"It *does* make dealing with them easier," Mary Maria said. "It's amazing how muddled their thinking can become with a bare breast staring them in the face. Pathetic, really."

"I don't care!" Bara growled. "Sisters are not to allow themselves to become fantasy sex-objects for breeders, whether it make your job any easier or not——"

Mary Maria flushed. "Surely you're not suggesting that I would——"

"I'm not accusing you of anything, Mary," Bara said more calmly. "I'm merely assuring that no such possibility can arise. From now on, all sisters dealing with the local breeders must wear sexually neutral dress. That's official doctrine, as of now. While I understand that this may deprive you of a certain useful psychological advantage, we must never forget that pragmatism is no justification for

136

arousing atavistic tendencies, either in the local breeders, or in ourselves. Do you understand what I'm saying?"

"Yes, Bara," Mary Maria said, properly chastened. "But surely you don't think—"

"No reflection on you at all, Mary," Bara said sincerely. "You're not . . ." She paused. You're not Cynda Elizabeth, she had been about to say. But there was no point in surfacing *that* problem with someone who was subordinate to them both.

She shrugged, and smiled at Mary Maria, brushing the unsavory business aside. "Now then," she said in a more businesslike tone, "I believe we should open our blitz with the standard sort of anti-faschochauvinist material . . ."

"We'd better stick with more subtle stuff at first, though," Mary Maria said. "Faschochauvinism is very subtle here, what with women almost dominating the political and economic structure."

Bara frowned. "I wouldn't exactly call the posturings of these Pacifican buckos, as they call themselves, subtle," she said.

Mary laughed. "They certainly have no low opinion of themselves as desirable sex-objects," she agreed. "Unfortunately, neither do Pacifican women."

"Well, that's what we'll work on initially," Bara Dorothy said. "Forget economics and politics and concentrate on male sexual dominance." She allowed herself a small smile. "Our friends from the *Heisenberg* have done an excellent job of pushing these buckos into even more sexually arrogant attitudes than they possess naturally. They've synced male faschochauvinism into support for their bloody Institute. Very well. Let's rub the Pacifican sisters' noses in it. Falkenstein is polarizing the breeders in support of his own cause, and it's already tending to polarize the sisters against him, though they have no positive focus. Let's give it to them. Let's make Femocracy the leader of the opposition to the Institute on this planet."

Mary Maria pondered that a moment. "Excellent," she finally said. "The Transcendental Scientists *have* given us a perfect local issue to polarize the sisters around. We'll build our campaign around that. I'll get right to it."

As Mary Maria left, Bara Dorothy swiveled her chair around and regarded the large map of Pacifica. What a prize this planet is! she thought. The center of the Galactic

Media Web! Feminize Pacifica, and the ultimate goal of a Femocratic galactic civilization will become achievable in decades, not centuries.

And the situation is perfect—a woman is already head of government, and women already have a superficially dominant economic status, so the change will be very subtle when Sisterhood controls the Pacifican Web product. We'll maintain "News of the Galaxy" and the entertainment exports with the tremendous pool of local talent, only the underlying mythic substructure will change. And the beauty of it is that the Pacifican sisters are so much better at that kind of thing than we are. What a contribution they'll make to the cause of Sisterhood after liberation!

And that, she thought, is perhaps the greatest strength of Femocracy. The only change we seek is the awakening of full consciousness in sisters everywhere. No imposed political hegemony from outside—just fully conscious sisters on every human planet exercising their rightful dominion in their own ways, liberated from the animalistic breeder faschochauvinism that nearly destroyed the Earth.

Our unity is one of shared consciousness, not of an imposed political order, not the simian territorial aggression that's the only kind of unity breeders can understand. In Sisterhood, diversity becomes a strength, not a source of weakness and conflict in the endless breeder battle for a total supremacy that no tribe of them can ever achieve. That's why our victory is inevitable.

Bara Dorothy sighed. Someday, perhaps, we'll be able to clone ourselves like those damned Transcendental Scientists. Then there will be no further need for breeders at all and the grand dream will become a reality—a galaxy of women, a humanity permanently at peace, a unity of Sisterhood infinite in time and space, enduring for as long as the stars continue to shine.

A very rapidly cut montage of clips from old tapes and ancient Terran films: a prehuman simian smashing the skull of another hairy hominid with an animal bone; a Roman legion pillaging a village of Gauls; mounted Cossacks whipping Jews to their knees from horseback; a Nazi SS squad machine-gunning men, women, and children in a village square; a screaming woman running down a jungle road clutching a napalmed baby while helmeted soldiers look on with professional indifference. Over all this, intermittent quick flashes of nuclear explosions.

Woman's voiceover: "From the prehuman past to the final Holocaust, history has been the story of man's inhumanity to man—and to woman."

The sequence ends with a series of shots of various Terran cities being vaporized by thermonuclear explosions.

Woman's voiceover: "The final glory of the phallic urge to power—the last war, the one that nearly destroyed the planet that gave us birth. But what could have been humanity's last sunset became the dawn of a new age . . ."

A series of shots smoothly dissolving into each other: women in animal skins suckling babies around a campfire; the Madonna cradling the Christ child in her arms; a pirouetting ballerina; a female nurse tending the wounded in a field hospital; Russian peasant women scything wheat; women marching down an urban street; Carlotta Madigan addressing the Pacifican Parliament.

Woman's voiceover: "For the history of humanity has also been the unsung story of woman. Woman, the giver of life; woman, the inventor of love; woman, the guardian of home; woman, the healer of broken bodies and spirits; and now, at last, woman, the bringer of peace."

A medium shot on a hollow-eyed man dressed in rags, squatting on a heap of rubble. Two tall bright-eyed women in shorts and tunics stand flanking him as the camera moves in for a tighter shot on the man's psychically ravaged face.

Man (speaking directly into the camera): "What can I say? For millions of years, we ruled the Earth and fought for glory and the final result was . . . *this*. We believed in peace, too; we believed in it so strongly that we fought ten thousand wars and piled up a mountain range of corpses to achieve it." He shrugs. "We tried. We failed. We saw no other way. Now we are few and tired and destroyed by our own hand. Now there is nothing for us to do but listen to our wives and daughters and mothers and sisters whose counsel we never sought and hope that *they* can find the path that has eluded us since we came down from the trees to become killers of the plain. We give up. We hand on the torch to cleaner hands . . ."

The young women help him, tottering, to his feet. Cut to a series of shots of the broken cities of Earth, new buildings beginning to rise from the rubble, bright-eyed women bustling about everywhere—ending with a long zoom down the shattered skyscraper canyons of New York which becomes a shot of the Statue of Liberty, eerily still intact, the noble lady holding her torch aloft haloed by a rising sun . . .

Man's voiceover: "And now, Transchauvinist Science brings you the latest wong-throbbing episode of *'Soldiers of Midnight.'* Hang on to your whackers, buckos!"

A full shot of a languid harem scene, all gauzy draperies and rose-colored light. A man reclines on a couch—bare-chested, with bright red nipples, wearing only filmy blue pantaloons, and dreamily sniffing a yellow flower. He starts at an off-camera commotion.

A moment later, two similarly dressed men stumble backwards into the frame, pursued by three huge women dressed in skintight black with enormous rubbery red dildoes sprouting from their crotches, over four feet long and thick as a man's arm. The women grip these gigantic dildoes with both hands and use them as exceedingly awkward clubs with which to batter the retreating men, buffetting them about the face and buttocks to the sound of much shrieking.

But the dildoes are so long, rubbery, and heavy that the women bumble and stumble about as they slap at the men with the things, crazily off-balance. Two of the women accidentally bump into each other and react angrily. They begin to fence with each other, battering their rubber cocks against each other in a gross parody of a swordfight. The third woman, still chasing the men, lets go of her dildo for a moment as she turns to look. The rubbery appendage droops, its head drags on the floor, and the woman, looking the wrong way, trips over it, and goes flying head over heels into her battling sisters. They all fall to the floor in a tangle of bodies, where they belabor each other with the dildoes like pillowfighting children while the man on the couch continues to sniff his flower with a superior attitude . . .

Suji Corwin glanced out the window in boredom. Arching over the low skyline of residential Valhalla, the permaglaze dome loomed grayly, keeping out the biting cold of

Thule, but not the everlasting somber twilight that hovered over the antarctic continent like a perpetual fog of gloom. Inside the little rented room, twelve women sat in a circle delivering their pallid opinions on the state of the universe, which today seemed to revolve around the new programming that Femocracy was pumping into the net. It seemed to Suji that most of them were as bored by all this as she was.

I wonder why they're dabbling in Femocracy? she thought. *Are their buckos acting strangely lately, like Ron? Are they offended by much of the Transcendental Science programming like "Soldiers of Midnight"? Or are they just curious about what it's like for women to sit around together without buckos and form their own silly little secret society? Or is everyone just a media critic these days?*

"Did you catch 'Soldiers of Midnight'?"

"Yeah, I laughed my guts out."

"So did Bill."

"Your bucko thought it was funny?"

"Uh-huh. He was surprised that Femocrats had a sense of humor."

"I'm surprised that there's a man who can laugh at his wong," said Marta, a big heavy-set woman whose remarks usually seemed more pointed than those of the others.

Beth Louise, the Femocrat who had started this little group, grimaced ironically. "If they don't laugh *with* us, they have to face the fact that we're laughing at *them,*" she said, "And they can't admit that. Typical breed—male defensive reaction."

"Yeah," said Olivia, the other member of the group who tended to dominate conversation. "Even down to hedging it with that old garbage about Femocrats—meaning women —not having a sense of humor."

"Seems to me it's the *buckos* who've lost their sense of humor these days," Suji blurted. "They've gotten so *serious* since these Transcendental Scientists began polluting the net." *Let me crack a joke about "Soldiers of Midnight" or laugh at "Space Opera," and Ron freezes like the damned icecap,* she thought. *And the way he watches those Transcendental Science documentaries so religiously. If I want to get off with him while one of them is on, he bites my head off.*

"Men have always been the humorless half of the

species," Beth Louise said. "How else could they look at ten thousand years of faschochauvinist history with a straight face?"

"What's that old saying, 'A stiff wong knows no conscience'? Well, come to think of it, it has no sense of humor either."

"Yeah. Did you ever *laugh* while you were getting it off with some bucko?"

"Oh, shit! Instant wong-wilt!"

Suji joined in the general laughter, getting more into the spirit of things. Maybe there was something going on here, after all. Buckos did seem to be off on their own crazy vector these days, thanks to the un-Pacifican garbage that was being pumped into their heads by those creeps off the *Heisenberg*. Their wongs were still seeking the same familiar berths, but they seemed to be going a little mano in the head. Maybe it *is* time we women got together and straightened this mess out, Suji thought. Maybe there's something to this Sisterhood stuff, after all.

A full shot on a very stylized laboratory. Bubbling beakers, sparking apparatus, ominous flashing lights in the background. In the foreground, a line of four men dressed as Transcendental Scientists with cavernous vampire makeup around the eyes are dancing to syncopated music. Behind them and to the right, three grotesque figures mimic their steps in a hideous robotized parody: a Frankenstein monster, a rotting male corpse, a Trilby in a diaphanous white gown with dead looking eyes. All three are wired into a gothic control console emitting intermittent sparks.

Transcendental Science chorus (singing horribly):

> "Rooty-too-toot
> "Rooty-too-toot
> *We* are the boys from the *Institute* . . ."

Cut to a closeup on a woman who looks superficially very much like Carlotta Madigan, the towers and bridges of Gotham in the background.

Woman: "Very funny, right? No? You say what an Institute of Transcendental Science will do to Pacifica is no fit subject for humor? You say what the boys from the

Institute have *already* done takes the fun out of our little musical comedy? You say your bucko's acting strangely? You say he's hiding leather underwear under the bed and manacles in the closet? You say he's starting to talk like Faust, masturbate with model spaceships, and ordering you to vote for an Institute of Transcendental Science?"

The woman's face becomes knowing, conspiratorial. She winks at the camera. "Well boys will be boys, and they love their new toys. It's happened before, on many planets. Once the boys from the Institute set up their mad doctor labs, whole *armies* of good buckos find themselves marching off into the never-never land of superscience fiction pan-piped by their peters. But of course it can't happen here. Or can it, sisters? Maybe it'd be wise to plug into some of those new tapes Femocracy has donated to the accessbanks and find out what Faustian faschochauvinism is going to mean to *you* . . ."

Roger Falkenstein picked idly at his wahfish almondine, looking across the table at Royce Lindblad, who was sneaking a glance around the crowded restaurant, watching the people who in their turn were sneaking glances at *them*. Could it be that this was Lindblad's subtle way of making a public statement? Having a meeting had been Falkenstein's idea, but lunch together in a public restaurant had been Lindblad's suggestion. Falkenstein decided to venture a probe.

"You're not afraid to be seen publicly with me, Royce?"

"Afraid of what?" Lindblad said cautiously.

The Sealane was a small restaurant fronting on a small downtown side street and specializing in Pacifican seafood prepared in various ancient Terran modes. There were sidewalk tables, but Lindblad had chosen a booth at the rear of the main dining room, more or less out of sight of the lunch-hour crowds on the street. Happenstance, or a calculated compromise?

"Afraid of the conclusions that might be drawn . . ." Falkenstein said. "Afraid of Carlotta's reaction . . ."

Lindblad flushed. "I'll be damned if I'll let a simple lunch be politicized," he said. "By you or Carlotta or the effing Femocrats or anyone else. This idiotic polarization has gone far enough, and if I'm making any statement, that's it."

Falkenstein nodded. "If I'd thought our presence would cause the Femocrats to go this far, I'd have withdrawn from Pacifica," he lied.

Actually, of course, the current situation had been projected long ago, and the Arkmind predicted a favorable outcome. By syncing their psychosexual propaganda into opposition to the Institute, the Femocrats had made a ghastly mistake, for they had layed themselves wide open to the converse proposition—a vote *against* the Institute was a vote *for* Femocracy, female dominance, and the psychic castration of the Pacifican bucko.

Theoretically, that would split the planet right down the middle and make any vote too close to call, but the Femocrats had inevitably ignored the facts that most Pacifican women were heterosexual and that the buckos ruled the bedroom as dominant sex-objects. In the crunch, enough women would vote in favor of their own buckos' manhood to provide the necessary swing vote.

Which was why Falkenstein had now moved his own base of operations from the Cords, where the mission had been successfully completed, to Gotham, where the critical lobbying would be taking place in the next two weeks. Beginning today with the pivotal Minister of Media, who now sat there studying him skeptically.

"You know something Roger," Lindblad finally said without any real hostility, "I think you're full of jelly-belly oil. Nothing is about to make you give up, especially when the Femocrats have played right into your hand."

Falkenstein found himself laughing unguardedly. Lindblad had a way of suddenly reminding him that despite his surface appearance of arrested adolescence, he wasn't the second most important political figure on the planet simply because he was the lover of Carlotta Madigan. Indeed, Madigan might be the planetary Chairman at least in part because her lover was Royce Lindblad.

"Since we understand each other, Royce, perhaps we can work together on this," Falkenstein said. "Surely you share my distaste for what the Femocrats are doing . . ."

Lindblad shrugged. "I won't try to con you about that," he said. "What we've got now is the Pink and Blue War at its most loathsome."

"Well, wouldn't you like to get rid of the Femocrats

before any permanent damage is done? You see how these people work. By the time their ship is repaired, they'll have a sufficient political base among your women to force Parliament to vote on any move to expel them, a vote that would be a showdown between men and women. Their permanent presence here will soon be a fait accompli."

Lindblad sighed. "All right, Roger," he said. "What are you really getting at?"

"Force such a vote now, before it's too late," Falkenstein said. "Introduce a resolution yourself giving the Femocrats thirty days to leave Pacifica, withdrawing their media access, and confining them to their ship in the meantime. Every man on the planet will surely support you. And at this point, surely enough buckos can carry their women's votes to push it through, if it's strictly a vote against Femocrat meddling."

"Carlotta would never agree . . ." Lindblad said.

"Hasn't it occured to you that you could ride to the Chairmanship *yourself* on such an issue if she didn't?"

Lindblad drummed his fingers on the table. He's tempted, Falkenstein thought. He's really tempted. He held his breath as Lindblad pondered the proposition in silence.

"No good, Roger," Lindblad finally said. "Don't think I don't see what you're trying to do. Maybe I should resent it more than I do, but . . ."

"Good lord, Royce!" Falkenstein snapped. "Is your loyalty to the woman *that* absolute?"

Lindblad flushed. He frowned. He shrugged. "Just maybe it is," he said. "But on this, it's not really being tested. My position would be the same as hers for pragmatic political reasons. If Carlotta and I split publicly on this, it would tear the planet apart. And we have no legal basis for withdrawing the Femocrats' media access or confining them to their ship. No, it can't be done unless . . ."

"Unless . . . ?"

Lindblad smiled sardonically at Falkenstein. "Unless it's a resolution to kick both you and the Femocrats off the planet," he said.

Falkenstein paled. "You wouldn't . . . you couldn't . . ."

Lindblad laughed wickedly. "Just playing with you, Roger," he said. "That'd be an even bigger mess. You'd have men voting to kick you out just to get rid of the

Femocrats, and women voting to kick out the Femocrats just to get rid of you. People couldn't figure out what they were voting for or against. Parliament wouldn't vote it up *or* down; they'd table it forever. It'd be the worst of both possible worlds."

"Then why did you ever bring it up?" Falkenstein said shakily. "Just to watch me squirm?"

Lindblad gazed at him with an amused crooked little smile. "Call it a quid pro quo," he said. "You people have a lot to teach us about science and technology, and I admit that I want to learn . . ." He laughed. "But when it comes to the politics of democracy, Roger, let alone its philosophical essence, we're the adults and you're the children. Haven't you ever thought about what you have to learn from *us?*"

Lindblad laughed at Falkenstein's bemusement. He called for the waiter with what seemed like a deliberately imperious wave of his hand. "Perhaps you'd care to discuss it over dessert," he said.

Falkenstein sighed inwardly. I don't think I really understand this man, he thought. I wonder if I ever will. Strange geography, a totally nonmammalian ecology, even the totally homosexual culture of the Cords had impinged upon Falkenstein's consciousness only as so much relevant data. Only now, sitting in an ordinary restaurant with the Pacifican he had thought he had gotten closest to, did he finally feel like a stranger in an alien world. Strangest of all, he couldn't quite figure out why.

". . . and now, back to 'Talk with the Falkensteins' . . ."

A medium shot on Roger and Maria Falkenstein, dressed in white, outlined sharply against a black backdrop blazing with stars. A woman's face, tense and strident-looking, appears in the upper right quadrant of the screen.

Woman (belligerently): "My name is Laura Wintergreen, I'm a mining tech in Thule, and I want to know why you faschochauvinist bug-brains are pumping puke like 'Soldiers of Midnight' into the net. Seems to me the men on this planet are narcisstic enough without meddling off-worlders filling their adolescent minds with—"

Falkenstein (smiling at Maria): "Have I stopped beating you yet, my dear?"

Maria (with a false laugh, and looking rather uncomfortable): "I've been meaning to talk to you about that, Roger."

Woman (angrily): "Cut the patter, Jocko, the sisters of this planet are getting a little sick of it! Why don't you get off Pacifica if you've got such a whanger on for the romance of interstellar space?"

Falkenstein: "Would it be safe to assume that you're a Femocrat sympathizer, Laura?"

Woman: "Would it be safe to assume that you're a faschochauvinist Faust, *Roger?* You can wager your wong I'm a Femocrat sympathizer, bucko!"

Falkenstein (archly): "For a Femocrat sympathizer, you seem to have a peculiar obsession with the male genital organ."

Woman (stammering): "Maybe . . . maybe that's because you all think with your wongs!"

Falkenstein (mugging at the camera): "And as we all know, two wongs make a right!" He laughs heartily as an earnest middle-aged man's face replaces the woman's face in the upper right quadrant.

Man: "I'm Harry Ginzer, and I don't think your last call was so effing funny, Dr. Falkenstein. It's an all-too-typical example of the kind of pathology Femocracy is creating on this planet, and as a scientist, you should take it more seriously."

Falkenstein (deprecatingly): "Come, come, Harry, a man should have a sense of humor about such people, a reasonably thick skin."

Man: "Easy for an off-worlder like you to say; those creatures aren't turning *your* women into crazed ball-cutters. But a Pacifican bucko would have to have a skin like a godzilla to just laugh it off with a bad pun like that."

Falkenstein: "Perhaps you're right . . . but it's really none of *our* business . . ."

Man: "Oh isn't it? You've promised this planet an Institute of Transcendental Science, and a lot of us take that promise very seriously. And now these Femocrats come along and try to use the women of Pacifica to take it away from us. Don't you have any sense of responsibility? Don't you feel any solidarity for the Pacificans who believe in you?"

Falkenstein (pondering): "I never thought of it that way before . . ."

Maria (somewhat woodenly): "He's right, Roger. As a woman, I can better see how the Femocrats are trying to poison female minds here, and as a Transcendental Scientist, I can see that if they succeed, it will cost this planet its Institute."

Man: "Listen to your wife, Dr. Falkenstein. Femocracy is the enemy of every man and woman who wants to see this planet join the forefront of human evolution."

Falkenstein: "Thank you very much for your thought-provoking comments. Perhaps our next callers will have more to say on this topic . . ."

An exterior shot on the shimmer-sceen entrance to a large silver building, a grander version of the Transcendental Science lodge in the Cords. A plaque over the entrance proclaims: "Pacifican Institute of Transcendental Science." A man exits, bare-chested in a Pacifican bucko mode, but wearing a high-collared black cloak reminiscent of a Transcendental Science tunic. The angles of his face are like hard steel slabs, and his eyes are dead-looking and deeply sunken.

Cut to a tracking shot; the camera follows this man as he boards a floater and skims down a typical Gotham street. But the scene on the street is far from typical. Men move haughtily down the center on floaters, motorcycles, powerskates, many wearing the high collars of Transcendental Science, all of them ramrod-stiff with cold eyes focused on some internal vista, arrogant zombies. All the women are confined to the peripheral glideways, slinking along with stooped shoulders, and some walking hand-in-hand. The lighting is grim and ominous, the atmosphere thick with unwholesome sexual tension.

Cut to an interior shot of a luxurious Gotham tower living room—plush couches, deep carpeting, a panoramic window looking out over the city. A beautiful red-haired woman sits on a couch, a smoldering sexual vision, bare-chested, wearing only a filmy skirt. The arrogant man from the previous shot enters, flips off his cloak, throws it on the rug imperiously, strides over to the couch, towers over the woman, snatches her up into his arms, and kisses her with a cold inhuman passion.

They stand there for a long moment kissing. The man's hands begin to roam over her body, cupping her breasts, sliding between her legs. Their hips grind into each other rhythmically. The man moans hoarsely and slowly bends her backwards toward the couch . . .

Suddenly the woman breaks away, dances across the room, and stands there, hands on hips, her body a paradigm of desirability, her face tilted upward proudly, a thin smile creasing her lips.

Woman: "No!"

Man: *"No?* What do you mean, *no,* Lysistrata?" He gestures commandingly. "Come here, woman!"

Woman: "No means *no.* We've decided. No more getting off for you, bucko, until you mend your ways. We're tired of making love to cold machines. Transcendental Science or *us!"*

Man (angrily, moving toward her): "Stop this foolishness . . ." He leers at her cruelly. "There are always *other* women who'll be more cooperative . . ."

The woman removes her skirt and runs her hands over her bare flesh tantilizingly.

Woman: "Not any more. No woman will get it off with any man until the Institute is banished from this planet forever. What'll it be—your minds or your wongs?"

Man: "I'll show you what it will be!"

He dashes across the room, grabs her, throws her down on the couch, and leaps on top of her. The woman offers no resistance. She just lays there like a slab of dead meat as he groans and writhes atop her. After a few minutes, he stops, defeated.

Man: "How long do you think you can keep this up? You have needs, too . . ."

A closeup on the woman's smiling face.

Woman: "And we have *sisters* to fulfill them. Think about *that* while you whip your whacker, bucko!" She laughs and twists her face into a parody of ecstasy as the frame freezes.

Woman's voiceover: *"Lysistrata,* sisters! Stay plugged in and see just how powerful Sisterhood can be!"

Karla Mantee laughed. She snuggled closer to Angela on the loungecouch, and kissed her briefly on the lips. "Tell 'em, sisters!" she said, waving a fist at the screen.

"Who needs men? There are plenty of women around who know how to give women what they need. Let 'em all whip their whackers!"

Angela scowled. She pulled away from Karla, and shook her head in that gesture of wiser disapproval that Karla knew so well.

"What's the matter, Angela?"

"That," the older woman spat, nodding towards their net console.

Karla eyed her uncertainly. "But that's great . . . *isn't* it?" she said somewhat plaintively. "It's going to give Pacifican lesbos a whole new army of lovers!"

Angela snorted. *"A whole new army of lovers,"* she mimicked sarcastically. "Now *there's* a wonderful turn of phrase for you!"

"I said something wrong?" Karla asked innocently.

Angela sighed. She smiled ruefully and put a warmly protective arm around Karla's shoulders. "It's not you, babe," she said. "But there's an ancient saying: when politics intrudes in the bedroom, love goes out the door. Or words to that effect."

Karla cocked her head at her lover. Angela was older and more sophisticated than she was, and she knew it, and it was part of what drew Karla to her. But sometimes it made her awfully hard to fathom. "You mean it's bad because bucko-lovers wouldn't be sincere if they got it off with us just to make a point with their men?"

Angela nodded. "There *is* that," she said. She scowled again. "But that's the least of it. What really worries me is that these effing off-worlders are telling Pacifica that every Pacifican lesbo is a natural ally of theirs, as if it were impossible to be a lady-lover and a real Pacifican too. That we all think with our crotches. It fucking well *insults* us. And it's not going to make life any easier."

"Hey, I never thought of that . . ." Karla said.

Angela grimaced. She hugged Karla briefly, and gave her a little smile. "I've got a feeling you're not going to be the only one," she said. "Sisterhood is powerful—but so is the stench of a big vat of rancid jellybelly oil."

The lights of Gotham dwindled away behind the boat, a handful of stars cast from the sky, a ghostly sheen of light rippling on the waters. The only sounds were the waves lapping at the bow of the boat, the wind snapping the sails, the keening of the lines. Now at last Cynda Elizabeth knew what it was to be truly alone on the naked surface of an alien planet; like the tall blond man guiding the boat over the surface of the sea, Pacifica was frightening and seductive, exotic yet deceptively tranquil, breathing with the oceanic rhythms of raw creation.

Why am I here? Cynda wondered. This is an insane risk. If Bara found out . . .

Perhaps that was part of it. Something about this planet moved her toward risk, perhaps for its own sake, perhaps because she yearned to taste its reality before that which made it the world it was was swept away by the irresistible tide of history.

She had seen much on her tour of the planet, yet she had been allowed to touch nothing. The rolling green plains, the icy beauty of Thule, the sere desert Wastes, the endless emerald isles of the Island Continent—they had all unreeled themselves around her like a travelogue tape while she remained encapsulated in her own reality. Surrounded by sisters, traveling, eating, even sleeping in a communal body, all under the watchful eyes of Bara's unseen agents.

Contact with the Pacifican sisters had been limited to speeches and formal meetings; never alone, never on a one-to-one basis. Cynda felt that she had seen everything and knew nothing. As for the Pacifican breeders—the mission had moved around the planet as if Pacifican men did not exist.

But these strange creatures *did* exist, striding through the streets like ancient machos, roaming the world at will, working side by side with their women everywhere, bursting with a confident energy of a sort she had never seen before, so utterly unlike the few pale breeders of Earth—and although her mind could hardly contain the concept, unlike the machos of long ago, too. Almost as if they were sisters inside, trapped in alien bodies. Though they didn't seem to *feel* trapped in their hard-muscled bodies; they seemed to glory in it, and in the way the sisters looked at them . . .

"Let's just drift for a while," Eric said, tying a line to the tiller and lowering the sails. He leaned back against the gunwale of the open cockpit, his bare chest slick with salty spray, glistening in the starlight. Cynda felt a thickness in her throat, a queasy lightheadedness rising from her chest.

"Are you glad you decided to sneak away from your keepers, Cynda?" he said, staring at her with an insinuating smile. "How do you like what you see out here, away from the city?"

"It's strange . . ." Cynda said softly. "It's not like Earth at all. Maybe Earth was like this long ago, before the Holocaust, before humans poured over every centimeter of it . . ."

Eric nodded. "That was the dream of the Founders," he said. "A place where men could keep their civilization without . . . without overwhelming the planet. I hope we'll always keep it that way." He frowned. "But you people wouldn't understand that . . ."

Cynda looked out over the dark waters as the boat drifted in a ragged circle at the whim of the sea. The city lights seemed so long ago and far away. Earth, the ship, the mission, her sisters, the past—these were an even dimmer reality. All that existed was the boat and the stars and the sea and two humans lost in the dark immensity, and the only real time was now.

"Perhaps we might learn," Cynda said.

Eric smiled at her, arched his back, and shook his long blond hair. "*You* might learn, Cynda," he said. "You're not like the rest of them."

"I'm not?"

He grinned and suddenly seemed to flow across the cockpit toward her. All at once he was sitting by her side. She could smell the strange heavy scent of his body. He flung an arm over the gunwale behind her, his bare skin not quite touching her shoulders. Her muscles tensed; something told her to pull away, but she resisted, and sat there staring up at the stars, unable to move, unable to look at his face.

"They wouldn't be sitting here alone in a boat with . . . a *breeder*," he said, sneering the last word contemptuously.

"What do you mean by that?" Cynda blurted, suddenly knowing all too well why she was here, knowing that he knew, too . . .

"You know what I mean," he said huskily. With an almost subliminal movement, his arm touched her shoulders.

Her body quivered as if from a jolt of electricity. The bubble of queasiness that had been rising from her chest into her throat burst, filling her with a giddy, lightheaded freedom. I'm going to do it, she realized. I don't care. I have to. Why shouldn't I?

"Tell me about your breeders, Cynda," Eric said softly. "Have you ever gotten it off with one?"

Cynda flushed. "It's our duty to produce a viable embryo if we can," she said. "Radiation has made it very difficult. It was my duty . . ."

Eric nodded. He moved closer. She could feel the hardness of his body against her side. "Did you enjoy it?"

"I felt nothing," Cynda said, but it was a twisted half-truth. The male creatures in the breeding chambers were no more than appliances. One ordered them to expose their piercers and prepare them for insertion, then one lowered oneself onto the organ and pumped rhythmically until the semen was deposited. A mechanical act as prescribed, nothing like honey-eating with a sister; no one felt anything. Even the breeders were repelled by sexual contact with others not of their own kind; they had been conditioned that way for generations.

"I could make you feel something," Eric said. "I could make you feel something you've never felt before."

Cynda glanced downward into the vee of his white pants. She could see the long shape of his piercer tight against the cloth. His eyes caught the line of her gaze. He laughed. He took her hand. "On Pacifica, you can touch, too," he said, and he suddenly thrust her hand between his legs onto the mysterious maleness of his body.

Cynda cried out wordlessly. A spasm of tension passed through her body, leaving a sweet lassitude in its wake. Yes, she thought. Why deny the inevitable? Why deny the truth? No one need ever know.

"Show it to me," she whispered. "I want to see your piercer."

Silently, he took off his pants, revealing his full nakedness. Cynda's eyes were drawn by the angular architecture of his hips to the alien fascination. She reached out hesitantly and touched the bare skin of his organ. It throbbed and twitched under her touch, a thing alive. How marvelous! She had never touched one with her hand before. How warm it was! How sensitive! How utterly strange!

153

Without removing her hand, she looked up into his eyes. There was kindness there, but she also sensed that he was laughing at her inside. There was understanding, but also something cruel and cold. The combination was overpowering. She wanted . . . she wanted . . . she knew not what.

"I . . . I don't know what to do," she said softly. "Show me." He grinned, and now the cruelty and laughter was more open, and it sent shivers up her spine as his expression seemed to somehow emphasize the colossal muscles of his arms, so dangerous, so enticing. He cupped her face in his hands and drew her mouth down. He slid through the surprised resistance of her lips. It choked her. It felt warm as roasted meat and smooth as velvet. He moved it inside her mouth uttering little soft cries.

It was the strangest thing that had ever happened to Cynda Elizabeth. It frightened and repelled her. It made her mouth go soft and her body throb with flame. It was like eating honey and like nothing else in the universe. She had to fight back a retch and yet she wanted to swallow it whole.

After a long time, he curled his hands in her hair and drew her head up to face him. He was breathing heavily, and his eyes had a faraway dreamy look. Cynda found her own breath coming in counterpoint to his.

"And now . . ." he murmured.

He bent over her, undid the fastenings of her shirt and trousers, and silently worked them off her body. Then they were naked together, under the starry skies, the boat rolling beneath them in complex rhythms. Now I'm going to get it off with a Pacifican breeder, Cynda thought, with a strange, almost mindless calm. With a *man*. Out here where no one can see.

She waited for Eric to lie down on his back and offer up his piercer. "Well?" she finally said. *"Well?"* He looked genuinely puzzled. Am *I* going to have to show *him?* Cynda thought. She touched his chest and gently pushed him backwards. He resisted.

"Oh," he said with a little laugh. "No, lady, that's not my style." And he moved forward against *her* resistance now, pressed his strong hard body against her, and pushed her over onto her back against the gunwale.

Then his full weight pressed upon her, and with a

liquid thrust of his entire lower body, he pierced her to the core.

Cynda screamed. She moaned. Waves of sensation traveled up her body from the junction of their union as he began pumping his piercer in and out of her with the motion of his whole body. She groaned in fear and delight; her arms fell over the side of the boat, her fingertips gently caressing the rippling surface of the water as the motion of his heavy body slammed her up against the hard edge of the gunwale again and again.

Her head lolled back, her eyes closed, and for a fleeting moment the fantasy came—the great hairy macho violating her flesh with slavering animal savagery. But then it was gone, and she was just *there*, right now, in a place she had never been before. He was brutal, quick, and hard; then languid, tender, and slow; then urgent and building; then easy and smoldering again. He was unexpectedly subtle, varying rhythms like a master musician.

Her eyes flicked open and closed at random, her head rolled back and forth, her hands flailed at the water, then relaxed into its cold caress. Whirling patterns inside her eyes. Images of his flushed face. Stars swirling overhead at crazy angles. The edge of the gunwale cutting into her back. Wet coldness at her fingertips. An enormous weight pulsing against her. A building, keening, rising wave of unbearably sweet tension that—

—broke into a flash of painful pleasure exploding from her lips in a wordless scream—

Gasping for air, drifting back from a nameless somewhere, she saw his face as he groaned like a savage. She felt a tremendous spasm ripple his body, and he burst like a fountain inside her, rolled his eyes, sighed once, and it was over.

Cynda Elizabeth had gotten off with a Pacifican . . . *man*. It had been nothing like doing it with a Terran breeder, nothing like the machos in the history tapes, and not much like her secret fantasies either. It had been itself, unique and strange, nothing more, nothing less.

She sat there quietly for a long time, ignoring the man beside her, staring at the far-off lights of Gotham, trying to decide just how she felt. There had been a physical pleasure she had never experienced with a Terran breeder or a sister; a fleshly rightness, a natural mindless flow, a visceral sense that this was the way it was meant to be, out here in the anonymous dark. Yet the mental dimension of what had happened was twisted, unwholesome, terrifying, and in some way demeaning.

Finally, she looked at Eric. His strong face was utterly relaxed, but something in his eyes seemed to be laughing at her. Strangely, he seemed even more alien to her now, after the ultimate physical intimacy she had experienced. Unfathomable, his mind occupying some unguessably different dimension. A bucko, she thought. A Pacifican bucko . . . Great Mother, what kind of creature really is that?

"Well?" he said, his voice seeming to come from very far away.

"Well what?"

"Well, did you enjoy it?"

"I . . . I don't know . . ."

He laughed ironically. "Well at least that's a unique response," he said.

"Are you playing with me, Eric? Have you been playing with me all along?"

He looked directly into her eyes and now there was no humor in his face at all. Something unstated, something true, seemed to pass between them. "I'm just as sincere as you are . . . sister," he said.

She forced a laugh, touched his knee briefly, and looked out over the water, away from the lights of the city, out to the eastern horizon, where the brilliant starry sky abruptly vanished into the impenetrable black sea, a crisp hard line between the commonality of galactic space and the singularity of this dark unknown world. And here we are, she thought, two humans bobbing on the interface. What kind of creature are you, Eric Lauder? Great Mother, what kind of creature am *I*?

Like a wraith on her rented floater, Maria Falkenstein roamed the night streets of Gotham, moving through the city but unable to touch it, isolated from the people by who she was and why she was here. Since she and Roger had come here from the Cords, she had taken to these lonely nighttime wanderings while he was off politicking, searching for she knew not what, perhaps nothing at all.

Cafés drifted by, bright with lights, humming with

people. A crowd poured out of a theater in a babbling roar. A man in a jump-harness touched down on the street a few meters away, then bounced onward on another long arc. A group of teenagers on powerskates bracketed her on both sides, zipped off down the street, and across a bridge to the next island. Maria turned off the busy street and onto a byway that led over a bridge to a small island, a wooded hill that rose sharply out of the bay.

The road spiraled up around the island, which was apparently a park. Warm yellow lights illuminated the pathway, and here and there blue bongowood benches were set into manicured alcoves in the wild shrubbery. Pacificans sat on some of these benches: lovers, old people talking, children playing some obscure game with balls and little figurines. The top of the hill was a clear circle of green lawnmoss, and the city stretched not far below in all directions.

It was not a cold mountaintop view that reduced the maze of brightly lit streets and the faerie traceries of the bridges to an abstract holoview panorama, but something more subtle, above the city yet part of it, preserving the human dimension. The people on the streets were part of the pattern, the boats and hovers skimming around the bridges seemed almost close enough to touch. Gotham lived below her; the noises of the city were a metropolitan babble, not a distant hum.

Maria turned off the float unit at the top of the hill, the floater settled to the ground, and it suddenly came to her that she wasn't searching for anything on these excursions into the alien city, she was fleeing —fleeing into anonymity, fleeing from Roger and herself, from what they were and what they were doing to this planet that seemed so thoroughly at peace with itself.

"Talk with the Falkensteins," she thought bitterly. Talk with Roger while he uses me as a prop. Free media access, the sacred Pacifican right. She wondered what those people down there would say if they knew that the last program had been a scripted exercise in cynical deception. That the ludicrous raving Femocrat and the self-righteous bucko had been actors off the *Heisenberg*, that the whole thing had been scripted by psychopoliticians and refined by the Arkmind.

She shook her head. Some of them surely must have

guessed, she thought. I sounded false even to myself. "As a woman, I can see how the Femocrats are trying to poison minds here . . ." And what are *we* doing, Roger? What about us?

Maria knew all the right answers to that one. Political necessity. Future human evolution riding on what happened here. The end justifies the means. And the Femocrats *were* a poison, a social carcinoma that had to be kept from spreading at all costs.

But Roger, in the process of fighting that poison, aren't we becoming the very thing they accuse us of being? In fighting a lie, aren't we turning it into the truth? *Faschochauvinism*, the loathsome catchword they use to justify their own disgusting gender fascism . . . but isn't stuff like "Soldiers of Midnight" faschochauvinism? Haven't the psychopoliticians constructed an entire scenario based on polarizing the men against the women? Haven't you been trying to play Royce Lindblad off against his own woman, Roger? Aren't you using *me* as a model of the dutiful wife supporting her husband against her own sex? And how many women have managed to get through an Institute? Is it really all a matter of intrinsic mental differences, or could the Femocrats have chanced upon a small truth?

Maria sighed as she looked out over Gotham. It seemed to her that these Pacificans had something among themselves that no off-worlder could quite understand. The buckos preened and paraded their sexual wares like the hated faschochauvinists of the Femocrat fantasies, and yet only a Femocrat or a fool could deny that women were more than equal here. The women dominated their men politically and economically, yet the balance was not far from equal. Their absolutism about their legal principles was a tactical weakness, and yet, in another sense, was it not a kind of strength?

Maria turned on the float unit and the floater rose off the Pacifican ground. I'm running from something, she thought, but am I not finding something, too? A people at peace with themselves. A society in some ways more complex than our own, a delicate balance of fragile improbabilities that we're trampling upon in the service of our hard, clear, evolutionary certainties. Perhaps the Femocrats are right about us, and we're right about them. And only these Pacificans have found a clear path, a world between.

A cool wind blew in off the bay as Maria started down the hill. She glanced upward for a moment at the bright stars above the city. They seemed cold and hard and very far away.

10

A PANORAMIC SHOT OF A PUBLIC SQUARE UNDER ONE OF the larger permaglaze domes of Valhalla, centering on a huge screen set up on the central lawn. A silver-on-black banner reading "Pacificans for the Institute" is strung above the screen between two trees, and a low podium has been set up in front of it. From the podium, a man in the gray workclothes of a Thule tech harangues the vast crowd that fills the square, his face mirrored in gigantic realtime on the screen behind him.

Thule tech: ". . . here in Thule where our very existence and the economy of the entire planet depends upon the highest technological level we can achieve!"

The crowd roars. It is almost entirely male, hardy no-nonsense types wearing functional workclothes. Here and there large placards wave above their heads. "Pacificans for the Institute." "Back to Earth, Femocrat Mothers!" "Vote for the Future!" "Ban Big-Mouthed Bitches!" The placards are all uniformly lettered in silver on black, and indeed they seem mass-produced.

Thule tech: ". . . the Managing Director of the Transcendental Science Arkology *Heisenberg*, Dr. Roger Falkenstein!"

The crowd cheers loudly as Falkenstein's face appears

160

on the giant screen; cool, smiling, unruffled, an impressive contrast to the tumult in the square. The camera moves in on the screen as Falkenstein begins to speak so that he fills the entire frame, speaking directly to the electronic audience.

Falkenstein: "Thank you very much, I'm overwhelmed by the support that Pacificans for the Institute are demonstrating all over the planet as I speak to you now . . ."

A quick intercut series of shots of male crowds all over the planet: Good Old Mountain Boys in a logged-out clearing, Gothamites in a domed amphitheater, an amorphous human sprawl along a bank of the Big Blue, a small island covered with male humanity. All wave the same mass-produced silver and black placards. Each shot centers on a large screen with Falkenstein speaking from it in realtime and a "Pacificans for the Institute" banner.

Falkenstein: "Your laws forbid us from participating in Pacifican politics, but they do not forbid *you* from making your views plain. *We* cannot officially endorse Pacificans for the Institute, but *you* can support us as a spontaneous expression of the good sense of Pacificans everywhere. We stand ready to serve you. Give us the permission we need and we will transform Pacifica together . . . matter will form itself to your command . . ."

A shot of the dead brown desert Wastes as a city grows magically from the sands, springing into being from nothingness with unreal speed.

". . . artificial suns will warm the frozen south . . ."

Three small yellow suns appear in the lead-gray sky over the frozen white plain of Thule. The sky turns a brilliant blue. A billion years' worth of mile-thick ice vanishes in an instant, and lawnmoss, trees, and fields of grain spring into existence on the bared brown earth.

". . . 'and death shall have no dominion.' "

A shot of a group of ancient, wizened men and women, as backs straightened, gray hair turns blond, red, and black, and lines vanish from faces, like a long-term time-lapse shot run in reverse.

Cut to Falkenstein's face; cool, confident, intelligent.

Falkenstein: "All this and more! We seek no political dominion, no disruption of the wise and just way of life you have evolved over the years. No pitting of man against woman, no pollution of the body politic with a ludicrous

and perverted female fascism that is already the laughingstock of every truly civilized world. We are not ideologues,
we are teachers. We are not demagogues, we are scientists.
We are not wild-eyed godzilla-brained raving sexual
chauvinists—but we know who is, and so, my friends,
do *you!*"

An almost subliminally fast flashed shot of Cynda
Elizabeth's face, contorted in a grimace of rage. Then a
rapidly cut montage of crowd shots all over the planet
as thousands of male throats break into a continuous
growling roar . . .

A series of wide-angle shots on shouting male crowds
waving placards, each one in a different area of the
planet; ugly, angry mob scenes made that much more
ominous by a subtle red filter and an exaggerated soundtrack with almost subliminal dubbed-in animal growls. Another series of shots, these extreme closeups of male faces
—features contorted by rage, hair wild and disarrayed,
spittle spewing from their lips, a montage of masculine
bestiality.

Cynda Elizabeth's voiceover: "Boys will be boys . . ."

Cynda Elizabeth's almond-eyed face appears—calm,
wise, infinitely tolerant, and more than a shade patronizing.

Cynda Elizabeth: ". . . or *something*. But as we all know,
as Dr. Falkenstein has told us, Transcendental Science
seeks no pollution of the Pacifican body politic, and
wouldn't *dream* of arousing wild-eyed godzilla-brained raving sexual chauvinism. So these buckos we've just seen
obviously aren't a mob of faschochauvinist savages, they're
just figments of our female imagination! *Sure* they are!"

A closeup of a blond young woman, with a busy Gotham
street in the background.

Woman: ". . . never seen anything like it. Men screaming like animals for something they call *science?* Falkenstein's got them thinking with their wongs . . ."

A closeup of an older gray-haired woman sitting behind
a desk.

Woman (somberly): "There's never been anything like
this on Pacifica before. Men and women have always gotten along in a civilized manner here until the *Heisenberg*
showed up. I've never placed much credence in Femocratic theories before, but after seeing what Transcendental

Science has provoked in our men in a few short weeks, I'm
beginning to wonder whether there might not be something to the notion of an inherent male urge to dominance
through violence . . ."

Closeup on a grimy, plain-looking woman standing by
some gray machinery.

Woman: "It's getting hard to work with the buckos
now. They get surly when they're given directives by female supervisors. They tend to stick to themselves. They
use the slightest excuse to launch into tirades against
Femocracy. They're not behaving normally. It's time the
government put a stop to this . . ."

Closeup of a ravishing black-haired woman leaning
against the side of a sailboat.

Woman: "It's thoroughly ridiculous. I can't get off with a
bucko anymore without getting into some insane political
argument. I'm beginning to wish I *was* lesbo so I could get
off with someone who would treat me like a human being.
Why is Carlotta Madigan stalling? Why don't we vote to
kick these faschochauvinist troublemakers off the planet
already?"

A medium shot on Cynda Elizabeth. She shrugs.

Cynda Elizabeth: "We're not here to tell the sisters
of this planet what to do. We're here by fortunate accident, and we wouldn't have even gotten involved if we
hadn't seen the vicious hand of off-world faschochauvinism
at work. But as long as this alien presence remains to
bring out the atavistic macho beast that lives in even the
most civilized man, as long as Transcendental Science
manipulates this faschochauvinist monster for its own ends,
we'll stay on Pacifica to fight it, as long as the women
of this planet will allow!"

Carlotta Madigan rolled away from Royce and lay
there by his side in the darkened Lorien bedroom, breathing raggedly, filmed with sweat, her loins aching from the
sorriest bout of lovemaking she had ever experienced with
him.

Her head pounded with frustration and her mind swam
with loathsome images. Royce puffing and groaning atop
her like some fucking machine. Ugly shouting men's faces.
Her legs clamped like pincers around his waist as she
ground her pelvis against him, trying to get herself off and

to hell with everything else. Carla Winkler calling her a traitor to her sex. Horrid flashed fragments from Transcendental Science porn operas—women screaming in terror, men in hard black leather, angry thrusting cocks, flesh violating flesh, chrome violating rubber.

Royce touched a gentle hand to her thigh. "Sorry," he said lamely.

"*Sorry?*" Carlotta snapped. "What do you have to be sorry about? *You* got off, didn't you, bucko?"

Royce jerked his hand away. "Up yours, too!" he said. "You weren't exactly synced into pleasing me either, you know!"

"I wanted you to eat my honey."

"Well, that just didn't happen to be what—wait a minute! *Eat your honey?* What in the fucking hell is that? That's straight out of some effing Femocrat dictionary!"

Bowb a bumbler! Carlotta thought. So it is. So it bloody well is. She turned on a soft yellow light and they lay there on the bed glaring at each other.

"What the hell is going on, Royce?" Carlotta said, trying to control the tone of her voice, reaching for sanity.

Royce grimaced. The angry lines on his face softened somewhat. "Speaking as your bucko, I'd say that you're becoming a narcissistic selfish bitch who can't get it off because you can't sync your body behind any real feeling for me . . ."

"*What!* You egotistical effing—"

Royce held up his hand for peace and smiled ruefully at her. "But speaking professionally," he said, "I think we're both suffering from the same strange new brand of media cafard that's infected the whole planet."

"Media cafard?" Carlotta said. "What do you mean, media cafard?" *Media cafard* was a sardonic pseudo-medical term for plug-in overload, a condition where someone had been plugged into the net for so long that they stopped relating to ground-level reality. What the hell did *media cafard* have to do with this crummy lay?

"Well, call it reverse media cafard with a moebius twist," Royce said. "Tell me, Carlotta, what was going through your head while we were trying to make love, if you can call it that?"

"Great grunting godzillas!" Carlotta muttered. "Were you reading my mind?"

Royce shrugged. "Just my own," he said.

"You, too?"

"Uh-huh."

"But this is ridiculous!" Carlotta said. "We love each other. We've been together for years. We're *Pacificans*, we're the masters of the media. And you're telling me that a lot of stupid, primitive off-worlder slok is capable of getting inside our heads and screwing up our love life?"

"I have to *tell* you? Quality of the product has nothing to do with it; what we're dealing with here is white-out media overload. The Femocrats have been pounding the idea that men are primitive selfish beasts into every woman's head. It may not get to you on an intellectual level, but the images get graven into the subconscious by sheer force of repetition. Some ancient Terran dictator called it the theory of the Big Lie. Shout a lie into people's ears long enough and loud enough and they'll eventually start acting on it, no matter how outrageous it is. And *he* didn't even have primitive television to work with!"

It's true, Carlotta thought. And the Transcendental Scientists are doing the same damned thing. Femocrat-fomented women are trying to cut your balls off by denying you an Institute, buckos! Your wong is your weapon, so use it, boys, Goddamn, it's even come between Royce and me!

Carlotta bounced off the bed and began pacing the bedroom in small circles. "We've got to stop this, Royce!" she said. "We've got to stop it *now*, before the whole planet ends up in the psycho ward, you and me included."

Royce got up and started pacing with her. "But how?" he said.

"I don't know," Carlotta said, "but we've got to think of *something*. Let's go get some air."

But *what?* she wondered as they walked down the hall to the veranda. Both sides have gone beyond subtle media blitzes into straightforward political campaigning. It's the Pink and Blue War with no holds barred, and emotionally it's a real war between the sexes already. She grimaced. The only way to make things *worse* would be to force immediate votes on the issues, which would be so close that the losing party just might not accept it in a democratic spirit, and then constitutional government itself might start to crumble . . .

Outside on the deck, the air was warm and moist on her bare skin. Traceries of cloud fleeced across the starry sky. Waves lapped the shore, painting the waterline with ephemeral translucent foam. The whole bloody business seemed so ridiculous out here in the tranquil world of sea and sky. Royce's naked body gleamed silver in the starlight. Just me and my bucko, Carlotta thought, that's the way it's supposed to be. Why can't they leave us alone? Why can't we *make* them leave us alone?

"You know, the Femocrat ship is almost repaired," Royce said, sinking down in a bongowood chair and looking out to sea. "We *could* try to squeeze an expulsion vote through, and if you made it a vote of confidence in yourself . . ."

"Leaving what?" Carlotta said, sitting down beside him. "Ten million women convinced they'd been power-tripped by men and howling for my blood? Look at the reverse—if we squeezed through a vote to expel Transcendental Science, ten million men would be convinced that Pacifican women had bitten off their balls."

Royce nodded. "I *did* playfully threaten Falkenstein with the third alternative," he said.

"*Third alternative?*"

"Kick both their asses out."

"But I thought you were convinced we had to have Transcendental Science . . . ?"

Royce shrugged. "I was . . . I am . . . I was only torturing him a little. Besides, if we combined the issues, we'd never even get it to the floor. Still . . ."

"Still *what?*"

"Still it did manage to terrify him . . ."

Suddenly something began to tease at the edge of Carlotta's consciousness. The Femocrats wanted one thing, the Transcendental Scientists another, and one good definition of political compromise was something that displeased both sides in equal measure . . .

"They're both pushing hard for quick conclusive votes, aren't they?" she said slowly.

Royce nodded. "I'd give it two weeks at the outside before you're handed a Parliamentary petition demanding votes," he said.

"Coitus interruptus . . ." Carlotta muttered.

Royce looked at her narrowly. "Is something percolating in that Machiavellian brain of yours?"

"Maybe . . ." Carlotta said. "I mean, what we're faced with is two media blitzes and political campaigns building to a quick showdown . . ."

"So?"

"So what if we screw up the timetable?"

Royce fingered his lower lip. "What are you getting at?"

"Try a sexual metaphor," Carlotta said. "Men and women fucking madly, harder and harder, the energy building to an orgasm . . . well, what happens to that energy level if orgasm is delayed by, oh, say six months?"

"Oh-ho!" Royce exclaimed. "Either it drops to a lower sustainable level or they fuck themselves into exhaustion before anything conclusive happens."

"Right," Carlotta said. "The Femocrats and the Transcendental Scientists simply couldn't keep up this level of hysteria if everyone knew that the conclusive votes were six months off. If they tried, everyone on both sides would see that they were gibbering maniacs in a month or two."

Royce stood up and began pacing the veranda. "Very sharp," he said. "We could call it the Madigan Plan. Postpone the final vote on the Institute for six months. Let the Femocrats do their damndest in the meantime. Yeah, they'd have to tone it down for the long haul."

"Do you think we could get it through Parliament?"

Royce stood by her chair and touched a hand to her shoulder. He grinned. "Are you kidding, babe?" he said. "The Delegates would fall all over themselves to vote for anything that would prevent a showdown at this point. Oh, they'd buy it all right. There's just one thing . . ."

"What's that?" Carlotta asked uneasily.

"I think we should let an Institute of Transcendental Science function in the meantime."

"*What?*" Carlotta shouted, bolting to her feet. "No way! They'd just use it to build a bigger political base, what they've done in the Cords writ large."

"But it *would* make it a matter of put up or shut up," Royce insisted. "Right now, they're promising us the universe on a golden platter. Let an Institute function for six months, and we'll *know* how much of it is real and how much is so much jellybelly oil."

He sat back down again and stared up at the stars. Carlotta knew what was running through his mind. Despite everything, he was still hooked on the Faustian grandeur of Transcendental Science; he still refused to give that fantasy up.

"We *do* have our own scientists," she said. "Someday we'll be able to develop everything Transcendental Science has on our own."

"Sure," Royce said. "A century from now. Two centuries . . . three . . . Even if it were true, imagine what a boost we'd get from just six months of an Institute here . . ."

"It'd be political suicide," Carlotta said coldly. "Let them set it up in the Cords, and we'll end up with a chauvinistic mano elite. Put it in Gotham, and it'd be a center of political troublemaking. Stick it in Thule, where the natural student body is, and we'd have a cancer at the heart of our economy."

"If we *don't* allow an Institute to function during the trial period, the men of this planet won't buy any Madigan Plan," Royce said. "The Femocrats would be allowed total freedom to do their thing, but the Transcendental Scientists wouldn't. It'd never get through Parliament."

"Meaning *you* won't support it wholeheartedly!" Carlotta snapped, slamming her bottom down into the chair beside him.

Royce looked at her belligerently. "If you insist on putting it on that level—*yes!*"

They sat there in stony silence, Royce looking up at the damnable stars, his jaw set in a hard line of resolution, Carlotta not deigning to look at him, her eyes mesmerized by the wavelets nibbling at the sandy shoreline.

Rugo waddled out onto the veranda, whonking a happy greeting that they both ignored. The bumbler stood between their chairs. He nuzzled Carlotta's thigh with his beak. "I'm not in the mood, Rugo," she grunted, pulling away. The bumbler reached up and rubbed his feathery head against Royce's shoulder. "Cut it out, Jocko," Royce snapped irritably.

Rugo looked at Carlotta, then at Royce, then at Carlotta again. If he had had hips and hands, he would have put his hands on his hips indignantly as he squawked his wounded outrage. "Whonk-ka-whonk ka-whonkity whonk!"

"Shut up, will you, Rugo!" Royce snapped.

"Whonk, whonk, ka-whonk, whonk, whonk!" The bumbler's feathers ruffled angrily as he harangued them.

"Will you stop yelling at us like a goddamn godzilla!" Carlotta shouted.

Chastened, Rugo finally subsided. But Royce's face broke into a great grin. "Godzillas!" he said, rubbing Rugo's head. "Jocko, you're a genius!"

"Huh?"

Royce broke into wild whooping laughter. "Godzillaland!" he finally managed to say. "Let them set up their goddamn Institute in effing *Godzillaland!* Can you see it?"

Now Carlotta started laughing. Festering jungle where the temperature never fell below 110 degrees. Giant godzillas rampaging through the trees, bellowing their endless threats day and night. And the crazy whackers who actually *liked* living there! Oh, it was delicious! Let Falkenstein try to build himself a political base among those maniacs! Two thousand kilometers from anywhere! It'll turn the whole thing into a planetary joke.

She got up and hugged Royce. "Godzillaland it is!" she giggled. "The Transcendental Institute of Godzillaland!"

"Then we've got ourselves a Madigan Plan?"

"We sure do!" Carlotta said. "Godzilla-brained faschochauvinist Fausts!" she laughed. She broke up entirely. She began stomping crazily around the veranda, grunting and bellowing like a godzilla. After a moment, Royce joined her, and they stood there, rolling their eyes, bellowing, and flailing their forearms at each other, until they collapsed into laughter into each other's arms.

"Whonk-ka-whonk? Whonkity whonkity whonk?" Rugo stood there cocking his head from one side to the other, quite certain that they had both gone insane.

"Good, perfect, we'll run it as is tonight," Royce Lindblad said, turning off the comscreen and punching up the latest depth-poll figures from the Parliamentary computer. Forty percent of the population were now against the Institute, overwhelmingly female; 42 percent were in favor of expelling the Femocrats, almost all male; 87 percent wanted an immediate vote on both issues. Logically, the figures were all bad, and seemed to predict a disastrous and crushing defeat for the Madigan Plan.

But Royce's gut-feeling went against the logic of the polls. For now at last the Ministry of Media was about to take an active political role in the conflict. For too long these effing off-worlders had used the net for their own purposes, while the Ministry of Media itself was hamstrung by the Constitution into serving as their unwitting allies, acting as the guardian of free media access while unable to function politically.

But now these bastards were going to get a lesson in how *Pacificans* could use the net for *Pacifican* political purposes. Which was why the current depth-poll figures didn't mean a damned thing. Starting tonight, the very media blitz techniques that had worked so well for Transcendental Science and the Femocrats would be used as weapons against them.

The tape that Larry Cristensen had produced to announce the Madigan Plan was a minor masterpiece. Open with choice cuts from the most rabid straight propaganda that the Femocrats and Transcendental Scientists had pumped out lately, edited into a building montage of total craziness, while slowly building up the sound level of dubbed-in mob noises to an animal roar. Then bits of their silliest entertainment tapes flash across the straight propaganda cuts as a laugh-track begins to white-out the mob-roar with gross guffaws and giggling hysteria. *Then*, a hard cut to just Carlotta, explaining the Madigan Plan as the voice of sweet reason. Finally a quick series of endorsements of the Madigan Plan from already-committed Delegates, carefully balanced between male and female.

Royce grinned. He got up and walked to the window of his Ministry office. He wondered how the Femocrats and the Transcendental Scientists would react to the Madigan Plan. If *I* were either of them, I'd keep my big mouth shut, he thought. If both sides lie low, the Madigan Plan will sail through without affecting the political balance. But if either side opposes it, we and the other side will come down on them like a sixty-ton godzilla. Of course, the best of all possible worlds would have the Femocrats alone oppose the Madigan Plan. Then it passes over their dead political bodies, but the vote would be close enough so that Falkenstein might be willing to offer some real concessions for our support.

And that's what you really want, isn't it? he thought.

An Institute without the Pink and Blue War, under effective Pacifican control, Transcendental Science without the Transcendental Scientists. And who knows? What might we do with a six-month trial period? How would they select their student body? How long would it really take for trained Pacifican scientists to acquire enough knowledge of the Transcendental Sciences to function independently?

Royce returned to his net console. Might not a small bending of mortality solve the whole problem once the Madigan Plan was passed? A little espionage? Isn't Falkenstein really asking for it . . . ?

He plugged into Harrison Winterfelt, the Minister of Science, on a secure scrambled comcircuit. "I want you to prepare a little list for me, Hari," he said. "Physicists, biologists, pharmacologists, electronics experts, the whole scientific spectrum. Good competent people in every scientific area."

Winterfelt's craggy, wrinkled face screwed up in owlish confusion. "You want twenty volumes of *Who's Who in Pacifican Science,* Royce? What for?"

"Use the Parliamentary computer to narrow it down through a set of parameters," Royce said.

"What parameters?"

"No senior people," Royce said. "No previous or present gov connections. None of them politically active in Pacificans for the Institute. Eidetic memories would be nice but not essential. And when you've got a list, run psych checks on them. I want only strong, apolitical, technically oriented personalities—in other words, people who would be most resistant to all forms of mind control."

Winterfelt cocked an inquisitive eyebrow. "What the hell is this for, Royce?" he asked.

"I'm not sure yet," Royce said. "Call it a contingency plan. I'm not telling you any more than you need to know because I want the tightest possible security maintained on this. You do likewise. Involve only enough people to get the job done, break it down so no one knows what the total project is but you and me, and don't talk to anyone but me about it."

"Not even Carlotta?"

Royce paused, sensing that he was about to cross some vaguely defined personal Rubicon. "Not even Carlotta," he finally said. "Because it would be political suicide for her to have known should word of this ever leak. Because there's one more parameter . . ."

"What now?" Winterfelt asked uneasily.

"The final list must be all male," Royce said.

Winterfelt whistled. Comprehension began to dawn in his large eyes. "*Now* I see what you're getting at," he said.

"Well, don't even tell *me*, Hari," Royce said, unplugging from the circuit. He leaned back in his lounger and gazed out the window at the setting sun.

Pacifica is going to retain control of its own destiny, and the off-worlders had just better watch their own asses, he thought. The Madigan Plan was going to pass, and that was part of it, exiling the Institute to Godzillaland would be another part, and the active intervention of the Ministry of Media yet another. Espionage might very well enter the equation, too, before all this was over.

At this moment in time, the situation was full of imponderables. How would the Femocrats and Falkenstein react to the Madigan Plan? How would Institute students be chosen? How much could Carlotta be told, and when?

But somehow, at least within Royce's own psyche, the situation had been altered. Now he was acting instead of reacting. Now something *Pacifican* was going to emerge between the opposing off-worlder forces. Now the lines of power were beginning to form a new geometry, with the Ministry of Media as one of the major foci. I've got the tiller in one hand and the boomline in the other, he thought. I'm getting the feel of the wind and the current, and I'm going to sail us through this storm. I'm going to do what I know best.

"Leave us alone," Bara Dorothy said curtly. When the junior staff members had left the office, she glared across her desk at Cynda Elizabeth. Mary Maria sat on the edge of the rumpled gilded bed as far away from them as possible, trying to look inconspicuous, though Cynda sensed that, as the sister who worked closest with the Pacificans, both male and female, she might be both a pragmatic and psychic ally. But for that very reason, she might be reluctant to disagree openly with the mentor.

"I say again, Bara, we'll be making a big mistake," Cynda said. "This Madigan Plan is going to pass no matter what we do. Why do you insist on fighting a losing battle?"

"The purpose of this mission is to win the *war*," Bara Dorothy said coldly. She nodded at the map of Pacifica, a forest of silver pins in all the right places. "Everything has been going according to plan, we have the momentum —and now this Madigan Plan throws the whole timetable off!"

"*But we can't do anything about it!*" Cynda insisted.

Bara steepled her fingers. "What would you have us do then, Cynda Elizabeth?" she said testily. ......

"Support the Madigan Plan or at least remain neutral. That way we're guaranteed six months of free operation, and we don't alienate Pacifican public opinion."

Bara looked sharply at Mary Maria. "Do you agree with this?" she asked.

"The . . . the public relations analysis seems accurate . . ." Mary hedged nervously.

Bara slammed a fist down on the desk. "Great Mother, how can you two be so dense!" she shouted. "*What* public? *What* Pacificans? Are the *sisters* of Pacifica in favor of a six-month trial period for the Institute? No! Of course not!"

"But . . . but they *are* in favor of the Madigan Plan . . ." Mary Maria said.

"Because that traitor to her sex Carlotta Madigan has linked permission for us to remain with permission for an Institute!" Bara snapped. "Just as she's trapped the breeders into voting to let us remain."

"Then you're *admitting* that we can't afford to have the Madigan Plan lose?" Cynda said. "Because it'd mean *we'd* be thrown off the planet, too."

"And *you've* just told me that the Madigan Plan is going to pass no matter what we do," Bara Dorothy said slowly.

"I don't understand . . ."

"*That*," said Bara Dorothy, "is painfully obvious. The point is that the Madigan Plan is a fait accompli, and we must therefore act *now* in ways that will maximize our future position under it. The goal of this mission is to have the sisters of Pacifica take control of the planet, and when that time comes, the breeders will be a hundred percent against us anyway."

"But what does that have to do with opposing the Madigan Plan?" Cynda said confusedly.

"Face reality, damn it!" Bara said. "We're going to have a functioning Institute here for six months. Our campaign has been built up for an immediate showdown that isn't going to happen. We're forced to slow our pace while holding the support of the sisters for the long haul. The Madigan Plan is a compromise, and a *compromise* is something we can't support. Now more than ever we must take an ideologically pure stance against the faschochauvinist Institute—*because the damn thing is going to exist*. From here on in, our whole campaign must be based on fighting the faschochauvinist evil of the Institute. We have to be able to say, 'we told you so' every step of the way. How better to establish our future credibility than by opposing a trial period for the Institute from the outset, even at the supposed cost of exiling ourselves from the planet? Great Mother, we might even pick up some *breeder* support if Falkenstein is heavy-handed enough! Can't you see that?"

Cynda Elizabeth sighed. It was a flawless analysis; the only trouble with it was that it was wrong. And it was wrong for reasons that Cynda dared not mention to Bara Dorothy or anyone else.

It was wrong because Bara Dorothy had never gotten it off with a Pacifican man. She still thought of Pacifican men as local versions of Terran breeders or worse—atavistic machos for the moment, easily convertible to tame mano breeders once the Pacifican sisters fully seized power. And even Cynda's three secret assignations with Eric had shown her how simplistic that view was, how circumscribed by a strange sort of historical chauvinism.

Oh, all the macho tendencies were there in the nakedness of the night; that was graven in the male genes here as elsewhere. How could a creature whose greatest pleasure came from thrusting a hard piercer into a soft receptive flower fail to sync into a posture of sexual dominance when flesh met flesh, unless he had been conditioned against the natural geometric congruencies for generations? But this same Pacifican male as often as not could work under a female superior, vote for a female Delegate or even Chairman, and form a stable relationship with a socially and economically superior sister without resentment. An atavis-

tic macho when piercer met flower, he was something else
again when mind met mind. And this was the natural order
that Pacifican women enjoyed.

And though Cynda trembled when she thought about it,
it was not hard to think of this arrangement as something
beyond faschochauvinism or Femocrat doctrine when her
own body flowed so easily into the Pacifican mode. I like
having his piercer plunging deep inside me, she thought. I
even like sucking it—even though I've been conditioned to
think of it as perverted and politically regressive.

How much stronger, then, was the sexual bond that
linked *Pacifican* sisters to their men? Didn't they have all
the pleasure of the macho piercer without the pain?
Weren't Pacifican men and women linked by something
beyond mere faschochauvinist dominance patterns?

Wasn't this "Madigan Plan" really a "Madigan-Lind-
blad Plan?" Eric was quite an ordinary man—what must
it be like for Carlotta Madigan and a man like *Royce
Lindblad?* Bodies linked piercer to flower as in the atavistic
past, but minds linked together as near-equals. *Almost as
sister-to-sister!*

"Well, Cynda?" Bara Dorothy said coldly. "Do you
want to register any further objections?"

"I've got to admit that your logic is irrefutable, Bara,"
Cynda said wanly. How could you ever understand, Bara?
she thought. Never having felt a man atop you, his piercer
plunging into your depths? How could you ever understand
that the sisters of this planet want that even while they're
demonstrating for Femocracy? Without having felt it yourself, how could you ever understand that a piercer in your
flower, the way it's supposed to be, is as strong as ever
Sisterhood was? That what Pacifican women want most is
precisely what they had before we or the *Heisenberg* ever
came to this planet—*their men the way they were!*

Roger snapped off the net console and began pacing in
small circles around the living room of their Gotham hotel
suite. "So the Femocrats are against the Madigan Plan,
are they?" he muttered. "So Cynda Elizabeth is going to
address Parliament before the vote, is she?" Maria Falkenstein had never seen her husband this agitated before. And
over what?

"I don't understand," she said. "Isn't passage of the

175

Madigan Plan a foregone conclusion? Isn't it to our advantage?"

Roger came to rest nervously on an arm of the couch on which she sat. "Yes, it's a foregone conclusion," he said. "No, it's not what we want."

"Why not? We'll get to set up our Institute."

"Yes, my dear, but on a temporary basis under constant Femocrat media pressure. If we had been able to force an immediate vote on a permanent Institute, we had a good chance of winning it. Thanks to the Femocrats, the buckos were solidly behind us, and they probably would have swung enough female votes to squeak us through. But this . . . now we'll have to win a vote six months from now under radically altered conditions."

"But once we've had an opportunity to show this planet what an Institute can mean—"

"To be sure," Roger said. "But the problem is that this trial period is going to present us with a dreadful paradox."

"I just don't see that . . ."

Roger studied her in a most peculiar manner, almost as if he were debating something within himself, holding something back that he feared to tell her.

"Come on, Roger," Maria said uneasily. "Are we keeping secrets from each other now?"

Roger sighed. He slumped forward. After a moment, he sat down on the couch beside her. "Security versus political pragmatism . . ." he said hesitantly. "The Femocrats are opposing the Madigan Plan on the grounds that the Institute will be a training academy for a male faschochauvinist elite, and they're going to attack us and our Pacifican supporters on that basis for the next six months."

"So?"

Roger stared down at the plush blue rug. "So under this Madigan Plan, we're going to have to risk giving them evidence that would substantiate that charge," he said quietly. "For unavoidable security reasons . . ."

"*What?*"

"I said—"

"I know what you said. But what are you talking about?"

"Consider the situation," Roger said, distancing himself into his cold lecturing mode. "An Institute disseminating advanced knowledge coexisting with a highly active Femocrat mission on the planet in an unstable political situation. A horrendous security problem. Obviously, we must make absolutely certain that every single Pacifican student totally understands the peril of allowing our advanced knowledge to filter into the hands of anyone who is not a dedicated Transcendental Scientist willingly and unquestioningly accepting total Institute discipline."

"I still don't see—"

"No Pacifican women may be admitted as Institute students," Roger said, suddenly staring her full in the face. "We'll sprinkle in a few women off the *Heisenberg* among the student body for appearances' sake, but we cannot allow—"

"What? That's the most—"

"Further," Roger said loudly, cutting her off, "the entrance screening, even for the men, must be incredibly rigorous, and *even then* they must be given psyconditioning and continuous depth-reinforcing, and be thoroughly monitored for a considerable period before they're allowed to learn anything of technological significance." He smiled ruefully at her. "You may now call me a deceitful faschochauvinist bastard," he said.

"After what you've just said, that would be totally redundant," Maria said icily. "I might, however, add 'disgusting' to your list of mea culpas. I might also add that as a female Institute graduate, I find it personally insulting."

"Maria, Maria . . ." Roger crooned, trying to place a hand on her knee. Maria angrily pulled away. "Don't you see that this has nothing to do with you or any female Institute graduate—"

"Who of course are legion!" Maria snarled sarcastically.

"Exactly the sort of female emotionalism that proves the point!" Roger snapped. He paused. He sighed. "I'm sorry," he said, "that was uncalled for. But you *must* understand, Maria. The women of this planet are and will be under tremendous Femocratic pressure, and the psychosexual balance is skewed abnormally toward female dominance in the first place. One female Institute graduate won over to Femocracy, just *one,* and what will we have? Cloning or the black-hole drive or advanced genetic engineering techniques in the hands of Femocracy? Choose your own nightmare! Call it faschochauvinism if you must, but we simply can't afford to take the risk."

Roger shrugged and threw up his hands. "That's why I must speak out against the Madigan Plan in Parliament in the strongest possible terms. That's why I must warn the planet that the Femocrats are ruthless Machiavellian meddlers who would not hesitate to tell the most outrageous lie in the service of their pathological ideology and should therefore be banished at once." He sighed. "Not because I believe I can influence the vote, but to help destroy their credibility beforehand in case—"

"In case they should happen to find out what's going on and tell Pacifica the truth!"

"Precisely," Roger said. He smiled warmly at her. "You *do* understand!"

Maria sighed, and all her righteous anger whooshed out of her with it. For despite the loathsomeness of what Roger had told her, the cold, hard political logic of it was inescapable. The Femocrats would be no more troubled by scruples or moral doubts than Roger or the Arkmind itself. It was the logical, scientifically sound, fail-safe policy to follow. Anything else would indeed be "female emotionalism."

Or perhaps, just perhaps, something that transcended both scientific logic and female emotionalism. Mutual trust, an organic sense of oneness between men and women, the body politic and the private psyche, which if it failed would be called folly, but which if it prevailed must surely be called wisdom. Something that, left to their own devices, these strange Pacificans might actually have, she thought. Something that we with all our advanced knowledge have not yet been able to program into an Arkmind.

"Yes, I understand, Roger," she said. "But there are times I wish I didn't."

The high curving sweep of the visitors' gallery was jammed with more people than Carlotta Madigan had ever seen at a Parliamentary session before. Every seat was filled, and solid masses of people stood in every available aisle space. The media booth behind her was crammed with cameras, and every single Delegate was there in the flesh. Everyone who could be here in the flesh *was* here, and she doubted that there was a single adult on the planet who was not plugged in electronically. As a political act, the vote on the Madigan Plan would be anticlimax, but as a media circus this session would probably draw the highest rating in Pacifican history.

The reasons sat in temporary seats at either side of her: Roger Falkenstein and Cynda Elizabeth, together in the same room for the first time, in the Parliamentary chamber itself, studiously ignoring each other's existence. In the right front row of the visitors' seats, Maria Falkenstein sat with a small delegation from the *Heisenberg*, and sixty degrees around the curve of the row sat a grim phalanx of Femocrats in identical severe blue tunics. The tension in the chamber was so high that you could all but smell the ozone in the air.

The audience had been eerily quiet during the perfunctory Parliamentary debate on the Madigan Plan. The main event would be the speeches of Falkenstein and Cynda Elizabeth; all else was meaningless tedium in this perspective, and even the Delegates acknowledged it. Only five of them had bothered to ask for the floor, and their speeches were short pro forma endorsements of the Madigan Plan, which were received with bored indifference. Partly this lack of real debate was the realization that everyone was waiting for the main event, that the planetary audience was in no mood for political-speeches-as-usual.

But partly, Carlotta thought, it's because no Delegate wants to take a stand on the real issuses if it can possibly be avoided. With the exception of the delegation from the Cords, every Delegate, male or female, had to face a constituency that was more or less evenly divided between men and women; a strong public stand either way would cost as many potential votes as it would gain, and that was the major reason why the Madigan Plan was assured of overwhelming passage. A neutral vote for the Madigan Plan might not arouse fervent support in any Delegate's district, but it wouldn't turn half their constituency against them either. Which was why Falkenstein's and Cynda Elizabeth's speeches would be strictly for show. *This* decision, at least, was entirely in Pacifican hands; the off-worlders could change nothing.

"Well let's get on to the main event," Carlotta said. "Both Cynda Elizabeth and Dr. Falkenstein have asked to briefly address this body. Cynda Elizabeth will speak first. Not, I hasten to add, because of the principle of ladies first. We tossed a coin."

A ripple of nervous laughter swept the chamber, undertoned by a rather ominous rumble. It guttered away into silence as Cynda Elizabeth rose, looking, strangely enough, more like a nervous schoolgirl than a fanatic firebrand.

"You will be shortly voting on a proposal that would allow our mission to remain on your planet for six months while permitting an Institute of Transcendental Science to function on a trial basis for the same period," she said in a thin hesitant voice. "We gratefully accept the invitation extended to us and we intend to accept it, come what may. But we must in all conscience oppose the legislation currently before you and urge its rejection."

She paused as if waiting for a reaction. When none came, she continued in a higher-pitched and louder tone of voice which seemed to Carlotta to be a mere simulacrum of heightened emotion. "This plan equates free media access for Femocratic principles with the functioning of an Institute of Transcendental Science as if they were somehow mathematical equivalents in a balanced democratic equation. *And they are not!!* Such a proposition insults Femocracy, insults Pacifican women, and ultimately outrages the principle of free political decisions freely arrived at which this planet professes to hold sacred!"

There was a scattering of loud lonely applause from the Femocrat section and a few fanatic supporters in the gallery. When it quickly died of embarrassment, Cynda Elizabeth lowered her voice to a more reasoned tone, but that, too, seemed like a scripted bit of mechanical business.

"Femocracy has operated and will continue to operate entirely in the open on Pacifica. What we have to say, we say openly on the net, under the same constitutional provision that protects all free discourse on your planet. And that is *all we* intend to do. Any political or social change which our presence here may effect will be entirely the result of ideas we have openly put forth for your own consideration . . ."

Her voice rose again for dramatic emphasis as she shot a scornful glance at Falkenstein, who stared straight ahead with a perfectly blank expression. "A functioning Insti-

tute of Transcendental Science, on the other hand, will be
an instrument of ruthless, covert, faschochauvinist, un-
democratic subversion! It will operate as a state within a
state. It will choose its Pacifican student body according
to its own secret parameters, and it will not hesitate to
use secret mind-control techniques. The result will be a
small elite of faschochauvinist agents possessed of advanced scientific knowledge and dedicated to the service
of an expansionist ideology determined to expunge your
way of life and replace it with a faschochauvinist puppet-
regime controlled by Transcendental Science. It has happened on every planet which has allowed these creatures a
foothold. Do you think it can't happen here? Vote down
this proposal! Save your planet for yourselves! If you
don't, you won't be able to say we didn't warn you!"

A peculiarly unfocused sound reverberated from the
visitors' gallery. The Femocrat delegation was on its feet
trying to lead the cheering and applause. Applause there
was, and a scattering of boos, too, but also a snarling
undercurrent of rumbled indignation and outraged pride.
It seemed a somewhat insulting speech to Carlotta, especially toward the end, and a rather wooden performance.
Her eyes chanced to fall on Maria Falkenstein, who sat
statue-still, staring blankly at God-knew-what with a
strange stricken expression on her face, almost as if this
mediocre speech had touched some secret Femocrat inside
her.

"Dr. Falkenstein?" Carlotta said, after the equivocal
audience reaction had died away. Falkenstein rose slowly
and dramatically to his feet, a thin sardonic smile creasing
his lips, somehow totally in command before he even
opened his mouth.

"I'm afraid I must oppose this proposal, too," he said
with an easy ruefulness that seemed expertly designed to
establish instant rapport with the great electronic audience. He shrugged. "I had worked out such a marvelous
speech explaining why, too. But I've been totally upstaged
by my worthy opponent." He favored Cynda Elizabeth
with a witheringly patronizing smile.

"After what you've just heard, I'm afraid that any
further explanation on my part would be totally redundant.
Were I great Shakespeare himself could I draw with words
a more cogent argument for expelling Femocracy from

your planet forthwith than this farrago of bile, pathology, and outright *lies* which it has just been your displeasure to witness?"

Falkenstein paused to let the rumble of audience reaction wash over him, and when he spoke again, the rueful sarcasm and easy counterpunching was gone, and his voice was steel-hard and gleaming, his eyes burning directly into the cameras.

"I don't know about you, but if I hear the word *faschochauvinist* one more time, I will probably vomit from boredom. If this planet *must* continue to be showered with intellectually vapid invective, can't we have some variety? Might I suggest *swine*? Beast? Motherfucker? Or that secret swear-word they love to keep to themselves—*breeder*? It all amounts to the same shrill mindless man-hating scream of 'Fuck You,' anyway!"

Boos, cheers, hisses, raucous laughter.

"And aside from shrieking their sexually twisted frustrated rage at the top of their lungs, what does Femocracy offer this planet but a splendid thesaurus of Machiavellian distortions and bald-faced lies? Femocracy operates entirely in the open on Pacifica? Then how did the Femocratic League of Pacifica spring into existence overnight? Spontaneous combustion, no doubt! Femocracy seeks only to engage in free intellectual discourse? Then what about what they've done to men on their own planets? Their *breeders*, as they call them—a handful of genetically downbred wretches kept in cages like animals and subject to unspeakable atrocities . . ."

Falkenstein paused, as if calming his own outrage. "But why go on?" he said more quietly. "People who will deliberately downbreed half their own species into mindless stud animals will obviously do or say just about anything. If you can bring yourself to do *that*, what's a little lying and subversion?"

He shrugged. "If this proposal passes, the lies they will then spew forth will escalate into purebred lunacy. No doubt we can expect to hear that Institute students have their brains scooped out and replaced with electronic circuitry. That we barbecue children and serve them up for breakfast. That we force initiates to roll in their own ordure, drink human blood, and swear allegiance to the devil. If you vote to subject yourselves to this pathology, we will abide by your decision. We will demonstrate the value of a Pacifican Institute of Transcendental Science to you with deeds, not empty words. And no amount of vicious, unfounded lies will sway us from our dedication to the scientific enlightenment of all humans everywhere. The profession of teacher is the noblest of all, and if vilification by ignorant primitives is the price we must pay to justify our claim to that calling, then so be it!"

The cheering for Falkenstein was much louder and so were the boos and catcalls. Brrrr! Carlotta thought. That was one brilliant, ugly speech, and the response to it was just as powerful both ways and almost as unwholesome. Anger was now the unifying theme in the Parliament chamber—anger evoked by Falkenstein against the Femocrats, and anger evoked by Falkenstein against himself. Black energy seemed to pulse off the visitors' gallery, but she also sensed something else, a potential that might be seized . . ."

She had originally planned to call the vote immediately after Falkenstein finished without any speech from her. But now her instincts told her otherwise, and she found herself glancing into Royce's eyes for some subliminal confirmation. Seated in the first row of Delegate seats, Royce nodded back. Okay, bucko, she thought, here's one for Pacifica!

"Well now, we've just heard our off-world friends call each other faschochauvinists, liars, subversives, and shrill, mindless Machiavellian monsters," she said conversationally, without rising. "I forget who called what which." The ugly mood broke at least for the moment into good-natured laughter.

"But who really cares who called what which?" Carlotta said cavalierly. "They've been shouting the same crap in our ears for a long time now, and here we are, conducting democratic business as usual. Oh, some of us may have gotten caught up in one side or the other, but we're all still *Pacificans,* aren't we? Listen, think, vote, and abide by our democratically arrived-at decisions. That's what electronic democracy is all about, and I don't think I'm bragging unduly when I say that I believe that every Pacifican understands it. . . ."

Carlotta glanced from Falkenstein to Cynda Elizabeth and back to the audience. She shrugged. "But I don't think these people have the faintest idea of what electronic democracy is all about. Both sides are convinced that they are in possession of the absolute truth and that therefore we should tell the other side to shut up before they pollute our impressionable adolescent minds with ideological garbage. The notion that we are undecided as a people on these issues and therefore should allow our time-tested democratic processes a decent interval in which to reach a democratic decision apparently seems terribly naïve to these galactic sophisticates."

Carlotta paused. The chamber was quiet now, but it was not a tense and ugly silence; it seemed to her that it was the receptive quiet of good sense and reason.

"But I wonder who is naïve and who is sophisticated," she said. "Those who seek to choke off continued debate? Or those who listen, evaluate, vote, and abide by democratic decisions democratically arrived at? True believers lusting after converts? Or the people who have done the most to make the Galactic Media Web the arena of free interplanetary discourse it is today? Everyone seems to want to enlighten we poor primitive Pacificans one way or the other. Shall *we* enlighten these poor benighted offworlders and return the favor with a demonstration of the freest democratic system in the human galaxy in action? Shall we force them to participate in Pacifican democracy at work whether they like it or not? *Shall we vote?*"

The applause was the loudest yet; heartfelt yet decorous, bright and cleansing. Soon it became a chanting of "Vote! Vote! Vote!" from the gallery as well as the Delegates. This isn't the voice of a mob, Carlotta thought, this is the voice of a democratic Parliament and a democratic people. This isn't for me, this is for *us*.

Something caught in her throat. Pride and embarrassment mingled behind her burning eyes. This is what it's all about, she thought. This is what makes it all worthwhile.

"Ayes for the resolution, nays against," she said, in a quavering attempt at technocrat neutrality. When the wall screen behind her showed that the resolution had passed 98 to 5, the chamber was filled with loud yet dignified applause, as Delegates and spectators alike cheered their Chairman, their government, and themselves.

We haven't yet forgotten how to be Pacificans, Carlotta thought as her vision blurred with tears. If I'm voted out of office tomorrow and never return, I'll have this moment to remember, and it will have been enough.

11

Roger Falkenstein stood near the helicopter at the edge of the jungle clearing that passed for the Hollywood liner port, cool and relaxed in the murderous heat as the last batch of Institute recruits, sweating profusely and starting nervously at every crash and thump from the surrounding jungle, were loaded aboard. The ambient temperature was up around 120 degrees and the humidity hovered around its usual 100 percent, but the modified inertia-screen that enclosed his body kept his skin at a nice dry 70 degrees. *If forcing us to locate the Institute in this jungle lunatic asylum was really meant as anything more sinister than a joke, it's been a dismal failure,* he thought. *The more hostile the natural environment, the better our technology looks, and the security problem is certainly minimized out here two thousand kilometers from anything,* surrounded by a godzilla-infested rain forest, where the sparse local population were far too obsessed with producing their endless godzilla epics to give much thought to anything more serious.

Falkenstein boarded the helicopter, nodded to the pilot, and the copter lifted clear of the jungle and headed northwest toward the Institute, about twenty kilometers of impenetrable jungle beyond the bizarre town of Hollywood. Almost at once, they were flying above the peculiar sprawling metropolis itself.

From the air, Hollywood seemed to be a huge city, a vast eclectic smorgasbord of every architectural style ever conceived by the mind of man. Here a few square blocks of Arabian Knights palaces, there the recreated skyscrapers of ancient New York. Medieval terrestrial castles and the glass towers of Heldhime. Downtown Gotham and the legendary Tivoli amusement gardens. The Luxor of the Pharaohs and the Rome of Julius Caesar.

In actuality, the few thousand whackers who inhabited the town lived in a cluster of environment domes at the eastern edge, and all else were flimsy half-scale mock-up shells of exotic buildings which existed in order to be periodically smashed to bits by rampaging godzillas for the benefit of the cameras and the delectation of the galactic audience. Indeed, just below, a fifty-meter green horned colossus and an even larger monstrosity with a huge mouth full of gnashing teeth were rolling about the streets of ancient Babylon, locked in mortal combat as hanging gardens and ziggurats crumbled from random kicks. Even inside the helicopter, the titanic bellowings and gruntings were quite harrowing to the Gothamite recruits.

But not to Falkenstein, who had long since developed a casual indifference to the crazed environment of Godzillaland, though his first encounter with this unsettling reality had been something else again.

The shuttle from the *Heisenberg* had landed at the Hollywood liner port with the Institute construction party, and he and Maria had stepped outside into a choking, enervating blast of soggy heat. Immediately before them was a high green wall of trees, vines, and underbrush that gave off an overpowering stench of rank rotting fecundity. Things howled, bellowed, grunted, and crashed in the nearby jungle, sounds of menace almost too horrid to be credible.

"Great suns!" Maria said. "I don't believe it!"

"Lindblad or whoever is responsible for this certainly has a mordant sense of humor," Falkenstein said, wiping sweat out of his eyes with the back of his hand.

Suddenly a terrifying series of monstrous roars and bellows issued from the jungle before them, and a moment later something huge came crashing through the under-

187

growth toward them, erupting into the clearing in a green explosion of vegetation.

The thing was mottled green and brown and it stood forty meters high on tree-trunk legs which ended in huge clawed feet. It stood upright like a man, balanced on a huge tail tipped with three sharp two-meter spikes. The small-eyed head was mostly mouth; when it screamed its outrage at them, thick drool sprayed from triple rows of teeth, and a tornado of unbelievably fetid breath assailed Falkenstein's nostrils even as he and Maria shrank back toward the shuttle.

Then another beast slithered toward them along the path broken through the jungle by the first. This creature was low-slung, shiny green, sinuous as a snake, and the tail-end of its seemingly endless body was nowhere in sight even after thirty meters of the thing became visible. It had huge yellow eyes, a grim-lipped mouth, and a scimitarlike horn growing from where its nose would have been. Black drops of venom dripped from its red forked tongue.

Bellowing, hissing, and screaming, the godzillas advanced into the clearing as the Falkensteins ran for the shuttle. Then all at once both of them abruptly froze still as statues. The low-slung godzilla sank to its belly. The bipedal monstrosity held a forelimb aloft in a grotesque parody of a military salute.

In the sudden silence, Falkenstein was aware of raucous human laughter. He took a careful second look at the immobilized godzillas. A long-haired man, naked save for black shorts, sat on the neck of the low-slung green creature, laughing uproariously. Perched in a saddle strapped to the neck of the saluting biped was a blond woman, also wearing only shorts, and also laughing her damn fool head off.

"Welcome to Godzillaland!" the woman shouted.

"Welcome to Hollywood!"

The two whackers broke up again at their asinine prank, and only now, after the first flash of visceral terror had passed, did Falkenstein notice the small black control consoles at the bases of the godzillas' heads. Of course! he remembered. The del gado boxes. The people here implanted electrodes directly into the brains of these monstrosities. With their control consoles, they could maneuver these great creatures like so many protoplasmic robots.

That was how they made their godzilla epics, directing the monsters by remote control. It had never occured to Falkenstein that anyone would want to use this technique to turn these huge stinking things into *riding steeds,* nor could he have imagined a state of human dementia that would find such a foul joke as had just been inflicted on them *funny*.

But that was five weeks ago, Falkenstein thought as the helicopter passed over the northwest edge of Hollywood, where workers mounted on bipedal godzillas were recreating a simulacrum of classical Athens from the flinders of its most recent epic destruction. Now nothing that the whackers did was capable of surprising him or the Institute staff, and once they had understood that, they had lost their taste for humor at the expense of the Transcendental Scientists. There was now an unstated agreement between the Transcendental Scientists and the whackers to regard each other as different sorts of maniacs and leave it at that. None of the whackers displayed the slightest interest in the Institute. They weren't even interested in the inertia-screens—they professed to enjoy the horrible jungle heat.

More dense jungle passed beneath the helicopter, and then all at once they were over the Institute. A perfect circle three-quarters of a kilometer in diameter had been burned free of jungle by an orbital laser from the *Heisenberg*. A huge silvery disc of a building had been erected in the middle of this cleared zone—the Institute proper, a standard temporary planetary structure identical to the one in the Cords except for scale. When the Pacifican Institute of Transcendental Science became a permanent institution, permanent structures would be built in a Pacifican architectural style at a more suitable location—ideally a small island in the Island Continent a discreet distance from Gotham.

A few small domes and discs surrounded the main building inside the clear zone. The periphery of the zone itself was surrounded by a single strand of cryowire strung on poles. This projected a powerful electrical field which effectively held off the wild godzillas that infested the jungle; not coincidentally, it also prevented anyone from leaving the compound except by air.

And now that the final batch of recruits has arrived, we can seal the place off from outside contact completely for the next five months, Falkenstein thought as the helicopter touched down in front of the main building. A hundred and eighty male Pacificans, fifty staff people, and twenty *Heisenberg* women masquerading as Pacifican students in a closed environment, very much like an experiment inside a sterile test tube, without even general access to net consoles to contaminate the process. A battle every step of the way, Falkenstein thought as he led the Pacificans across the bare earth toward the building, but at last we have it!

The recruitment procedure had presented the final difficulty with the Pacifican authorities, but now, at last, that too was over. Tens of thousands of applications had poured in—a data-processing nightmare—but it had enabled Falkenstein to turn down the Ministry of Science's suggestion that *it* select the student body behind an impenetrable smokescreen of the Pacificans' own democratic rhetoric.

In actuality, the last thing Falkenstein wanted was Pacifican scientists certified by the government. The students finally selected were scientific neophytes with high intelligence, no existing permanent ties to women, a high susceptibility to psychomolding techniques, and records of at least some sympathy for Pacificans for the Institute. A relatively high proportion of them were manos from the Cords, and lower-grade Thule techs were also strongly represented. If some small chance of a security leak yet remained, it had certainly been minimized by the parameters constructed by the Arkmind, and the psychomolding program would reduce even that minimal margin for error to as close to absolute zero as any scientific procedure could approach.

Inside the building, in the large lobby that overlooked the wall of jungle beyond the cryowire barrier, Falkenstein gathered the recruits around him for a brief welcoming speech before turning them over to the waiting staff from psychomolding. The sweat on their faces was rapidly drying in the cool building, and they seemed quite happy to be inside.

"Welcome to the Pacifican Institute of Transcendental Science," Falkenstein said. "My apologies for this unpleasant location, but believe me, that was the choice of your government, not us! However, I do think you'll find the isolation conducive to study, and the local environment

190

an inspirational lesson in how what you will learn can transform the brute uncaring universe into a more suitable matrix built by the mind and hand of man."

Almost as if on cue, two huge godzillas, one bipedal, the other a squat low monstrosity with a great armored head, emerged from the jungle tearing and clawing at each other. They rolled against the invisible electrical barrier, uttered horrendous screams of pain, fear, and outrage, and crashed back into the jungle in panic, their original dispute forgotten.

"So much for the forces of brute nature," Falkenstein said with a thin smile. "And now I'll turn you over to our input personnel, who will show you to your quarters and begin your initiation into that great quest for total human mastery over matter, energy, time and mind which we now all share. Welcome to the Institute, and good luck!"

Ideal, Falkenstein thought as the psychomolding people divided the recruits up into small groups and led them away to begin their processing. *If only I had thought of it, we could've wired up some godzillas of our own and put on a similar show for* all *the entering students!*

Walking down a corridor past classrooms, labs, and tape playback facilities, Maria Falkenstein had a strange sense of split reality. *How like the Institute where she had studied this place was, and yet how different!*

The curriculum was essentially the same—psychesomics, contextual physics, psychohistory, genetic design, time theory, projection, and so forth—but here they were being taught linearly, *not* holistically. Instead of studying the basic areas simultaneously so as to emphasize the basic unity of all knowledge that was the essence of Transcendental Science, the Pacifican students were being taught sequentially, and the sequence was a major element of the total psychomolding process.

First a solid week of nothing but psychesomics, the science of the mind-matter interface. The electronic and chemical matrix of consciousness itself, psychosensory determinism, evolutionary psychesomics, and all the rest. With their sophistication in the media arts, the Pacifican students were soon experiencing a deeper understanding of their own mental processes, helped along by long ses-

191

sions in the Think Tanks and continuous doses of brain-eptifiers to maximize the chemical matrices of their minds.

In this heady state, while the cogency of Transcendental Science was self-evident in their own consciousness-fields, they had a week of nothing but psychohistory poured into their minds. The evolution of human cultural matrices as determined by the sensorium-environment interface. The history of human societies as the evolution of environmentally determined self-sustaining shared consciousness-patterns, leading to tribalism, chauvinism, nationalism, and war. The shattering of these fixed patterns in the twentieth century as the result of an exponentially evolving technological environment, leading to a positive feedback between consciousness and the environment, leading to the expansion of man into space. Leading to neonationalistic planetary cultures and social cancers like Femocracy on the one hand, and Transcendental Science on the other, the next evolutionary step toward total human freedom from environmental determinism, human and physical.

Capped with a ruthless psychohistorical analysis of Pacifican culture itself. Electronic democracy as the result of dispersion and abundance. Female economic power as the consequence of universal distribution of citizens' stock. Male sexual attraction to older, dominant women as compensation for loss of the genetically mandated male supremacy in economic and political spheres. Female desire for sexually dominant buckos as compensation for lack of socially dominant male figures. The vulnerability of female Pacificans to Femocracy as a function of this peculiarly Pacifican sexual balance. On and on, exposing every nook and cranny of their culture to cold scientific logic, while subtle euphoriants were added to the students' brain eptifier formulas.

Only after depth analysts had certified that this psycho-molding process had been successfully completed were the Pacifican students exposed to the areas of Transcendental Science from which advanced technology flowed. And even then, the curriculum was kept mostly theoretical while *more* psychomolding went on.

Maria understood all too well the strategic reasons for this perversion of Transcendental Science. But *perversion* it is, she thought, peering into a classroom as she passed by. The entrance parameters and the lack of female students she could justify to herself on security grounds as the Femocrats continued their campaign against the Institute with the beginnings of a subtle emphasis on female supremacy. Even the heavy psychomolding and manipulations of brain-eptifier formulae might be justified in the name of desperate expediency.

But it seemed to her that this politically motivated sequential teaching of the Transcendental Sciences violated the very essence of Transcendental Science itself, defeated the very purpose for which the *Heisenberg* had come to Pacifica in the first place. For if one word described the world-view of Transcendental Science, that word was *unity*. Matter, energy, time, and mind as states of each other, to be understood in terms of each other, to be studied holistically and simultaneously, so that the consciousness of the Institute graduate truly transcended the compartmentalization of traditional science. That was the essence of Transcendental Science, and that was what was being violated here.

Maria reached a viewing balcony at the periphery of the building. Here Pacifican students sat, singly and in small groups, studying or talking. Outside, the shadowy Godzillaland jungle was ominous and alien under the late afternoon sun. Unseen monstrosities shook the trees with their passage. Now and again a great fanged head or a huge expanse of scaly hide showed itself for a moment. It was an awesome yet repulsive vista—the mindless, savage, uncaring universe incarnate. Yet it was also somehow . . . Pacifica itself in all its fertile untamed promise.

But the Pacifican students for the most part had learned to ignore it. Bright-eyed, loquacious, flush with the adolescent pride of their new knowledge, they sat around discussing their studies with innocent enthusiasm, obsessed with the brave new universe inside these walls, the world outside no more than a holodiorama at the periphery of their consciousness.

What are we creating here? Maria wondered as she walked among all these enthusiastic innocents. A class of people who are no longer quite Pacificans yet not truly Transcendental Scientists. An elite of clever superficial simulacrums of ourselves, alienated from their own planet, yet not quite sharing in the consciousness that binds together the people of the Arkologies.

She had never thought much about the people of the planetbound Institutes, but now, standing among them, it occurred to her that they must be lonely and alienated folk, neither fish nor fowl, their feet planted in the soil of their own peoples whom they dominated as synthetic outsiders, their minds towering into the stars forever just beyond their reach. Do we give as much as we take away? she dared to ask herself.

One Pacifican student stood apart from the others, hands pressed against the transparent wall, staring out at the jungle under the purpling sky. He was short and wiry, with large nervous eyes, and his slight body seemed to vibrate with an unresolved tension that somehow, in this moment, drew Maria to him.

"What do you see out there?" she asked, approaching him.

He shrank into himself. His expression became guarded. "Jungle," he said. "What should I see? Am I missing something?" He was making a great effort to sound neutral, but a bitter tension in his voice could not help but filter through.

"I mean as a Pacifican. What does it mean to you?"

"You want me to explain what it feels like to be a Pacifican?" he said sharply. "But I thought you understood that. You've taught us all about ourselves here." He started nervously, as if suddenly aware that he had let something dangerous slip. It only made Maria empathize with him all the more. Perhaps she wanted to like him. Perhaps she wanted him to like her.

"Only analytically, from the outside," she said. "The essence is yours alone, isn't it?"

"Is it?" he blurted. "Have you left us that much?"

"You know better than I do," Maria said sympathetically. "What do you mean?"

"Look, we're *Pacificans,*" he blurted. "Media psychodynamics may not be psychesomics, but do you think anyone who's had a smattering of it can't recognize subliminal mind-molding, even when it's raised to something quite beyond us, even when we're—" He cut himself short, terrified by his own words. He turned away from her and stared out into the jungle.

"You were saying . . . ?"

"Nothing. I've said far too much already." He turned

194

to look at her, his pleading eyes at war with the belligerent set of his face. "You're going to report this, aren't you?" he said. "It'll be analyzed and evaluated and . . ."

I have to, Maria thought. Somehow this man has escaped full psychomolding undetected. He's a potential security risk, a random, unpredictable factor. Yet she found herself speaking otherwise. "No," she said. "I'm not going to report you. This was just an idle conversation."

"I'm not sure I believe you."

"We're not all . . ." Maria shrugged, her mind unable to form the right word.

But the Pacifican seemed to understand anyway. "I'd like to believe that," he said. "You people really do have something, but . . ."

"But so do you," Maria said.

"Or so we thought," the Pacifican muttered, turning his face once more to the jungle world of fang and claw.

"Pretend we never spoke," Maria said, turning away. A strange sadness came over her, mingled with an ill-defined trepidation, yet also a sense of satisfaction she could not quite define, as if for a fleeting moment the barrier of politics and lies, culture and manipulation, had been transcended. How sad, she thought, that we must both pretend it never happened.

Carlotta Madigan sat in her Parliament office still trying to dig herself out of the mountain of pending business that had accumulated during the time the whole gov had been totally obsessed with the Femocrat–Transcendental Science crisis.

The situation still existed: the Femocrats were flooding the net with anti-Institute propaganda, Transcendental Science was still countering with its own media blitz, Pacificans for the Institute and the Femocratic League of Pacifica were still politically active, male-female relationships were still souring, but the passage of the Madigan Plan had at least taken the immediacy out of the crisis. Now at least there was nothing that the administration had to *do* about it, and she was at last able to find time to deal with the ordinary day-to-day business of her office in some coherent fashion.

And there was plenty that had to be dealt with! The proposal to set up a govcorp to bring down the Gotham-

Cords airfares. A precipitous drop in the wheat market. The whole tangled question of—

"Carlotta! Plug into news channel four—*right now!*" Carlotta swiveled her chair to face the net console. Royce's face had appeared on the comscreen, and he looked *really* agitated.

"Can't it wait?" she said irritably. "I've got a—"

"Plug in now, talk later!" Royce said sharply. "I'll keep this circuit open."

"Shit," Carlotta muttered under her breath as she plugged into the news channel, "this had better be effing *important.*"

On the screen was a nervous wiry man with big feverish eyes, whose face seemed to pulse with an unwholesome tension, speaking in a rapid-fire shrill voice.

". . . and so I managed to stow away on a helicopter taking some Institute staff to the liner port, and from there I caught a liner before they even knew I was missing, I think . . ."

A two-shot, showing Nancy Muldaur, a well-known newshound, interviewing whoever-it-was. "Well, what would have happened if you had just told them you wanted to leave?" she asked.

"I don't know," the nervous man said. "I don't know *how* far they would go . . ."

"Surely they wouldn't have tried to keep you at the Institute against your will? That would be *kidnapping,* wouldn't it?"

Now just a closeup on the man, more angry than frightened now. "Look, I don't think you understand what I've been telling you," he said. "They're *brainwashing* people. They've chosen their students for susceptibility to mind-molding techniques, and that's what they're doing! They don't want the people of Pacifica to know what's going on, and that's putting it very mildly! There are no private net consoles. They've got an electronic barrier around the Institute, supposedly to keep godzillas out, but it also keeps the so-called students *in.* How do *I* know how far they'd really go? You think I wanted to find out the hard way?"

Another two-shot including Nancy Muldaur, looking slightly skeptical while asking her next question. "This . . . ah, so-called brainwashing . . . what *is* it, specifically?"

"It's hard to describe unless you've gone through it.

196

For one thing, all the students are constantly being fed drugs. Brain-eptifiers to enhance the chemical matrix of consciousness, they claim, and it certainly *does* sharpen your mind—but who knows what *else* is in the formula? For another thing, it's what they're teaching and the way they teach it. For the first two weeks they don't teach any real science at all. They fill your head full of theories of consciousness that sync into their own mindset, and then they teach you so-called psychohistory which is pure Transcendental Science propaganda dressed up as scientific objectivity. And during the whole process, you have these sessions every day with so-called tutors who are really brainwashing experts evaluating your reaction. I tell you— I tell the people of Pacifica—that's no *school*, that's a brainwashing academy!"

Shrill and unstable as the Institute "escapee" sounded, what he was saying rang true to Carlotta. It was full of emotional conviction, and she could hardly put such tactics past Falkenstein and his crew. A great hollow bubble built up in her gut. There was only one possible question that might defuse this thing before the Madigan Plan blew up in everyone's face. "Ask him how come it didn't work on *him!*" she muttered at the screen.

Nancy Muldaur, pro that she was, obliged her and asked the question that must have been on the minds of the millions of Pacificans plugged into the interview. "No offense, Mr. Carstairs, but what made *you* so special? If this Institute brainwashing is all you say it is, why didn't it work on you? Why are you alone sitting here and warning us?"

The camera moved in for a closeup on Carstairs. The look of confusion on his face seemed utterly genuine, utterly ingenuous, even appealing in its lack of guile or facileness. "To tell you the truth, I don't really know," he said after a long pause. "I *have* studied some media psychodynamics, and I kept that off my application because I thought that might disqualify me, so maybe I had more insight into the process than the other students. I don't have a degree or anything, I just picked it up from a friend I once lived with, so there's no way they could've found out . . ."

He paused, and when he spoke again, his voice was much calmer. "Also, I was curious about those brain-

197

eptifiers . . . not really suspicious then, just intellectually curious. So as an experiment, I stopped taking them for a few days. My mind seemed to get clearer. Things that they had taught me didn't seem so self-evident any more . . ." He shrugged. "I'm not saying that's the reason," he said appealingly. "Maybe I was just lucky . . ."

"Maybe you're not the only one," Nancy Muldaur said as a closeup of her replaced Carstairs on the screen. Carlotta could see the newshunger in her eyes as she spoke directly to the camera. "This clearly calls for a complete investigation. And you can be sure that if one isn't immediately forthcoming from the government, this news net will—"

"Enough!" Carlotta muttered, unplugging from the news channel. "I get the picture!"

Royce peered at her ruefully from the comscreen. "Well?" he said ironically. *"Important?"*

"Disasters are always important," Carlotta sighed. "And this one puts us right back where we started."

"If we're very, very lucky," Royce said. "The Femocrats are going to go utterly berserk over this, and who knows what Falkenstein's counterblitz is going to be like. I only hope we *do* end up no worse than we started before we got the Madigan Plan through." He grimaced. "But I doubt it. This looks like escalation time."

"We're going to have to close down the Institute right now," Carlotta said. "No government can tolerate *this* kind of shit and still call itself a democracy."

Royce shook his head firmly. "No way," he said. "On the basis of unsubstantiated charges? Before we can gauge the political reaction? Do that, and Pacificans for the Institute will be howling for your blood."

"You think it's not true, Royce?"

He shrugged. "Who knows?" he said. "All I know is that we'd better not take a stand until we know the truth. I mean, this Carstairs character didn't sound like the most stable person on the planet to me . . ."

But he *is* telling the truth, Carlotta thought. I know it in my bones. Nevertheless, Royce's analysis was correct. We're back in the shit again, and once more we have to temporize. But not for much longer. Not for bloody much longer!

198

"What do you suggest, O master of the media?" she asked.

Royce frowned. "Announce that the matter is under investigation. Get the facts. Wait for the full political reaction to develop before saying anything."

"Too weak," Carlotta said. "We've got to make *some* immediate dramatic gesture."

Royce shrugged. "Then announce that I'm going to Godzillaland to investigate the situation personally," he said. "I'll stay around for a few days to handle the media aspect and then fly down and have it out with Falkenstein."

"Leaving me to sit here as the muck hits the exhaust . . ."

Royce forced a wan smile. "At least you won't have godzillas to contend with."

Carlotta sighed and managed a small grin back. "Just a planetful of people bellowing like them," she said.

12

A CLOSE UP OF CARSTAIRS, THE INSTITUTE DEFECTOR, taken from the news channel footage; angry, righteous-looking.

Carstairs: ". . . chosen their students for susceptibility to brainwashing techniques, and that's exactly what they're doing! They don't want the people of Pacifica to know what's going on, and that's putting it very mildly . . . ."

A hard cut to a closeup on Cynda Elizabeth. She is holding a large sheaf of documents and she waves it for emphasis as she speaks.

Cynda Elizabeth: "It certainly *is*, Mr. Carstairs, and there are a few things even *you* don't know either! I have here a list of one hundred and eighty verifiably Pacifican Institute students, and all of them are *male*. Furthermore, we've been able to trace connections between ninety-seven of them and Pacificans for the Institute. And Transcendental Science's faschochauvinist treachery goes even further than *that*. There is the matter of the twenty so-called female Institute students. No record of their prior existence on this planet can be found. Only one conclusion can be drawn—they're not Pacifican sisters at all, but spies off the *Heisenberg* itself!"

A series of panoramic shots of Pacifican women demonstrating and marching—in downtown Gotham, the streets of Valhalla, a town on the bank of the Big Blue, a village in the Island Continent.

Cynda Elizabeth's voiceover: "So what we have in God-zillaland is exactly what I predicted when I opposed passage of the Madigan Plan—a Transcendental Science brainwashing academy with an all-male student body chosen for their faschochauvinist tendencies to begin with, and infiltrated by secret agents from the *Heisenberg*. Overt faschochauvinism, drugs, mind-molding, spies, lies, and duplicity! A total effort to subvert Pacifican society through the creation of a brainwashed male faschochauvinist elite!"

A closeup on Cynda Elizabeth, oozing an I-told-you-so smugness.

Cynda Elizabeth: "If there was ever any doubt in the minds of the sisters of Pacifica that this so-called Institute should be closed immediately, this certainly removes it. The sisters of Pacifica are demonstrating everywhere today, and their demand is simple and clear: close the Institute now, and banish Transcendental Science from this planet forever!"

A panoramic shot of the public entrance to Parliament, thronged with marching people. The camera moves in closer, revealing that they are all women organized into massive, orderly picket-lines. Their placards repeat the same three phrases over and over again: "Femocratic League of Pacifica," "Close the Institute Now!" and "Banish Faschochauvinist Fausts!"

Cynda Elizabeth's voiceover: "The sisters of Pacifica are on the march, and they will not rest until the last faschochauvinist Transcendental Scientist has left this solar system! We call on the government to *close the Institute now!*"

Chanting pickets: "Carlotta Madigan, *close the Institute now! Carlotta Madigan, CLOSE THE INSTITUTE NOW!*"

A closeup of a man's wong and balls. A huge knife wielded by a female hand slashes across the frame and severs them from his body. Cut to a medium shot on a woman looking very much like Cynda Elizabeth as she waves a bloody knife in one hand and the male organs in the other with a demented look of triumph.

Harsh male voiceover: "Don't kid yourselves anymore, buckos, *that's* what it's all about."

Cut to a panoramic shot of a large male crowd filling Seaside Park in downtown Gotham, angry, shouting, and waving placards that read "Pacificans for the Institute," "Fuck Femocracy!" and "Bucko Power!" The camera moves in for a shot on the stage that has been set up on a green hillside in front of the crowd. Behind the stage is a huge screen. On the screen is the previous shot of the Cynda Elizabeth lookalike waving the knife and the gory male organs triumphantly. On the stage is a big angry-looking man wearing a tight black suit with a decidedly neomilitary cut.

Man in black: "Women have always been equal on Pacifica—*more* than equal! They have economic power and political power and the Chairmanship itself—but now that's not enough! Now they want . . . *that!* Our effing *balls* on a silver platter!"

The crowd roars its ugly defiance.

Man in black: "You want to see what they want to turn us into? Have a look at buckohood, Femocrat-style!"

A huge ugly woman leads a man up on stage by a steel chain attached to a collar around his neck. The man wears a short fluffy blue skirt and pink tights. His hair is dyed a hideous pastel pink and set in high-piled ringlets. He minces across the stage to the uneasy laughter of the crowd. The woman yanks him forward by his leash.

Woman: "Tell them how wonderful it is to be a Femocrat breeder, you balless bucko!"

Man in the skirt (in a thin falsetto): "Yes mistress. We *boys* all *love* being Femocrat breeders. Our mistresses take good care of us and give us pretty dresses to wear and we don't have to worry about *anything*, we don't even have to *think*. All we have to do is kiss their boots, and we *love* licking our mistresses' boots clean . . ."

He falls to his knees and begins slobbering over the booted feet of the woman holding the leash. After a few moments of this, she kicks him across the stage, where he lies in a heap, whimpering. The crowd boos, hisses, and curses. There is very little laughter.

Man in black: "Do we want to lick our women's boots?"

Crowd roar: "NO!"

Man in black: "Do we want an Institute?"

Crowd roar: "YES!"

Man in black: "Are we going to take any more shit from the Femocrats and their fellow travelers?"

Crowd roar: "NO!"

Man in black: "Are we going to kick their fucking asses off our planet?"

Crowd roar: "YES!"

Man in black: "And are we going to take a good hard look at how this planet's being run? We've given our women political and economic power, and what are they giving us? A kick in the balls! Who are the natural leaders and rulers of Pacifica?"

Crowd roar: "WE ARE!"

Man in black: "And what do we want?"

Crowd roar: "BUCKO POWER!"

Man in black: "And what are we going to take?"

Crowd roar: "BUCKO POWER! BUCKO POWER!"

Man in black: "Say it again! Say it loud enough to be heard in Parliament, all over this city, all over this planet!"

The camera pulls back for a panoramic shot of the crowd, chanting, waving placards, stamping its feet in thunderous unison.

"BUCKO POWER! BUCKO POWER! BUCKO POWER! BUCKO POWER!"

As Eric turned the sailboat around and headed back toward the lights of Gotham, a sadness overcame Cynda Elizabeth, tinged with something utterly alien that she could not begin to fathom.

It wasn't just that their getting it off had been so cold and perfunctory this time, nor, she thought, was it entirely the dreadful images that had filled her mind as his body slammed hers to the cockpit deck, as his piercer plunged in and out of her like some weapon of vengeance —crowds of Pacifican breeders chanting "BUCKO POWER! BUCKO POWER!" to the rhythm of his piercer in her flower, as if every man on the planet were watching him pierce her to a sadistic cadence of encouragement.

Nor, indeed, was it entirely the utter conviction that Eric, too, had the same images in his head, that he had felt his body moving to a planetary chant of "BUCKO POWER!"

No, she thought, the horrible fact is that some sick

part of me *enjoyed* the fantasy. There was something about this whole Bucko Power thing that both raised a bubble of nausea in her gut and sent unwholesome shivers up her spine, and the dichotomy terrified her and filled her with an unfocused self-loathing.

"Eric?"

He turned to face her, his expression cold and distant.

"What were you thinking about when we were getting it off?"

He frowned and looked away over the dark waters. "You don't want to know . . ."

"But I think I *do* know . . ."

He looked at her again, his mouth twisted into a sneer. "Oh, really?" he said sardonically.

"Bucko Power . . ." Cynda Elizabeth blurted.

He raised his eyebrows. "I can imagine what *you* think of bucko power . . ."

"Can you?" Cynda said ingenuously. "Then maybe you'd like to tell me, because I'm feeling very confused."

"What is this?" Eric snapped. "Are you finally trying to trap me into an ideological argument so you can push your Femocrat jellybelly oil down my throat? I thought we agreed—"

"But do you really believe in this . . . this . . ."

"Faschochauvinist crap?" Eric said angrily. "Do you believe in *your* faschochauvinist crap?"

I'm not so sure anymore, Cynda wanted to say. "That's different," she said lamely instead. "Women aren't out in the streets yelling for flower power . . ."

"Oh aren't they?" Eric said. "Then suppose *you* tell *me* the difference between Bucko Power and Femocracy?"

"Why . . . why . . . they're as different as any two things can be!"

Eric sighed. He stared out at the approaching lights of the city, mirrored now in the shimmering water. He spoke more softly.

"Look, Cynda, Earth had a long history of male domination—okay, I admit it—so Femocracy was the natural outcome of women grabbing for power after a lousy war on a planet where they had none. But here women have always had things their own way and men have fooled themselves into believing they were equals because their wongs made them kings of the bedroom. So on Earth, it took a terrible war to get women to seize power from men who had fucked things up, and here it took you effing Femocrats to wake up the men of this planet by making our women flex their political muscles to keep us down where we've always been. I'm a man, so I've got a self-interest in Bucko Power. You're a woman, so you've got a self-interest in turning buckos into effing breeders. Power against power, the rest is just jellybelly oil."

"The law of the jungle . . ." Cynda muttered. "Evolutionary warfare between the sexes that goes on forever?"

Eric grinned at her cruelly. "Not forever," he said. "Like the Transcendental Scientists say, there are intrinsic differences between the sexes. We're bigger and stronger. We ruled for millions of years—even you Femocrats talk about the male will to power, don't you? If we weren't the natural leaders, would we have been on top for most of human history? When it's power against power, biology determines the winner, and we both know who that will be, don't we?"

Cynda shivered as if an unseen wind had blown in off the sea. "You really believe that?" she said. "You really believe in . . . in . . . in male *supremacy?*"

"Don't you?" Eric said slyly. "Here you are, the leader of the effing Femocrat mission, getting it off with me, even with all that Femocrat garbage pounded into your head. Why? Because every woman wants a *real man* on top of her—deep down, in her body, in her effing *genes*, no matter what kind of jellybelly oil her head is filled with. Look at the way we're built, Cynda: men big and strong, women small and weak. My wong, built to thrust inside your body, and you built to take it. Doesn't your own body tell you all you really need to know about Bucko Power?"

"But . . . but that's just *sex*, Eric," Cynda said uncertainly.

Eric snorted. He looked out at the city again, the buildings, islands, and bridges now clearly outlined by their own lights. "Yeah, that's what we used to think on Pacifica," he said. "Democracy. Equality. All that highsounding crap. Until *you* came along and convinced our women that we're faschochauvinist beasts who have to be controlled for our own good. Well, if we have to be either *breeders* or faschochauvinists, there's no real choice, is there? Now that we've got the name, we have to play the game—to win."

He looked her full in the face. He smiled. "You know," he said, "it's almost as if Bucko Power is what our women really wanted all along, deep down. I mean, they've sure gone out of their way to provoke it, haven't they? Haven't *you?*"

Cynda shuddered as Eric steered the boat toward its quiet secluded mooring. She found that she had no easy answers anymore, that her compulsion to talk had been replaced by a welcoming of the dark quiet of the night. Could he be right? she wondered. Could there be atavistic genes in *women* as well as men? Could millions of years of male faschochauvinism, of macho domination, have been the result not merely of a male genetic predisposition to power, violence, and dominion, but of a genetic flaw in the human species as a whole? A *female* genetic predisposition to *reinforce* macho faschochauvinism against the best interests of Sisterhood and the race as a whole? Biological coding in both men and women that synced together to form a racial tendency toward . . . *Bucko Power?*

How could you explain why it took millions of years for Sisterhood to finally arise without it?

Eric tied the boat up at the dock and automatically helped her ashore. Cynda took his hand just as automatically—now, however, very much aware of the unconscious mechanical response. *Can it be true?* Is what we have to fight this strong and deep in all of us? *In sisters, too?*

"Shall we meet again, Eric?" she asked. "Or can there be nothing but war between us now?"

He kissed her on the lips with ironic tenderness. "Why not let the game go on a little longer?" he said. He laughed harshly. "And may the best man win."

Skimming low over the endless green jungle, then skirting around the southern periphery of Hollywood to avoid a massive twelve-godzilla fight scene being shot in a mock-up of ancient Venice—lumbering monsters smashing bridges, swamping elegant gondolas, crunching the Doge's palace—Royce Lindblad brought the *Davy Jones* down in the midst of the cluster of environment domes at the edge of town where the whackers actually lived.

Sweating profusely in the skin-rotting wet heat, he made his way down the bare earthen main street as quickly as possible, past rows of electronically immobilized godzillas standing like hideous statues of themselves, to the air-cooled sanctuary of Hollywood Central.

Here, under the largest dome in Hollywood, were the editing rooms and interior soundstages, the technical facilities and the producers' offices, an untidy jumble of makeshift huts, warehouses, and bungalows in a constant state of flux like the fungoid growths under the green canopy of the Godzillaland jungle.

Lauren Bates, longtime number-one producer of godzilla epics and unofficial Mayor of Hollywood, met him just inside the main gate, surrounded by a gaggle of whackers, male and female, wearing only the ubiquitous Godzillaland shorts. Lauren, with his thinning gray hair and incipient paunch, was getting a little long in the tooth for this costume, Royce thought, as Bates gave him the glad hand and ushered him through the crowd of whackers to the privacy and relative sanity of his own bungalow.

Still the same lunatic asylum, Royce thought as he sat down gingerly in a chair made from the foot of some monstrosity too gigantic to even contemplate. No sign at all of Institute influence here, or for that matter of the political storm that was raging over the rest of the planet. Godzillaland, as always, seemed a world unto itself. But still, it paid to check with Lauren before descending upon Falkenstein—Bates always knew the smallest detail of everything that went on here.

Bates's office was furnished with standard desks, chairs, and loungers, but also with barbaric items made of bits and pieces of the local godzillas. Hideous still-shots from a hundred godzilla epics papered the walls, and piles of scripts and shooting schedules were everywhere. Bates himself paced restlessly as he talked, fingering scripts, clipboards, bits and pieces of bric-a-brac and clutter.

"Now, I know you're here about this Institute flarf, Royce," he said. "The net is full of that slok, but I've got something of far greater cosmic impact to talk to you about. As a matter of fact, those Institute jockos were the source of my inspiration. *Godzillas in Space!*

Think of it, Royce! We build a half-scale mock-up of the
Heisenberg in orbit and eight—no, make it an even
dozen—of the biggest godzillas we have *utterly demolish*
it, while gonzos in Transcendental Science suits are power-
less to stop them with all their superweapons! Totally the
ultimate! And maybe with this one, we even pick up the
Femocrat market—"

"Lauren, for—"

"I know, I know," Bates said, holding up his hand.
"Cheap it won't be, what with the boosting costs. But
godzillas in *zero-gee*, Royce! I *guarantee* it'll earn out, my
word—"

"Lauren, I didn't come here to discuss Ministry sub-
sidies!" Royce snapped. "Don't you have any ideas of
what's happening outside this bonker bin? Don't you
realize there's a political crisis going on?"

"You mean that Pink and Blue War slok?" Lauren
said. "The rest of the planet is foaming at the mouth over
the most boring jellybelly oil imaginable, and they call
us whackers? We *make* godzilla epics, we don't *star* in
them. We *control* godzillas, we don't act like them. But of
course everyone knows *we're* crazy."

"You have a point," Royce admitted sourly. "You mean
none of it has affected the people here, even with the
Institute right next door?"

Bates shrugged. "We leave them alone, and they leave us
alone," he said. "Oh, a few of their staff people drift in
once in a while to watch the shooting, but if they start
whonking at us, they suddenly find themselves conversing
with a sixty-meter godzilla doing a tapdance. We've got
those gonzos conditioned to keep their yawps shut around
here. Live and let live, bucko!"

"And the Pacifican students? What do they seem like?"

"Zilcho, jocko!" Bates said. "Never seen a one. All
studious, hard-working lads, I guess. Either that, or the
Transcendental gonzos have them all wired for control
like godzillas. Hmmm . . . bet the Femocrats never thought
of *that* one . . ."

Despite himself, Royce smiled. Somehow, under the
present circumstances, the very up-front weirdness of this
place was a fresh breath of sanity. The whackers might
be crazy in their own way, obsessive even, but they didn't
take any of it *seriously*, not the way the rest of the planet

was becoming humorlessly and pathologically obsessed. A pity there aren't enough of them to form a real political base, he thought.

"Well, I guess I'd better go check out the Institute and get it over with," Royce said, rising.

"Yeah, sure, but what about *Godzillas in Space?* I tell you, the export market will—"

"Too expensive, Lauren, you're out of your mind," Royce said genially. He grinned. "Tell you what, though, if I don't like what I see up at the Institute, I'll give you the place to play with. Take *twenty* effing godzillas and *really* demolish it. I'm not sure about the export market, but I have a feeling it'd be a big hit on Pacifica."

"No, no," Bates said excitedly, "the Femocrat planets will eat it up, we can crack the market at last! Flasho, Royce! *Revenge of the Godzillas,* we can call it." He peered at Royce owlishly. "Are you serious?" he asked. "Should I put a writer on it?"

Nervously, somberly, Roger Falkenstein found himself trailing Lindblad around the Institute like a junior officer tagging along behind some auditor from the Council. He had known from the net announcements that this was going to happen, but he had not known when, and Lindblad had simply dropped in from nowhere, announced in no uncertain terms that he was going to inspect the place starting now, and that even the slightest hint of noncooperation would be taken as proof of the Femocrat charges.

Lindblad stuck his nose in everywhere and asked questions that seemed both sharply pointed and crafted to establish an almost paramilitary authority. In the records office, he had compared the student rosters to some documents he had brought which might have been the list the Femocrats had had. In the pharmacy, he demanded an explanation of the brain-eptifiers and their effects on human consciousness. When Blatski responded with a technical explanation obviously far over Lindblad's head, he had peremptorily ordered a complete report sent to the Ministry of Science within ten hours.

Lindblad sat in on classes in psychesomics and psychohistory without venturing a word in response. He cornered random students and asked them disconnected cryptic questions. Who is your Delegate? What's your love-life been like? What are your favorite entertainment programs? Why did you apply for admission?

Clearly this is no political cosmetic job, Falkenstein thought as he followed Lindblad into one of the viewing balconies. He's really serious about this, he's really sharp, and if he finds out the real truth, we're in deep trouble. Although Lindblad had never gone quite so far as to support the Institute, he had more or less openly opposed those who sought to impede its operation, including, perhaps, Carlotta Madigan herself. Moreover, he does seem to have a basic sympathy with our ultimate goals, and I do believe he wants to be with us in spirit. An overtly negative report from Lindblad would be a political disaster.

Now Lindblad was approaching Anne Marshak, a psychomolder from the *Heisenberg* masquerading as one of the female students. Falkenstein's stomach sank. If she doesn't convince him that she's a Pacifican . . .

"Hello, I'm—"

"I know, you're Royce Lindblad, and you're inspecting the Institute," Anne said ingenuously. "How can I help you?"

"Just a few simple questions," Lindblad said. "What's your name and where are you from?"

"Anne Marshak, from Salo. That's an island about sixty kilometers from—"

"Know the area very well," Lindblad said brusquely. "Used to sail there to watch the marinerdyles breed. Dozens of them at a time rising to the surface and battering each other with their sails. You can hear them going at it clear across the lagoon. You ever sail out and watch them getting it off?"

Anne managed a slight blush. "Well . . ."

"Oh, come on, everyone on Salo does it . . ."

"Well, once or twice when I was still a teenager . . ." Anne admitted with an engaging show of shyness.

"That's all," Lindblad snapped.

"That's all?" she said.

Lindblad shot a sidelong glance at Falkenstein. "That's quite enough," he said.

Without knowing how or why, Falkenstein was convinced that some disaster had just occurred. Something had to be done to counteract whatever mistakes had been made, and it had to be done *now*. I've got to assume the worst, Falkenstein decided. I can't afford to underestimate his intelligence. I've got to win him over now *despite* what he apparently knows. I've got to finally convince him that what Transcendental Science has to offer completely transcends the limited imperatives of local politics.

"As long as you're here, Royce, perhaps you'd like to see some of our really advanced work," Falkenstein said. "Once you've completed your own evaluation, of course."

Lindblad looked him squarely in the eyes. "Sure, Roger," he said. "Why not? My evaluation is now completed. You might as well do your damndest. You're going to have to, after what I've seen today."

Falkenstein blanched. "Don't draw any hasty conclusions on incomplete data," he said.

"Wouldn't dream of it," Lindblad said, continuing to stare at him with an unwavering gaze. "You'll take me on your grand tour, and then we'll have dinner, and once we've digested everything, we'll talk deal." Lindblad grinned ironically and bowed from the waist with a beckoning flourish of his arm. "Lead on, Potemkin," he said.

Royce Lindblad took a final sip of wine, leaned back in his chair, steepled his hands in front of his face, and peered over them across the table at Roger Falkenstein. A sense of power flowed through him, both Falkenstein's and his own.

I could close this place down instantly, he thought, and Falkenstein knows it, though maybe not how or why. Lauren Bates, the utter lack of net consoles, and the electronic perimeter fence verified that the students were cut off from the outside world as a matter of policy. The classes had been, more or less as Carstairs had described, and the Ministry of Science would soon tell the full tale on the brain-eptifiers. The male students seemed like definite Bucko Power types, and a thorough checkout through the parliamentary computer would probably prove it.

But the so-called female student from Salo had been the clincher. Anyone from anywhere near Salo knew that there was no marinerdyle breeding ground there, and every Islander knew that marinerdyles bred under water, not on the surface. Therefore "Anne Marshak" was a ringer from the *Heisenberg,* and so, no doubt, were all the other "female students," and that would be pretty easy to prove, too.

But the legalistic strength of the case is almost beside the point, Royce thought. If I support Carstairs's charges, the Institute is finished, because it will be tried not in a court of law, but politically before Parliament. I've got the power of life or death over the Institute now, and Falkenstein knows it.

The little VIP tour that Falkenstein had favored him with had been an obvious acknowledgment of that power, an attempt to balance out the new equation by revealing more of the science behind the technology and the further technology that such knowledge implied.

The inertia-screen wasn't just portable airconditioning; it was based on the total mass-energy isolation of a closed system, which implied gravity control, inertialess propulsion, and who knew what else. In its obvious form, the "matter transformer" was a mere parlor-trick, but what possibilities it opened up in areas as diverse as dirt-cheap instantaneous construction and tachyon transmission! Even "psychesomics," perverted here into a sophisticated form of brainwashing, implied the total conscious control of the parameters of human consciousness itself, the ability of the mind to lift itself by its own mental bootstraps. And the "genetic design" they used as a catchword phrase was based on the ability to synthesize DNA molecules perfectly to order, to custom-tailor existing organisms, or create new life itself off chemicals on the lab shelf—let alone the apparently very real prospect of physical immortality!

For the first time, Royce felt he understood what Transcendental *Science* implied, as opposed to mere advanced technology. They had opened up so many arcane areas that even *they* might take centuries to fully exploit what they already knew. And knowledge increased exponentially—the more you had, the easier it was to get more.

If Falkenstein had sought to impress him with the utter insanity of Pacifica's turning its back on all this, he had succeeded admirably. To isolate ourselves from Transcendental Science would be to turn ourselves into a planet of backward primitives within a generation, Royce thought.

A historical park in which a frozen moment of the past was preserved, quaint and intact forever, for the delectation of tourists from the ongoing *real* human civilization. And that's the source of *your* power, Roger, he thought.

"All right," Lindblad said finally, "let's talk about reality."

Falkenstein cocked an innocently inquisitive eyebrow at him. His wife Maria, who had said almost nothing during the generally silent meal, frowned and began to rise as if to leave.

"Why don't you stay, Mrs. Falkenstein?" Royce said. "Secrecy and jellybelly oil time is finished, and you might as well hear this."

"I'm not sure I *want* to hear it," Maria Falkenstein said, looking at her husband.

"At least it might help refute the charge of a male faschochauvinist cabal deciding the fate of the Institute and Pacifica," Royce said half-seriously. Because we are going to deal here, and I think we both know it.

"Do stay, Maria," Falkenstein said, the mock innocence gone now, his eyes hard and observing. "Your council may prove useful."

Maria Falkenstein sank back into her chair. Outside the window of the Falkensteins' private dining room, the Institute seemed to float in the darkness; a silvery disc, self-contained and isolated from the jungle backdrop like a spaceship under the starry skies. The image seemed to neatly sum up the situation—a self-contained alien presence orbiting the planet silently, pregnant with both promise and menace.

"Charges have been made," Royce said, "and now we both know that they're true."

Falkenstein inhaled deeply. Maria's face was cold and unreadable. "You mean the Carstairs charges?" Falkenstein said. He smiled thinly. "Aren't they self-invalidating? Obviously, *he* wasn't chosen for loyalty to the Bucko Power movement, and he could hardly serve as an example of our successful brainwashing!"

Maria Falkenstein frowned, as if in disgust. Could it be that even *she* is sick of this crap? Royce wondered. "Forget it, Roger," he said. "I've verified that your so-called female students are plants from the *Heisenberg*. I've observed your teaching procedure, and I'm a media pro, remember? I've gotten a feel for the political bent of your real students. Tomorrow I'll have a report from the Ministry of Science on the drugs you've been feeding them. Do you *really* want to wait for definitive proof in the form of a Ministry of Justice indictment? The game's up, Roger; I'm on to you."

Falkenstein exhaled. "You're mistaken, Royce," he said calmly. "Like the Femocrats, like poor Carstairs himself, you've misinterpreted some isolated data into—"

"Enough, Roger!" Maria Falkenstein suddenly snapped. "Can't you see that you're just insulting the man's intelligence? No one is fooling anyone any more!"

Falkenstein goggled at his wife in shocked bewilderment. Well, well, well! Royce thought. Finally a crack in *their* façade! "Listen to the lady," he said. "You've got nothing to gain by trying to lie to me further."

Falkenstein sat there, stunned. For the first time, Royce saw the man out of control of a situation; confused, ambivalent, uncertain. Human.

"Oh, good lord, Roger, enough of this!" Maria Falkenstein said. "If you're not willing to admit the truth, *I* am. It's all true, there are no female students, the—"

"Maria!" Falkenstein yelled, his face flushing with anger, outrage, and something very much like bucko indignation.

Maria Falkenstein seemed to retreat into a cool shell in the face of her husband's anger. "Think what you like, Roger," she said calmly. "It's been said, the moment is past, and the situation is altered. You said my counsel might prove useful, and I believe it just has. But you're still Managing Director of the *Heisenberg*, you can order me to leave . . ."

Royce watched Falkenstein fighting to calm himself, torn by conflicting emotions. Maria Falkenstein had given him a tactical victory, injected the necessary reality into the dialog, and he was grateful for her good sense. Yet there was also something quite unseemly in her open defiance of her husband in the face of an adversary. It made Royce sympathize with Falkenstein, it made him admire the man as he reached for self-control, calmed himself, and found it.

"Very well," Falkenstein said coldly. "As Maria has said, the moment is past, and the situation is altered. But

I ask you to consider *why* we've done what we've done, Royce."

"All right, Roger—why?"

"You've seen the potential power—"

"I know, I know," Royce interrupted. "You can't afford to risk having your knowledge diffused to the Femocrats. Spare me the repetition. I agree."

Falkenstein looked at him peculiarly. "If you agree, then why do you object to—"

"Because *we're* not the effing Femocrats!" Royce snapped. "You've been using the damn Femocrats to justify every lousy thing you've done on this planet. You're fighting them so hard that you've become exactly what they've always claimed you were in the process. Well, that's *your* business. When you start treating *Pacificans* like enemies, it becomes *mine*."

"We're not your enemies, Royce."

"Maybe not," Royce conceded. "Maybe you've just become so paranoid that you've forgotten how to act any other way. But you and the Femocrats have inflicted your paranoias on *my* planet, and it's got to stop. And I tell you right now, the way you're running this Institute is not acceptable to me."

"You have specific objections, Royce?"

"Yeah, I have specific objections. First of all, you've politically screened your student body, and that's tantamount to interference in internal Pacifican affairs, and *that's* illegal. Second, you've outright *lied* about the female students, and that comes close to violating the news access laws. Third, the way you're mind-molding the students comes close to being an act of war. Fourth, what you've done has precipitated the present crisis which jeopardizes the Madigan Plan, makes Carlotta and me look like idiots, and imperils your own position. And *that's* just plain stupid, Roger."

Royce paused, waiting for some reaction, realizing now just where this was going to go. *I've got to control the student body,* he thought, *or at least get some Pacifican scientists into this place. We've got to have people in here who are Pacificans first and Transcendental Scientists second. That's the nonnegotiable bottom line.*

Roger Falkenstein studied him silently, and it was Maria Falkenstein who finally spoke. "He's right, Roger. We've made a political mess of things. We've grossly under-estimated the political sophistication of these people, and now we're paying for it."

"What do you suggest, Maria?" Falkenstein said icily.

"I don't know," she said. "But I think Mr. Lindblad is ready to make some suggestions of his own, and I think we should weigh them very carefully."

"Very well," Falkenstein said harshly, making an obvious effort to choke back his anger. "You're doing the talking now, Royce . . ."

"First of all, if I don't leave here with an agreement that satisfies me, I'll report the facts as I see them now," Royce said. "I'll publicly call for the closing of the In-stitute myself, and I'll use the Ministry of Media to make damn sure it gets through Parliament. Do you doubt that I can do that?"

"I don't doubt that you *could*, but I'm not so sure you *would*," Falkenstein said. "I think you realize that the importance of the Transcendental Sciences to your planet transcends transitory political considerations. I think you may be bluffing."

"If you really believe that, your so-called science of psychohistory is just so much jellybelly oil because you just don't understand Pacifica," Royce said. "You're so effing caught up in your own self-importance that you don't see that Pacifican electronic democracy is as important an advance in the art of politics as any advance you've made in science. Maybe you can't see that because *politically* you haven't evolved to *our* level. Any scientific discovery can be made again. But what we've built here is unique and complex and fragile, and if we let you destroy it, it could be gone forever. And believe me, Roger, nothing you have to offer is worth *that*."

"And if I say that we'll leave here unless the Institute is allowed to continue on our chosen basis?"

Royce grinned crookedly. "And leave the Femocrats to work their will uncontested on the media hub of the human galaxy? *Now* who's bluffing, Roger?"

Falkenstein managed to laugh, which sent a flash of admiration for the man through Royce. "Very well," he said. "Let's talk terms."

This is it, Royce thought. I've got to play this just right, not too much, and not too little. "The present student body must be dismissed and replaced by a new one chosen by the Ministry of Science," he said.

"Out of the question!" Falkenstein snapped. "You expect me to give you total control over admissions?"

"Okay, there's room for compromise," Royce said. "The Ministry will give you a list of approved applicants by number, not name; you can screen them however you like and reject anyone you find unsuitable. But since you won't know their names, you won't be able to apply any political parameters."

Falkenstein stroked his chin reflectively. "We might be able to live with that," he said.

"It's to your advantage. Taking admission out of your hands will defuse most of the charges against you and make it one hell of a lot easier for me to preserve the Madigan Plan."

"Very well," Falkenstein said. "Conditionally accepted."

"Secondly, you may only give the students such brain-eptifiers as pass Ministry of Science approval."

"No problem," Falkenstein said. "Despite the paranoid propaganda, those drugs really *do* do nothing but improve brain function, and if your scientists are at all competent, they'll find that out."

"Third, all students are to have free access to net consoles. That's their constitutional right, and totally non-negotiable."

"Very well."

"Finally," Royce said, "I don't like the way you're teaching things here. Seems to me you're establishing a mind-set before you get down to teaching anything concrete, and that does come perilously close to brainwashing . . ."

"No!" Falkenstein said sharply. "That goes too far! You will not be permitted to dictate our methodology. We will not consider putting dangerous knowledge in the hands of people who have not been properly prepared to handle it. You know the reasons. We have to have *some* semblance of security, and you're leaving us little else."

Royce pondered that for a moment. Carstairs had resisted mind-molding simply because he happened to have some training in media psychodynamics. Surely a crash-course in the same should do the same thing for the psychically stable, politically neutral Pacifican scientists screened by the Ministry of Science. And it really didn't matter if *some* of them were affected. We're so close to an agreement . . . we've got to take this one small risk.

"Okay," he said, "I'd concede that point for the sake of an agreement. Do we have a deal now, Roger?"

Falkenstein got up and began pacing in small circles. "Perhaps," he said. "*If* you agree to two conditions of mine . . ."

"I'm listening."

Falkenstein stopped pacing, put his hands on the table, leaned forward, and stared at Royce. "We *must* have some assurance that nothing we teach the Pacifican students will be passed along to the Femocrats," he said. "As I understand your laws, there's nothing to prevent any Pacifican Institute graduate from selling information to them."

"I can handle that," Royce said. "As Minister of Media, I act as agent for all Web transactions, and I can construe the Femocrat mission on the planet as an extraplanetary customer. As we both know, the Femocrats have zilch in the way of galactic credits. I will guarantee that no cut-rate technology sales to the Femocrats or anyone else will be approved. You have my word on it."

Falkenstein sank back into his chair. "Is that the official word of the Pacifican government?" he asked.

"It's the word of honor of Royce Lindblad, Minister of Media of Pacifica," Royce said stiffly. "That will have to do."

Falkenstein pondered a moment. He sighed. "Very well, then," he said quietly, "we have an agreement. But just one more thing . . ." He paused. He glanced at his wife, who had been listening to all this with a face of stone. He looked back at Royce. "No female students," he said. "That must stand. We can't risk that."

Maria Falkenstein blanched. She seemed to be about to say something, but her husband caught her short with a cold withering stare.

This is sure going to make it harder to sell the total package, and Carlotta is not going to like it, Royce thought. But he couldn't honestly say that he didn't understand Falkenstein's position. The thought of such advanced technology in the hands of the Femocrats made his stomach quiver, and with what was going on, he couldn't honestly say that any woman on the planet could be totally reliable politically. That thought itself deeply disturbed him, but there it was, and he couldn't deny it.

"I don't like it, Roger, and it's going to make things a lot harder for me politically," he said. "But I suppose I have to accept it, don't I?"

Falkenstein sighed. His face, his whole body, seemed to melt into relaxation. "Then we have an agreement," he said. He filled the three empty wineglasses on the table and held his own aloft ceremoniously. "Shall we drink to it?"

Royce picked up his own glass. He leaned back in his chair. I've done it! he thought. I've won. I've sailed us into safe harbor. He clinked glasses with Falkenstein. "To better days!" he said.

"If you *gentlemen* will excuse me . . ." Maria Falkenstein said acidly. She shot a vicious glance at her husband and stalked out of the dining room.

Seething with rage and ill-understood confusion, Maria Falkenstein paced the narrow confines of their bedroom as Roger entered, his face contorted with anger, and slammed the door shut behind him.

"That was an amazing performance you put on in there," he snapped. "What's gotten into you?"

"You *asked* me to stay!" Maria shot back belligerently.

"To lend your support, not to interfere in my negotiations with Lindblad!"

"You asked for my counsel and you got it! You also got an agreement, now didn't you, Roger? Despite my stupid female interference, perhaps even because of it. If I hadn't spoken up when I did, you might *still* be trying to treat him like some naïve primitive when all the while he was smarter than you were."

"*What?*" Roger shouted. He sat down on the edge of the bed and gaped up at her. "I don't believe I'm hearing this!"

Neither do I! Maria thought in numb amazement. I've never spoken to you like this before, I've never even *thought* of doing it. Somehow that thought by itself tapped some inner core of anger that gave her the courage to go on.

"While you've been interfering in the local culture, *I've* had plenty of time on my hands to take a good look at what we're meddling with," she said. "Lindblad is no fool and these Pacificans are by no means intellectual inferiors. They may be far behind us in science and technology; but how far behind them are *we* when it comes to political sophistication, to constructing a society that works for *everyone*, to justice, to simply living together as human beings?"

"This is preposterous!" Roger said. "What's wrong with *our* society? What's wrong with the way *we* live together as human beings? Great suns, Maria, have *you* become infected by the Femocrat pathology?"

Maria sank down into a chair near the door, as far away from Roger as possible. No, she thought, if I've become infected with anything, it's *Pacifica*. The way men and women treated each other on this planet before we interfered. The way their political system continues to function even under this terrible stress. Their willingness to accept negative pragmatic consequences to stay true to this concept of constitutionality, this esthetic of justice. Their ability to compromise. We have so little of that, whatever it is. So little that we can't even quite conceive of what it is we're lacking. So little that you don't even feel the loss, Roger.

"Femocracy?" she said. "No, when it comes down to what the Pacificans have, they're at least as pathetic as we are."

"Pathetic? We're *pathetic*? What are you talking about?"

"Nothing you would understand, Roger," Maria said. "I can't say I really understand it myself. I only know that these are a noble people, nobler than we are in ways I've not yet been able to fully understand." She laughed bitterly. "Instead of inflicting our Institute on them, perhaps we should petition them for teachers. Though I'm not at all sure that what they know can really be taught."

Roger stared at her in bewilderment. Suddenly he seemed so distant, so brittle, so . . . so diminished in her eyes. One of us has become a stranger, Roger, she thought. And I think it's me.

Roger shook his head, got up, and turned down the bedclothes. "I've had about enough of this," he said. "Let's go to bed. Perhaps you'll be more rational in the morning."

Maria stood up. She looked across the room at him. Her eyes burned——whether from sadness or anger or sense of loss, she couldn't say. Her mind was a roaring vortex of confusion. She felt a rage pulsing up hot and red from her unexamined core, and a strange wistful tenderness equally beyond her previous experience. All that was clear was her immediate need to be alone.

"I think I'd better sleep in the living room tonight, Roger," she said.

Roger looked at her in numb amazement. "My wife!" he snapped. "An Institute graduate! Raving at me with female emotionalism! Look at you, Maria, you're acting like some primitive irrational planetbound Pacifican!"

"What's wrong with that?" Maria shouted. "What in hell is wrong with that?" She ran from the bedroom, slamming the door behind her.

❦

13

THE SKY WAS A CLOUDLESS BLUE OVER LORIEN LAGOON, the sea was tranquil as glass, Rugo was down on the beach communing with a flock of wild bumblers, and Royce beamed at Carlotta Madigan as they sat together on the veranda as if he had just won a sailboat race. Everything was the very picture of natural ease and domestic bliss.

And Royce, her bucko, her closest political ally, her alter ego, had just told her that he had unilaterally made a deal with Roger Falkenstein behind her back, had sold her out to Transcendental Science.

How am I supposed to react? Carlotta wondered. Am I supposed to rant and rave and tear my hair? Cry? Royce was no help; he just sat there grinning as if he expected a pat on the head and a hearty "Well done, bucko!"

"I must admit I don't quite know what to say, Royce," she finally answered. "Up yours? Drop dead? Et tu, Brute?"

"You're pissed off?" Royce asked with infuriating innocence.

Carlotta looked down at Rugo, waddling along the beach with his fellow bumblers. "Did you hear that, Rugo?" she shouted. "The man asked me if I'm pissed off!" She looked back at Royce, who was frowning now, apparently having finally gotten the message. "Yes, Royce," she said thickly. "I am pissed off. I am hurt. I am amazed. In fact, bucko, you could say I'm fucking infuriated!"

"What's wrong with you, Carlotta?" Royce snapped, reacting to her anger with a mixture of wounded innocence and superior annoyance. "It's the best possible thing that could've been done under the circumstances. What would *you* have done differently?"

"Closed the bloody Institute!" Carlotta yelled. "In fact, that's what I'm going to do anyway. You can forget this stupid deal of yours."

"*You* can't close the Institute," Royce said angrily. "Only a vote of Parliament can, and you know it."

"When you make your report to Parliament on the net, believe me, there'll be enough votes to close it down," Carlotta said. "Politically screened students! Brainwashing! Phony female students! Lies! Treachery! By the time we're through, even the mano Delegates won't be able to vote against closing the Institute."

"I won't do it," Royce said evenly.

"*What?* What did you say?"

"I said I won't do it."

Carlotta stared at Royce as if he were some strange new species of animal. What in the world has gotten into him? "*Why* won't you do it?" she said tensely, fighting back her rage.

"First because I gave Falkenstein my word of honor, and second because I'm right and you're wrong."

"Royce! Royce!" Carlotta shouted. "What did they feed you there?"

"Will you stop shouting and listen to me for a minute!" Royce snapped. He got up and began pacing in small circles. "We've got a deal with Falkenstein now whether you like it or not, and that means it's in his interest to cool it. But if I double-cross him, he'll fight us like a godzilla with an ironbush thorn up its ass. And the Femocrats will move in for the kill. By the time you bring it to a vote, the issue won't be the treachery of the Institute, it'll be Femocracy versus Bucko Power, men versus women, a split right down the middle in every Delegate constituency on the planet! If you were a Delegate in that situation, how do you think *you'd* vote?"

"I'd—"

"I'll tell you how you'd vote! You'd vote against the resolution, but first you'd make it clear that you were doing it only to force an electronic vote of confidence on the issue. That way, only *Carlotta Madigan* would have to face the electorate on the issue, and she'd be out on her ass because she'd be running against her own damn Madigan Plan! Net result: the Institute stays open, you're out of office, and the planet is put through the most polarizing electronic vote of confidence possible. *Very clever, lady!*"

Royce sat down. He smiled ruefully at her. "Go ahead," he said, "tell me I'm wrong."

"I can't," Carlotta said. "But the deal you've made is no better. In return for some control over admissions, I'm supposed to endorse an all-male student body? How do you expect me to sell something like *that* when it makes my own blood boil?"

"Simple," Royce said. "We just don't mention it. We just announce that Falkenstein has agreed to accept Ministry of Science control over admissions and pat ourselves on the back for having won a victory. We don't confirm the charge. The hand is quicker than the eye."

"That is loathsome, Royce," Carlotta said. "That *is* faschochauvinism. Besides, even if I could do it without vomiting, what's the point? In less than four months, the trial period will be over and we'll be right back where we started."

"At which point, we call for the ouster of both the Transcendental Scientists and the Femocrats."

"*What?*" Carlotta shouted. He's gone whackers! she thought. That's what all this is. Falkenstein's fed him something that's turned his mind to mulch. "You're starting to gibber, bucko," she said. "If that's the net result, then what are we putting ourselves through all this shit for?"

"For a Pacifican Institute of Transcendental Science," Royce said.

"*Huh?*"

"Run by Pacificans, staffed by Pacificans, with a student body of male and female Pacificans, and no offworlder meddling," Royce said. "You never gave me a chance to tell you what else I've done."

"Great grunting godzillas, there's *more?*"

"I've got a list of middle-level Pacifican scientists

screened for stability and political neutrality. They'll be put through a crash-course in media psychodynamics to counteract any Institute brainwashing. We'll slip them into the new student body. In four months, they may not know as much as the *Heisenberg* people, but they should know enough to put us in the Transcendental Science business for ourselves."

"An all-male spy corps, I gather?"

"Obviously."

"And this is the keystone of the vast political edifice you've built up on your own behind my back?" Carlotta said. "Who's the Chairman here, anyway? You've been a busy little bucko, haven't you?"

"I've been doing my job," Royce said stonily. "I've done what I thought best."

"What you thought best!" Carlotta shouted, bolting to her feet. "I thought I was the effing Chairman! I thought we were *a team!* Now you tell me you've committed my administration to some godzilla-brained scheme without even bothering to consult me!"

"Yeah, well *I* thought *I* was the Minister of Media, not just your tame errand boy!" Royce snapped. He rose, and they stood there glaring at each other, nose-to-nose, toe-to-toe.

"That doesn't mean you can commit this administration to a policy without my authority!" Carlotta said.

"I didn't commit your effing administration to anything, Carlotta! I committed *me*, Royce Lindblad, Minister of Media of Pacifica. I gave Falkenstein *my* word, not yours. I made it clear I wasn't speaking for the whole government. For once in my life, I made a personal political decision on my own. *Falkenstein* seemed to think the support of the Pacifican Minister of Media was worth something on its own, without the great Carlotta Madigan, even if you don't!"

"And if I tell you I think what you've done stinks? If I tell you that it's *my* independent decision to come out for the closing of the Institute now?"

Royce paused. The anger seemed to drain out of him. He walked over to the railing of the veranda, leaned up against it, and stared out over the tranquil turquoise sea. "You're an independent human being, Carlotta," he said quietly. "You're entitled to go *your* way if you think it best. And so am I."

Carlotta came up beside him. A flock of boomerbirds overhead began honking in chorus, and for once the sound seemed sad and mournful, a far-off dirge. "But you wouldn't support me, would you Royce?" she said softly. "We'd be on opposite sides. You'd do what you could to keep the Institute open."

"I made my decision and I gave my word," Royce said, turning to her. "What am I if that means nothing? A Terran breeder on a chain? Can't you respect that, Carlotta?"

"Bucko Power . . . ?" Carlotta muttered sardonically.

Royce laughed, and for a flash, he was her bucko again, the breeze ruffling his long hair, the sun shining golden through his eyelashes, and Carlotta sensed that this was not a death; that which bound them together was stronger than what was now driving them apart. Stretched a little thin by the pain of this moment, perhaps, but yet alive.

"You could call it that," Royce said softly. "I love you, and at least as far as I'm concerned, no political hassle is going to change that, babes. But I'm the second most important official on this planet, and if *I* didn't have the balls to stand on my own against my woman when I thought I was right, what would that say about Pacifican men? If you can't live with that, what does it say about you? About us? About what we're supposed to believe in?"

"Am I really like that?" Carlotta asked. "Have I really kept you in my shadow?"

Royce shrugged. He touched her arm. "I think maybe *we've* been like that," he said. He smiled at her. "Besides, you're one hell of a lady, and you're usually right."

A strange feeling came over Carlotta. Without Royce's support, any move on her part to close the Institute now would be an utter disaster. Her own Ministry of Media would be against her, and the man who had done so much to get her past other crises would be on the other side. And this deal with Falkenstein, this plan to infiltrate the Institute with male spies personally loyal to him, stank of faschochauvinism and the pathology of the Pink and Blue War. She was blocked, she was hamstrung, and it was Royce who was doing it to her.

Yet she felt her body bending closer to his, as if caught in his magnetic field. She found herself putting her arm around his waist and slipping her hand around to the inside of his thighs. And it was not lust that moved her. Somehow, in some unfathomable way, the respect that he was demanding flowed freely from her heart. Confronted, shouted down, stalemated, she had never quite felt this proud. It was as if the child she had never had had suddenly revealed himself as an adult, an equal entity. Loss there was, but it was a thing of the ego, and what replaced it came from the heart, a kind of love for him that she had never felt before.

"So be it, then," she said. "If you think this is the price of your manhood, I can fight you politically if I have to, and still love you, you obstinate, wrong-headed, faschochauvinist son of a bitch!"

Royce laughed and moved his body against hers. The boomerbirds soared off toward the west, and Rugo leaped into the sea with an ungainly splash. Everything was as screwed up as it could be, and yet two warm tears flowed down her cheeks in the bright sunlight, and in this moment of all incongruous moments, she felt a oneness with him beyond all understanding, a unity in conflict that surpassed anything she had known before.

"How about a tender loving grudge-fuck?" Royce whispered in her ear. They laughed, and they kissed, and they clung to each other even as a lone white cloud passed across the golden disc of the sun.

For two days political and domestic life had hung in limbo for Royce Lindblad while Carlotta tried to sort things out and reach a position of her own. He had announced the public portion of his agreement with Falkenstein to a good deal less effect than he had projected. The Femocrats could not possibly have become more rabid, and the Bucko Power movement was now not to be mollified by anything less than the expulsion of Femocracy. Royce half-believed Falkenstein's claim that it now had an indigenous life of its own.

So he had spent most of the time monitoring the net, searching for political movement that was not forthcoming, and setting up the crash course in media psychodynamics for the corps of infiltrators, while Carlotta tried to count nonexistent noses in favor of a showdown vote to close the Institute.

Their hours together since his return from Godzillaland

had had a certain unreality. If anything, their lovemaking had been more frequent, more prolonged, more intense, more tender, as if to fill the long silences and bridge the gap between them via the only remaining effective medium. It seemed to Royce that Carlotta was both trying to humor him out of a brittle sense of noblesse oblige and trying to transcend political differences with a very real, if exaggerated, personal tenderness. As a result, even their genuinely loving sex did not entirely escape having political overtones.

So they had spent their off-duty hours making love, and during working hours Carlotta had kept to her office in the Parliament building while Royce closeted himself in his office at the Ministry plugged into the net, as they went their separate political ways. The tension was becoming unbearable; *something* had to break soon.

Royce was listening to a progress report from the Minister of Science when all the screens on his net console began strobing red and all audio channels began shouting, "PRIORITY OVERIDE! PRIORITY OVERIDE!"

What now? Royce wondered bleakly. "We'll continue this later," he told Harrison Winterfelt, unplugging him from the circuit and plugging his comscreen into the priority channel. The strobing and shouting ceased immediately and Bill Munroe from news monitoring appeared on comscreen, harried and excited.

"What?" Royce asked curtly.

"Strike in Thule," Munroe said. "It's on all the news channels. Plug into any of them."

Royce shrugged. "That's for the Ministry of Labor, not me."

"Not *this*," Munroe said. "Maybe I'd better play it back for you from the beginning. Gov channel okay? No differences in any of the coverages."

"Okay," Royce said. "But what's this all about?"

"Effing Femocrats!" Munroe grunted. "Look!"

On the newsscreen, a panoramic shot of a big pit mine under a medium-sized permaglaze dome. Outside the dome, the whirling whiteness of a full-bore Thule blizzard. Inside the dome, the great shovelers and conveyors stand idle and abandoned like frozen godzillas of steel. Lines of female pickets wearing the workclothes of Thule techs cordon off the machinery and the lip of the mining pit.

Picket signs read "Ban Faschochauvinist Fausts Now!"
"Close the Institute!" and "Femocratic League of Pacifica."

Announcer's voiceover: "A general strike called today
by an ad hoc committee of female workers in Valhalla
has effectively paralyzed most mining and industrial activ-
ity in Thule."

A series of shots: female pickets outside another pit
mine, a deep-mining complex, half a dozen factories under
Thule environment domes. In two of the shots, a few male
workers appear to be counterpicketing, unorganized, without signs.

Announcer's voiceover: "Male workers appear to be
avoiding confrontations and are not attempting to cross
the picket lines. No incidents of violence have been reported. Susan Willaway, spokesman for the striking female
workers, explained the purpose of the strike at a rally
held in Valhalla three hours ago . . ."

A medium shot on a sandy-haired woman addressing
a large female crowd from a makeshift podium.

Susan Willaway: ". . . no woman will go to her job here
in Thule until the faschochauvinist Institute of Transcendental Science is closed and the *Heisenberg* is sent back to
wherever it came from! Let's see how *Bucko Power* can
keep the mining and industrial heartland of Pacifica producing with half a work force! Thule sisters, unite against
the Institute! Work is power! No work while the Institute
remains open!"

A panoramic shot on the wildly cheering crowd of
women, without local audio.

Announcer's voiceover: "The Ministry of Labor estimates that the strike has the support of at least seventy-five
percent of the female Thule work force . . ."

Royce's auxiliary comscreen came alive. It was Carlotta.
"Have you—"

"Yeah, yeah, just a minute . . ." Royce said. He turned
off the news channel audio. "Unplug from this circuit,
Bill," he told Munroe. "And thanks." He turned his full
attention back to Carlotta.

"Well, that changes things, doesn't it, Royce?" she said,
her agitation undertoned with a certain smug satisfaction,
or so he thought.

"Does it?" Royce said dubiously.

"Good lord, Royce, all our heavy industry and most of

our mining operations are in Thule!" Carlotta said. "A few days of this, and the whole planetary economy will start to shut down. Everything else aside, we've *got* to close the Institute now or we'll have mass unemployment and a crunching depression."

"Give in to a bunch of Femocrat-fomented strikers?" Royce said angrily. "You should get in touch with Cynda Elizabeth and demand that they call this thing off or else!"

"Or else *what!*"

"Or else we'll kick their asses off the planet forthwith!"

Carlotta grimaced. "That would only egg the strikers on. We've got to give in now, and I have the authority to do it on my own if I have to. I'll declare a state of—"

"It'd solve nothing, Carlotta, wait and see," Royce said. Roger Falkenstein's face appeared on the main comscreen. Oh-oh, he thought, it looks like we won't have to wait very long! "Falkenstein's calling me," he told Carlotta, "and he does not look happy."

"Well, that's something anyway," Carlotta said sardonically. "Patch me in, monitoring only."

"Right," Royce said. He cleared a monitoring channel from his net console to Carlotta's, so that she was plugged into Falkenstein's call but he wasn't plugged into her. Carlotta's tensely pensive face remained on his auxiliary comscreen as he plugged in Falkenstein's audio.

"What's the meaning of this strike in Thule, Royce?" Falkenstein said angrily. "I thought we had reached an agreement."

"We have, Roger, and it still stands."

"Well, what are you going to do about this situation?" Falkenstein demanded. "Our Arkmind projects that your economy will begin to falter within a week if this situation continues, and there'll be mass unemployment within two. At which point, the economic pressure to close the Institute will become overwhelming, and—"

"There's nothing I can do," Royce said. "The right to strike is protected by the Constitution." Although, he mused, a strike for a non—work-related political goal might skirt perilously close to insurrection . . . might pay to check it out with the Ministry of Justice . . .

"Is it?" Falkenstein said slowly. "You mean you have no legal means of bringing this strike to an end?"

"Looks that way to me, Roger," Royce said, knowing

what the inevitable response would be, and half-welcoming it. There could be only one viable political counterweight to this Femocrat strike, and Falkenstein was certainly smart enough to perceive the obvious. It would escalate the situation further, but it would certainly remove knuckling under to the Femocrats as a real alternative.

"Well then, Royce, I trust you understand how . . . how the buckos of Thule are likely to react to this vicious tactic . . ."

"I have some vague idea," Royce said sardonically.

"Not that I myself or any of my people would interfere in your domestic politics, of course . . ."

"Oh, of course not, Roger. No more than the Femocrats would. No more than they already have."

"And under the present circumstances, no less," Falkenstein said. "After all, I cannot in all conscience attempt to restrain our independent Pacifican supporters from . . . taking congruent action. That in itself could be construed as interfering in local politics, couldn't it?"

"For sure," Royce grunted.

"None of this need affect our agreement, though," Falkenstein said. "You understand my position?"

"All too well, Roger, all too well."

"I'm very sorry it's come to this . . ."

"So am I," Royce said, unplugging from the circuit . . . *I think.*

"You two boys seem to understand each other very well," Carlotta said, frowning. "Would you mind letting me in on the inner meaning of your cryptic conversation?"

"Isn't it obvious?" Royce said. "Now the male workers will 'spontaneously' counterstrike for retention of the Institute and expulsion of the Femocrats."

"Oh, fuck," Carlotta groaned. "Of course."

"That's what I meant when I said that knuckling under to the female strikers would solve nothing," Royce said. "In a few hours, we'll have the female and male workers on strike together for mutually exclusive goals. Give in to one side, and you just guarantee that the other strike will continue."

"Great grunting godzillas, what do we do now?" Carlotta said. She looked at Royce pensively, uncertainly. "It *is* 'we' on this one, isn't it, Royce? We *are* together on this?"

"On the need to stop both strikes without giving in to either side?" Royce asked carefully.

"On the need to stop both strikes quickly, whatever it takes," Carlotta said. She sighed. "I suppose under the circumstances, it amounts to the same thing, doesn't it?"

"Yeah, babes," Royce said. "Keeping the economy from being chewed to bits has to be number one. I'm with you on that, boss-lady."

Carlotta smiled at him, pantomimed a kiss. Royce laughed and blew a kiss back. Awful as this situation is, it does have its personal compensations, he thought. At least we're synced together again in the face of adversity. But *what* adversity!

"Well, any brilliant ideas, bucko?" Carlotta asked grimly.

Royce shrugged. "You could call Cynda Elizabeth and tell her there's going to be a counterstrike," he suggested. "Tell her that I can get Falkenstein to call off his if she'll end hers."

"Fat chance," Carlotta said. "Cynda Elizabeth must have known there'd be a counterstrike before this started. I have a feeling that both Transcendental Science and the Femocrats will not be unhappy to have this situation continue to some awful showdown. Shit . . ." She fingered her mouth reflectively.

"There *is* one possibility," she said. "We have no legal means of ending these strikes, but if we could get away with construing them as civil insurrections . . ."

"You've been reading my mind again, babes," Royce said.

Carlotta smiled at him. "Feels pretty good, doesn't it?" she said. "As good as anything can feel under these circumstances."

Royce laughed. Despite the gravity of the crisis, he felt an enormous release of tension. For now, at least, the stress was coming from without, not within. Now they were really working in sync again, at least for the moment, for whatever it might be worth politically.

"You get onto Cynda Elizabeth, I'll check with the Ministry of Justice," he said.

"Right babes," Carlotta said. "Good to have you aboard again."

"Likewise," Royce said. "Now all we have to do is figure out some way to keep the boat from sinking."

A tracking shot on Roger Falkenstein and a squat, dark-haired man in a pseudo-military black tunic as the camera follows them down a long hall in the Institute.

Falkenstein: ". . . in keeping with our policy of non-interference, we take no position for or against the men striking in Thule . . ."

Man in black: "You won't even take a position on the Femocrat strike?"

Falkenstein: "That's different, Mike. The female strike is openly backed by the Femocratic League of Pacifica, an obvious Femocrat front, and they've declared open warfare on us. Their strike may be legal, but it is certainly directed against the Institute, and therefore we have no compunction against calling for its swift termination by any means necessary."

Man in black: "But you still won't officially support the strike organized by Pacificans for the Institute?"

Falkenstein (somewhat impishly): "That would be *illegal*, Mike. Of course, we totally support your *goals*. But we believe that the buckos of Pacifica are men enough to determine their own destiny without our advice or endorsement. However . . . we *do* think it appropriate to show the people of Pacifica what this planet stands to lose if the Femocratic League of Pacifica succeeds in using economic blackmail to drive us from this planet . . ."

Cut to an exterior shot just outside the Institute building. Six male Pacificans are operating a control console connected to a mesh of thin wire fifty meters in diameter on thin wooden poles over a large heap of earth.

Falkenstein's voiceover: "A form of matter-transformer used in instantaneous construction. Matrix patterns of various constructs are stored in a computer memory. The desired construct is chosen and the transformer assembles it electronically out of an equivalent mass of raw matter . . ."

A silvery field of force envelops the area under the mesh. When it clears a moment later, a replica of the Institute building, forty meters in diameter, has appeared, seemingly from nowhere.

Falkenstein's voiceover: ". . . a building . . . or a hover . . ."

The field of force appears again, and when it clears this time, the model building has been replaced by a sleek blue hovercraft.

Falkenstein's voiceover: ". . . or even a piece of heroic statuary . . ."

The force field transforms the hovercraft into a piece of monumental sculpture: four Pacifican buckos in realistic full color looking upward as a stylized Transcendental Scientist hewn in black obsidian raises an open palm toward a hologram of the galactic starstream which floats magically overhead.

Falkenstein's voiceover: "I rather like that, don't you? I think we'll keep it."

Cut to an interior shot in a small infirmary. An old man lies in a bed surrounded by life-support machinery. Three Pacificans in white smocks hover over him, reading his life-signs, administering injections.

Falkenstein's voiceover: "Here Pacifican students are learning the many complex techniques involved in rejuvenation. The result might justly be called an indefinite lifespan and perpetual youthful vigor. However, for all Pacificans to benefit from these techniques, we will not only have to train people in all the necessary sciences, but we will have to train *teachers* in all these areas in a *permanent* Institute, so that your planet can eventually develop the corps of thousands of Transcendental Scientists that will be needed."

Cut to a small darkened room where a Pacifican student lies on a couch under the watchful eye of a Transcendental Scientist. An electrode band around his brow is wired to a small console. In the middle of the room is a small-scale and quite fuzzy holoprojection of a Gotham street scene: ethereal buildings, vague crowds, tiny dots that might be hovercrart or hydrofoils skimming over the nearby shimmering waters.

Falkenstein's voiceover: "This is frontier technology, even for us. The subject's brain is synced into a computer which operates a holoprojector, thereby transforming thoughts into visible images. The technology is not quite perfected, and the training necessary to operate the device successfully is quite arduous. But the possibilities are staggering—new forms of psychotherapy, new artforms and media technologies, ultimately perhaps an electronically augmented form of direct mind-to-mind communication."

Cut back to the tracking shot on Falkenstein and the man in black as they walk down the seemingly endless corridor, past a long series of open doorways through which a myriad arcane activities are briefly visible.

Falkenstein: "One of the charges against us is that we're creating a scientific elite, and to that I must plead emphatically guilty. What, after all, *is* an elite but an ever-growing community of enlightened, idealistic, and dedicated men leading their people onward toward infinity?"

Cut to an exterior shot of the statue grouping outside—the stylized Transcendental Scientist leading the Pacifican buckos onward to the stars—from a low angle, emphasizing the upward thrust of the piece's lines.

Falkenstein's voiceover: "As we now pass this torch of knowledge to Pacifican Institute graduates, so will those graduates become an elite passing the torch on to their entire people. This is the great upward sweeping spiral of human evolution—upward and onward, time without end, worlds without limit. If this be Faustian faschochauvinism, let us make the most of it!"

Bara Dorothy smiled across her desk at Cynda Elizabeth. The little breeder-loving fool drummed her fingers nervously on the desktop, apparently still unable to grasp how perfectly the strategy was working. But then she had been against calling the strike in the first place, Bara thought. She seemed to have lost her clear sense of the true purpose of the mission long ago.

"I still don't see why you're so pleased," Cynda whined. "The strike strategy has been a dismal failure. The Institute is still open, Falkenstein has countered with a male strike, and now the government *can't* close down the Institute without a direct confrontation with the breeders."

Bara Dorothy shook her head impatiently. "What is the purpose of this mission?" she asked, as if quizzing a dull little girl.

Cynda Elizabeth stared at her blankly.

"Not to close the Institute," Bara Dorothy continued, "but to unite the sisters of Pacifica in Femocratic consciousness so that they will seize power and establish a Femocratic government on this planet! Great Mother, Cynda, have you forgotten that?"

Cynda opened her mouth, then nibbled her lower lip as if she had been about to say something, and then thought better of it.

"Therefore," Bara said, "the present situation is ideal. The strikes have drawn the line between sisters and breeders with utter clarity. Everything that Falkenstein does now to mobilize this loathsome Bucko Power movement behind him will also mobilize the Sisterhood behind *us*. As the strikes begin to wreck the Pacifican economy, even that traitor to her sex, Carlotta Madigan, will no longer be able to equivocate. There will be a victor and a vanquished—and *soon*."

"But how can you be so sure that the *breeders* won't win?" Cynda said. "They're half the population, and they're in a position of rough equality."

"*Democratic politics!*" Bara snorted. "You've become infected with the local ideology, Cynda! You think this issue will be decided by *votes?*"

"But that's the way they do things here . . ." Cynda said fatuously.

"That's the way they *did* things here!" Bara replied triumphantly. "But the fate of this planet will now be decided by *power*, and power here, as everywhere, is in the hands of Sisterhood! The breeders of this planet may now unite against us, but they're still *macho breeders*, which means that the Pacifican sisters are their *sex objects*. Whereas fully conscious sisters have no sexual need for breeders. So when the final confrontation comes, the breeders' own contemptible piercers will force them into capitulation."

"But . . . but most Pacifican women are heterosexual," Cynda said. "They want men as much as men want them."

For the moment, you little fool, for the moment, Bara thought. "Unfortunately, that's quite true," she said. "Therefore, it's time to raise Pacifican Sisterhood to full consciousness, to erase their atavistic craving for the local breeders. Then they will be truly united in total Femocracy; then they will fully come into their own rightful power and make that power felt—*decisively!* Mary Maria is already preparing material for the media campaign."

Cynda Elizabeth frowned. A sickly look came into her eyes. The filthy little breeder-lover! "What's the matter now, Cynda?" Bara Dorothy said slyly, twisting the knife a little deeper, daring the little pervert to reveal her true atavistic feelings. "Do you feel *sorry* for the stinking macho swine? Do you lack the will to fight through to final victory? Are you a secret *breeder-lover* at heart?"

Emotions flashed across Cynda Elizabeth's face: a flush of anger, a tremor of fear, a white-skinned effort at control. You're such a transparent little fool, Bara thought.

"If . . . if those are official charges, bring them officially," Cynda stammered. "Otherwise . . . otherwise keep your innuendos to yourself!"

"That's the spirit," Bara said sardonically. "Come on, cheer up, I'm not bringing any charges." Not yet, she thought. She laughed almost gaily. "Come on, sister, let's enjoy this moment together. At last we can unfurl our true banner openly and unite proudly with our Pacifican sisters behind it. Doesn't that thrill you? Don't you want to stand up and cheer?"

She laughed long and loud in the face of the dirty little pervert's hollow-eyed silence.

14

A STOCK HISTORICAL SHOT OF ANCIENT TERRAN NAZIS; phalanxes of male troops in black uniforms goose-stepping across the screen to the thunder of steel-soled jackboots on concrete, arms outstretched in phallic salute. A slow dissolve to an exactly similar shot on a Bucko Power demonstration marching to the same beat, emphasized by the continued jackboot thunder from the Nazi soundtrack. The chant of "Bucko Power! Bucko Power!" fades in on the soundtrack to the marching rhythm, and as it does huge surreal wongs sprout from the crotches of the Bucko Power marchers in hideous parody of the Nazi salute, their glans replaced by clenched fists.

Cut to a closeup on a Falkenstein lookalike, superimposed on ancient stock footage of war-rockets blasting off from their pads; as each rocket spouts flame and rises, his eyes roll in orgasmic ecstasy. Cut to stock footage of a line of ancient tanks lumbering across a blasted landscape. A line of gigantic naked male figures is superimposed behind them, so that the tanks, with their long erect cannon, become their genital organs. As the cannon fire in ragged sequence, the male figures arch their backs in ecstasy.

Female voiceover: "Throughout human history, men have openly identified their sexual organ with war, domination, vengeance, and violence. They've *cocked* their guns, *screwed* their adversaries, *pierced* their enemies, *unzipped* their avengers, and in general *fucked people* over, and hardly ever *pricked* their conscience over it."

An extreme, ludicrous, clinically unwholesome shot of a disembodied penis pounding in and out of vaginal lips. Intercut with this a series of shots—a sword plunging into a stomach, a fist smashing a face again and again, a closeup of the blazing muzzle of a machine gun, arrows plunging into an animal carcass in rapid-fire sequence—all set up, in angle and rhythm, to sync into the gross shot of sexual penetration.

Female voiceover: "That's why most women have always secretly perceived sex with men as violation, submission, bodily pollution, and rape . . ."

A series of rapidly cut shots: a woman being raped by a soldier against the shattered wall of a building, a naked women on her knees sucking the penis of a cold man in black leather, a woman being buggered on a laboratory table by a man in a white smock, ending in a loathsome closeup of a ravaged vagina leaking blood and semen.

Female voiceover: "The piercer *penetrates* your flesh, the man *pounds* away at you, *crushing* you with the weight of his body, and then he *shoots* his alien fluids into the deepest recesses of your being."

An extreme closeup of a bloody wong pumping away directly at the camera.

Female voiceover: "Sex for the male is an act of aggression and conquest by its very biological parameters! Aggression and sex are united in the very essence of maleness. The piercer is the primal weapon of faschochauvinism, and the heterosexual act is the primal mode of violent macho fascism. A woman *cannot* allow a piercer inside her body without reinforcing this rock-bottom faschochauvinism with her own energy!"

A rapidly cut reprise of previous footage: marching Nazis, tanks-as-male-organs, a fist smashing a face, a woman being raped by a soldier, the blazing muzzle of a machine gun, a Bucko Power march, a bloody pumping wong.

Female voiceover: "When you allow a male to stick his piercer inside you, *this* is what you're submitting to, millennia of it, time without end! Getting it off with men is donating *your* precious energy to the beast itself! But there is another way, and hundreds of millions of sisters have found it . . ."

A series of crystalline, misty, artful shots of two strikingly beautiful women making love in an ethereal meadow, lush with green grass, rich with a profusion of multicolored blossoms. The shots melt and dissolve into each other sensuously, overlapping into a tender visual fugue, the visual analog of the ancient baroque music playing behind them. Mouths moist and gentle between thighs. Graceful fingers cupping tender breasts. Lips meeting lips in achingly sweet caresses. A hymn to lyrical self-contained female sexuality that climaxes into a complex multiply overlapping mandala composed of all the possible variations of woman-to-woman sexual ballet.

Female voiceover (husky and sensuous): "When sister touches sister, there are no penetrations, no violent dialectic between the hard and the soft, the giving and the taking. All acts of love become congruent with each other, and the only power that exists is the tender loving power of bodies, minds, and hearts synced together, the power of sisterhood united . . ."

A series of shots of Terran animals fading rapidly into each other: a noble stag with a great crown of antlers, surrounded by his harem of does; a magnificent peacock fanning his tail for an adoring hen; a great male gorilla pounding his chest at an intruder as females and young ones cower behind him; a lordly black-maned lion leading his pride across the veldt as he roars terror at the sky. Finally, a Cro-Magnon man, noble of countenance, powerful of build, his great arm draped protectively around his mate, who holds a suckling babe in her arms.

Male voiceover: "From the ancient forest of the north, to the tropic jungles and the primeval veldt, the male virtues of courage, honor, and protectiveness have been graven in the genes of all the warm-blooded species that evolved on the planet Earth. Essential buckhood is something we share not merely with all human men in all times and places but with the great timestream of Terran evolution. Older than our species itself, it has taken us from the primal forests of our birth to our foreordained heritage in the stars."

The Cro-Magnon man becomes a toga-clad Greek, a medieval armored knight, an ancient astronaut in his gleaming spacesuit, a Transcendental Scientist, a Pacifican bucko, while the woman and child, going through similar transformations, remain at his side.

Male voiceover: "And throughout this long march, woman has remained at man's side, the hidden driving force behind the upward evolution of the species. For graven in the male genes is the urge to compete with his fellows in the fulfillment of the ideal of manly virtue, and what he competes *for* is the favor, love, and admiration of women. Women have been the *judges* of the manly virtues. They have chosen the brave, the strong, the just, and the wise to breed the next generations, and so they have been the creators of what we are today."

Cut to a panoramic shot of a street scene in some modern Terran city, the buildings shabby-looking, the pavement in disrepair. The camera zooms in and out, catching closeups of men and women: the men wispy and vapid-eyed, the women mannish, hard-eyed, feverish-looking.

Male voiceover: "But when this evolutionary dialectic breaks down as it has on Earth, the inevitable results are the decay of the gene pool and a third-rate culture declining toward inevitable barbarism. For the bucko virtues are the essence of what has brought our species from the trees to the stars. When they are shunned by women as faschochauvinist, when men forget who they are, men and women alike begin the inevitable slide back down into the tarpit of racial devolution . . ."

A medium shot on a virile, intelligent-looking Pacifican bucko, as he slowly devolves into a frail-looking Terran breeder, an emaciated mindless hulk, a hairy, slack-jawed prehuman simian.

Hard cut to a phalanx of such ape-men shambling across a plain, whipped along by women dressed as Femocrats. The sky darkens, fills with stars, and a Transcendental Science Arkology appears above the ape-men. The creatures pause, their backs straighten, and they march off in rough unison in a new direction. As they march faster and faster, the hair melts from their bodies, they walk fully erect, the Femocrats drop their whips and become Pacifican women marching by their sides. As the sun rises, the procession becomes a Bucko Power demonstration marching triumphantly through the streets of modern Gotham.

Male voiceover: "Here on Pacifica, these same forces are now at work. There are those who would reduce your manhood to simpering effeteness, to a pale cowering shadow of what a man is meant to be. But there are buckos with the will to resist, to be men among men, to lead this planet on into the great galactic civilization to come, men for whom 'Bucko Power' is not a rag of shame but a badge of honor . . ."

Cut to a shot of naked men marching down another Gotham street, eyes resolutely forward, penises erect and proud. Women watch from the sidewalks. Some, ugly, fat, thoroughly repulsive, and dressed in the Femocrat mode, jeer and curse. Others, beautiful, lithe, wearing sexually provocative clothing, watch quietly with adoring eyes.

Male voiceover: "And their ultimate allies are the real women of Pacifica themselves! For as long as men have the courage to be themselves, as long as buckos march proudly under their own true banner, flesh will call to flesh, male will call to female, and those women who are worthy will be proud to follow where their men lead. For only the brave deserve the fair, and only the fair are worthy of the brave!"

A medium shot on the front rank of naked marching men as they raise their fists into the air.

Chanting men: *"What do you want?"*

Female chorus: "BUCKO POWER!"

Chanting men: *"What do you want?"*

Female chorus: "BUCKO POWER!"

A panoramic shot of a vast crowd of beautiful nude women, writhing provocatively, stroking their own bodies invitingly, pumping their fists rhythmically into the air.

Women (chanting imploringly): "BUCKO POWER! BUCKO POWER! BUCKO POWER!"

Superimposed on this shot, the serene, knowing, intelligent face of an idealized Pacifican bucko. This noble male head flashes through a series of transformations, becomes a ram, a bull, an eagle, a stag, a black-maned lion, a man again.

"BUCKO POWER! BUCKO POWER! BUCKO POW-ER! BUCKO POWER!"

"It's revolting, Roger," Maria Falkenstein said. "I can't even bear watching the pathological filth you're pouring out."

Beyond the cooling comfort of her inertia-screen, the midday heat of Godzillaland seemed almost visible as molecules of steam transpired by the rank green jungle just beyond the electronic barrier. Monstrosities thrashed and bellowed just out of sight as the Falkensteins walked from the Institute building toward their private quarters, yet it seemed to Maria that what was going on behind the silvery Institute walls was no less feral, no less savage, and no less mindless than the jungle world of tooth and claw that surrounded their little island of so-called civilization.

"Perhaps you prefer the Femocrats' brand of pathological filth?" Roger said irritably. "You certainly seem less than affectionate lately."

"That has nothing to do with it," Maria said, avoiding his gaze. It was certainly true that she was finding his touch difficult to bear, and even his company irritating. Indeed, she found herself wondering whether the loathsome and unprincipled media war that both sides were now waging had not even poisoned *their* own lives together. Not that she believed that the putrid Femocrat propaganda had warped her own perception of the male of the species in general and Roger in particular, but could Roger *really* direct such a campaign to arouse the worst sort of narcissistic male power-fantasies—and, yes, vicious faschochauvinism—without syncing into such latent feelings buried deep within his own psyche? Without exposing and exacerbating such unconscious pathology festering in the roots of our own society?

Certainly the *Pacificans* have a deeper, more stable, and more just sense of psychosexual equilibrium than we do, she thought, and even *they* have been thoroughly poisoned by this war of competing faschochauvinisms. Can we *really* do it to them without doing it to ourselves?

"Well, maybe it *does* have something to do with it," she said. "Aren't you in the very process of fighting the Femocrats, becoming the very caricature of male faschochauvinism they portray? Aren't you playing right into their hands by allowing their propaganda to become a self-fulfilling prophecy?"

"Rubbish!" Roger snapped. "We didn't start this. We wouldn't have even tackled this planet if the Femocrats hadn't targeted it first. Now that they've revealed their true colors openly, we have no alternative but to counter-attack with equal vigor. You've got to fight fire with fire!"

"Really?" Maria said sardonically. "I thought you fought fire with *water*."

"Ridiculous semantic sophistry!" Roger snapped.

"No, it isn't!" Maria said angrily. "If you try to fight fire with fire, you just create a greater conflagration and burn down the very thing you're trying to save. And that's precisely what's happening here! The Femocrats shriek their nauseating antimale propaganda and you shriek back with equally vile male supremacist filth which validates everything they say about men, just as what *they're* doing validates your Bucko Power bile! Where can it end, Roger? Where can you possibly expect it to end?"

"With their defeat and our victory!" Roger snarled, his face contorted into a hideous mask of anger, a vein throbbing in his right temple. "With the crushing of their strike and their expulsion from Pacifica!" Never before had he appeared even remotely this ugly in Maria's eyes.

"And how do you expect *that* to be accomplished?" she said scathingly. "By the triumph of . . . of *Bucko Power?*"

"If necessary," Roger said coldly.

Maria stopped dead in her tracks. She touched him on the shoulder, bringing him up short, and stared directly into his face, feeling the outrage building inside her. "You're really serious about that, aren't you?" she said. "You're perfectly willing to destroy the delicate psycho-sexual balance of this planet and replace it with wild-eyed male faschochauvinism in order to preserve our position here?"

"In a word," Roger said, *"yes!"*

"And what about the Pacificans?" Maria shouted in his face. "What about a way of life that has worked for three hundred years for men *and* women? Are these people nothing but pawns on some cosmic chessboard?"

"You're shouting at me, Maria!" Roger shouted.

"So I am," Maria said, with a colder, more controlled anger. "But then you've just admitted that you're willing to commit cultural genocide, and I would think that's something worth shouting at."

"Cultural genocide! What rot! If the psychosexual balance on this planet weren't abnormal in the first place, none of this would even be necessary."

"Oh, really? From our pinnacle of psychosexual equality, health, and justice, you've passed judgment on Pacifica and found it wanting?"

"Great suns, Maria, if you'd clear your mind of all this female emotionalism, you'd realize that the men of this planet are psychosexually arrested adolescents," Roger said petulantly. "If they functioned as proper adult males, do you think they would have even permitted the Femocrats to land? Pacifican women have historically dominated the buckos to an unwholesome degree, and while our methods may seem slightly extreme, all we're really doing is restoring the natural balance."

"Female emotionalism!" Maria screamed. "You stand there spouting faschochauvinist slok and you have the temerity to lecture me about *female emotionalism!*"

"Stop shouting at me, Maria!"

"Stop shouting? I've just begun to—"

Suddenly, with a series of sharp bellows and a great crashing of underbrush, two big bipedal godzillas exploded from the jungle, stumbled into the electronic barrier field, howled in pain and outrage, and stood there on their massive hind legs, waving their atrophied forelimbs at each other futilely, threatening each other with guttural roars and gnashing teeth.

"That's us, Roger!" Maria shouted over the din. "Two brainless godzillas shrieking and screaming at each other! That's what we're turning this whole planet into—a feral, stinking jungle infested with enraged monsters thirsting for blood!"

Evenly matched and knowing it, the two godzillas stood there for long moments, bellowing imprecations without attacking. Finally, they turned their backs on each other, and with a last chorus of animal rage, disappeared back into the jungle along their separate vectors.

"No more of this, Roger," Maria said. "I can't take it."

She turned and began walking back toward the Institute building.

"Where are you going?"

"I'm moving into the Institute dormitory," she said over, her shoulder. "At least till you come to your senses. I have met the enemy, and he is us."

Tears filled her eyes as she walked away without looking back. I'm running away from Roger, she thought, but where am I running to? Our own damned Institute—what a gesture of futility! I've got to get out of here for a while. I've got to find someplace where I can be alone and think. Gotham, maybe. Things seemed to make more sense there. Maybe the Pacificans have an answer. We surely don't. I'm not even sure we know what the question is.

Trembling with tension, Cynda Elizabeth parked her floater on the deserted residential street and walked down the footpath through the dense copse of trees to the hidden and secluded dock where Eric moored his sailboat. He was waiting for her at the end of the dock when she reached the shore; standing hands-on-hips, his hard masculine body armored in the black pseudomilitary tunic that had become a fad with Pacifican men lately, a silhouette of razor-edged darkness against the brilliant nightscape of the city. A tremor of dread went through her; that dark figure looked so distant and ominous against the lights of Gotham, and his pose seemed a deliberate ideogram of macho defiance.

"Well, so you actually had the balls to show up," he said. "Have to give you credit for that, at least."

Cynda reached out to touch him, but something stopped her, as if he had surrounded himself with an impenetrable psychic barrier, and the gesture died in mid-air. "What's wrong, Eric?" she said lamely.

He laughed bitterly. "What could be wrong?" he said. "The lady is here to get it off with me, isn't she? The fact that she's trying to turn every woman on the planet off men shouldn't matter, should it?"

"That . . . that's not my doing . . ." Cynda stammered. "I tried to stop—"

"You're the leader of the Femocrat mission, aren't you?"

Cynda sighed. "In name only," she said. "You have no idea—"

"I guess not. And frankly, I don't give a damn."

"Look," Cynda said, "could we go out on the boat and—"

Eric glared at her. "We're not going anywhere tonight," he said. "This is it, lady! You've used me for an effing dildo for the last time."

Cynda's knees trembled. Wearily, she sat down on the hard wooden dock and looked up at Eric, who towered above her, still locked into his arrogant stance of outraged machohood. "I haven't used you, Eric," she said. "Really I haven't."

He crouched down beside her, balanced on the balls of his feet, the tight fabric at the seat of his pants hovering above the splintery weathered emeraldwood of the dock. "Haven't you, Cynda?" he said. "I plug into the net. I've seen what you're putting out. What we've been doing is an act of macho aggression, isn't it? A metaphor for war and faschochauvinist domination? 'Perverted,' by your own standards."

"No! I mean, I'm not like that!"

"No? Then what *are* you like, lady?"

"Great Mother, I don't know any more!" Cynda sighed.

"Well, then I'll tell you!" Eric snapped. "You're an effing *pervert*, Cynda. You hate men. You think you're a superior creature. You believe that wongs are disgusting organs attached to inferior *breeders* whose proper place is kneeling at your feet licking your fucking boots . . ."

He smiled cruelly at her and fingered the fly of his trousers. "But the thing is, your body wants that disgusting weapon of faschochauvinism inside you," he said. "You despise men, but oh, how you love *cock!*" He undid the front of his pants and worked his piercer free of the clothing with one hand. It grew huge and hard and somehow menacing as he waved it at her.

"Look at it, lady, and tell me you don't want it up you," he said. "Tell me you don't want to put it in your mouth and suck it till it fills you with loathsome male seed!"

"You're being disgusting!" Cynda cried, unable to take her eyes off the throbbing piercer, even while her flesh crawled away from him.

"Sure, I'm being disgusting," Eric said. "That's the

whole point, isn't it? You consider what you want to do disgusting and perverted. Your body wants it, but your mind is out there telling the world just how disgusting it is. Your cunt is out of sync with your brain, you're all fucked up inside, and that's exactly what it means to be a pervert, isn't it? *Hypocrite* is just another word for it."

"That's not so!" Cynda insisted.

Eric stood up, his piercer waving free in the warm night breeze above Cynda's face like some ghastly banner, like some foul faschochauvinist ensign. Yet she found her eyes transfixed by it, and her lips wanted to—

"Then straighten out, Cynda," Eric said. "Put your mouth . . ." He stopped short, laughed sardonically. "Put your *mind* where your mouth wants to be. Stop the crap you're putting out. Don't try to keep other women from being the same damn thing *you* want to be."

"I . . . I tried, really I did," Cynda said. "But I couldn't, it's out of my hands."

"Jellybelly oil!"

"It's the truth!"

"Well then, take yourself out of *their* hands," Eric said more softly.

"What do you mean?"

He shrugged. "Defect. Ask for political asylum. Tell the whole damn planet that what you've been saying is a lie. Come over to our side."

"*Your* side? Whose side? Falkenstein's? Bucko Power's?"

Eric held his piercer centimeters from her lips, stroking it languidly. "*This* side," he said. "The side your body's on already."

"I can't do that," Cynda said. He brushed the head of his piercer teasingly over her lips. An electric shock passed from her lips to her groin and her mouth flowed forward. Eric laughed and danced back half a step.

"Why not?" he said.

Why not indeed? Cynda wondered. Admit it, you hate Bara. You've begun to hate what we're doing here, you're no longer sure we're even right. And you're a *breeder-lover*, Cynda, a dirty, perverted breeder-lover. You want that piercer inside your flower, you want to suck on it, you haven't eaten honey once since you came to this planet. He's right, that's what you are, a *pervert*. What's stopping you? Why won't you go all the way?

She looked up at Eric, a dark figure of knowing macho arrogance, thrusting his piercer at her like a weapon, the perfect image of all that was loathsome faschochauvinist pride.

He *is* using it as a weapon, she realized. What we're saying may not be the whole truth, but it isn't a total lie either. *This* is what we're fighting on this planet, and this is what Falkenstein has called forth in the Pacifican breeder. *This* is what the men of this planet will become if Bucko Power wins out. This is the face of the beast. Great Mother, help me, I feel myself drawn toward it, but I know that it's wrong, a flaw in my own genes, in his, in both halves of our divided species. Perhaps Sisterhood isn't the only answer, but it's the only one I know, and this . . . *this* is surely something worth fighting, in the world, and in myself.

Slowly she rose to her feet. "I am what I am, Eric," she said. "And you are what you are. I thought perhaps it could be different, but I can see that it's not."

Eric stared at her harshly. Slowly his expression softened—to regret, sadness, embarrassment. Clumsily, he tucked his piercer back into his pants and closed them with a gesture of finality. "I guess so," he said quietly. "I guess I just made a fool of myself."

Cynda shrugged. She smiled wanly. "Maybe the way things are just made fools of both of us," she said. "Maybe we're all just a flawed species, men and women. But I know that I still believe in some kind of Sisterhood, no matter how flawed. I can't betray that, Eric. Not for you, not for my own sexuality, not for anything. I'm sorry."

"So am I," he said. "I may believe in Bucko Power, but I can't say that *this* bucko feels very powerful right now."

She touched him briefly on the cheek. The lights of the city mocked the darkness behind him, and overhead the stars were lonely points of light lost in a cold immensity. "I guess this is goodbye," she said.

He sighed and nodded his silent agreement.

"Try not to hate me too much," Cynda said, and then she was running down the dock, staggering with sadness and seething with rage at she-knew-not-whom.

White clouds with just a hint of gray in their fluffy underbellies scudded rapidly across their course as Royce put the *Davy Jones* on another northward tack, zigzagging the sailboat east toward Gotham against a stiff westerly wind.

Of all the times for Royce to win the endless argument and get her to make the slow trip from Lorien to Gotham under sail, this period of shrill and frozen crisis had seemed the most unlikely to Carlotta Madigan. Perhaps it was a mutually agreed-upon symbol of the altered nuances of their relationship; perhaps it had had something to do with the realization that under these circumstances, the economy straining from the Thule strikes and no path of action presenting itself; her time was less valuable than she wished it to seem.

But as they sailed toward Gotham, tacking endlessly, north, south, north, against the prevailing winds, Carlotta began to understand what Royce meant about using the trip to think, about learning from the dynamics of wind, tide, and inertia. How like the political events of the past months this is! she thought. The wind blowing squarely against us, conning the ship of state on an endless series of diversionary tacks, clinging to some semblance of a true heading only by balancing the forces off against each other.

And now that process seems to have reached a dead end. How can we find a clear channel now, and how can we steer Pacifica through it, past the jagged rocks of destruction on either side?

She studied Royce, intent now on balancing off the tension in the boomline against the inertia of the tiller, internalizing the forces within our own relationship, she thought. And we seem to be making it work, with give and take, zigs and zags, and a little accommodated tension between us. Why can't we apply the same process politically, as Pacificans together? All at once, something hopeful began to glimmer just beyond her conscious grasp . . .

"I wonder, Royce," she said, "if we shouldn't just construe these strikes as civil insurrections and proceed on that basis . . ."

Royce shrugged. "According to the Ministry of Justice, a 'civil insurrection' has to involve an extralegal attempt to violate a law or the Constitution," he reminded her. "Way they see it, these are legal strikes, period."

"But what about Parliament?" Carlotta said. "I doubt

the strikers would defy a resolution of Parliament, even if it *was* on shaky legal grounds."

"Hmmmm . . ." Royce muttered. "The depth polls *are* interesting. Thirty percent of males support the Bucko Power strike, and about the same percentage of women support the Femocrat strike, and virtually all men are against the Femocrat strike and all women against the male strike. But something like twenty-seven percent of the total population is fed up with both strikes, and that vote *isn't* sexually polarized . . ."

"And that figure should grow every day as the economy continues to deteriorate."

"For sure . . . but it's still not enough to make a majority of the Delegates brave enough to pass a resolution to end the strikes—not when they can avoid taking any position with a nice safe legalistic cop-out."

Royce twisted the tiller and shifted the boom over. The sail flapped and luffed for a moment, then filled again as he established a southern tack. "Damn!" Carlotta said. "Why do we have to let Transcendental Science and the Femocrats control the parameters? Why can't we find an effing *Pacifican* position that isn't either-or?"

Royce eyed her speculatively. "*I* thought I had, but you didn't agree," he said.

"You did? I didn't?"

"Infiltrate the Institute with Pacifican spies," he said. "Get what we can during the trial period, then kick *all* of them off the planet. But you thought that was fascho-chauvinist jellybelly oil, remember?"

"Uh . . ." Carlotta muttered. "But we're on a different tack now, aren't we?"

"Aha!" Royce said. "At last you see the ineffable wisdom of my devious mind."

"Not quite, bucko!" Carlotta said. But pieces of the puzzle were beginning to fall into place. "But I'm beginning to see that maybe you and I really *do* agree on the basics, and maybe the two of us sitting in this boat have the essence of a real *Pacifican* position between us."

"We *do?*"

"Look, neither of us wants a Femocratic Pacifica, and neither of us wants some elite male Transcendental Scientist caste lording it over the planet, right? Keeping

251

Pacifica Pacifican is number one. Isn't *that* an issue which transcends this out-worlder-fomented sexual polarization?"

"Not if your idea is to kick all the off-worlders off the planet immediately," Royce said. "I won't support any move that will cut us off entirely from the Transcendental Sciences. I meant it, and I haven't changed my mind."

A slight flash of anger passed through Carlotta, but she instantly suppressed it. Her mind was cool and analytical now, reaching for compromise, not conflict. Tacking against all opposing winds, even if they came from within. "All right, all right," she said, "so let's agree to disagree on that and see if we can't fit even the disagreement into a Pacifican position, since it's exactly the gap we have to bridge anyway."

"If that's what you're selling now, I'm buying, babes."

"Okay, okay," Carlotta said rapidly. "So what's this Pacifican thing we're trying to restore and preserve? The democratic process. Equity between men and women. A smooth psychosexual balance."

"Liberty and justice for all," Royce said sardonically.

"Oh, so you think that's just a tub of jellybelly oil?"

"I think it's just words and fancy rules, Carlotta. What we had here didn't depend on that. The real Pacifican thing is—or was—a feeling, something in the soul. Community, trust, I dunno . . ."

After a long moment's silence, Carlotta sighed. "Yeah, Royce, it's just that feeling that we've lost," she said softly. "Why can't *that* be a political issue? If these off-worlders have proven anything, it's that they can't comprehend the thing that makes Pacifica Pacifica."

"Pacifica for the Pacificans?" Royce said archly.

"Well, why not?" Carlotta answered, and suddenly everything clicked into place. "Pacifica for the Pacificans, and in the Pacifican way! Why not make that feeling the issue?"

Royce grinned. "The logic is a little fuzzy," he said, "but I can sure see the media blitz!"

"The fuzzier the better!" Carlotta exclaimed. "Goddamn it, we'll *go* with your plan to infiltrate the Institute, we'll put your deal with Falkenstein into effect unilaterally, tell the planet we have done something, and demand the strikes be ended. Trust will be the issue—Pacificans must

252

trust Pacificans, not any bunch of godzilla-brained off-worlders!"

"Amen to that," Royce said.

"We'll fudge the real isues!" Carlotta said. "We won't say *anything* about infiltrating the Institute or setting one up on our own. The only issue will be Pacifica for the Pacificans, and anyone who disagrees is a traitor to the Pacifican way of life, a pawn of off-world meddlers, period!"

"Well, that sounds dirty enough to me," Royce said. Once again, he shifted the boom and changed tacks. "The only trouble is," he said as the sailboat headed northward, "that right now that's precisely what nobody's buying."

"Then we'll effing well *sell* it to them!" Carlotta said sharply. "And we'll make ending the strikes the test issue. Anyone in favor of continuing the strikes is an un-Pacifican son of a bitch! We'll introduce a resolution in Parliament and force the Delegates to stand up and be counted."

Royce sighed. "But they're sure to vote it down," he said.

"Then screw Parliament!" Carlotta snapped. She smiled. She grinned. She laughed. *Of course!* "That's exactly what we'll do," she said.

Royce cocked an inquisitive eyebrow at her.

"We'll *really* screw Parliament," she said. "We'll introduce a resolution to end the strikes and make damn well *certain* it's voted down. Then we'll have an electronic vote of confidence, and we'll use the campaign to build a third force, a Pacifica for the Pacificans movement, good old-fashioned local nationalism. Then when I win the vote of confidence, there'll be a new Parliament elected in which we'll have sufficient Delegates representing our third force to block *anything* the Bucko Power creeps or the Femocratic League of Pacifica tries to do."

Royce goggled at her in amazement. "That's a lovely scenario," he said, "but it can't happen. It breaks down at the electronic vote of confidence. How in hell can you hope to win it?"

"By ending the strikes *after* the resolution fails but *before* the electronic vote," Carlotta said. "The Delegates who voted down the resolution will look like perfect asses. They'll be thrown out and replaced by our people."

Royce shook his head numbly. "And how do you expect to accomplish this miracle of ending the strikes?"

Carlotta laughed. "When you start playing really dirty, life becomes a lot more simple," she said. "We'll use the campaign to cover a trip down to Valhalla. We'll tell the male strikers that unless they end their strike, we'll both come out for closing the Institute while permitting the Femocrats to remain on Pacifica, and we'll tell the female strikers the exact opposite. And of course if anyone makes these threats public, we'll deny everything and call it un-Pacifican off-worlder lies."

"Whoo-ee!" Royce said. "That's some game of bluff! If we get called on it . . ."

"We won't," Carlotta said confidently. "Because 'bluff' is too timorous a term for it. Why not call it what it is—*blackmail.*"

Royce laughed. "You said it, I didn't," he said implishly. He giggled. He leaned over and kissed her on the lips. "You can be one mean lady when you have to be, peerless leader," he said approvingly. He shook his fist at a lone boomerbird passing overhead. "Pacifica for the Pacificans, jocko!" he shouted.

"Pacifica for the Pacificans!" Carlotta yelled back. The stern of the sailboat left a foaming white wake in the water, the wind half-filled the sail, and suddenly the zigzag tacking course seemed somehow appropriate; despite the worst efforts of the countering wind, it *was* a way to safe harbor. With a tiller in one hand and a boomline in the other, you could find a way to work your will against tide and wind, outside forces, and the blind hand of fate.

Royce grinned at her. "I'll make a sailor out of you yet, Carlotta Madigan," he said.

"What the hell do you mean by that?" she blurted reflexively. He didn't bother to answer, but she thought she was beginning to understand.

15

A SERIES OF SHOTS RAPIDLY CUT IN EVER-INCREASING tempo: the *Heisenberg* in orbit, a rape scene from "Soldiers of Midnight," Falkenstein's smug face, the grounded Femocrat ship surrounded by Pacifican security forces, a lesbian sex scene from the Femocrats' *Lysistrata*, Cynda Elizabeth, demonstrations, marches, rallies, striking pickets. On the soundtrack, an unintelligible babble of voices that grows ever louder, shriller, and more strident to the building rhythm of the cutting, as the sequence ends in a split-screen shot of a man and women screaming at each other with the animal voices of the mob, faces purpling with rage. Dissolve to a similar shot of two godzillas bellowing at each other with the same brainless mob voice.

Cut to a closeup of Carlotta Madigan; cool, calm, smiling her best Borgia smile.

Carlotta: "Welcome to Pacifica, the galaxy's first real-life *human* godzilla epic. See men and women tearing at each other like jungle beasts! Watch the economy of the media hub of the human galaxy disintegrate! And finally, observe the Delegates to the most democratic Parliament known to man crawling on their bellies like reptiles!"

Cut to a panoramic shot of the Parliament chamber,

emphasizing the screens above the Chairman's seat as Carlotta calls the vote.

Carlotta: "All those in favor of declaring both strikes in Thule civil insurrections and empowering the Chairman to act accordingly to end them, aye; those opposed, nay."

Numbers flash across the tally screen as the Delegates vote, finally resulting in 31 ayes and 72 nays. Blue and pink strings materialize, attached to the crotches of the male and female Delegates respectively. The camera slowly pans upward along the tangled skeins, through the dissolving dome of the chamber, to reveal Roger Falkenstein and Cynda Elizabeth as leering puppet-masters controlling the Delegates.

Cut back to the closeup on Carlotta Madigan.

Carlotta: "Thus has Parliament expressed the will of the Pacifican people! Or *has* it? Is this what you really want, Pacifica?"

A series of shots slowly dissolving into each other: mining equipment rusting under a pall of snow beneath a shattered environment dome; moss and vertigris covering the rotting machinery of an abandoned factory; a street in Gotham filled with gaunt-bellied, rag-clad, starving wretches; a field of wheat searing to straw under a cruel sun.

Back to the closeup on Carlotta Madigan, bristling now with righteous indignation.

Carlotta: "Well, that's what your Delegates have voted for by refusing to support my determination to end these godzilla-brained strikes! The economy is already falling apart. Unemployment will soon reach twenty-five percent. Food production will soon begin to suffer. Everything we've built on this planet in three hundred years is turning to *shit!* And for what, fellow Pacificans, *for what?*"

A tracking shot on an army of goose-stepping men marching across the screen from left to right. They wear skin-tight blue uniforms and brandish immense rubbery cocks. Cut to a similar shot on an army of women goose-stepping from right to left. They wear skin-tight pink uniforms and their crotches are steel traps with gleaming jagged teeth that gnash and snap to the marching rhythm. The armies meet and clash in ludicrous combat. Men batter women with their penile clubs. Toothed steel vaginal mouths snap shut on giant wongs, severing them in fountains of gore. The battle becomes an ideogram of insane sexual hostility.

Carlotta's voiceover: "So as to continue fighting the Pink and Blue War, the most idiotic and self-defeating conflict in the entire crazed history of the human race!"

Cut to a closeup on Carlotta, grimacing ironically.

Carlotta: "Do you remember what a dumb joke the Pink and Blue War was to this planet a few months ago? Now *we're* the clowns doing idiotic pratfalls in a comic opera satire of ourselves, the laughingstock of the galaxy, while we tear our economy and society to pieces in the process!"

The camera pulls back to a longer shot on Carlotta, revealing Lorien lagoon in the background, gentle waves, blue skies, a flock of passing boomerbirds.

Carlotta: "Now, as your Chairman, I face an electronic vote of confidence on the issue of ending these strikes, and I stand here on the veranda of my home wondering why I'm bothering. Why should I continue to expend my energy in the service of a planet that seems bent upon its own destruction?"

The camera moves in for a closeup as she shrugs, as her eyes seem to stare off into some distant vista, growing soft even as her expression hardens. Superimposed over this closeup of Carlotta is a series of lyrical shots slowly dissolving into each other: the Big Blue River, a sapphire ribbon winding through fields of golden grain; a cluster of emerald islands under a deep blue sky gilded by the setting sun; the shaggy green shoulders of the Sierra Cordillera capped with brilliant white snow; the ghostly sheen of the Thule icecap under a hard black sky brilliant with pinpoint stars; finally, Pacifica itself, breathtakingly organic and alive against the black velvet of space.

Carlotta's voiceover: "Let the Transcendental Scientists call it female emotionalism; let the Femocrats call it an atavistic impulse; I'll call it love for this planet and be done with it. So I submit myself to your vote of confidence, but make no mistake about it, this is also a matter of *my* continued confidence in *you*. And of your continued confidence in yourselves as Pacificans."

Just Carlotta now, speaking directly into the camera.

Carlotta: "These ruinous strikes must be ended, and *now!* Regardless of your temporary allegiances to off-world ideologies, the future of your planet demands that men and women alike now vote as *Pacificans* and for *Pacifica*. If I win this vote of confidence, I kid you not, I will move with all possible speed and with all the powers that the office of Chairman commands to end these strikes at once. And I tell you just as plainly, if I lose this vote of confidence, you can all go to hell without my further assistance—I'll never run for public office again. That's how strongly *I* feel about this planet we all love. What about you, my fellow Pacificans? Are you willing to destroy this planet for the sake of words and slogans and alien ideologies?"

A slow dissolve to a shot of Pacifica, a vision of fragile life-quickened complexity against the hard uncompromising simplicity of perpetual galactic night.

Carlotta's voiceover: "Or will we in this hour of decision stand together, men and women, buckos and sisters, and speak with one voice that will be heard from the streets of Gotham to the forests of the Cords, from the Island Continent to the jungles of the Horn, from the banks of the Big Blue to the icebound wastes of Thule? The voice of *Pacificans* speaking for *Pacifica!*"

A medium shot on a hard, strident-looking woman standing on a small Gotham bridge, the Parliament building visible in the background across the bay.

Woman: "How the eff can any sister really trust Carlotta Madigan when she refuses to take any stand at all on the *real* issues?"

Female interviewer's voiceover: "But you say you *are* going to vote for her anyway?"

Woman (shrugging at the Parliament building): "What's the choice, *those* gutless wonders? They've got their cowardly fingers stuck up their asses. At least Madigan's willing to put her career on the line to end the strikes."

Female interviewer's voiceover: "You mean you're in favor of closing the Institute but *against* the Femocratic League's strike?"

Woman (smiling ironically): "Babe, I've been a lady-lover all my life, I'm as lesbo as any of these effing Femocrats. But that doesn't make me any less of a Pacifican. Show me what their stupid strike has accomplished except to give the Bucko Power fanatics an excuse for a strike of their own and make every lesbo Pacifican's patriotism seem suspect. . . . (somewhat sheepishly) Besides, I've just been layed off. . . ."

Cut a closeup of a tall, long-haired mano type, leaning against a bongo tree.

Mano: "I haven't decided whether to vote for Madigan or not. I'm all for Pacifica for the Pacificans, and the damn Femocrats *started* this mess; remember, the buckos are only striking to stop their power-trip against the Institute. So if Madigan tells me how she's going to end both strikes without caving in to the Femocrats, she's got this boy's vote. Otherwise . . ." He shrugs.

Cut to a full shot on two huge bipedal godzillas, immobilized by del gado boxes. A male whacker is mounted on one, a female on the other.

Male whacker: "You bet your wong we're voting for Carlotta Madigan, boyo! The Institute's our next-door neighbor, and it's not bothering us a bit. As for Femocracy . . ." He sticks out his tongue and makes a ripe raspberry noise.

Female whacker: "We don't need lames telling us who to get it off with; we don't need fancy scientific toys; and we *sure* don't need a bunch of shit-brained fanatics shutting down the whole damn Pacifican economy! Only thing I've got against Carlotta Madigan is she doesn't go far enough . . ."

Male whacker: "Yeah, what we *should* do is ship about thirty godzillas down to Valhalla and let the effing strikers try shouting their slogans at *them!* Same intellectual level, right, and it'd make a flash epic. Pacifica for Pacificans, boyo! But then the rest of the planet thinks *we're* crazy!"

They manipulate their controls and the two huge godzillas rear up suddenly, bellow, and salute with their tiny forearms.

Both whackers in chorus: "Pacifica for the Pacificans!" They break up into roaring laughter. "Godzilla Power!"

Cut to a two-shot on Carlotta Madigan and Royce Lindblad sitting side by side in Carlotta's office. They're both smiling slightly, their arms are touching, they radiate an aura of togetherness, and they seem to be speaking to each other, rather than to the camera.

Carlotta: "Well, babes, in the past few days, a lot of

people seem to be coming to their senses. *We've* had our disagreements, too, in the past few weeks, but . . ."

Royce: "Who wouldn't, with the crap that's being shoved down our throats? But I think that all Pacificans— faschochauvinist macho Fausts and ball-cutting crypto-Femocrats alike—are beginning to see that these strikes are hurting everyone except for a few fanatic off-worlders who couldn't care less about the Pacifican economy anyway."

Carlotta (looking at the camera now) : "And we've come up with an equitable formula for stopping them."

Royce: "That's right. While Parliament has been sitting on its hands, *we've* been doing some hard negotiating with Roger Falkenstein and we've forced him to accept the following modifications to the Madigan Plan . . ."

Carlotta: "The present student body of the Institute will be dismissed. The new student body will be chosen not by the Transcendental Scientists but by the Pacifican Ministry of Science. Their names will not even be revealed to the Transcendental Scientists, so there will be no possibility of political screening on their part. No drugs may be given to the students without prior Ministry of Science approval. I am implementing this agreement as of today on my personal authority as Chairman of Pacifica. As far as I'm concerned, this puts the Institute under effective Pacifican control, and removes any further excuse for the Thule strikes."

Royce: "I've been convinced that Pacifica must have an Institute of Transcendental Science all along, and as far as *I'm* concerned, this is the Pacifican way of doing it!"

The camera moves in for a closeup on Carlotta.

Carlotta: "I've based my campaign on a promise to end these strikes if I win, but with this agreement now in hand, I've decided that *action* speaks louder than words. There are now two days till the electronic vote. Royce and I are going to Thule immediately and we won't come back until we've ended these strikes. If we haven't accomplished this by election day, I say vote me out of office forever! But when we end these strikes— and we effing well *will*— I say that anyone who votes against me *then* is voting against sanity, against reason, and against Pacifica itself."

The camera pulls back for a two-shot on Royce and Carlotta.

Royce: "We negotiated this agreement as a *team,* we're going to end these strikes as a *team,* and we hope you'll think of us as a team when it's time to vote. Not for a woman or a man but for two *Pacificans* who love each other, who respect each other, and who are working to make this planet what it is meant to be once more— *Pacifica for the Pacificans!*"

Royce and Carlotta put their arms around each other, smile at the camera, and kiss briefly.

Carlotta: "If *that* be treason to my sex, I say let's make the most of it!"

Her mind honed to keen-edged clarity by the forces converging on this pivotal moment of personal and planetary destiny, Carlotta Madigan strode into the cavernous silent machine shop where the strike committee awaited her. Five tough-looking women in gray jumpsuits sat on chairs around an empty workbench, their arms folded sullenly across their breasts, their hostile eyes tracking her as she walked deliberately across the echoing concrete floor past the rows of paralyzed engine lathes.

Well, you brought this on yourself, she thought as she stood before them. Despite the success of the last net appearance, the vote was still going against her, even as Royce had predicted. Howls of rage were still echoing, not only from the Femocrats and their supporters, but from the overwhelming majority of Delegates, who felt that she had exceeded her authority. The 40 percent support that the polls now showed—hard-core Pacificans for Pacifica and people with enough sanity left to vote their bank balances—was a hopeful sign, but the only real chance of winning the vote of confidence lay right here and now, in stunning the 60 percent against her by ending the strikes forthwith. This was the moment of truth, and no fucking strike committee was going to be allowed to stand in her way.

"Well, what's your proposal?" said a hard-faced, sandy-haired woman who Carlotta recognized as Susan Willaway, both the strike leader and a heavy in the Femocratic League of Pacifica.

Screw diplomacy! Carlotta thought. She remained standing, assumed a belligerent hands-on-hips posture. "No *pro-*

posal, sister," she said. "I'm here as the head of government to *order* you to end your strike."

"Don't *sister* us, you effing breeder-lover!" Susan Willaway snapped. "And don't think you can order us around either. You think you and that faschochauvinist Lindblad can—"

"Shut your fucking face!" Carlotta roared. She perched on the edge of the workbench and stared the strike committee down. "You *are* going to obey my order, and now I'm going to tell you why."

"Oh, really?" Susan Willaway sneered to the nervous laughter of the rest of the strike committee.

"For sure," Carlotta said coldly. "Because you'd find the alternative totally unacceptable. If I *don't* leave here with your agreement to bring this strike to an immediate end, I will come out immediately for the expulsion of the Femocrats and the retention of the Institute."

All five women laughed, and the tension seemed to go out of them. "Some threat!" a lanky redhead said. "The lame duck Chairman is going to take a position against us. We're just *terrified,* sister."

"So you don't think I have a chance of winning the vote of confidence, do you?" Carlotta said, forcing a tone of confident superiority into her voice.

"Do you?" Susan Willaway said with equal disdain.

"By a landslide if I end these strikes," Carlotta said, "and that's exactly what's going to happen."

Now they regarded her as if she had gone totally around the bend. "You'll win if you end the strikes and you'll blackmail us into ending the strike after you win the vote," Susan Willaway said. "Seems to me your reasoning's a bit circular, *sister.*"

Carlotta paused. She forced a smile. Now it's time for the little self-fulfilling prophecy, she thought. Royce, don't let me down! "Seems to me you haven't looked at the numbers, *sister,*" she said. "I just unilaterally implemented an agreement to keep the Institute open for the duration of the Madigan Plan. Which means every bucko on the planet is going to vote for me."

"And every sister will vote against you," sneered a heavy-set committee member. "You think we're *afraid* of that kind of total polarization?"

No, Carlotta thought, that's exactly what you stupid bitches think you want! "I'll pick up enough female votes to win if you continue this strike," she said. "In fact, I'll get them over your politically dead bodies—when the male workers here end *their* strike unilaterally."

"*What?*"

Carlotta laughed. "What do they have left to strike about now?" she said. "I've given them what they wanted." She paused. "At this very moment, Royce is finalizing our agreement with them to do just that."

That brought them up a little short; the logic of it was self-evident, even to these politically naïve ideologues. If only Royce can close the loop on this self-fulfilling prophecy.

"And *that's* supposed to get you female votes?" Susan Willaway said, only a shade less confidently. "You openly sell your sisters out to the Transcendental Scientists and you've got the endorsement of the faschochauvinist strikers to prove it, and you expect a single sister to vote for you? You're pathetic, Carlotta Madigan!"

"And you've got your brain so far up your cunt you forget that there are Pacifican women who don't think the way you do," Carlotta snapped. "You're looking at one right now, you asshole! Twenty-five percent of the female electorate is unemployed now, thanks to these strikes. How many of those votes do I have to pick up to win with the buckos solidly behind me? Ten percent? Five? Three? You think three percent of those women aren't going to vote against you to get their jobs back? Are you really that stupid? You think every woman on this planet is a bug-brained fanatic like yourself?"

"You're disgusting!" Susan Willaway shouted.

"You're a traitor to your sex!"

"You're a tool of the faschochauvinists!"

They were screaming like godzillas with ironbush thorns up their asses now; in other words, they were on the run.

"Continue your strike, and you'll see just how disgusting I can really get," Carlotta said. "Give me a chance to make you godzilla-brained cretins the villains of the piece —the *only* ones keeping this planet from going back to work. The subversive pawns of the Femocrats. Un-Pacifican lesbian man-hating destroyers of the Pacifican economy. *Traitors!* And don't think I'd be beyond having you *indicted* for treason, either."

Carlotta smiled sweetly as the committee members balled their hands into impotent fists. "You know, I'm doing you a favor," she said. "I'm giving you a political out. The male strike is over, period. Continue *your* strike, and all you do is provide some cheap propaganda for the Bucko Power creeps and make my inevitable political victory a victory for Transcendental Science. Contrary to what you think, I don't want that any more than you do. But goddamn it, sisters, I'll take what I can get if you force me to!"

Carlotta stood up. "Enough," she said. "You agree to obey my order now, or the next step is the Ministry of Justice."

The committee members exchanged frustrated angry glances for a few moments. Susan Willaway finally spoke in a sullen, subdued voice. "If we end our strike, you'll announce it as our own voluntary decision?"

"We'll announce the end of both strikes simultaneously," Carlotta said. "You can all come up smelling like patriots."

"You guarantee a simultaneous end to the Bucko Power strike?"

Carlotta nibbled at her lower lip. Well what do I have to lose? she thought. "I told you that already," she said.

The committee members began muttering among themselves. After a few moments, Susan Willaway cut them off with a peremptory wave of the hand. No doubt as to who was really running *this* show! She glowered at Carlotta. She bit her lip. "On that basis, it seems we have no choice," she said quietly.

"None whatever," Carlotta said, fighting back a triumphant grin and extending her hand instead. Susan Willaway drew back with a disgusted snort. "Up yours, you traitor!" she snarled.

"Likewise, I'm sure," Carlotta said blithely. She turned her back and walked slowly out of the silent machine shop, knowing that the morning would see it humming with life, knowing that the vote of confidence was now won, knowing that she had once more steered the ship of state on a *Pacifican* course between the hard rocks of competing off-worlder ideologies. That is, she thought a shade more uncertainly, if Royce has had the same luck I have!

The glacial ice outside the environment dome marched on to infinity, a brilliant sheet of bluish sheen under a cloudless sky. Inside the dome, Royce Lindblad hunkered down with the three-man strike committee on the tread of a huge digger parked at the lip of an enormous pit mine, terraced with spiral roadways, littered with idle earth-moving behemoths. From the ice outside, to the crater of the pit mine, to the machinery itself, the scale of everything was surreally enormous, and the sense of isolation from the rest of the planet was thereby heightened. Yet this cruel and inhuman landscape was the industrial heartland of Pacifica. Here were the sooty mines, ugly factories, fumes, gases, and effluents that allowed the rest of the planet to function as an esthetic blend of natural and urban ecology.

And here were three tough gritty men who represented a work force that spent half the year in this grimy and frozen workshop of the world. The slavies of Pacifica, yet also its laboring aristocrats, making more money in half a year here than most Pacificans made working full-time. Enough to spend the other half of their lives as vacationers in the warm sun of the Island Continent.

Maybe that's why the strikes came here, Royce thought, and maybe that's why the Thule workers seem so indifferent to the mass unemployment afflicting the rest of the planet. When this is over, all it will cost them to catch up economically is the sacrifice of a month or two's vacation. *They* can afford a long ideological strike; their whole way of life is geared to it.

"Well buckos," Royce said easily, "I'm here to tell you that you've made your point. The Institute stays open at least through the trial period, so it's time to call off your strike."

"That's not quite the way we see it," Mike Lumly said. A squat, powerfully built man, he was one of the leaders of the Bucko Power movement, perhaps with a direct link to Falkenstein himself. Berliner and Como, the other two members of the strike committee, were his nominal equals, but seemed less politically oriented, local window-dressing for a movement that was probably directed by Falkenstein through Lumly. Royce wondered just how much leeway even Lumly had.

"Well then how *do* you see it?" Royce asked genially. He expected little trouble ending the male strike; it was Carlotta who had the heavy work cut out for her.

"We're all for what you and Madigan have done," Lumly said, "and we're even willing to swallow letting the effing Femocrats remain on Pacifica a while if that's what it takes to keep the Institute open. But the way we read it, Madigan implemented the agreement with Falkenstein without a Parliamentary majority, so if she loses the vote of confidence, we're no better than right back where we started from, maybe worse. We end our strike now and the unilateral Femocrat strike will force the new Parliament to close the Institute to save the economy."

"So," said Berliner, "we've decided to stand pat at least through the vote of confidence and see what happens."

"Yeah," said Como. "There's no percentage in relaxing the pressure now."

"But there is," Royce said. "If these strikes aren't ended before the vote, Carlotta will lose. But if they are, she wins for sure, and we can guarantee you that the Institute will stay open."

"Talk to the Femocrat strikers, not us," Lumly said skeptically. "They end their strike, we'll end ours. Otherwise—"

"Carlotta's doing that right now," Royce said. "And I can guarantee you that the women here will be back to work tomorrow."

"What?"

"Doesn't make sense. How do you expect to pull that off?"

Royce favored them with a we're-all-buckos-together smile. "Simple," he said. "Carlotta's told them that you've already agreed to end your strike, implying she's going to win the vote of confidence no matter what they do. So if they continue *their* strike, they're the heavies, and Carlotta wins over their dead bodies. We've got the little ladies tied up in knots, buckos!"

"We?" Lumly said harshly. "Where do you and Madigan come off announcing that we're going to end our strike? It's a *lie*, Lindblad, and you know it."

"Is it, Mike?" Royce said. "If that little lie ends the

Femocrat strike, doesn't it become the truth? You going to throw away a political victory like that just because Carlotta had her fingers crossed?"

"I don't like being used this way," Lumly said stubbornly.

"Aw, come off it, Mike," Como said. "We're getting what we wanted, aren't we? So what if it takes a little fancy footwork?"

"Yeah," Berliner said. "I think it's kind of cute."

"Quid pro quo," Royce said. "Carlotta wins the vote of confidence, and you get what you were striking for in the first place. Or have you forgotten just what that was?"

"I still don't like it," Lumly said. "It means ending our strike without really settling anything. The Institute's still temporary, the Femocrats are still here, and the only clear winner is Carlotta Madigan."

"Aw, for shit's sake, Mike!" Como said irritably. "What is this, your own personal ego-trip? Royce here delivers what he promises, and we've got no reason to keep striking."

"Yeah. And if we do, guess whose dead bodies Madigan wins over *then?* If the women go back to work and the Institute stays open, what the fuck do we claim we're striking for?"

"To kick the Femocrats off the planet! To make the Institute permanent. For Bucko Power!"

"Effing jellybelly oil, and you know it!"

Royce just sat there letting the two Thule techs go at Lumly and do his own work for him. It seemed to him that Lumly was parroting some line layed down by Falkenstein —that now Falkenstein, like the Femocrats, wanted this crisis to continue to a conclusion. That Bucko Power, once a means, had become an end for men like Lumly and perhaps for the Transcendental Scientists themselves. But it also seemed that plenty of men who supported the Institute, even Bucko Power types like Como and Berliner, still had the pragmatic detachment to know the difference between tactical means and open-ended godzilla-brained ideological demands. And that gave him a hope beyond winning this essentially inevitable tactical victory.

"Look Mike, we both agree to go along with Royce here and end the strike," Berliner finally said. "This is a democratic committee, and we outvote you, if you want to have it that way."

Como nodded in agreement. Lumly looked at Berliner, at Como, at Royce, meeting unsympathetic eyes at every station of the way. He frowned. He shrugged. "Okay," he said without any enthusiasm, "I guess I might as well make it unanimous."

"You won't be sorry," Royce said. He reached out his hand. Como and Berliner shook it with enthusiasm. Lumly handled it as if it were a moribund discray which might still have some sting left.

"I hope you're right, bucko," he said. "I only wish I knew where you and Madigan really stand."

"I thought we had made that pretty damn clear," Royce said.

"I'm not talking about these strikes, Lindblad, I'm talking about the big picture, the real issues. Ever since the *Heisenberg* came to Pacifica, you and Madigan have zigged and zagged, bought time and equivocated, and nobody really knows which side you're on. Bucko-to-bucko, Lindblad, where do you really stand?"

"Do I look like a Femocrat, bucko?" Royce said archly.

Como and Berliner laughed. "No, but your lady does, and she's the boss," Lumly said.

"She's the *Chairman*, Mike, and I'm the Minister of Media. We work together, we're a team, and believe me, Carlotta Madigan's no crypto-Femocrat! You really think I'd be getting it off with someone who was?"

"You telling me that the administration's going to come out on our side when the trial period's over and it's time to really decide?"

"Our side?" Royce said evasively. "*Whose* side?"

"The Institute. Your brothers. Bucko Power."

Royce paused, pondering how much he could afford to reveal. But anything said to Lumly would no doubt get back to Falkenstein, so while his heart longed to tell these buckos the whole truth, his mind told him that he dared not. "When this trial period is over, we intend to move to expel the Femocrats," he said. "And I'm personally convinced that there must be a Pacifican Institute of Transcendental Science."

"Then you *are* on our side!"

"Maybe more than you can understand right now,

bucko," Royce said. "We're on *Pacifica's* side. And I think
that's where your heart is, too. We've been trying to steer
a *Pacifican* course, a middle way. And I hope that by the
time this is over, we'll all be on the same side again. Not
as men and women but as Pacificans together. The way it
was. The way that worked. The way it was meant to be.
You think about that, buckos, and see if I'm not right."

Lumly snorted contemptuously, but the other two men
were silent and thoughtful, and Royce thought he could
sense a certain longing in them for the way things were, for
the time when men and women were Pacificans together,
when the ballet of the sexes was a dance of love, not war.
How could a man *not* want that in his heart of hearts?
What were men without the love of their women? What
were women without buckos beside them?

The shrill and frustrated creatures so many of us have
become.

Royce looked out over the gleaming white wastes of
Thule, where cold hard glaciers ground implacably against
each other, warring in sterile mindless stalemate like
Femocracy and Bucko Power, and the shape of the Parliamentary campaign to come appeared to him like a contrasting vision of green, organic fecundity.

Let them grind each other to bits with their own fanatic-
ism, he thought; let them rant and scream at the mind
and the crotch. While we speak softly and to the heart,
for the fields of Columbia, and the forests of the Cords,
and the green islands of home, for what this planet has
been for us and what we have been for each other. In the
end, with patience, and love, and grace, they'll spend
their energy against each other, and only the Pacifica of
our hearts will remain.

A medium closeup on Carlotta Madigan. Triumph shows
on her face, but it is tempered by a softness, a modesty,
even a humility. Behind her is a holo of a chain of green
islands floating in a sun-shimmered sea.

Carlotta: "My fellow Pacificans . . . tradition would
have me thank you for the enormous vote of confidence
you have just given me, but truth be told, the victory is
yours, not mine. The confidence you have expressed is in
yourself as Pacificans. In Thule, the most ardent supporters
of both Femocracy and Bucko Power have ended their

strikes to preserve the economy of the planet we all love. Even they have come together as Pacificans for Pacifica, and in this moment we are all brothers and sisters again . . ."

The hologram behind her dissolves into a panorama of the white Thule icecap under a curtain of fat, lazy falling snowflakes.

Carlotta: "Now there will be a new Parliamentary election, a bitterly fought campaign between candidates totally convinced that their way is right. The issues that divide us, men from women, lover from lover, will once more inflame our passions and divide us once more in political conflict. This is right, this is just, this is what democracy is meant to be . . ."

Behind her, the scene changes again: the wooded mountains of the eastern Cords rise above the sere brown desert of the Wastes like the eternal promise of spring.

Carlotta: "But democracy is also the middle path, the way between, the *only* means by which a divided people may find a new collective center and heal the wounds of its collective soul. And so I ask you in this coming time of strife to stand back and consider not only that which divides us but that which binds us together as well."

In the background, the Big Blue River winds between golden fields of ripening grain, and the thin white wake of a hydrofoil draws a calligraphic line between the lush banks.

Carlotta: "Amidst the shout and fury of Bucko Power and Femocracy, there will surely also be still clear voices calling for sanity, for the triumph of neither extreme. Men and women who remember what we had and who we are and what we must once again regain . . ."

Behind her, just the cold black star-speckled blackness of interplanetary space.

Carlotta: "I'm not telling you how to vote, my fellow Pacificans, I'm just asking you to remember what you have achieved today and to listen . . ."

A pinpoint of light grows in the center of the void, becomes a blue disc, then a bright mottled marble of blue, white, green, and brown, then the living planet of Pacifica challenging the darkness—fair, luminous, revolving with a stately grace, a huge and lovely orb backlighting Carlotta Madigan's pleading face.

Carlotta: "Listen to more than the claims and charges of Transcendental Science and Femocracy. We are a great people, blessed by our planet, ennobled by our history. made whole by our love, and today, if only for a moment, we have shown each other that we can be that again. I ask you only to listen with your hearts, to that clear inner voice, to Pacificans speaking as Pacificans for Pacifica, in the fullest confidence that if you do, the torch we have re-kindled together today can never die. Thank you all, and goodnight."

16

In her element now, commanding the kind of struggle she was trained to wage, Bara Dorothy sat behind her
desk, evaluating the district-by-district demographic data,
filling in the names of Femocratic Delegate candidates on
her master list as field operatives called them in, and
watching the total picture rapidly taking shape on the new
map of Pacifica that had been set up on the wall behind
her.

The planet had been divided up into Delegate districts,
color-keyed to the demographic balance. The overwhelmingly male Cords districts were a deep blue. Scattered
about Gotham, the Island Continent, and Thule were light
sprinklings of deep red districts, where sisters outnumbered
breeders by decisive margins, and there were similar
sprinklings of deep blue in Godzillaland, the Wastes,
Gotham, the Island Continent, and the Big Blue Valley,
where the breeders had what seemed like prohibitive margins. Perhaps another 20 percent of the districts were evenly
divided between pale blue and pink—here breeders and
sisters respectively held slight demographic edges, though
not enough to be really decisive. The bulk of the planet
was neutral white—in the majority of districts, the statis-

tical margin for error was greater than the deviation from an even 50–50 split.

Silver pins marked those districts in which the Femocratic League was already fielding candidates, and new pins were being added rapidly. Black pins marked districts with declared Bucko Power candidates, and Falkenstein's strategy was also swiftly taking shape. He was fielding candidates in all the deep and pale blue districts and most of the white, while avoiding the red and even the pink. But Bara Dorothy planned to run candidates in every district that wasn't solidly in the male column, including even the pale blue.

For the imponderables just might give us enough of the marginally male districts to control a slim Parliamentary majority, she thought. Every district has at least one wild-card candidate representing neither the League nor Bucko Power. If we can hold a solid female vote, these uncommitted candidates could siphon off enough breeder votes to give our people pluralities even in some of the marginally male districts. If you're not for us, you're against us, she thought, Bucko Power candidates and so-called "neutrals" alike . . . That just might confuse enough stupid breeders who might otherwise vote Bucko Power into voting for the wild cards . . .

As she had ordered, Mary Maria entered the command center to finalize the media blitz. As she had definitely *not* ordered, Cynda Elizabeth entered a few steps behind her. Cynda had been acting even more regressively than usual lately, if that were possible—arguing sullenly with every little decision, frequently in front of subordinates, almost taking a perverse public pleasure in pointing out that Bara's strike strategem had been a dismal failure, as if determined to emphasize her titular position as Leader, even as her real authority faded swiftly away. But since she *was* the titular Leader and had not yet committed an overtly regressive act, there was little that Bara could do about it. She couldn't even exclude her from this meeting, though she longed to. But some day soon, you'll make a real slip, you dirty little breeder-lover, and when you do . . .

"Well Mary, do you have a finalized media scenario?" Bara said as the two of them sat down in front of her desk, pointedly ignoring Cynda Elizabeth.

"I think so," Mary Maria said. "But the conditions of this election aren't exactly ideal. Seven days from beginning to end pretty well neutralizes our superior organization on a local level."

Bara Dorothy scowled. "Are you giving me excuses in advance? I would think that the exact opposite is true. We've got cells everywhere, whereas Falkenstein has to build a party organization almost from scratch."

Mary Maria fidgeted nervously. "Oh, Falkenstein's got worse problems than we do," she said. "On a party-to-party basis, we've got him beat. It's all these independent candidates that neither of us control. These damn Pacifican elections just aren't set up for party-to-party confrontations. *Every* candidate for Delegate gets a full-time local net channel, and the independents are people who have spent *years* becoming well-known locally. The Pacificans vote for local personalities, not political parties. They've never even *had* planetary political parties. Great Mother, even *Madigan* doesn't have a coherent political party behind her!"

"Well, they've got a planetary party *now*, don't they?" Bara snapped. *"Us.* Two parties, counting Falkenstein's Bucko Power front. Where's the problem? We've got a superior organization and an ideological position with a mass following—that should only help us smash both Falkenstein and this anarchic collection of so-called 'local personalities.' We're introducing sophisticated party politics into a primitive political matrix. How can we possibly not prevail?"

Mary Maria nodded, though somewhat more sycophantically than Bara would have liked. "That's essentially my analysis, Bara," she said. "I'm not saying we can't win, I'm saying that our media campaign has to emphasize our planetary platform. Forget about centrally produced campaign material for each local candidate and concentrate on selling Femocracy itself with a *planetary* media blitz."

Bara shook her head in agreement. "Vote for Sisterhood, not for a sister," she said. "That's essentially it, isn't it?"

"Very good!" Mary Maria exclaimed, with what seemed like real enthusiasm this time. "Maybe we can use that! And we should stick to three essential points and hammer them home: a vote for us is a vote *against* faschochau-

vinism, a Bucko Power vote is a vote *for* faschochauvinism; and most critically, a vote for an independent candidate is a vote for Carlotta Madigan, a traitor to her sex.
That's the essence of what I've layed out."

"Leave your detailed plans for me to study," Bara said,
"but it sounds good." Better than you realize, she thought.
It would be a mistake to become obsessed with the numeri-
cal outcome of this or any other election. Femocracy
could never decisively win an election on a planet where
breeders had equal rights. Every election should be seen
as merely a means for strengthening the unity and numbers
of Sisterhood and raising the consciousness of the local
sisters to the point where the will to power overrode any
residual squeamishness about electoral processes or constitutional niceties. Final victory could only come via some
sort of coup, and Mary Maria's scenario for this election
would serve to move Pacifican Sisterhood in that direction,
if nothing else.

Mary Maria sat a fat folder on Bara's desk and began to
rise. "Just a minute!" Cynda Elizabeth said. "I've got
something to say, and you'd better listen!"

What now? Bara Dorothy thought. Mary Maria glanced
uncertainly at Bara, at Cynda, at Bara again.

"You can go now, Mary," Bara said.

"No!" Cynda snapped. "This is for the record, and I
want a neutral witness."

Bara studied Cynda for a moment. The little breeder-
lover's face was pink with anger and tight with tension.
Perhaps this is the moment, Bara thought. Perhaps now
she's ready to go too far at last. A witness might not be
such a bad idea. "Very well," she said, "Mary stays. Deliver your pronouncement . . . *Leader.*"

Mary Maria sank back into her chair with a bemused
expression. Cynda Elizabeth seemed to calm herself somewhat, and when she spoke, her tone was cold and mechanically official.

"As Leader of this mission, I hereby express my official
disagreement with the policy you have decided to follow
in this election. It is my considered opinion that it will
result in a Parliament once more controlled by Carlotta
Madigan, in the eventual alienation of a majority of the
Pacifican population, in our eventual expulsion from this

planet, and therefore in the failure of our mission. If you go ahead with it, I want my dissent in the official record."

Bara gaped. She chuckled. She could hardly believe Cynda's stupidity or her own good fortune. "Let me get this straight," she said. "You're forcing me to declare this a doctrinal matter and formally overrule you?"

"That's right," Cynda said firmly. "The responsibility for the failure of the mission is now yours."

"And for the success as well," Bara said. "You *do* realize what that will mean, Cynda Elizabeth? You'll be officially on record as opposing my doctrinal interpretation, and you will be charged with impeding the implementation of a successful policy. The penalties—"

"—are the same as you will face for overruling me if this mission fails," Cynda snapped. "One of us will be vindicated, and the other will be disgraced, demoted, anathematized—"

"Or worse!"

"Or worse!"

This was just *too* easy! Bara Dorothy stared across the desk at Cynda Elizabeth, failing to fathom what was going on in that warped mind. She could not believe that Cynda had handed her the weapon of her own destruction. Did she seriously believe that the mission could fail? Was she planning to defect? Or had this atavistic Pacifican society finally snapped her sanity?

"I'm happy to stake my chances on success if you're stupid enough to stake yours on failure," Bara said. That in itself might be construed as an overt regressive act that would permit Cynda's arrest and detention, she thought. But if the Pacifican media found out about it . . . It was tempting, but not worth the risk. "Would you care to enlighten me with your brilliant analysis?"

The backbone seemed to go out of Cynda Elizabeth. She slumped backward in her chair, shook her head, and regarded Bara Dorothy woodenly. "I can *tell* you, Bara," she said, "but I'm afraid *enlightening* you is far beyond my meager capacity. Only events can do that, and even then . . ."

She shrugged. "For what it's worth, and for the record, Carlotta Madigan is a heroine to this planet now, and Lindblad is a hero. She staked her career on ending the strikes, and she won. Falkenstein has no real issue to fight her on for the moment, but he'll try because we're forcing him to contest this election. He'll split the bucko vote with her and—"

"Precisely!" Bara said. "They'll split the breeder vote between them and we'll capture the sisters!"

"Not if you run against Madigan, too," Cynda said. "The Institute fanatics will vote for Bucko Power candidates and the committed Femocrats will vote for ours, but the people between—"

"*What* people between, you little idiot!" Bara snorted.

Cynda sighed. She stared at Bara quizzically. "You really *don't* understand, do you?" she said. "To you, they're invisible. The Pacificans. The women who love men. The men who love women. People who care more about each other and their own planet than Femocracy or an Institute." She laughed. "That's who's going to defeat you, Bara—invisible people. Millions of them."

"A handful of atavistic pseudonationalistic reactionary primitives!"

Cynda smiled softly. "That's right," she said. "But not just a handful. A *planetful*."

Bara shook her head ruefully. There was no point in reasoning with Cynda Elizabeth now; the little wretch was clearly unbalanced, totally subverted by this outmoded Pacifican romanticism. Her doom was sealed, but she was so pathetically deranged that Bara now found herself taking little pleasure in the certainty of her destruction.

"I suppose you want *that* in the record, too," she said.

Cynda nodded quietly, with an idiotic show of calm confidence.

Bara sighed. "You may not believe this, Cynda," she said, "but I really do feel sorry for you. What you're doing to yourself is beyond my comprehension."

Cynda smiled ironically. "I *told* you that you were beyond my poor powers of enlightenment," she said.

A panoramic shot of a large crowd of female strikers picketing a factory in Valhalla. Bright sunlight streaming down through the environment dome paints the scene in vivid hues and bathes the strikers in an aura of cheerful and positive energy. Cut to a tighter shot of a small group of sullen male pickets around a pit mine, shot through a blue filter which leaches color and energy from the scene and creates an atmosphere of brooding, ugly tension. Super-imposed over this is a closeup of a leeringly triumphant Roger Falkenstein. This superimposition dissolves into one of Royce Lindblad, his expression an unwholesome blend of glee and craven subservience, which in turn dissolves into a closeup of a slump-shouldered, deenergized Carlotta Madigan.

Belligerent female voiceover: "What happened in Thule, sisters?"

The male picketers wave their fists and chant as if in answer: "Bucko Power! Bucko Power!"

Cut to a medium shot on Susan Willaway sitting on a workbench in a machine shop, her features contorted with righteous indignation.

Susan Willaway: "This is where Carlotta Madigan sold out her sisters to Transcendental Science's Bucko Power front! I was there! I saw the Chairman of Pacifica mouth-ing the orders of Royce Lindblad, who in turn was relaying them from Roger Falkenstein. And they admitted it to the whole planet on the net, remember?"

Cut to a two-shot on Royce and Carlotta.

Royce: ". . . we've been doing some hard negotiating with Roger Falkenstein and we've forced him into accept-ing the following modifications to the Madigan Plan . . ."

Carlotta: ". . . I am implementing this agreement as of today on my personal authority as Chairman . . ."

Royce: ". . . this is the Pacifican way of doing it . . ."

Carlotta: ". . . with this agreement now in hand, Royce and I are going down to Thule immediately and we won't come back until we've ended these strikes . . ."

Royce: ". . . the two of us have negotiated this agree-ment as a team, and we're going to end the strikes as a team . . ."

Royce and Carlotta smile at the camera and kiss.

Carlotta: "If *that* be treason to my sex, I say let's make the most of it!"

Cut to a closeup on a shrugging Susan Willaway.

Susan Willaway: "She said it herself, didn't she, and she certainly *did* make the most of it! The Madigan admin-istration secretly capitulated to Falkenstein, in return for which he called off the Bucko Power strike, leaving *us* no choice but to go along or be branded the sole destroyers of the Pacifican economy. And we all know the results—

the Institute stays open, the Madigan Plan remains in force, and Carlotta Madigan wins her vote of confidence—all courtesy of Roger Falkenstein and Transcendental Science! *Pacifica for the Pacificans indeed!"*

Cut to the previous two-shot of Royce and Carlotta kissing.

Carlotta: "If *that* be treason to my sex, I say let's make the most of it!"

A rapidly cut series of shots: the Institute building, a Bucko Power march, a cut from *"Soldiers of Midnight"* in which two men in black bugger helpless women, a two-shot on Royce and Carlotta in which Royce seems dominant and supreme.

Carlotta's voiceover: "If *that* be treason to my sex, I say let's make the most of it!"

A very rapidly cut montage of local Femocratic League of Pacifica candidates addressing crowds, talking to women in the streets, speaking into cameras. Superimposed over this is a still shot of Carlotta Madigan tinted a bilious blue-green.

Female voiceover, mimicking Carlotta with heavy irony: ". . . I'm not telling you how to vote, my fellow Pacificans . . ."

Susan Willaway's voiceover: "If that be treason to our sex, *I* say let *us* make the most of it!"

"Bucko Power on the march!"

A full shot of orderly ranks of men marching across the screen from left to right. Hard cut to similar phalanxes marching in the opposite direction, then back to the first shot. Back and forth, left, right, left, the rhythm of the cutting moving to the martial beat of the stamping feet.

Male voiceover: "Fresh from their victory over the repressive Femocratic forces in Thule, the buckos of Pacifica are now uniting to preserve Pacifican democracy from the impending Femocratic coup . . ."

Cut to an establishing shot of the interior of the Parliament chamber. Most of the Delegate seats are occupied by belligerent-looking women. The few male Delegates are effete types wearing lacy blue tunics. Armed female guards surround the floor of the chamber and stand among the Delegates. A squat, muscular, short-haired woman in a military uniform occupies the Chairman's seat and addresses Parliament.

Chairman: "Resolved that the media access laws, the right of assembly, the male franchise, and further elections be suspended until further notice in order to preserve the internal security of Femocratic Pacifica. In favor?"

A loud chorus of "Ayes."

"Opposed?"

A pregnant silence broken only by a series of ominous clicks as the female guards cock their guns.

Chairman: "I declare the resolution passed—*unanimously.*"

Cut to a medium shot of a graying, wise-looking Transcendental Scientist sitting by a very impressive-looking computer.

Transcendental Scientist: "Their record on other planets makes the strategy of the Femocrats in this election quite transparent. Since men are roughly half of any planetary population, Femocracy participates in democratic processes only to destroy them. Once they achieve even a temporary controlling majority in any government, they always act swiftly and ruthlessly to establish a permanent Femocratic dictatorship."

Cut to a two-shot of two men having a heavy political discussion at a Gotham sidewalk café.

First man: "Well, Carlotta Madigan doesn't want that! The effing Femocrats themselves are calling her a traitor!"

Second man: "Aw, that's the oldest trick in the book! They attack poor old Carlotta so enough saps like you will vote for fence-sitting nerds to split the bucko vote and elect a Femocrat Parliament. After all, what allows the effing Femocrats to stay here and subvert this election in the first place?"

First man (comprehension drawing on his face): *"The Madigan Plan!"*

Second man: "And you really think any *woman* is going to have the balls to kick the Femocrats off Pacifica?"

First man: "I guess what we need is a real *man* as Chairman for a change . . . Say, who *was* the last bucko Chairman?"

Cut to a closeup on Mike Lumly. The camera pulls back to reveal the large male crowd he is addressing in front of the main entrance to Parliament.

Lumly: "Who *really* ended the Femocrat strike that was destroying our economy? *(He jerks a thumb at the Parliament building.)* Those ball-less wonders?"

Crowd: "NO!"

Lumly (sardonically): "Our *lady* Chairman?"

Crowd: "NO!"

Lumly: *"Who* saved Pacifica?"

Crowd: "WE DID!"

Lumly: "And how did we do it?"

Crowd: "BUCKO POWER! BUCKO POWER!"

Lumly: "And what's the only answer to Femocrat subversion of this election?"

Crowd: "BUCKO POWER! BUCKO POWER! BUCKO POWER!"

Lumly: "And what's a man who votes for anyone but a Bucko Power candidate?"

Crowd: "A BALL-LESS BREEDER!"

Cut back to a reprise of the opening shots: phalanxes of men marching back and forth across the screen, left, right, left, the rhythm of the cutting and the marching feet creating a drumfire of righteous power and determination.

Male voiceover: "Bucko Power on the march! For freedom, for democracy, for Pacifica—and for a new Parliament with the *balls* to preserve them!"

A full shot on two feathery roly-poly bumblers—one wearing a silly pink ballet skirt, the other stuffed into a black leather uniform—as they whonk and babble at each other, bumping bellies belligerently. Cut to a similar shot on two humans in male and female clown suits, one wearing a mask that caricatures Roger Falkenstein, the other wearing a grotesque Cynda Elizabeth mask, as they squirt each other in the face with traditional seltzer bottles.

Cut to a long shot on a mixed crowd of men and women on a stylized mock-up of a Gotham street. The women wear enormous false pink breasts, the men wear giant red rubber wongs, and all of them are in clown makeup. A man creams a woman in the face with a gooey cream pie. The woman retaliates in kind. In a few moments, dozens of pies are flying through the air, then hundreds. Soon everyone is coated with white pie-filling as the great battle continues to escalate. Barrages of pies fall from the buildings. Finally, there is an ominous whistling sound like a missile falling, and an immense ten-meter cream pie falls from the sky onto the fray with a godlike splat.

Caption: "THE PINK AND BLUE WAR!"

Cut to a two-shot of Carlotta Madigan and Royce Lindblad as they walk together on the beach at Lorien lagoon.

Royce: "Boys will be boys!"

Carlotta: "And girls will be girls!"

They begin raving at each other in mock anger.

Royce: "And so's your mother!"

Carlotta: "And you're another!"

Rugo waddles into the frame from the left, stands between them, glances back and forth at the two of them in rather patronizing indignation, and delivers a sermon.

Rugo: "Whonk-ka whonk ka-whonkity? Whonk *whonk* ka-*whonkity* whonk? Whonk, whonk, whonka!"

Royce and Carlotta look appropriately chastened and embarrassed.

Royce (foolishly): "Well, you see, jocko, it's like this, we humans are having a very serious election campaign. The men are afraid that the women are going to bite their wongs off . . ."

Carlotta: ". . . and the women are afraid that the men are going to confine them to purdah . . ."

Rugo bounces up and down cackling.

Royce (indignantly): "It's *not* a joke; it's *serious!* Just ask Pacificans for the Institute or the Femocratic League of Pacifica, and they'll set you straight."

Rugo, disbelieving, continues to bounce and cackle. After a moment, he pauses, looks up at Carlotta, then at Royce, both of whom have put on expressions of mock anger. He shakes his head slowly, sadly. He makes cooing throaty noises. He grabs Royce's hand in his big flexible bill and places it in Carlotta's. He rubs his body against both of them, turns to face the camera, and whonks contentedly.

The camera moves in for a closeup of Royce and Carlotta, smiling together now. The frame freezes, then solarizes into an abstract ikon of loverly bliss. This slowly dissolves into a lyrical series of shots of lovers that melt into each other to dreamy romantic music. Two faces coming together in a kiss, silhouetted by a rich seascape sunset. A naked couple walking hand-in-hand through a forest in balletlike slow motion. A couple making love in a feather-soft white snowbank under a jeweled night sky.

Soft female voiceover: "Pacifica is for lovers . . ."

Mellow male voiceover: "And lovers are for Pacifica . . ."

A closeup on Rugo, looking dreamy and contented now. The camera pulls back for a longer shot, showing Royce, Carlotta, and Rugo ambling slowly together down Lorien beach. The camera moves in again for a two-shot on Royce and Carlotta.

Royce (sardonically): "But *men* will be *men* . . ."

Carlotta: ". . . and *women* will be *women*."

Cut to a closeup on Rugo.

Rugo (in a rather cute quacking voice): "But *humans* will be humans if they stop whonking at each other like bumblers."

Cut to a full shot on a Bucko Power candidate haranguing a small streetcorner crowd of men. His mouth, his arms, the fist-shaking gesticulations of the crowd—all are in jerky fast-motion. Moving in graceful contrasting slow motion, Royce and Carlotta move into the frame and bracket the speaker.

Speaker (in filtered mechanical voice): "Down with Femocracy! Power to the penis! We demand what we deserve."

Royce and Carlotta glance at each other meaningfully, shrug.

Royce: "He *asked* for it . . ."

Magically, they both produce cream pies and slam them in the speaker's face from both sides.

Royce and Carlotta: "Pacifica for the Pacificans!"

Cut to a similar shot of a wild-eyed woman hectoring a female crowd. Royce and Carlotta move into the frame, flank the speaker, and look questioningly at the crowd.

Speaker: "Sisters! Speak out for your rights! Tell these faschochauvinist dupes what you want! Let me hear it! Let me have it!"

Carlotta grins at the crowd and raises her hand like an orchestra conductor.

Crowd: *"Pacifica for the Pacificans!"*

Pies fly from both sides, creaming the speaker's face with white goo.

Cut to a two-shot on Royce and Carlotta walking on Lorien beach.

Carlotta: "Of course, this election is serious business."

Royce (fatuously): "In fact, I've never seen so many *serious* people shooting their damn fool mouths off in my life. If you believe what you hear, Carlotta's sold out the women of Pacifica to Transcendental Science and sold out the men to Femocracy, both at the same time. How'd you manage *that* trick, babes?"

Carlotta (waving her hands like a magician): "The hand is quicker than the eye!"

Royce: "And if you believe that, you must believe in the tooth fairy, too."

Carlotta: "Personally, I make a practice of believing in two impossible things before breakfast. Today it was Transcendental Science and Femocracy."

Royce: "Well, *we've* had *our* fun, fellow Pacificans . . ."

A huge hand shoves a big cream pie into the foreground of the shot as if handing it to the viewer.

Carlotta: "But come election day, it'll be *your* turn to throw the pie!"

Royce Lindblad giggled, turned away from his net console, and gave Carlotta a big grin. "They don't know what's hitting them!" he said. "Falkenstein's bellowing like a wounded godzilla, and the Femocrats won't even talk to newshounds. Their campaigns are disasters, and they can't even figure out why."

Carlotta shook her head, paced around his office, glanced at the depth poll figures on the access screen, and sat down on the arm of Royce's lounger. "To tell you the truth, I'm not sure why either," she said. "I thought this media blitz you layed out was crazy, but . . ."

"But it's working, isn't it?" Royce said somewhat smugly.

The depth poll figures might not be ideal, but the shape of the new Parliament was already clear. Planetwide, the projected vote now broke down as 23 percent Femocrat, 30 percent Bucko Power, 31 percent for the vague Pacifica for the Pacificans movement, and 12 percent undecided with two days of campaigning left. Neither Transcendental Science nor the Femocrats had a prayer of forming a new government, and a paralyzed Parliament would mean maintaining the status quo by default—a Madigan Chairmanship and a continuation of the Madigan Plan. And a considerable portion of the population, male and female, was at least temporarily coming to see the whole Pacifican Pink and Blue War as some kind of hideous joke.

"If there's one thing you can count on fanatics to do when it's escalation time, it's lose their sense of humor," Royce said. "They're screaming foul slok at us and each other and they just can't comprehend why we're just counterpunching with cream pies. And still less why it's working as well as it has."

Carlotta took another, longer look at the depth poll figures. "But I think we've milked the fun-and-games approach as far as we can," she said. "Seems to me, anyone who's *still* committed to Femocracy or Bucko power after all *this* is going to vote that way no matter what anyone does in the next two days. I'd expect the undecided to break roughly in thirds, so that's not going to affect the outcome either . . ."

"Yeah," Royce said.

"Which means no one will have the votes to oust me from the Chairmanship or repeal the Madigan Plan or dare to force a vote of confidence on *anything* for the duration of the trial period."

Royce nodded. "You could call it constructive paralysis," he said.

"But when the trial period is up, we've got to be in a position to get through a resolution expelling the Femocrats and Transcendental Scientists, or at least win an electronic vote of confidence and elect a new Parliament that will pass it if this one votes it down. So . . ."

"So?"

Carlotta got up and began pacing the office again. "*So* since the outcome of this election is already decided, we should start playing the endgame *now*. Get heavier and nastier so that the result of this election isn't just a cream pie, but a ringing endorsement of Pacifica for the Pacificans. Of me. Of us. Of the Madigan Plan. Of Pacifican nationalism." She grinned crookedly at Royce. "It's time to change the media blitz and make us heroes, babes."

Royce laughed. "I suppose I can hold my nose and do it," he said. "Carlotta Madigan and Royce Lindblad, saviors of the Pacifican way of life, champions of Pacifica for the Pacificans, the golden couple, and so forth . . ." He grimaced wryly. "As long as we don't start believing it ourselves."

Carlotta laughed. She looked down at him with what seemed like a perfectly straight face. "Why not?" she said archly. "Isn't it the truth?"

A medium shot on Royce Lindblad and Rugo. Royce is apparently involved in a serious conversation with the fat little bumbler, but he's whonking and squawking like a bumbler himself. Hard cut to a tighter shot on Carlotta Madigan as she flings a pie into the face of a male speaker. Cut to a full shot on two figures made up as clowns, their faces ludicrous caricatures of Royce and Carlotta, as they grope each other obscenely, squirt the camera with seltzer bottles, and finally heave a barrage of pies at a large hologram of Pacifica in the background.

Cut to a two-shot on Roger Falkenstein and Mike Lumly sitting in a viewing balcony at the Institute, with the Godzillaland jungle in the background.

Falkenstein (shaking his head in bemusement): "Can *you*, as a native Pacifican, explain the antics of your two leading politicians? Their serious political discourse seems to consist of soft porn, pie-throwing, and . . . uh, talking to dumb animals. Is *this* the traditional Pacifican way of choosing a government? Have our psychohistorians missed something?"

Lumly (righteously): "They've got nothing serious to say, so they're reduced to making public asses of themselves."

Falkenstein: *"Nothing serious to say?* In the face of an impending Femocrat coup? With the existence of this Institute at stake? The Chairman of Pacifica can contribute nothing more to the political debate than low humor, pretty pictures of the landscape, and xenophobic rantings about 'Pacifica for the Pacificans'?"

Lumly: "There's only one issue in this campaign: whether or not Pacifica is going to become a Femocrat dictatorship. Any Femocrat is going to vote for her own kind, and any real bucko knows that the only alternative is to support Bucko Power all the way. So who's left to vote for crypto-supporters of Madigan? Just a handful of fools who don't take the real threat seriously. So Madigan's campaign theme is nothing but honest: a vote for a Madigan supporter is a pie in your own face."

A triple split-screen shot. On the right, a long shot of the Parliament chamber, filled with female Delegates, sprinkled with armed female troops. On the left, the shot of Royce and Carlotta as clowns, heaving pies and squirting seltzer. In the center of the screen and dominating the shot, a rapidly cut montage of the wonders of Transcendental Science—buildings springing up instantly, an artificial sun transforming the icy wastes of Thule into a green garden, an ancient man blossoming forth with new youth and vigor.

Singing male chorus to the beat of marching feet:
"Which side are you on?
"WHICH SIDE ARE YOU ON?"

Two shots alternating with each other again and again: Nero playing his violin on a balcony while Rome burns below him and hairy barbarians pillage and rape in the flaming streets; Carlotta Madigan on a similar balcony overlooking Gotham, kissing Royce while a similar horde of barbarians—Neanderthals stuffed into black military tunics—rape women in the streets below and wave "Bucko Power" placards.

Female voiceover (sardonically): "Pacifica for the Pacificans!"

Ancient film footage of Nazi stormtroopers smashing windows and beating Jews with truncheons, Adolf Hitler addressing a frenzied Nuremburg rally, tanks rolling through the ruined streets of a city.

Female voiceover: "Germany for the Germans!"

A long shot on an altar atop a great stone pyramid. The steps are lined with bound captives, and at the pinnacle, an Indian priest rips out a beating human heart with an obsidian knife.

Female voiceover: "Mexico for the Aztecs!"

A rapidly cut series of shots of tremendous nuclear explosions vaporizing Paris, New York, London, Peking, Moscow.

Female voiceover: "Earth for machismo!"

Cut to a closeup on Susan Willaway, looking straight into the camera with righteous indignation.

Susan Willaway: "Throughout human history, rabid appeals to irrational nationalism have always been the last desperate resort of ideologically bankrupt demagogues. It took Femocracy to put a stop to it on Earth, sisters, and now that Pacifica is about to be liberated from faschochauvinism, why of course our own little tinhorn demagogue, Carlotta Madigan, dredges up this filthy jingoistic slime from the atavistic past and attempts to hide her treason behind a shit-smeared screen of nationalistic muck! It can't happen here . . . ?"

A series of shots of Bucko Power demonstrations—marching men, waving fists, distorted shouting faces—all to the terrible music of stomping jackboots.

Susan Willaway's voiceover: "But it *is* happening here! *Pacifica for the Pacificans!* But what kind of Pacifica for which Pacificans is Carlotta Madigan ranting for? Who is responsible for the continued existence of an Institute metastisizing its foul poison through the body politic like a loathsome cancer! Carlotta Madigan! Who sold out her sisters to Transcendental Science? Carlotta Madigan! Who is therefore responsible for the faschochauvinist animals rioting in our streets? Carlotta Madigan, and her Machiavellian breeder, Royce Lindblad!"

Cut to a closeup on Susan Willaway.

Susan Willaway: "Why has Carlotta Madigan failed to answer the charge of treason against her? Because she *has* no answer! Instead, she gives us circuses, the Madigan Plan, an Institute, outmoded nationalistic chauvinism, and calls it Pacifica for the Pacificans! And what kind of Pacifica will that be if she succeeds? Just what we have now— a Pacifica ruled by Falkenstein through Madigan's breeder, where Bucko Power fanatics are allowed to run riot in the streets, where democratic strikes by Sisterhood are broken by blackmail or force, where the beast reigns supreme! Pacifica for the Pacificans? Pacifica for faschochauvinist swine and their lackeys and dupes!"

A panoramic shot of a huge and orderly Femocratic League of Pacifica rally, in which the camera first focuses on a section of the crowd, and then slowly reverse-zooms upward and outward, so that the army of women seems to expand toward the horizon in all directions, filling the field of vision to infinity as if it covered the world.

Female voiceover: "But Sisterhood is strong, Sisterhood is united, and Sisterhood will not be fooled by meaningless slogans. Pacifica for the Pacificans . . . ?"

A tremendous amplified shout from the crowd: *"SISTERHOOD FOR PACIFICA! PACIFICA FOR SISTERHOOD!"*

A closeup of Carlotta Madigan seated in front of a large hologram of Pacifica, looking cool, tranquil, humbly satisfied with herself.

Carlotta Madigan: "Tomorrow you will vote, my fellow Pacificans, and thereby consign to well-earned oblivion the most vicious and un-Pacifican campaign in the history of our planet."

Behind her, a montage of Bucko Power demonstrations, striking workers, Femocratic League rallies, angry, animalistic, shouting male and female faces.

Carlotta Madigan: "Where once our political differences were economic and philosophical and settled in the democratic spirit of compromise, now they seem to revolve around the nature of our genitals and are not to be compromised at all. The Femocrats accuse Transcendental Science of subversion, and Transcendental Science accuses Femocracy of plotting a coup, and they both accuse *me* of treason and atavistic nationalism, and *I* accuse *them* of interference in our way of life, and, my fellow Pacificans, *all of us are right!"*

Behind her now, a shot of Pacifica as seen from far off in space, a luminous marble alone in the darkness.

Carlotta Madigan: "I rue the day that these off-worlders insinuated themselves into this solar system by lies, deceit, and trickery. If what they have both done to shatter our harmony is not subversion, *what is?* If what they have done is not interference in our way of life, *how much further must they go?* Were I not a traitor to both Femocracy and Transcendental Science, could I be true to the planet I love, could I sleep at night? *And with whom?* If an overriding faith in our own people, in what we've built together, in who we are, is chauvinistic nationalism, I say let us wave that flag and wave it proudly!"

Behind her, the camera zooms in on Pacifica till it becomes a huge globe. The planet stylizes into a circle of green, brown, white, and blue in the center of a black flag of space, waving in the breeze behind Carlotta against an azure sky.

Carlotta Madigan: "For while the gross excesses of this campaign must fill every reasonable Pacifican with disgust and loathing, I say we have much to be proud of, too. Without our total devotion to free media access, none of this vicious propaganda would have disturbed our tranquility. Were we not first, last, and always a democratic society, the government of Pacifica would have long since crushed this off-worlder subversion with an iron hand. Did we not still believe in our democratic instincts, in our planet, and in ourselves, this putrid mess would not exist."

The camera moves in for an extreme closeup on Carlotta Madigan, as she shrugs and smiles ruefully.

Carlotta Madigan: "Our apparent weakness is our greatest strength, and we all know it in our hearts. A great man said it all centuries ago: 'Democracy is the worst of all possible political systems—excepting all the others!'"

The camera pulls back for a longer shot on Carlotta as images fade into each other behind her—bustling Gotham streets, sailboats riding the breezes of the Island Continent, mano lumberjacks scampering up giant trees in their Superigs, men and women working together in a Valhalla machine shop, Columbians harvesting golden fields of grain.

Carlotta Madigan: "And I believe that this too shall pass. When the votes have been counted, and the shouting has died, men and women alike will have united to preserve Pacifican democracy. I think I know my own people better than any off-worlder ideologue can. I understand. You understand. Beyond *any* momentary issue, beyond any bug-brained ideology, you believe that in the end, reason, sanity, love, compromise, the spirit of our democracy—these must be preserved, and these shall prevail."

An extreme closeup on Carlotta Madigan as she cocks her head at the camera and grins.

Carlotta Madigan: "Femocrats and Transcendental Scientists alike will say that my people believe this because they are stupid. I believe it, too."

As evening moved toward midnight and the running vote tallies swiftly firmed up into certainties, a gloomy silence descended upon the Institute's main staff lounge. Soon no one was talking to anyone else, and least of all were any of the psychopoliticians daring to venture any opinion to Dr. Roger Falkenstein.

Their analyses had been useless, their strategy had failed, and not even the Arkmind had predicted *this*. Late returns might switch a close race here or there, but the shape of the new Parliament was now a certainty: thirty-one seats for Femocratic Delegates, twenty-nine or thirty Bucko Power seats, and something over forty for the loose coalition of independents backed by Royce Lindblad and Carlotta Madigan.

Sitting in front of the big net console, his depression and displeasure wrapped around him like a cloak of isolation, Falkenstein tried to understand what had happened, what had gone wrong, and he was in no mood to listen to any of the experts who had failed him.

One thing, at least, was clear—trying to paint Madigan as a dupe of the Femocrats had been a dismal tactical error, a stupid reflex-action to the Femocrats' attempt to portray her as a traitor controlled by Transcendental Science. Had we gone along with *their* gross error and *accepted* support for Madigan as support for us, he thought, the dominant Madigan faction might now be something of an ally. Instead, she's made it clear that this victory is going to be seen as a rejection of *all* off-world influence, a triumph of Pacifican nationalism. We were too ambitious, Falkenstein thought. We shouldn't have contested this election as an independent force, we should have let the Femocrats isolate themselves and quietly cooperated with Carlotta Madigan.

But we didn't, he thought, rising and raking the room with his gaze. That's the past, and it can't be changed. He noticed that the staff people were averting their eyes defensively, as if anticipating deserved recrimination. Recrimination might be deserved, but it was useless as well.

Falkenstein grimaced. The staff would be useless at least until tomorrow, when they would have digested the sour meal of failure and be ready once more to face the future.

Without a word to anyone, he left the lounge, walked down a series of empty brooding hallways, and stood in one of the viewing balconies overlooking the black Pacifican night. Beyond the electronic barrier, dark shapes thrashed and moved amid the deeper darkness of the jungle. Overhead, the stars were mere pinpoint abstractions, unreal and very far away. Somewhere up there the *Heisenberg* would be moving grandly across the impassive firmament, but now it was invisible, and Falkenstein could not remember ever feeling so isolated and alone. Only the ghost of Maria stood at his side, like the phantom presence of a freshly amputated limb, palpable only through the pain of its absence.

Since that day when she had left his bed for the dormitory, even the time they did spend together had become an unreal dull torment, filled at first with arguments, and then with a forced and artificial normalcy that, under the circumstances, seemed like the most painful sort of madness.

They were strangers to each other now—worse, the pain of that estrangement was made more poignant by the memory of what had been for so very long, and the conviction of each that the other was to blame widened the abyss with every passing hour.

Falkenstein longed to be with Maria in this moment of total loneliness, but the Maria he longed for was the Maria that had been. The Maria that was would only exacerbate his loneliness with the triumphant vindication of her emotionalism over his logic. Were it rationally possible to hate an entire planet, Falkenstein thought, I would hate Pacifica with the passion of an outraged cuckold.

He sighed, moved closer to the transparent wall of the viewing balcony, and collapsed into a chair. Such thoughts only divert my attention from the problem at hand, he told himself firmly. Hate, rage, emotion itself are hardly what's called for now. I'm faced with a situation, and I must think it through logically.

And things could be worse, he told himself, reaching for optimism. The *Femocrats* could be in control of the new Parliament. Instead, Carlotta Madigan is in effective control, and she's at least committed to keeping the Institute open for the whole trial period. The new student body is installed, the Institute is functioning, and the crunch won't come until the trial period is up, three-and-a-half months from now. The only operative question is the matter of a scenario for the interval between.

What to do . . . ? What can we learn from this current fiasco . . . ? He grimaced. *Maria* would say that this election proved that the Pacificans have become so fed up with off-worlder meddling that they've been pushed into uniting against us and the Femocrats alike. No doubt she sees this as the triumph of some rude sort of social justice, some superior Pacifican democratic esthetic.

But however wrong-headed that emotional value judgment may be, he reflected, the psychopolitical analysis is essentially correct. Maria understood that in a raw emotional way, and it would seem that Carlotta Madigan understood it with cold political precision.

Therefore, Falkenstein realized with instant clarity, the thing to do now is precisely . . . *nothing*. No more media blitzes till the climactic vote on a permanent Institute is at hand. Let the Bucko Power movement go its own way. Maintain a low profile for the duration. While—if we're lucky and they're foolish—the Femocrats continue to polarize the women against the men, make themselves the main enemy of the Pacifican nationalism that's been stirred up, alienate that middle 40 percent, perhaps enlarge it, and burn themselves out.

Falkenstein rose to his feet buoyed by new energy—energy and a new kind of hope. Politically, such a scenario might be mere temporizing, a pragmatic admission that forces beyond his control now dominated the situation, but on a *personal* level . . .

On a personal level, Maria would *approve* of this approach. She would see it as a vindication of her own feelings toward the people of this planet, as a personal compromise between them, as his loving attempt at a private rapprochement. It can bring us together again! he thought excitedly. The loss of this election can give me back my wife!

With the anxious ardor of a courting adolescent, Falkenstein searched the Institute building for Maria. She wasn't in the staff lounge, nor was she in the commissary or any of the viewing balconies, and her dormitory bed was empty. Some personal reticence, an unwillingness to display a private emotion publicly, his secret shame at the failure in his personal life, kept him from asking after her. So he searched the building in solitary silence, and only when he had satisfied himself that she wasn't there did the thought occur to him that perhaps he had underestimated the love that still existed between them.

Perhaps even now she was waiting in their private quarters to comfort him in what she would surely perceive as his hour of defeat. Of course! he thought. How stupid of me! Where else would your wife be when you needed her most? She's waiting there for me while I've been running around here like a fool. Perhaps she's even moved back in. Come to think of it, I do believe her clothing *was* missing from the dormitory.

He dashed out of the building into the sweltering Godzillaland night, not even bothering to pause to erect his inertia-screen. By the time he had covered the fifty meters of open space to their private habitat, his breath was ragged and his clothes rank with sweat. But he barely noticed either the monstrous heat or its sudden absence as he entered their cool quarters.

"Maria? Maria?" The living room was empty. The dining room was empty. The study was empty. "Maria . . . ?"

With a mounting sense of panic, Falkenstein entered the bedroom. Empty as well. Not a sign of her return.

Then he noticed the red message light on the panel of the small net console. Woodenly, he punched the recall button, and collapsed, slump-shouldered, on the foot of the bed, as Maria's face appeared on the utility screen—tense, drawn, quavering, but frozen into a mask of grim resolution.

"Roger, by the time you see this, I'll already be in a liner for Gotham. I can't stand it here any more. I can't stand what we've been doing, and I can't stand being so close to you and yet so far away. I don't know what I want to do; I only know I need time and space and aloneness in which to think. As I record this, I'm watching the election results, and what's happening has confirmed my female emotionalism with hard statistical data . . ."

Her voice became more shrill, and the line of her mouth hardened. "What we've done here is *wrong*, and now we're paying for it. I don't know what we can do about it, but I'm grateful to the people of Pacifica who seem quite able to preserve themselves. Failure seems to make the guilt I bear a little easier to take, but it's not enough, and I don't know what is . . ."

Her voice began to tremble, her mouth quivered, and her eyes filled with tears.

"I know this is cowardly of me, Roger. I should've faced

you in person. But sad to say, I'm not sure you would have let me go had I placed that power in your hands. So . . . so . . . goodbye for now, I'll call you from Gotham . . . and try to believe that in some way I still love you . . ."

The tape ran out and Falkenstein found himself sitting there staring dumbly at the dead screen. Fury, pain, loss seemed emotions too picayune with which to confront this unfathomable, unfaceable moment. They passed through him like transient electric shocks, leaving him drained of all emotion, leached of all possibility of thought, unable to even react. His being was as dark and cold and lonely as the dead and empty reaches of the space between the stars.

17

SKIMMING OVER THE CALM WATERS OF THE BAY TOWARD
Parliament on her floater in the bright blue morning, Carlotta Madigan wondered if the unreal tranquility which had
descended on Pacifica these past two months was a genuine
return to harmony or just the lull before a greater storm.

An exhausted ease had enveloped the planet since the
Parliamentary election, at least compared to the frenzy of
the previous months. Once more, the primary business of
government had become the economy, and cleaning up the
mess left by the Thule strikes seemed to have sucked up
any excess political energy left over from this rather eerie
cooling of the Pink and Blue War. The temporary raw
materials shortage had necessitated the setting up of temporary quotas and allocations, along with a complex system of standby gov price-fixing for virtually all manufac-
tured goods, and the sudden drop in disposable income
caused by the temporary mass unemployment had to be
cured by the prepayment of abnormally high citizen's
dividends.

Ordinarily, an economic package of this complexity and
scope would have meant a long, arduous debate in Parliament, but the whole thing had sailed through in four days
with hardly a murmur, giving Carlotta a strangely unset-

tling sense of her own enhanced power over the new Parliament. Naïvely, one could put it down to a quiet orgy of patriotic cooperation, but more realistically it seemed that both the Femocrat and Bucko Power factions were walking on eggs, neither side daring to do *anything* that might provoke her into a coalition of convenience against the offending party.

As a result, she had the virtual de facto power to rule by decree, and while this certainly made life easier, there was something quite unhealthy about it that made her perversely long for the more usual perpetual political tug-of-war.

Truth be told, this quiet interregnum was not quite what Carlotta had expected. The Femocratic League and Pacificans for the Institute continued to organize, but the mass rallies and heavy media blitzes had faded away, as if both sides had realized that their attempts to polarize men and women against each other had reached the point of diminishing returns in the last election, had created a third force more dangerous to both than each was to the other. She had to admit that she found such political flexibility and subtlety on the part of the off-worlders both surprising and somewhat unnerving.

For now the outcome was almost entirely in the hands of the handful of Pacifican scientists that Royce had secreted in the Institute. Unless the viability of a totally Pacifican Institute could be demonstrated by the end of the Madigan Plan period, polarization would swiftly become total as the 40 percent in between was *forced* to choose sides, and the electorate would be so evenly divided than an enforceable democratic decision might very well become impossible to make, and democratic government itself could collapse.

Carlotta reached the lip of the main Parliament landing, floated onto the shore, and paused for a moment, looking back across the bay at the island heart of the city. The brilliant morning sun sparkled off the towers and domes; the faery traceries of the bridges bustled with pedestrian traffic; floaters and hydrofoils scrawled their white-water calligraphy on the blue waters; the city was a picture of commerce, tranquility, and reassuring normalcy.

But behind that façade, what stratagems were being hatched, what plots were forming, what was really going on in the cafés and offices, the backrooms and the bedrooms? In quiet Ministry buildings, Royce and his spies were working on her secret plan for the confrontation soon to come. But what were the *other* sides doing behind the eerie truce?

"Well, where do we stand now, Hari?" Royce Lindblad asked somewhat nervously. "You know, we've only got a month to pull this off."

On Royce's office comscreen, Harrison Winterfelt grimaced owlishly. "Could be better, could be worse," the Minister of Science said.

"A statement that could be applied to any given day's weather or your love life," Royce said testily. "I'm interested in specifics, Hari."

"*Specifics* is mostly what we've got," Winterfelt said with a shrug. "Chemical formulas and cookbook techniques for their rejuvenation processes. Blueprints for their matter transformer. We know how they get from star to star so fast. An inertia-screen, we could build. The brain eptifiers are no trouble. But . . ."

"But what?"

"But basically what we've got is *technology,* not science," Winterfelt said. "We can reproduce their gadgets and drugs, and we've got their theoretical approaches down, too. But the *linkages* are another story. We can synthesize brain eptifiers and rejuvenation biologicals, but how do the damn things work on cellular metabolism and the mind-matter interface? What's the unified field theory behind the inertia-screen? And so forth. Our boys have some advanced basic theories and general approaches, and a lot of advanced technology on an industrial espionage level, but Transcendental Scientists they're not. Institute graduates have *six years* of study behind them, and even the best conventional scientists can't pick all that up in a few months."

Royce tried to understand what Winterfelt was saying, but the essence of it hovered just beyond his grasp. "But in practical terms, Hari, in terms of a media show that will win votes, can you give me enough to be really impressive?"

"You mean to *laymen?* For sure! Pacifican-built matter transformers and inertia-screens. We could race a ship around the system in record time. We can rejuvenate some famous old jocko. We can show the people a fifty-year quantum jump in technology. We can knock 'em dead."

Royce sighed and relaxed back in his lounger. "That sounds great to me," he said. "Congratulations are in order. So what's bothering you?"

Winterfelt frowned. "Look, we can convince the voters that Pacificans can set up their own Institute of Transcendental Science," he said, "but me, I'm not so sure. Cut off from the real thing, it'll take decades for our scientists to understand the new theories and new technologies well enough to put them together in a way that will continue to generate more on a Transcendental Science level. In the meantime, Transcendental Science itself will progress at its own accelerated rate. Without some *real* Institute graduates to guide us, it could take us a century or more to achieve real equality with the Arkology boys."

"But we *can* do it? We won't become a permanent backwater?"

Winterfelt shrugged. "Probably not," he said. "If we *do* go it alone, it'll be a tremendous boost for Pacifican science. Not just the stuff we've pirated, but the knowledge that we *can* do it because we *have* some of it and there are people out there a century ahead of us who we *can* catch with an all-out effort. A lot of the best brains will go into science the way they go into media now. In a decade, we'll be the number-two scientific power in the human galaxy." He looked at Royce owlishly. "But *number two*, Royce," he said, "not number one. Not for a century. That's the trade-off—a delay of a century in scientific progress for getting rid of all these damn off-worlders."

"And which way would *you* vote, Hari?" Royce asked.

Winterfelt smiled ruefully. "As a Pacifican, I'd say we can't afford any more of the past few months. As a scientist, I'd say being at the leading edge of galactic science immediately is worth any risk." He shrugged. "It's a *political* decision, Royce," said. "And as a politician, I'm glad that it's yours and not mine!"

"Thanks a lot, Hari!" Royce said. "But from where I sit the choice is obvious. There's no way we can keep the *Heisenberg* people without being stuck with a permanent Femocrat mission, and there's no way the buckos of this planet are going to sit still for *that*. Even if we *could* squeeze such a resolution through Parliament once, there'd be moves to repeal it every other week, and we'd end up changing Chairmen and Parliaments about as often as you change your underwear, with permanent Femocrat and Bucko Power parties forever, or until one side pulls off a successful coup. Thanks, but no thanks. What we're stuck with may not be the best of all possible worlds, but it's the *only* possible way for this one!"

"Well, I wish you luck," Winterfelt said.

"Thanks," Royce said dryly. "Within the month, this whole planet's for sure going to need it."

Masking her uneasiness with an artificial confidence, Carlotta Madigan surveyed the Delegates, glanced at the near-empty spectators' gallery, took a deep breath, and announced: "The Chair now has a resolution to introduce."

I sure hope you're right about this, babes! she thought, exchanging a quick glance with Royce, who now sat in the center of the ideologically rearranged Parliament. The Femocrats sat to her extreme right, the Bucko Power Delegates to her left, and the center block in the middle, and none of them, she thought, will be expecting *this*.

The Madigan Plan still had eight days to run, this was supposed to be an ordinary session dealing with the economic situation, and everyone, even those who counted themselves her allies, would be caught totally flatfooted. *Nobody* was going to like it. Once more, she was going to deliberately provoke a vote of confidence she couldn't win, and this time the resulting electronic vote of confidence would *really* be critical. Win or lose, there would have to be a new Parliamentary election afterward, because *no one* would be able to form a governing majority with *this* Parliament after the chaos this move was going to create.

"It's a setup," Royce had insisted when he broached the idea to her two days ago. "Falkenstein and the Femocrats will be caught with their pants down. Parliament is sure to vote it down, and they'll find themselves suddenly in the middle of an electronic vote of confidence a week before they expected it. Their reaction will be to attack you from both sides; we'll just let them gibber and scream, then hit them with the bombshell on election eve, and you'll win the vote of confidence in a landslide."

"Maybe," Carlotta had said. "But if we've got the

clincher, why not spring it *before* the Parliamentary vote and settle the whole thing without elections?"

"Because we *want* new elections."

"We *do?*"

"Don't we, Carlotta? Okay, we could expel Transcendental Science and Femocracy now with this ammunition with a cute little Parliamentary maneuver, without risking elections. But what would we have then? The same damn ideological power-blocks turning the next decade's politics into an endless bout of recriminations. Getting rid of the off-worlders isn't enough—we've got to get rid of their rotten legacy, too, and the only way we can do it is to shatter the Bucko Power and Femocratic blocks and elect a new Parliament that's overwhelmingly non-Femocrat, non–Transcendental Science, and pro-Pacifica. And if that means risks, we've got to take them."

"Of course, you realize this means chaos . . ."

Royce had smiled wickedly, nodded, and said: "For sure. Chaos is the dissolution of the existing order, and the existing order *sucks*. Now is the time for all good men to destroy political parties. Trust me, babes, let's take the chance."

And after sleeping on it, Carlotta had decided that he was right. There would have to be cauterizing new pain before the infection could be destroyed, in order for the injuries done to the body politic to have a chance to heal.

Carlotta glanced around the chamber one more time and took another deep breath. We who are about to lie salute you! she thought fatalistically.

"The Madigan Plan period ends in eight days," she finally said, "and at that time the legal mandate for both the continued presence of the Femocratic mission and the continued operation of the Institute will run out. Therefore, I've decided that, in order to prevent a period of total confusion during which the legal status of the Femocrat mission and the Institute would remain in limbo while we decided what to do next, a vote must be taken on these issues *now*."

The expected pandemonium broke over her. A low murmur whooshed through the chamber, cresting into a series of incoherent shouts. Virtually every light on her board lit up with Delegates demanding the floor.

"Order!" Carlotta shouted, turning up the amplification

301

of her microphone to override the din. "I've got the floor, I'm in the process of introducing a resolution, and you can damn well wait till I've finished before you lynch me."

The shouting faded quickly into a guttural murmur again, and then into an even more ominous silence as a hundred pairs of eyes glowered at her with shock, distrust, and no little hostility. *And you ain't heard nothing yet, kiddos!* she thought.

"The Madigan Plan was passed during a period in which the conflicting forces of Femocracy and Transcendental Science were threatening to tear this planet apart," Carlotta said. "The idea was to postpone the decision now before us so that we would be able to judge the practicality of a permanent Institute of Transcendental Science and a permanent Femocrat presence—and to judge them by deeds, not just words."

She frowned sardonically. "Well, since then we've had plenty of both!" she said. "As far as I'm concerned, both Femocracy and Transcendental Science have had their chances to demonstrate their goodwill and compatibility with our way of life, and they've both failed dismally. Therefore . . ."

She paused. The silence was a palpable quivering thing, a giant wave pausing to crest into a roaring, foaming breaker.

"Therefore . . . Resolved: that the Institute of Transcendental Science be closed forthwith; that all *Heisenberg* personnel be banished from Pacifica; that all Femocrats from Earth be likewise banished; and that both the *Heisenberg* and the B-31 be ordered to leave our solar system within two weeks of the passage of this resolution."

An animal roar of outrage rocked the Parliament chamber. Delegates leapt to their feet shouting and waving their fists, Femocrats and Institute supporters alike. The men and women in the center block for the most part sat there stunned and confused, babbling incoherently to each other.

"The floor is now open for debate on the resolution," Carlotta said with inane-sounding sweetness.

"If no one has any further words of wisdom to contribute to this most enlightening debate, I'll call for a vote on the resolution," Carlotta said with sardonic blandness.

Royce Lindblad sat in the middle of the bedlam as he

had throughout the whole endless and meaningless debate, silently admiring the way Carlotta was handling the situation. Using a high setting on her microphone to aurally dominate the cacophony, she had controlled the acrimonious debate—or at least kept some semblance of order—without once raising her voice or even bothering to respond to the shrill insults, threats, and charges flung at her from all sides. While the Femocrats ranted about "treason to her sex" and the Bucko Power boys raved about a "sellout of Pacifican buckohood," Carlotta had remained the voice of sweet reason, the statesman rising far above the ugly three-hour temper-tantrum.

And that, Royce thought, is what's going to come across on the net: a serene Carlotta Madigan democratically presiding over an unseemly Parliamentary chaos. The way she had rattled the bars of the cage with gentle patronizing sarcasm throughout the debate had admirably served to milk the situation for as much political capital as it was worth. No one realized it yet, but the media campaign to win the electronic vote of confidence had already begun.

Now a spent and confused silence prevailed. Perhaps, Royce thought, the Delegates are finally beginning to realize that they're in the process of being had, though they can't figure out how. The Femocrat and Bucko Power Delegates were not about to let this resolution pass, but by now they had to realize that the failure of the resolution was going to mean an electronic vote of confidence, and an election campaign under these confusing circumstances was not exactly what they wanted either. So no one wanted to end the debate, but no one had anything coherent left to say either, and perhaps the Delegates were also beginning to realize what public asses they were making of themselves.

Royce shrugged. Why not a small act of mercy? he thought. "Second the motion!" he called out. "I call for the vote."

A sullen murmur swept the chamber that guttered quickly into silence.

"Any other seconds?" Carlotta asked.

Dead silence.

"Objections to an immediate vote? Points of order? More speeches?"

Only a wordless snarl of discomfort.

303

"Very well . . ." Carlotta said neutrally. "Ayes for the resolution, nays against . . ."

Numbers flickered across the tote-screen behind her as the Delegates pressed their voting buttons. After a minute or two, the final tally appeared to oohs, ahs, and uncomfortable muttering: 31 votes for the resolution, 72 against. Even the centrist block had not held firm behind Carlotta Madigan.

Carlotta shrugged. "Motion defeated," she said with unsettling geniality. "The Chairman's motion having been defeated, an electronic vote of confidence is hereby scheduled for seven days from now." She laughed. She favored the chamber with an enigmatic smile. "The Chairman wishes to state at this time that she holds no hard feelings against those of you who voted against the resolution. No hard feelings at all, kiddos. This session of the Parliament of Pacifica is now adjourned."

For a moment the Delegates stared at her in stunned silence. Then dim comprehension dawned—somehow, Carlotta Madigan had tricked them again. But why? And how? Why would she deliberately force an electronic vote of confidence on an issue where the numbers seemed to be two-to-one against her? How have we been screwed this time?

A moment later, the floor broke up into dozens of little impromptu debates and shouting matches. Royce winked at Carlotta, and she winked back. Half a dozen Delegates caught the exchange and favored Royce with lizard-eyed stares. Royce shrugged and smiled back sweetly at them. You'll never figure it out, he thought. Not in a million years.

A full shot on Roger Falkenstein standing in front of the Institute building. Between Falkenstein and the Institute, lines of male Pacificans are trooping somewhat sullenly into four large helicopters. Falkenstein himself looks grim, his face taut with ill-concealed (or perhaps artfully crafted) anger.

Falkenstein: "Citizens of Pacifica! Although your Parliament has rightfully voted down the perfidious resolution, introduced by Carlotta Madigan, to close the Institute, it is my judgment that the Institute can no longer function in safety and security as long as Madigan is Chairman of

Pacifica. She has unilaterally attempted to abrogate two agreements concluded between her administration and Transcendental Science. Therefore, we have the same lack of confidence in her that your Parliament has just expressed and that I hope you too will express in the coming electronic vote of confidence."

Cut to a much longer shot on the Institute building, the lines of students entering the helicopters, and crews of *Heisenberg* personnel who are disassembling domes and outbuildings with matter transformers. One by one, the small buildings wink out of existence until only the bright silvery disc of the Institute itself remains.

Falkenstein's voiceover: "Though it pains me to do this, I am now dismissing the Institute's Pacifican student body and dismantling some of the facilities themselves. The teaching staff will be returned to the *Heisenberg*. The Institute will remain closed until Carlotta Madigan is defeated and the Pacifican Parliament grants us *permanent* permission to operate an Institute of Transcendental Science on this planet."

Cut to a closeup on Falkenstein, looking regretful but determined.

Falkenstein: "Should such permission not be forthcoming within thirty days, the *Heisenberg* and all within her will leave this solar system forever. Pacifica will be permanently excluded from the interstellar communion that will one day encompass all human worlds. Only the empty shell of the Institute building will remain as a monument to the shortsighted folly of your government . . ."

An exterior time-lapse shot of the silvery Institute building. Jungle undergrowth grows in the cleared area. Great trees shoot up, godzillas roam among them, vines begin to creep over the Institute building itself, until all is obscured by the renascent Godzillaland jungle.

Falkenstein's voiceover: ". . . and soon enough even that will sink back into the primeval slime . . ."

A series of shots slowly dissolving into each other: an artificial sun over a verdant Thule, great buildings springing up to form a fantasy city on the dun sands of the Wastes, an old man melting into a vision of youthful vigor, a great fleet of fancifully baroque Arkologies orbiting Pacifica.

Falkenstein's voiceover: ". . . and all that will be left to you is the sad lost memory of what might have been."

Cut to a closeup on Falkenstein, shrugging ruefully.

Falkenstein: "And for *what?* For some dim concept of planetary nationalism that was moribund before man reached the stars? To gratify the bloated ego of Carlotta Madigan? Because you fear growth and change? Perhaps not. I hope not. I think not. I cannot believe that you will let this happen when the time comes for you to vote—for a place in the forefront of human evolution, or for moral cowardice, primitivism, and ultimate retrogression. But the choice is yours. May you have the greatness to make it wisely."

In her hotel room high above the brilliant nightscape of Gotham, Maria Falkenstein sat on the edge of the bed listening to Roger shout at her on the comscreen.

". . . what do you *mean* you won't go? I'm your husband! And I'm also the Managing Director of the *Heisenberg,* and I've ordered all *Heisenberg* personnel to return to the Arkology until Madigan is defeated and Parliament grants us a permanent Institute! That certainly applies to you! What do you think Madigan and Lindblad would make of it if they learned you were still on Pacifica against my direct orders?"

"I don't know, Roger," Maria said. "I don't understand what's happening."

Maria sighed. She had come to Gotham in the first place to clear her head, to come to a better understanding of these people, to decide who they really were, who she really was, and what she must do. But now they suddenly seemed more alien than ever. What was happening now was incomprehensible to her. But at least now I've got plenty of company, she thought.

"What's happening is quite simple, Maria," Roger said testily. "Madigan has made a catastrophic mistake. She will surely be soundly defeated in this electronic vote of confidence. With her out of the way, this 'Pacifica for the Pacificans' movement will evaporate, and politics here will boil down to a straightforward confrontation between our supporters and the Femocrats. Therefore, we're forcing the electorate to face reality by closing the Institute and removing ourselves to the *Heisenberg*. Which is why *you* must return to the *Heisenberg* with me at once!"

Roger's angry face, his voice, his scenarios, his clear certain logic seemed to Maria like a pale spectre of the dead dim past, a thin surface reflection of the deeper, more complex, and far more ambiguous reality that now rolled over Pacifica and which writhed in convoluted tangles within her own mind. I can't go back, she thought. I'm not the same person anymore, and perhaps Roger isn't either. Or if he is, it only proves what a sleepwalker I was before I set foot on this planet. A human computer running on preprogrammed logic circuits. I can't be that any more, even if I want to. And perhaps I do . . . perhaps I do . . .

"I can't do that, Roger," she said. "I can't go back. It's too late for that."

"Maria, Maria, come to your senses!" Roger said, his voice plaintive now, but also patronizing. "What do you suppose you're going to do?"

"I don't know," Maria said forlornly. "I really don't."

Roger's anger burst through again. "I could force you," he snapped. "I could declare you mentally unbalanced and place you under protective custody."

"No, you couldn't," Maria said, more in sorrow than anger. "That would be kidnapping or worse under Pacifican law, and I'd go straight to the Ministry of Justice if you tried. You couldn't afford a scandal like that."

"Great suns, Maria, you're talking like one of these bloody Pacificans yourself!"

"Maybe I am . . ." Maria muttered. "Maybe I am . . ."

A cold steel shield seemed to come down behind Roger's eyes. "You're really serious about this?" he said flatly. "You won't come back to the *Heisenberg?* And if . . . if we should be forced to leave this solar system . . . ?"

"Oh, come on, Roger," Maria snapped, "you're not planning on that and neither am I. Madigan will be defeated, you'll push your resolution through Parliament, the Institute will be reopened, and . . ." And nothing will really be changed, she thought. Except what matters most to these people. You'll win out in the end, Roger. You always do. And that'll give me the easy way out. She shuddered. She wondered why she felt so trapped, so overcome by self-loathing.

"For once tonight you're making sense," Roger said coldly. "This *is* only a temporary withdrawal. If . . . if I can't convince you to listen to reason . . . at least will you promise me that . . . that you'll keep out of public sight . . ."

"Appearances are more important to you than reality now, aren't they?" Maria said sadly. "This isn't my husband speaking now, it's the Managing Director of the *Heisenberg*, isn't it?"

"*I* see no conflict in those roles even if you do," Roger snapped. "Will you please—"

"I'll stay out of sight for now to please you," Maria said. "It's the least I can do, isn't it?" And to please myself, she thought. Truth be told, I'm not very proud of who I am right now.

"It certainly is!" Roger said. "I'll keep in touch with you from the *Heisenberg*."

"You do that, Roger," Maria said. I only wish you really meant it in some kind of human sense.

"Goodnight, Maria."

"So long, Roger," she muttered, and unplugged from the circuit.

Afterward, she stood for a long time at the window, looking out at the lights of the alien city spread beneath her like a mocking reflection of the distant stars. From this vantage point, both seemed equally far away, equally abstract, equally beyond the reach of her heart. Suspended between the world she had known and the world she had come to love in some cold alienated way like a woman enamored of the image of a man she could never touch, Maria was alone in the Pacifican night, isolated from both worlds, trapped in the desolate reaches between.

18

A PANORAMIC SHOT OF THE INSTITUTE OF TRANSCENDEN-
tal Science as seen from the air; a silver disc abandoned
and isolated in an endless sea of green like a ruined temple
in some primeval Terran jungle.

Female voiceover: "Sisters of Pacifica! The Institute of
Transcendental Science now lies empty and abandoned.
Only Parliament can reopen it, and if we can prevent such
a resolution from passing for thirty days, the faschochauvinist Transcendental Scientists will leave Pacifica forever.
Falkenstein has trapped himself by his vainglorious attempt
to blackmail our planet into submission."

Cut to a closeup on Susan Willaway.

Susan Willaway: "But we cannot slack in our determination. If Carlotta Madigan should win this vote of confidence behind her smokescreen of false evenhandedness,
there will be new Parliamentary elections, and the dupes
of Falkenstein will wage an all-out campaign to seize control of the new Parliament."

A medium shot on Susan Willaway, her head and shoulders haloed by a large hologram of Pacifica floating in the
stellar blackness.

Susan Willaway: "That is *one* reason for consigning
Carlotta Madigan to oblivion. But there is another. The
Transcendental Scientists have now left Pacifica, so the

309

full weight of Madigan's determination to ban both Transcendental Science and Femocracy from this planet now falls *on our Terran sisters alone!* It is now revealed as nothing but an attempt to deny ongoing free media access to interstellar Femocracy! It is treason to both Sisterhood and Pacifica's own media access laws! The so-called Madigan Plan now stands revealed as the fraud it always was."

A long shot of male Institute students trooping into helicopters, taken from Falkenstein's own footage.

Susan Willaway's voiceover: "The student body leaving the Institute of Transcendental Science. That's right, sisters, all male, *buckos,* one hundred percent! Even *after* Madigan announced that our own Ministry of Science would control admissions, the Institute was *still* allowed to function as a faschochauvinist brainwashing academy *with the active and knowing collaboration of the Madigan administration!* In secret! After she lied to us in order to break our strike!"

Cut a closeup on Susan Willaway, smiling sardonically.

Susan Willaway: "If Falkenstein's stupid macho arrogance hadn't led him to close the Institute as a blackmail threat, we might never have learned of this perfidy on the part of Carlotta Madigan until a faschochauvinist scientific elite, brainwashed and controlled by Transcendental Science, was unleashed to rule our planet by superior military force!"

A series of shots of Femocratic League of Pacifica demonstrations and rallies and newschannel footage of the Femocratic Thule strikers.

Susan Willaway's voiceover: "But let's not give Falkenstein or Madigan *too* much credit for their stupidity. For it was the strength of Sisterhood which *forced* Falkenstein to take his desperate gamble and reveal the true treasonous nature of the Madigan Plan. And it will be Sisterhood which finally puts an end to the career of this traitor to her sex and her planet! Remember this treason on election day! Remember that only Sisterhood has saved Pacifica from becoming a Transcendental Science puppet-state! Down with faschochauvinism! Down with treason! *Down with Carlotta Madigan!*

Wearing a short yellow dress bought in a large Gotham boutique, Cynda Elizabeth wandered incognito through the

tense and sullen streets of the city. Ever since her confrontation with Bara Dorothy, she had spent much of her
time aimlessly walking the streets of the capital, as much
to fill her empty days as anything else.

Refusing to front for a policy with which she had registered her official opposition, she had been barred from all
strategy sessions and command decisions, and her sisters,
fearing ideological contamination, avoided her like a
plague-carrier. She had taken her stand, and now she was
very much alone, both at the Sirius Hotel and out here
among the Pacificans.

At first, she had fantasized about meeting another Eric,
satisfying her perverted desires one more time before the
mission failed and was expelled to an Earth where the only
men were pallid breeders, pale shadows of Pacifican
buckohood. At times, she toyed with the idea of defecting,
of finding her own destiny here among men and women
who openly shared in ease and pride what she must hide
forever within her soul.

But this notion always evaporated like morning mist in
the clear hard light of day. She was what she was, and
though these Pacificans might be a happier breed, Eric
had taught her that she could never be truly one of them.
And truth be told, what she now saw in the streets made
her wonder whether what she had perceived as the harmonious Pacifican psychosexual balance had ever really
existed outside her own perverted wish-fulfillment fantasies.

Every park seemed to have its own impromptu orator
hectoring a sexually polarized audience, condemning either
Femocracy or Bucko Power, but always, so it seemed,
Carlotta Madigan. In most cafés and restaurants, women
sat with women and men with men, and the occasional
mixed couple stood out like some atavistic anomaly. Every
day, there was at least one Femocratic and one Bucko
Power rally somewhere in the city. On the streets, men
and women eyed each other in passing with suspicion and
hostility. The Pacifica that had been now seemed like a
thin veneer of harmony that once had masked this bottomless reservoir of contending faschochauvinisms. Perhaps it
had only maintained itself by self-consciously ignoring the
genetic flaw in the human species itself.

Which *we* and the Transcendental Scientists have now
brought bubbling up from the racial tarpits of the past,

Cynda thought as she turned off onto a little side street lined with small sidewalk cafés. And that alone gave direction and a strangely altered sense of duty to the newborn confusion of her life.

For what she had seen on Pacifica had taught her that the true enemy was *faschochauvinism itself*, both the male half of the equation which Femocracy had vanquished on Earth and the female half which had destroyed the manhood of the Terran breeders and made love between men and women a perverted and impossible dream. If this mission failed, it would fail because the Pacificans, for all that had been directed against them, clung successfully to that narrow and fragile path between.

And when that happened, Bara and her ilk would be tarnished by that failure, her own position would be vindicated, and the sisters of Earth might be ready for some small voice of change. So she couldn't risk throwing that possibility away by destroying her credibility by being caught in a liaison with a Pacifican man. She had been lucky with Eric, but she dared not trust to such luck again. It was her duty—to herself, to her species, and in some elusive way to Sisterhood itself. Even, ironically, to those secret sisters who might long to dare what she had done.

If only Carlotta Madigan hadn't ruined everything by her incomprehensible blunder, Cynda thought more wanly. Men and women had been coming together again here until that disastrous Parliamentary vote. Now things were flying apart again and *no* conceivable outcome seemed inevitable or even possible . . .

Yet somehow, walking down this back street, Cynda once more had the illogical conviction that these people would in the end manage to preserve their own complex identity. Here, in these small cafés secluded from the clamor of the main boulevards, she saw that men and women still gathered together in couples, and above the cafés were three and four floors of apartments, where surely much private life must go on as it always did.

In the end, were not the Madigans and the Parliaments, the demonstrations, the propaganda, and the politics, only the quicksilver surface of a people's reality? Was not the real Pacifica *right here* on this quiet back street, multiplied by a thousand, by a million—the millions of interlocking private lives and personal realities that were the true

essence of any society, basically unchanging, like the subconscious underpinnings of surface human thought itself?

Like this tall, gray-haired older woman wandering up
the street toward her. How could any off-worlder really
know what was going on behind those haunted-looking
eyes? A Bara Dorothy or even a Carlotta Madigan might
take that expression as symbolic of the deep political conflict enveloping the planet, but couldn't she just as well be
pining for a lost lover or worrying about a sickly daughter
or even her job? Who knew what—

The woman paused as their paths intersected. Her eyes
lit up with an ironic flicker, and as they did, Cynda Elizabeth recognized that face. She had seen it on the net
dozens of times; only this strange context had masked
the woman's identity.

"You're Maria Falkenstein!"

"And you're Cynda Elizabeth!"

They stood there in awkward silence for a moment.
What does she see? Cynda wondered. The face of the
enemy? What do I see, a Transcendental Scientist? How
strange! she thought. We've been fighting each other for
months, and yet there's been no human contact. And here
we are, suddenly face to face in a back street in an alien
city, and it's the *human* reality that seems unreal.

"I . . . I thought you people had all gone back to the
Heisenberg," Cynda finally stammered.

"Everyone but me," Maria Falkenstein said. She
shrugged with a strange diffidence. "I suppose my little
secret will be all over the net by morning . . ."

"No . . ." something made Cynda say. "I'm . . . I'm
out of all that now . . . I . . . if you can understand . . ."

Maria Falkenstein smiled a strange little smile at her.
"I'm probably the only person on this planet who could,"
she said.

"You, too, eh?" Cynda blurted. You, too, *what?* she
wondered. Unexpectedly, incomprehensibly, she suddenly
felt a strange bond to this enemy of all she had believed
in, a communion that went beyond words or understanding. For some unfathomable reason, there seemed to be an
instant spark of sisterhood between them that had nothing
to do with either shared ideology or sexual attraction.

"This *is* peculiar, isn't it?" Maria Falkenstein said. "We
should be at each other's throats, shouldn't we?" She

laughed. "What would your people say if they saw us standing here like this? What would *Roger* say?"

"I hardly know what to say myself . . ."

"Well, then may I make a highly improper suggestion, one enemy to another, Cynda?" Maria Falkenstein said. "Let's sit down and have some wine together. This is too outré an opportunity to miss, don't you think?"

"All right," Cynda said woodenly. "Why not?" They found an outside table at the nearest café. Maria ordered a bottle of floatfruit wine, poured two glasses, and then they sat there staring silently at each other for long moments.

"Well . . .?"

"Well . . ."

"Why aren't you on the *Heisenberg?*" Cynda finally said.

"Why aren't *you* at the Sirius Hotel?"

Cynda frowned. She hesitated. But something began to loosen her tongue. Of all times, all places, all people, *here*, strangely enough, was someone she could talk to beyond political or ideological restraints. "I don't feel I belong there any more," she said. "I . . . I . . ."

"So you wander the streets of Gotham trying to connect up to the reality of this planet and you find you can't do that either."

"How did you know that?" Cynda said sharply.

Maria laughed, took a sip of wine. "I'm sitting here in the same place as you now, aren't I, *sister?*" she said. "Great suns, what a mess we've both made here! And what a mess we've made of ourselves in the process. I mean, here the two of us sit, and we can't even work up a good healthy rage at each other. We're committing treason to our causes at this very moment, you know."

Cynda took a long swallow of wine. "Or vice versa," she said. "I mean, this planet does seem to blur the hard edges. Take you. You're a Transcendental Scientist, but you're also a *sister*. I've always known intellectually that there were women on the Arkologies, but I've never confronted that reality before. What's it like being . . . being a free woman in a faschochauvinist society?"

Maria drank a gulp of wine. "Neither as faschochauvinist as you people think, nor as free as we like to pretend," she said bitterly. "Once more the truth lies in that ambivalent region between where only the Pacificans seem to be comfortable. I wonder how they do it."

"So do I."

"You *do?*"

"I think I'm learning to admire them," Cynda blurted. "Envy them, even." She drank more wine for courage, and perhaps to wash the taste of her own words out of her mouth.

"You, too, eh?" Maria said. "You know, I think the two of us have gotten a dose of our own medicine. We came here to tell them how to live, and we end up . . . floating in our own limbo. Perhaps there *is* some cosmic justice in the universe after all."

"That's why you didn't go back to the *Heisenberg?*"

Maria grimaced. "Tell me what I'm supposed to do now, and I'll tell you why I didn't go back to the *Heisenberg*," she said.

"You don't know?"

Maria shrugged and drank some more wine. "I knew I couldn't tolerate being around Roger," she said. "I hate what we're doing to this planet. I can't stand being a collaborator in it any more. I wanted to be alone to think . . . vague, isn't it? Hardly logical and scientific. And you, Cynda? Tell me, have you thought about defecting yet?"

"Defecting!" Cynda snapped. "Certainly not!"

Maria laughed tipsily. "Not even just a teensy little bit?" she teased. "Isn't that what we're really talking about? C'mon, old enemy, we can be honest about it with each other—who's to know? Tell me you don't find life here the least bit seductive . . ."

Cynda sighed, poured more wine, and belted it down. "All right, all right, so I've thought about it," she admitted. The wine, the months of hidden internal tension, the memory of Eric, the unreality of this situation must be going to my head, she thought. But what the hell, what the hell, sometimes you gotta talk to *somebody* . . .

"As long as we're being so honest with each other sister," she said, "I'm gonna tell you my deep dark secret— I mean, I've got to tell somebody who's nobody, and right now for me you're as close to nobody as anybody can get. I'm a pervert, I'm attracted to men. Buckos. *Real* men, not Terran breeders. I want them on top of me, I want their

315

piercers—" Great Mother! she thought, bringing herself up short. What am I saying?

"How shocking," Maria said sardonically.

"You're being sarcastic!"

"Maybe," Maria said, "but these days I'm not so sure. Just when I'm thoroughly fed up with what our own men have done, I meet a *Femocrat* who . . ." She paused. She studied Cynda Elizabeth. "But if that's true, why *don't* you defect?" she said. "Why torture yourself for something you no longer believe in?"

"But I *do* still believe in Femocracy!" Cynda insisted. "Earth is my planet, sisters are my people, and I'm proud of what I am!"

"*Including* your feelings for men?"

"No!" Cynda blurted. "I mean yes! I mean . . . look, we're far from perfect, and so are men, but if sisters like me run away, nothing will ever change. I'm a Femocrat. I want men. It's about time real Femocrats with these . . . these *feelings* stood up to the Bara Dorothys and tried to make Femocracy into something that works for everyone. *Defect?* Great Mother, the only thing I can defect from is myself."

Mother, what a conversation this is becoming! Cynda thought in amazement. And yet, if there really was such a thing as Sisterhood, wasn't *this* exactly it? Two women speaking their hearts across the abyss of culture, ideology, and conflict? Sisterhood is *truly* powerful, she thought. In some strange way, more powerful . . . more powerful than its twisted perversion of itself!

She looked across the table at Maria Falkenstein. "So *you're* going to defect?" she said.

Maria laughed bitterly. "How?" she said. "To what? If our side wins, Pacifica will just turn into what I'd be defecting from. If your side wins, it'll become something more loathsome to me than what I left."

"But what if the *Pacificans* win? If they succeed in expelling both Femocracy and Transcendental Science?"

Maria shrugged woozily. "You really think that can happen?" she said dubiously. "And even if it did, it would be over our dead bodies. And at the cost of losing their chance to have an Institute forever. Do you seriously think they'd tolerate my presence after that?"

"Who knows?" Cynda said. "You could try. I think you should, sister, I really think you should."

Maria Falkenstein shook her head and rose shakily from the table. "Ah. it's just a fantasy," she said. "Roger will win, or your people will win; these poor lovely bastards don't have a chance. We both know that, *sister*."

She started away from the table, turned, and looked back at Cynda Elizabeth. "In fact, this whole conversation has been a fantasy, hasn't it?" she said. "It's not real. No one would ever believe it happened, and soon enough we won't either. What a pity . . ."

"Maybe," Cynda Elizabeth said. "But good luck anyway, sister."

"You, too," Maria said, shaking her head ruefully. "We sure could use it, couldn't we?"

Then she was gone, and Cynda Elizabeth was alone once more, sitting at a table at a sidewalk café in a back street of an alien city. And how strange it was that of all the people in the galaxy, the one person who for at least a moment had touched her heart had been the wife of the enemy.

A closeup of Carlotta Madigan at her desk in the Parliament building, calm, plainly dressed, with only the prosaic office furnishings as backdrop.

Carlotta Madigan: "Good evening. Tomorrow I will face you once more in an electronic vote of confidence on the issues that have divided our planet for so many months. The polls show me running far behind. Every political analyst on this planet is certain that my resolution to expel the Femocrats and the Transcendental Scientists was an act of political suicide. I have been accused of everything from treason to deliberate falsehood to being the creature of Roger Falkenstein. Every voice on Pacifica seems to be screaming for my defeat. Yet thus far I have remained silent during this campaign . . ."

Now Carlotta smiles a confident, easy Borgia smile.

Carlotta: "Why? Because I've given up? Because I have no answers to these charges?" She laughs sardonically. "No, I haven't given up, and I don't lack for answers. Far from it, for as I speak to you tonight, I am utterly confident of victory. Because tonight Pacifica gets its answers, in *deeds*, not words. Why have I fought to maintain the Madigan Plan, admittedly using every trick in the book? Why did I break the Thule strikes? Why did I sit still for a secret agreement with Roger Falkenstein that permitted the Institute to function with an all-male student body selected by our own Ministry of Science? Pacifica wants an answer? Pacifica demands an answer? Well, Pacifica deserves an answer—and here it is!"

Cut to establishing shot of a spacious hall inside the Ministry of Science. Royce Lindblad and Harrison Winterfelt, the Minister of Science, stand in the center of the shot behind a small podium. To their right is a large screen. To their left, a long line of Pacifican scientists with various apparatus waiting to perform like contestants at a Columbian fair. A large mass of video and sound equipment and newshounds are visible in the foreground as the camera moves in for a two-shot on Royce and Winterfelt, emphasizing Royce.

Royce: "I'm speaking to you from inside the Ministry of Science. With me is Harrison Winterfelt, our Minister of Science, and the other men you see are all former students at the Godzillaland Institute of Transcendental Science."

The camera pulls back for a longer shot including some of the former Institute students and their apparatus.

Royce: "As you know, when the original student body was dismissed, the Institute chose its new student body from blind lists compiled by our own Ministry of Science. But as you *don't* know, and as Dr. Falkenstein didn't know either, many of these new students were trained Pacifican scientists acting under orders from Minister Winterfelt, myself, and Carlotta Madigan. Men capable of learning a good deal more than their 'teachers' may have intended." He pauses, smiles, shrugs.

"Unkind and unfriendly souls might go so far as to call them Pacifican spies. Hari . . . ?"

A closeup on Winterfelt, looking somewhat nervous.

Winterfelt: "I want to emphasize that *everything* we will demonstrate tonight has been constructed by *Pacifican* scientists working for the *Pacifican* Ministry of Science using information gathered by *Pacifican* operatives inside the Institute of Transcendental Science. Once this indeed may have been *Transcendental* Science, but it is *Pacifican* Science as of now."

318

Cut to a full shot on a display table. In a vase on the table is a single fragile blue flower. Beside it is a small cage holding a tiny red piperlizard. Between them is small metal box. At the end of the table is an even smaller box with a toggle switch. A short-haired scientist stands behind the table.

Scientist: "The inertia-screen, a device for isolating an area of space from all outside electromagnetic, chemical, and thermal phenomena: a heat-shield, an atmospheric barrier, a radiation screen, among many other applications . . ."

He throws the toggle switch. He picks up a blowtorch and envelopes the area around the flower and lizard in bright orange flame. He turns off the torch, revealing an unsinged flower and a lively chirping piperlizard. He dons a gas mask and sprays yellow vapor over the test area from a cannister. When the gas clears, the flower and the lizard are unaffected. He palms a small red sphere and flips it toward the lizard cage. There is a small loud explosion. Again the lizard and the flower are untouched.

Cut to a full shot on three scientists standing beside a waist-high control console. In front of the console, two thin wire grids are suspended on poles. Under the left-hand grid is a pile of earth. The floor under the right-hand grid is empty.

First scientist: "The matter transformer—a device for the instantaneous materialization of any desired object from raw atoms . . ."

He signals to the other scientists, who manipulate the controls. A silvery aura envelops the area under the left-hand grid.

First scientist: "Useful in construction . . ."

The pile of earth dissolves and is replaced by a small model of the Pacifican Parliament building. This in turn dissolves and becomes a model of the Institute building, then an apartment tower, then a model hovercraft, then a pile of earth again.

First scientist: "It can also be used to transmit the matrix pattern of any material object over any distance with the speed of tachyon transmission."

He places an oil painting of a sunset over the Cords on the empty floor under the right-hand grid. The other scientists manipulate their controls. The painting disappears and reappears instantly atop the pile of earth to the left, perfect in every detail. The first scientist removes the painting and puts it back under the right-hand grid.

First scientist: "One copy can be reassembled at the receiving end—or many."

The painting disappears again, but this time the pile of earth under the left-hand grid completely dissolves and in its place are dozens of copies of the painting, identical down to the scrollwork on the bongowood frames.

Cut to a medium shot on Harrison Winterfelt, including a portion of the screen beside the podium.

Winterfelt: "Two demonstrations of major items of Transcendental Science among many available here for newschannel taping after this formal presentation. But first, I'd like to show you tapes of three other demonstrations we could hardly bring into this room . . ."

The camera pulls back and recenters on the screen as a view of Pacifica from orbit appears on it. In the foreground of the shot is a standard Pacifican orbital liner.

Winterfelt's voiceover: "This liner has been equipped with an inertia-screen and a beefed-up fusion drive . . ."

A silvery aura envelops the stubby-winged craft. A thin blue flame erupts from the stern and the liner begins to accelerate very rapidly, exponentially, faster and faster, finally accelerating at a rate that should pulp its occupants to jelly. It goes into a polar orbit around Pacifica, disappearing over the north polar icecap and reappearing almost instantly over Thule. It continues orbiting the planet at incredible speed, the exhaust flame dopplering red when it moves away from the camera.

Winterfelt's voiceover: "Without the inertia-screen, the pilot of this liner would now be pulling dozens of gees, and would in fact be dead. But inside the inertia-screen, gravity remains normal. This is how Transcendental Science Arkologies sustain their enormous accelerations. By flying parabolic arcs past black holes, they can accelerate to near-light speeds within days in safety . . ."

Cut to another view of space, just a fiery sun floating in the star-flecked blackness. Pacifica swims into the frame behind it, a huge crescent filling most of the field of vision, and revealing that the sun is not distant and huge but tiny and orbiting no more than a few hundred kilometers from the surface of the planet.

Winterfelt's voiceover: "An artificial sun, a complex fusion plasma confined within an inertia-screen—and built by *Pacifican* scientists!"

Cut to a full shot on a naked old man, his chest sunken, his limbs withered, his skin a parchment of decay, his face almost a skull.

Winterfelt's voiceover: "Finally, a male Pacifican *before* rejuvenation by *Pacifican* medicine—and *after!*"

The shot dissolves into a similar shot on the same naked man. But now his hair is black, his body is sleek and well-muscled, his penis is erect, and his face glows with youthful vigor. In fact, he is Dov Ardisman, the famous porn opera star of forty years ago, whose tapes are still well-known classics of the genre.

Winterfelt's voiceover (as Ardisman grins his famous grin and salutes the camera): "Dov Ardisman rides again! I understand we can look forward to seeing his first comeback porn opera in three months."

Cut to a closeup on Carlotta Madigan, seated behind her desk, grinning sardonically, and waving an admonishing finger at the camera.

Carlotta Madigan: "O ye of little faith! While Femocrat supporters have been ranting about the evils of faschochauvinist Transcendental Science and Bucko Power fanatics have been demanding that we sell out our way of life for the wonders you have just seen, while the idiocy of the Pink and Blue War has torn this planet apart, a few *real Pacificans* have managed to keep their big mouths shut and do something about it! And so we can bid a not-so-fond farewell to Transcendental Science and Femocracy alike."

She pauses, and her face becomes more serious, almost stern.

Carlotta Madigan: "To the supporters of the Institute, I say *here* is *Pacifican* Transcendental Science without the Transcendental Scientists, without off-worlder machinations. Look what you've done to your women and your own love-lives—and for nothing! To our local home-grown Femocrats, I say *here* is the answer to your man-hating paranoia! The Transcendental Sciences have been liberated from male faschochauvinist monopolists, not by your strident posturings and *female* chauvinist demands, but by *Pacifican buckos*, working not for Transcendental

Science but for *Pacifica*—for Pacifican men and women alike."

She pauses again and assumes a calmer, more statesman-like expression.

Carlotta Madigan: "Following this electronic vote of confidence and the coming Parliamentary election, my first act will be to introduce a resolution calling for the establishment of a *Pacifican* Institute of Transcendental Science, staffed by Pacifican scientists of both sexes, with a student body equally divided between men and women. *Pacifican* Transcendental Science will be sold to all worlds with the galactic credits to pay for it. We have not only liberated Transcendental Science for ourselves, but for the species, for men and women everywhere."

A large hologram of Pacifica appears behind her now, floating triumphantly in the void.

Carlotta Madigan: "Finally, to those Pacificans, men and women alike, who have never succumbed to the gibberings of Femocracy or Bucko Power, who have supported me throughout this long crisis, who have kept this planet foremost in their loyalties, I say thank you with all my heart. And in the days to come, when your errant brothers and sisters return to the communion we have all shared, I ask you to welcome them back as Pacificans with open arms and generous souls."

Carlotta pauses and grins crookedly.

Carlotta Madigan: "As for me . . . well, what can I say? Tomorrow you will get the chance to say it all with your votes. So all I can say for myself now, with my world-famous modesty and humility, is . . . thank me, and good night."

19

Woodenly, Bara Dorothy scanned the roomful of sour, defeated faces. "Turn that damn thing off!" she snarled. A sister got up, turned off the net console, and sat down again.

Dozens of folding chairs crammed Bara's office; another score of sisters were standing around the room; virtually the entire Gotham staff had gathered here, and no one dared speak a word. Even Cynda Elizabeth confined her gloating to a thin satisfied smirk. *Seventy-four percent!* Carlotta Madigan had pulled 74 percent of the overall vote, and the preliminary breakdown showed that she had gotten 76 percent of the female vote. Total catastrophe!

Bara Dorothy glowered at Mary Maria, who quickly looked away. Bara started to snap something at her, thought better of it, and remained silent. It isn't Mary's fault, she thought. This wasn't a failure of the media blitz; after Madigan revealed how she had outfoxed the Transcendental Scientists, *nothing* could have defeated her. It isn't really my fault either, Bara realized. How could I have changed the outcome? Nevertheless, *I'm* going to take the blame for the failure of this mission, since Cynda Elizabeth has formally dissented from the policy we followed. Damn the dirty little breeder-lover!

As if to rub it in—*as if?*—it was Cynda Elizabeth who broke the deadly silence. "Perhaps this isn't all bad," she said loudly.

A great collective groan.

"No, really. The Pacificans have broken the Transcendental Science monopoly, haven't they? They've promised to sell everything they have freely on the Web. Now we can buy things we never thought we'd ever get—inertia-screens, matter transformers, genetic engineering techniques, rejuvenation. Maybe we didn't exactly win, but Great Mother, *Transcendental Scienc*e is the big loser! Now we can buy what they've been keeping from us, from Pacifica."

Expressions brightened somewhat. A buzz of conversation rippled around the room.

"With *what?*" Bara Dorothy sneered loudly. "Where are we going to get the galactic credits? You think Pacifica is going to *give* this stuff away?"

"We'll have to reevaluate our Web policies," Cynda Elizabeth said. "We'll have to take part in interstellar commerce, develop new technologies of our own that we can sell, maybe even entertainments, like Pacifica. In the long run, it'll be good for us, it'll force us to become more of a part of the galactic mainstream."

"Great Mother, what rot!" Bara snarled.

"It's the future whether you like it or not, Bara," Cynda Elizabeth said. "And we're going to have to learn how to adapt to it."

Murmurs of approval swept the room. As if things weren't grim enough, Cynda Elizabeth was getting to them with this subversive talk in their defeated depression. It had to be stopped! "You know we *do* have an upcoming Parliamentary election now," Bara said. "We *do* have one more chance to retrieve this situation before we slink back to Earth like whipped dogs!"

"How?" Mary Maria asked glumly.

"That's *your* department, Mary, now isn't it?" Bara snapped. "You've got about a day to come up with something." She paused, looked up, and addressed the whole room. "That goes for all of you," she said. "Enough defeatism! Back to your jobs! I've got work to do now, and so do you, so clear this room!"

Slowly, sullenly, the sisters trooped out of her office,

finally leaving Bara alone with her own dark thoughts. The fact of the matter was that Femocracy had no real issue left on this planet; Madigan had totally destroyed the movement's political viability. Only some maddened reaction by Falkenstein—

The comscreen of her net console came to life. It was Susan Willaway, local leader of the Femocratic League of Pacifica.

"What?" Bara grunted testily.

"I'm resigning as leader of the League," Susan said. "I'm also resigning my membership."

"What?"

"I feel like a fool!" Susan said angrily. "I feel like a dupe! I've been had. We've all been had. Carlotta Madigan has been right all along, and now she's proven it. I'm sick of all this; it's like awakening from a long nightmare. I'm going to run for reelection to Parliament as an independent and take my chances with my own people."

"You miserable cowardly traitor!"

"Traitor?" Susan snapped. "To *what?* Great grunting godzillas, the men of this planet have proven that they're Pacificans first and buckos second! What does that make Pacifican *women* if we can't admit we were wrong? And I'm not the only one, Bara; we're being flooded with resignations."

"Go suck a piercer, you dirty traitorous breeder-lover!" Bara screamed, unplugging from the circuit. "The whole stinking planetful of you atavistic chauvinist swine!"

Then she buried her head in her hands, kicked the leg of her desk, and wondered what it would be like to let herself cry.

A full shot on Roger Falkenstein standing on the bridge of the *Heisenberg*. He is flanked by two men—one tall, lean, and quite bald; the other a younger, heavier man with a full head of wavy blond hair.

Falkenstein (bristling with anger): "Citizens of Pacifica! Once more we have been betrayed and you have been duped by the cynical perfidy of the Madigan administration. Need I point out that the espionage committed by your government is a direct violation of the agreement concluded between the Madigan administration and myself—a bald-faced *theft?*"

The camera moves in for a tighter shot on Falkenstein, whose anger now takes on a somewhat sardonic edge.

Falkenstein: "No doubt those of you who saw fit to return Carlotta Madigan to office are now congratulating yourselves and your perfidious government for having successfully nationalized Transcendental Science. But it's not quite so simple as that, my friends. Jon Guilder, a very recent *graduate* of one of our Institutes . . ."

Cut to a closeup on the heavyset man.

Guilder: "It's taken me *six years* of very difficult study to graduate from an Institute as a truly qualified Transcendental Scientist. The notion that men who have studied for only a few months are qualified to run an Institute of Transcendental Science is just too ludicrous to arouse anything but pity. These pathetic Pacificans don't even know enough to know how *little* they know!"

Cut to a closeup on the tall bald man.

Falkenstein's voiceover: "Dr. Charl David, former Provost of the Wenigo Institute of Transcendental Science, now Chief Science Analyst of the *Heisenberg* . . ."

David: "Pacifican scientists have produced technological artifacts from plans stolen from our higher scientific civilization much as a preatomic society might successfully construct a nuclear generator from pilfered specifications. However, such a preatomic civilization would hardly then possess a true understanding of subatomic physics! Any more than Pacifica now possesses a true understanding of the Transcendental Sciences! A *child* could reproduce a great painting by an ancient master using a color-by-the-numbers kit, but that would hardly make him a Michelangelo or a Miranda! Indeed, certain Terran *birds* can reproduce a great oration verbatim without understanding a word of what they are saying, but no one would contend that they have become Churchills or Ciceros in the process!"

Cut to a two-shot on Falkenstein and David.

Falkenstein: "Well, how *would* you evaluate the worth of this stolen knowledge to isolated Pacifican science?"

David (diffidently): "Oh perhaps in fifty years they'll have some dim understanding of what they've stolen, and within two centuries they might even reach our present level . . ."

Falkenstein: "While the rest of the galaxy under our leadership—"

David: ". . . will of course have advanced to the total mastery of matter, energy, time, and mind. A two-century knowledge gap is a two-century knowledge gap!"

Falkenstein: "And the notion of a Pacifican Institute of Transcendental Science operating on its own without our guidance—"

David (sardonically): ". . . is roughly the equivalent of a Sumerian Institute of Biophysics!"

The camera moves in for a closeup on Falkenstein.

Falkenstein: "My Pacifican friends, you have been utterly duped by Carlotta Madigan. Test the true knowledge of your treacherous spies. Demand that your Ministry of Science publicly explain the unified field theory behind the inertia-screen, the molecular physics of rejuvenation, the true knowledge behind the stolen toys they have constructed for your befuddlement. And when their answer is silence, remember that the forthcoming Parliamentary election is your last chance to retrieve what your government has thrown away. Unless you elect a Parliament that returns control of the stolen knowledge to us, authorizes a permanent Institute under *our* terms, expels Femocracy forever, and ousts Carlotta Madigan, we will leave this solar system to its own pathetic devices forever. This is your last chance, Pacificans. You will not get another."

Royce Lindblad frowned at the comscreen, drumming his fingers nervously on the arm of his lounger. On the screen, Harrison Winterfelt shrugged fatalistically. "Don't blame *me*, Royce," he said. "I told you the truth in the first place."

"You mean this slok Falkenstein is putting out is *true?*"

"About as true as the show *we* put on," Winterfelt said. "We were exaggerating for political purposes and so is he. No, our boys *can't* go on the net and explain the science he's challenged us to explain. But savages doing a monkey-see, monkey-do act we're not either. Their timetable is grossly exaggerated for propaganda purposes, and with a little luck, we *can* achieve parity with them in less than a century."

"That's not exactly a flasho public answer to what they're saying, Hari," Royce grunted.

"Do we really need one? Is the political situation all that critical?"

"Yes and no," Royce said. "I'm not worried about the numbers. We'll have maybe a two-thirds majority in the next Parliament on expelling Femocracy and the *Heisenberg* boys. But I don't like the stink this is going to leave. We need a long period of healing, and if a third of the people end up feeling that a Pacifican Institute is a sham and a fraud, our politics will be poisoned by it for decades. Refighting the Pacifican Pink and Blue War will remain an obsession with a sizable minority, and if our Institute doesn't start showing real results faster than you say it can, the whole bloody thing could start up all over again."

"I wish I could help you, Royce," Winterfelt said. "But we've done all we can. And it certainly could've turned out much worse, couldn't it?"

"Yeah."

Winterfelt grinned crookedly. "And I suppose this is a pretty good argument for an increased budget for the Ministry of Science," he said dryly.

"Ordinarily, I'd tell you to go fuck yourself for making a pitch like that at a time like this," Royce said. "But you happen to be right, and I'm sure we can push through a resolution earmarking all the proceeds from selling what we do have on the Web for the research budget of the Pacifican Institute." He smirked sardonically. "Which, of course, will only increase the political pressure on *you* to produce results fast. Needless to say, we will not make this an issue in the current campaign."

"Needless to say," Winterfelt grunted uneasily. He laughed mirthlessly. "Now if we could bribe a ranking *Heisenberg* scientist into defecting, that would be money well spent," he said. "*That* would make it a whole new game. Know any takers?"

"Maybe I should take it up with Falkenstein," Royce said sourly. "Maybe I could offer him *your* job."

"Very funny."

"I wouldn't worry about it too much," Royce said dryly. "Even if one of those bastards was corrupt enough to sell out for money, he could make a lot more of it selling what he knew directly on the Web. No, Hari, it looks like *you're* the man in the scientific hot-seat for as long as your ass can stand it."

"Words cannot express how thrilled and relieved I am to hear you say that," Winterfelt sighed wearily.

A long shot on Bara Dorothy standing beside the gray hull of the Femocrat starship. To her left, arranged in rows like graduating students posing for a final class picture, are about thirty Femocrats, including Mary Maria but not Cynda Elizabeth.

Bara Dorothy (woodenly, awkwardly): "My name is Bara Dorothy, sisters, and I'm speaking to you as spokeswoman for all the unsung heroines who have labored so tirelessly and selflessly for a Femocrat Pacifica."

The camera moves in for a closeup on Bara Dorothy.

Bara Dorothy: "It now seems certain that Pacifica will shortly elect a Parliament that will expel us from your planet. Will all our efforts have been for nothing? In the long run, I hope not. For that same Parliament will also banish Transcendental Science forever."

She permits herself a small smile. "Judging from the bellows of outrage emanating from the *Heisenberg,* Roger Falkenstein hardly considers this outcome a smashing victory either. And within his defeated ranting is a small but telling truth."

The camera pulls back for a wider shot, including the rows of Femocrats, who stare into the camera with fixed expressions of dogged determination.

Bara Dorothy: "I too believe an independent Pacifican Institute will be a fraud and a sham, if not exactly for the same reasons. Need I point out that all the teaching personnel of the new Pacifican Institute will be male? No doubt there will be some female *students* for cosmetic purposes. But since the male Pacifican staff will control the technology stolen from the *Heisenberg,* the end result will be a male faschochauvinist elitist clique using its secret advanced technology like a priestly caste to dominate Pacifican society."

A closeup on Bara Dorothy.

Bara Dorothy: "When this faschochauvinist elite reveals its true face, I believe that the sisters of Pacifica will remember what Femocracy tried to do for this planet, and they will see the outcome of the forthcoming election as a tragic mistake, the right road not taken. On that day, you will realize that the struggle, far from being over, is only just beginning."

Cut to a series of shots dissolving rapidly into each other: a Femocratic League of Pacifica demonstration; ranks of marching women; a street scene on Earth where confident women bustle about their business; shots of four planets seen from space with marching women superimposed over them; and finally a spaceship much like the B-31 moving toward Pacifica.

Bara Dorothy's voiceover. "You may be turning your backs on us now, but Femocracy will never turn its back on *you*. Know that your comrades on all liberated planets will never abandon their Pacifican sisters! Summon us once more to your aid, and we shall return! Sisterhood is powerful, Sisterhood remembers, and Sisterhood is forever! Long live Sisterhood and long live our undying solidarity with those Pacifican sisters who will keep the faith through the long night of faschochauvinism that is now descending."

A vague sense of unease soured what should have been Carlotta Madigan's impending moment of triumph as she sat in her office reviewing the depth poll figures two days before the Parliamentary election.

The figures were encouraging, to say the least. Bucko Power and Femocratic candidates were contesting less than half the seats, and even these were trying to disassociate themselves from off-worlder connections in an effort to survive the impending landslide. Both off-worlder fronts were finished as coherent political forces. The total vote against them should top 70 percent.

And yet, Carlotta thought, there *is* that hard-core 25 percent, and anyone who still votes Femocratic or Bucko Power has to be intransigent indeed! When they're crushed in the election, they'll disappear as an overt political force, bitter and intransigent, to nurse their festering wounds in secret. And if our Institute is as slow to produce results as Winterfelt says it will be, the Bucko Power remnants will brood upon Falkenstein's parting shot. And the remaining Femocrat fanatics will remember their promise to return, maybe turn it into a filthy little cult. And the

Pink and Blue War could return, perhaps this time outside the democratic process . . .

Carlotta sighed. Maybe you're asking too much, she thought. You want to win without anyone being left to feel like the vanquished? You expect some magical balm to heal all the wounds of these many months without leaving noticeable scars? Not even Transcendental Science has medicine like that . . .

Her broodings were interrupted by her secretary's face on the intercom screen.

"What is it, Bill?"

"You've got a visitor."

"Is it important?"

"I think so . . . it's Maria Falkenstein."

"Maria Falkenstein?" Carlotta exclaimed. "But I thought they were all recalled to the *Heisenberg*? What's *she* doing here? What's she want?"

"I don't know, but she says it's important . . . should I . . . ?"

"For sure, send her in," Carlotta said. Great grunting godzillas, what's *this* all about? she thought. What *now?*

Maria Falkenstein wore a tan pants suit that might have been bought in any store in Gotham. There were slight bags under her eyes, and although her face was much more tanned than Carlotta had remembered, there was a gray pallor beneath it. She looks like she's been under tremendous stress, Carlotta thought.

"May I sit down?"

Carlotta nodded silently at a chair, steepled her hands as Maria Falkenstein sat down, and waited for her to begin whatever-it-was.

"I suppose you're surprised to see me here," Maria said, wringing her hands nervously.

Carlotta nodded silently, not knowing how to react, or indeed what she was supposed to be reacting to. There was a haunted look in Maria Falkenstein's eyes, a great sadness, but behind that there seemed to be a strange tranquility that went beyond mere resignation.

"I've left Roger, you know . . ."

"No, I didn't," Carlotta said inanely, arching an eyebrow.

Maria nodded. "I have," she said. "Weeks ago. I've been in Gotham ever since, trying to understand your

331

people, and what we've done here." There was absolutely none of that Transcendental Science arrogance; indeed, she seemed almost humbled, and quite contrite.

"And just what cosmic conclusions did you reach?" Carlotta asked, somewhat sarcastically.

That seemed to get a small rise out of Maria; her eyes sharpened a bit and her voice hardened slightly. "I'm *here*, not *there*," she said. "When Roger ordered us all back to the *Heisenberg*, I couldn't bring myself to go. I felt I had to stay behind."

"Why?" Carlotta said sharply. "To what end? Soon enough, Parliament will vote to expel all Transcendental Scientists from Pacifica, and that will mean *you*."

Maria Falkenstein looked down into her lap. "I . . . I hope not . . ." she said softly.

"*What?*"

Maria looked up at Carlotta, and now there seemed to be pleading in her eyes. "I'm not your enemy," she said.

"You're not?"

"Not any more . . ." Maria sighed. "You know, this is pretty difficult for me, and you're not exactly making it any easier."

"Under the circumstances, I don't feel exactly relaxed either," Carlota said somewhat less harshly. "Especially since I have no idea what this is about. Would you mind explaining why you're here?"

Maria shrugged. "You could call it a new understanding, if you could feel some kindness toward me. Or just a guilty conscience if you can't."

"A guilty conscience?" Carlotta said softly. By now she was convinced this was no Falkenstein ploy. This woman had really left her husband, she really was here against his orders, and whatever emotion was gripping her, she was sincere, and it was costing her.

"You have to understand who I am and where I come from," Maria said plaintively. "I'm a woman of the Arkologies, that's common enough, but I'm also a female Institute graduate, and that's quite rare." She frowned crookedly. "A great source of pride to my husband— to have an Institute graduate for a wife. So you see, I was an anomaly to begin with; I had a much easier time of it than most of our women—an Institute graduate *and* the wife of a Managing Director of an Arkology."

Most of our women are . . . well, just wives—because of
the genetic differentiation between the sexes, or so we're
told. And our society functions smoothly and optimally,
so one didn't question this until . . . until . . ." Maria
paused and studied Carlotta speculatively. "Do you understand what I'm trying to say?" she asked.

"I think I'm beginning to," Carlotta said, feeling sympathy for the woman growing within her.

"And then we came here," Maria said. "And I saw that
things could be different and still work. Femocracy repelled me, but it also forced me to take another look at my
own culture, to see that there *was* a subtle male chauvinism
at work within it, and not merely a logical application of
the scientific principles of psychobiology."

She looked Carlotta straight in the eye, and what Carlotta saw in her face seemed like affection, an affection
directed toward *her*. "And I saw you," Maria said. "You
and Royce. A woman who ruled a whole planet and a
man who stood by her side in strength, not weakness. A
whole planet like that. An alternative to both male and
female faschochauvinism. Scientifically backward, maybe,
but on another level so far beyond what we—"

Carlotta laughed good-naturedly. "We're neither as simple nor as perfect as we may seem," she said. "As witness
the events of the past half-year," she added more darkly.
"Events in which you people played no small part!"

Maria Falkenstein hung her head in rather touching
contrition. "I know," she said softly. "We took something
that worked and tried to change it for our own ends. And
so we meddled and schemed and we used all the techniques of our superior science . . ." She looked up at
Carlotta and shook her head. "And we almost succeeded,
didn't we?" she said. "We almost destroyed the harmony
of Pacifica forever."

"You came reasonably close," Carlotta admitted dryly.
"And I'm not so sure at least some of the damage isn't
permanent."

"That's why I'm here," Maria blurted. "Maybe you
won't believe this, but my mind was divided from that first
day when I saw how you and Royce could be with each
other. I believed in the future Transcendental Science is
building, and I think I still do. But I saw that Pacifica had
something that *we* lacked, even as we had a vision that

333

you lacked. How far did we have a right to go in the service of our vision? Roger and the others saw no limit, but I . . . I felt we had no right to destroy what worked so well here and so badly in our own society."

She shrugged. She grimaced. "How pious and self-serving all this sounds now, after the fact!" she said. "But please understand, I was a dedicated Transcendental Scientist, I believed in what we were doing, I loved my husband, I trusted in his wisdom . . . it was no straight and easy path for me from there to here."

"And just where is *here?*" Carlotta asked.

"I want to help," Maria said. "I want to make amends. I want to do my part to repair whatever damage we've done, damage that I admit I've collaborated in."

"You mean you're telling me you want to *defect?*" Carlotta exclaimed. "Is that what this is all about?"

Maria nodded silently, avoiding her eyes.

"Could get difficult . . ." Carlotta said uncertainly. But in her heart, she had already decided.

How difficult it must have been for this woman to have reached this decision! she thought. To put her world, her past, what she had been, and the man she had loved behind her for the sake of . . . *what?* Principle? Contrition? A new awareness of herself? The small-minded might call this treason, Carlotta thought, but there was an elusive and touching loyalty here that went beyond planet or ideology, treason or defection. Home is where the heart is, however you get there.

"I could be of great assistance to you . . ." Maria suggested. "Believe me, I could more than justify the political risk . . ."

Carlotta studied her speculatively for a moment. She thought of that potential embittered 25 percent of the voters. She thought of Roger Falkenstein's prediction of failure for the Pacifican Institute of Transcendental Science. Perhaps Transcendental Science *does* have a medicine to heal our wounds without leaving scars, she thought.

"I believe you, Maria," she said, reaching out and taking her hand. "Welcome aboard." Maria looked up. She smiled wanly. She nodded silently.

"So Sisterhood *does* turn out to be powerful after all, doesn't it?" Carlotta said. She laughed. "But not quite the way the Femocrats mean it," she said. "You could twist

semantics a little closer to the truth and call it the Sisterhood of man."

A very long aerial shot of the silvery disc of the abandoned Godzillaland Institute of Transcendental Science.
As the camera zooms in on the Institute, six helicopters
parked in front of the building become visible. Tiny
figures scamper from the helicopters toward the Institute as the camera zooms in closer: men and women
carrying crates, chests, and items of equipment into the
empty building.

The shot centers on a stationary female figure standing
just in front of the entrance to the Institute, and the
camera zooms in much more rapidly now into a closeup
on this woman, who is revealed as Maria Falkenstein. Her
face is calm, determined, perhaps a bit contrite.

Maria Falkenstein: "Citizens of Pacifica . . . or I should
say my fellow Pacificans, for I'm going to have to get
used to that . . . as you no doubt know, I am Dr. Maria
Falkenstein, Institute graduate, late of the Arkology
Heisenberg. Pending Parliamentary approval of a permanent position, I have accepted a provisional appointment as
acting Provost of the Pacifican Institute of Transcendental
Science, contingent upon approval of my application for
Pacifican citizenship. As you see, the Institute is now being
reopened under my direction, and applications for admission will now be accepted by the Ministry of Science."

She pauses, staring at the camera, as if waiting for the
enormity of her announcement to sink in.

Maria Falkenstein: "My people came here with a vision
of a transcendent human future and a dedication to
spreading our advanced knowledge throughout all human
worlds. Unfortunately, we also came with a righteous
conviction that this end justified any means. Even more
unfortunately, a Femocrat mission arrived with an even
more ruthless dedication to thwarting that goal, and soon we
were all caught up in a conflict that strained Pacifican
society to the breaking point."

She becomes openly humble, painfully apologetic.

Maria Falkenstein: "For my part in what happened, I
can only humbly beg your forgiveness. But despite the
efforts of Femocracy and Transcendental Science, it was
you who in the end prevailed. And for that, I can only

offer my heartfelt thanks to you for what you have taught me."

She pauses and smiles ruefully. "I learned how men and women could live together in justice and equality. I learned that it takes more than logic and knowledge to make a people whole. I learned how a free and democratic people could retain control over its own destiny despite overwhelming odds against them. I am learning from you still . . ."

The camera pulls back for a longer shot, including the entrance to the Institute as Pacificans pass back and forth through the shimmer-screen.

Maria Falkenstein: "Now I offer my own knowledge in return. You have been told that without guidance from a true Institute graduate, your native Pacifican Institute can only be a pale shadow of the real thing, and I must tell you that this is true. The Femocrats have told you that a male faschochauvinist scientific elite will in time come to dominate Pacifica, and I say this shall not be, and I am here to prove it."

The camera moves in for a closeup on Maria Falkenstein; determined, resolute, some of her old pride regained.

Maria Falkenstein: "I stand before you now as Provost of a truly *Pacifican* Institute of Transcendental Science, as an Institute graduate capable of guiding that Institute to scientific parity within decades, not centuries, and as a woman. To the Femocrats, I say, *here* is the leader of your male faschochauvinist scientific elite! To my former colleagues, I say *here* is an Institute graduate and a Pacifican, who will share our knowledge with all mankind as knowledge was meant to be shared. To you, my fellow Pacificans, I promise to dedicate the rest of my life to the great adventure we are now embarking upon as fellow Pacificans and human beings."

The camera pulls back abruptly as her composure cracks and tears well up in her eyes.

Maria Falkenstein: "And finally . . . and finally . . . to you, Roger, I say . . . I say . . . I'm sorry if you think I've failed you. I'm sorry if . . . I hope one day you'll understand . . . I loved you and a part of me loves you still . . . I'm sorry, Roger, I'm sorry that this had to be . . ."

A sob wracks her body, and she covers her face with her hands as the camera jerkily reverse-zooms into a discreet long shot on Maria Falkenstein as seen from far, far above, a lonely isolated figure standing in a clear space in the wild greenery of the everlasting jungle, like a figure out of an ancient tragedy framed by a spotlight in the center of some vast and bewildering planetary stage.

20

AFTER ALL BUT SHE HAD BOARDED, CYNDA ELIZABETH
paused atop the embarkation ramp of the B-31 for a last
glimpse of Pacifica to carry with her across the abyss of
time and space to Earth.

Fewer than two hundred people had bothered to see the
Femocrat ship off, and most of these were newshounds
and media crews, and even *their* turnout was unimpressive
considering the planet's multitude of news channels. So
final and complete was their defeat and discrediting after
the defection of Maria Falkenstein that their departure
wasn't even a major news item.

A defection for which *I* was at least partly responsible,
Cynda thought, and strangely enough, she felt no little
comfort in that. At the end, she had after all managed
to leave some small trace of herself on the future destiny
of the planet and in the life of one true sister—and for the
better, not the worse. Now the Pacifican Institute of
Transcendental Science would be truly Pacifican—a joint
effort of men and women together with a woman and a
Transcendental Scientist in charge.

As for Maria Falkenstein herself, Cynda, perhaps more
than anyone, could empathize with the course she had
taken, for it was the mirror-image of the choice she her-

self had been forced to make. Maria had forsaken the man she had loved for the new destiny that called her, and Cynda had forsaken the possibility of finding the kind of man who might fill her heart for her duty as a Femocrat and a human being. Maria's sacrifice took her away from the world she had known to work out a new life on a new planet, and Cynda's sacrifice was bringing her back to her own world as a transformed stranger, a potential agent of change. There was symmetry in that, a rough sort of cosmic justice.

And when the arguments and counterarguments had ground each other down, Cynda was sure that Femocracy would be forced to realize that it could no longer afford to stand aloof from the commerce and discourse of the Galactic Media Web. Not with the Pacificans openly trafficking in the formerly secret knowledge that Sisterhood had coveted for over a century. Femocracy could now not afford not to buy the inertia-screen, the matter transformer, rejuvenation, and all the rest. Even an ideologue like Bara Dorothy was beginning to see that isolation from the Web would mean that the Femocratic planets would become a primitive backwater while the rest of the galaxy swept onward and upward.

And in order to buy, Femocracy would have to sell. In order to sell, Femocracy would have to produce wares that could compete on the interstellar market. And in order to do that, Femocracy would have to learn how to adapt itself to the galactic mainstream, to grow, and to change.

Who can say where that may one day lead? Cynda Elizabeth thought. Who can say that one day it may not be possible for a Sister and a Femocrat to openly walk the streets of Earth with her *man* and yet remain both a Sister and a Femocrat? There are other Sisters on Earth who have felt what I feel, a few strongly enough to have braved punishment by acting out what was in their hearts. How many of us are there? Who has even dared to try to find out? Femocracy is going to have to change, and if Sisterhood is truly powerful, may it not one day be strong enough to accept even breeder-lovers like me as Sisters and true comrades? Who can say that I may not live to see that new world?

Cynda looked out across the broad Columbian plain

for one last time. Fields of golden grain rippled in the breeze beneath an unclouded sky. In the distance, the Big Blue River flowed toward Gotham, that alien city where for a while at least she had found her own true nature in the arms of a man. She wondered what Eric might be doing now, whether he would be watching this departure on the net.

She sighed. That had been, and now it was over, and the equivocal future called to her. For the moment, it was enough to remember what had been, and to know that wherever she was, a world existed somewhere where men and women lived and loved, free, equal, and together.

She waved goodbye to no one in particular and stepped into the ship.

The inertia-screen was on, the drive cut in, and on the main viewscreen of the *Heisenberg's* bridge, Pacifica began to dwindle rapidly. A huge living world of blue sea, mottled green and brown land, swirling white cloud-banks; then a smaller abstraction of itself like a planetary holo-map; finally a bright blue marble glowing against the black velvet of space like a huge and precious sapphire.

As Dr. Roger Falkenstein stood there watching the planet recede, it seemed to him that some psychic umbilicus that linked him to Pacifica, to Maria, to what had been, was being stretched, thinned, and stressed, and he almost physically steeled himself against the moment when it would snap. Indeed, he wished it *would* snap, whipping his bitterness and confusion out of the center of his being and down the long corridor of the void to oblivion.

But that moment of release never came, and how foolish it was to hope that mere kilometers or light-years or parsecs could magically clear his mind of what had transpired down there on Pacifica. Around him, the bridge crew bustled about the task of readying the *Heisenberg* for deep space, and in the decks below many of the Arkology's personnel were already entering the blissful nothingness of Deep Sleep. All was as it had always been, and yet everything had changed.

No longer would the Arkologies and Institutes be able to hold their knowledge unto themselves. No longer would centrally controlled Transcendental Science spread from planet to planet as a great unifying force. That day was done; the Pacificans would see to that.

Ongoing human evolution could no longer be guided by the best minds of the species; now it would become chaotic, multifocused, as the forefront of knowledge was transferred to the random marketplace of the Web. Only the Pacificans, the masters of the Web and the subverters of the great plan, would be capable of exercising any control, and *their* idea of control was no control at all, precious knowledge sold to any and all bidders.

The only alternative was to try to beat the Pacificans at their own game; dispense gratis via the Web the knowledge and technology that they would be selling. At least that way, by selecting planets with some care, *some* pattern could be maintained at least for a while, and social cancers like Femocracy could be kept from the leading edge of technology. It was a far more subtle and limited form of guidance, restricted as it was to positive reinforcement, but it was now the only way, and the Council would have to accept it as the only viable policy. And perhaps in time, with the responsibility for the destiny of the species that they were unwittingly assuming, the Pacificans themselves would learn the wisdom of care, restraint, and a coherent guiding vision.

As for Roger Falkenstein's personal life, it existed only as pain, a pain that was becoming a gaping void, but not swiftly enough by far. Losing Maria was still like the shock of a sudden amputation; a part of him was gone, and the wound was still too fresh for him to feel anything but the whited-out pain of his loss.

Only now, as Pacifica became a brilliant blue ball of light mocking him from the darkness, as Maria disappeared forever beyond the veil of space and time, did small coherent thoughts begin to flit around the periphery of his massive pain—and yes, anger.

Was *I* in some way responsible for this? Falkenstein wondered. Was there some lack in me as a man that enabled this planet to insinuate itself into my wife's psyche and finally take her from me as surely as if Pacifica were a newer and fresher lover? Was there some emptiness in our life together, in the very society that made us, that Pacifica was able to fill? Was I mistaken? Was I wrong? About *what?*

341

In the viewport beyond Pacifica, stars and everlasting night extended to infinity in space and time. Now, in his pain and his loss, Falkenstein felt a new sense of humility in the face of that overwhelming cosmic countenance. Perhaps the universe was in the end too vast to be entirely encompassed by any living mind. So, too, the mysteries of the human heart. Perhaps where certain knowledge ended, the glimmerings of true wisdom began.

Before them, the great orange ball of the sun hovered just above the western horizon, painting the clouds purple, mauve, and gold, glazing the sea with fire, casting long deep shadows eastward from the green islets of the Island Continent, illumining the yellow undersides of a flock of boomerbirds flying high overhead.

Carlotta Madigan sat in the cockpit of the *Davy Jones*, the boomline in one hand and the tiller in the other, sensing and controlling the forces of wind and water where they converged inside her own body, while Royce watched proudly. Not, however, without a certain gentle smugness.

"You're definitely getting it," Royce said as Carlotta steered the sailboat into the mouth of Lorien lagoon. "I'll make a sailor out of you yet."

"It looks like it, doesn't it?" Carlotta said contentedly. "I think everyone's learned a lot about tacking these past few months."

Royce nodded. "Pacifica has, you and me have, babes, men and women here have, but I wonder how much seamanship those poor off-worlders have picked up . . ."

The house hove into sight, and on the beach, Carlotta could make out a fat brown shape launching itself onto the water and paddling out to meet them. A distant excited whonking echoed across the lagoon.

They were home for the moment; the planet was more or less at peace, and the man beside her seemed much older in a way that sat very well on his tanned bare shoulders. Bucko and lover, helpmate and teacher, second soul and stranger, they had passed through the changes, alone and together, and the ties that had bound them to one another in stasis were transcended now by something at once more fragile and yet stronger than what had been in its very unsettledness. Like the interplay of wind and water, their relationship could only be an ongoing dialectic of constancy and change now, for the vector sum would never again be *hers* or *his* to command, but a shared true course through the seas of change for as long as they sailed together.

She laughed. She craned her neck and without letting go of tiller or boomline kissed him briefly on the lips. "To hell with everyone else, bucko!" she said. "All I know is that we're learning how to sail this boat together!"

They laughed together, and Royce reached for her, and they hugged each other, and kissed, and suddenly the boom was swinging free and the boat whirling crazily in the water.

"Duck!" Royce shouted, and threw her to the deck as the boom whistled over her head.

"Whonk-ka-whonk ka-whonkity whonk!" Rugo had come alongside and was protesting indignantly as he paddled and puffed to avoid colliding with the out-of-control boat.

Royce lifted himself off Carlotta, grabbed the boomline and tiller, and quickly restored control. "Bucko Power to you, lady!" he laughed. "You were saying something about learning to sail this boat?"

With a gross ungainly flapping of stubby wings and a great splash of water that soaked them both, Rugo leapt into the boat.

Carlotta cocked her head at the clumsy bumbler, who stood there showering them with water as he shook his body dry, then grinned crookedly at Royce. "You were saying something about Bucko Power, jocko?" she said.

They laughed and Carlotta snuggled into Royce's shoulder as he steered the boat toward its mooring under the purpling sky. Rugo curled up between them. A sudden puff of wind bellied the sails. Soaked and shivering slightly now in the sunset breeze, huddled together for warmth like little children, they sailed into the safe harbor of home.